LEGEND OF THE GOLDEN CITY

TREASURE HUNTERS ALLIANCE
BOOK 2

MICHAEL WEBB

Published by Whatup Publishing LLC 2023

Cover design by jeffbrowngraphics.com

ALSO BY MICHAEL WEBB

Get a FREE prequel novella to the Shadow Knights series - Shadow Knights: Origine - by signing up for my mailing list at www.subscribepage.com/michaelwebbnovels

1

"This is gonna be the last time you see me in a dump like this." Denton slumped onto the bar, barely avoiding knocking over his ale—how many mugs had he had? Couldn't be sure. What started as a celebratory dinner had turned into drinks, and then more drinks, and then the crowded room spinning around him. The cool surface of the bar pressed against his flushed face. "My life's gonna be different now."

"Is that right?" The bartender sounded bored.

Maybe Denton had already explained his future of wealth and riches. He couldn't remember. A cool sea breeze blew through the open windows, perking him up. With some effort, he sat up again. "You'll see. I will come back and buy this bar."

"You'd be doing me a favor," the bartender said.

Denton spent a lot of time in inns, and the Salty Lodge was better than most. At the far edge of the seaside town of Marris, the beds were cheaper, and the patrons minded their own business, busy with arguments or gammit. Lanterns along the walls flickered cozy light through the room. Near the window, a broad-shouldered man in a dark cloak sipped from a glass of whiskey.

"What does a man have to do to get service around here?" another patron barked, a short, balding man with an angry pink scar where his right ear should have been. "Another ale, Calum!"

The bartender poured a mug and slid it across the bar to the one-eared man. "Keep your pants on, Tomas. It's a busy night."

"Not so busy that you can't indulge some drunken ramblings, I see."

"Ramblings?" Denton barely noticed the slur in his own voice. "You're speaking to a future Lord of Palenting!"

Tomas laughed. "Don't be ridiculous. A man like you wouldn't last a week in Palenting."

"As if you'd know."

"Of course, I'd know. I know every city in Terrenor, and then some. Tell him, Calum."

The bartender rolled his eyes. "Tomas thinks he's a mercenary for hire instead of a traveling salesman."

"Salesman!" Tomas' face turned red, the scar at the site of his missing ear remaining pale. "I'm a collector of rare goods! A dealer! Closer to a fine goods curator than a salesman." He took an angry swig of his ale.

"Ha!" Denton raised his mug to Tomas. "You know a thing or two about rare goods?"

"More than a thing or two." Tomas chuckled as he stood and walked closer. "What? You have something of interest?"

Denton grinned. "More than interest. I have something a salesman like you can only fantasize about."

"I'm not a salesman," Tomas forced through gritted teeth. "Fools like you always think they have something remarkable. I've wasted plenty of time on nonsense."

"Fool?" Denton smacked the bar with his palm, the sound echoed through the room. "You'll regret disrespecting me."

The sound caught the attention of the other patrons in the bar. By the window, the man in the cloak set his glass of whiskey down.

"All right, lads," the bartender said. "I think you've both had enough."

"No," Tomas leaned forward, holding up a hand. "I'm curious. What does this fool think he has?"

Denton puffed out his chest. He was always hotheaded, but booze made it worse. This salesman was getting in his face, doubting him the way everyone doubted him—*but now everything will be different.*

"I don't *think* anything," Denton said. "I know what I have. The Key of Kytalia."

Tomas' eyes widened. They flicked to the bartender, then back. His lips made as if to speak, but nothing came out.

Denton grinned. *Now, I've got his interest.* A laugh from the salesman shattered his hope.

"Kytalia? Ha!" The cackle was boisterous. "The City of Gold is a myth. You're even more foolish than I thought." He clapped Denton on the shoulder, drained the remainder of his mug, then dropped a few tid on the bar. "I'm off to bed, Calum."

Denton scowled at the salesman's back as the man ascended the stairs. "Another round," he grunted.

After a pause, Calum poured another ale.

The cold drink did nothing to ease Denton's irritation. *Idiot man has no idea.*

A gaze burned into his back, leaving him fidgeting. "What're you looking at?" he snapped at the dark figure by the window. Appearing unfazed, the man picked up his whiskey and drained the rest.

Denton worked on his ale, listened to the crashing waves and mused over his upcoming change in fortune. His vision grew increasingly blurry the longer he sat. When the mug emptied, he waved his hand for another.

"I think you've had enough," the bartender said.

Denton clambered to his feet. "I'll be the judge of that." The room tilted and his stomach lurched. *Yeah, maybe he's right.*

He stumbled toward the stairs, but before he arrived, Tomas descended the final step and walked to the door of the inn. The salesman made eye contact, flashing a faint grin as he pushed the door open and left.

Denton considered chasing after the man to pick a fight, but with his fuzzy vision, it probably wasn't the wisest idea. Instead he ascended the stairs to his rented room on the second floor of the Salty Lodge.

He fumbled with the door to his room, then pushed it open and left it that way while he found a lone candle on the small dresser. After several strikes of flint, the candle flickered to life.

His bed looked welcoming, small but soft. The perfect size to sleep off the alcohol before he left in the morning. Footsteps sounded behind him.

"Where is it?" a threatening voice whispered from the doorway.

Shoved forward, Denton's knees slammed into the hard wooden floor. The terror racing through him numbed any pain. He spun and looked up.

A hulking shadow loomed over him. The whiskey drinker from the bar lowered his cloak. The flickering light of the candle cast the man's face in shadow. He sneered down at Denton. A long vertical scar ran over his left eye.

"It's you!" Denton gasped. "Y-you—"

"I'll ask you once more. Where is it?"

"M-my brother will hear about this!" Denton stammered.

"He certainly will." Before Denton could respond, the man grasped his arm and hauled him to his feet. "Tell me where the Key is."

"The Key is mine." Denton's mind reeled while thoughts of riches and power slipped through his fingers. Whimpered words dribbled from his lips. "I tracked it down! It belongs to me!"

"Tell me." The man twisted Denton's arm behind his back.

Denton squawked in pain as it burned through his shoulder. "It's not here."

"You're lying." He twisted harder.

Denton swore. Something popped in his shoulder and a spasm of pain ran down his side . His resolve to resist shattered with the crack of his body. "Stop! Stop! Okay, I'll tell you." Tears blurred his vision. "It's—it's in the dresser."

The man released his arm. Denton groaned as he crumpled to the ground. He wanted to get up, to fight back, but his arm screamed and his legs wouldn't cooperate.

"There's nothing here." The man tossed the clothes from the dresser.

"What?" Denton's breath caught. "I put it there for safekeeping! The second drawer!"

"There's nothing."

"I swear, I did!"

"You're lying to me." The man turned around. "Where is it?"

That doesn't make sense. Denton scrambled backward, pain shooting down his arm. Terror ran like ice through his veins. "I'm not lying. I swear! It must've—"

The man on the stairs. His smirk. Cold sliced through his impaired thoughts, bringing clarity.

"The salesman from Palenting!" Denton gasped. "He stole it just now! I saw him leaving the inn!"

The man's eyes narrowed. "You flaunted the object's presence to the entire bar like a fool. Then you let it disappear."

"It's not my fault!" Denton pleaded.

The man stepped forward, then pushed on Denton's injured shoulder with his foot.

Pain burned behind his eyes as he groaned and thrashed. When the spots cleared from his vision, the man still loomed over him with a coil of rope in his callused hands.

"Please," Denton whispered. His heart froze in his chest. "Not that. Please."

A cruel grin split the man's face. "There's still a price to pay."

2

The sun hung high and fell in golden beams against the vertical rock face. Peter rubbed his hands together then blew into them to warm up. Though it was still early in the wiether season and the deep cold had yet to arrive, the morning chill clung to the rock and numbed his hands at the touch.

"Here, take this." Sephiri handed him a canteen of hot tea.

"Oh, perfect." Peter didn't drink—just held the canteen until feeling returned to his hands.

"All right," Rylan shouted from high above their heads. "This is the place!"

Kira stepped back, craning her neck. "You sure you're tall enough?"

"Watch it, Kira!"

Kira covered a laugh with her hand, strands of blonde hair trailing over her arm.

Sephiri stayed seated, but her gaze focused on Rylan. If he screwed up, she'd be the one to make sure he didn't break his bones.

Secluded in the foothills north of Palenting, the crag made

the perfect destination for Peter and his friends on a beautiful Weekterm day. Tiny features and cracks covered the four-story rock face, creating enough routes to the top that they never got bored.

It was something they never could've done before Sephiri introduced them to the Source. A four-story fall wasn't so bad if you had a cushion of air to catch you at the bottom.

Rylan pressed his toe into a tiny, jutting rail on the rock, then sprung his stocky form up toward the hold above his head. His grunt reached the ground as he hung from his fingertips.

Peter, Sephiri, and Kira watched, leaning forward.

"His arm's shaking," Peter said. "He's gonna lose it."

Rylan pulled hard on the rock and heaved himself up to a more secure position.

Sephiri exhaled in relief.

High above, Rylan whooped, then continued up the rock face at a steady clip.

"He can just muscle through moves like that," Kira said. "It's not fair."

"He probably didn't see that crimp you used," Sephiri said. "I sure didn't."

Kira laughed. "Fair point."

Kira climbed with her brain more than anything else: positioning her body to use side holds in ways Peter never considered. Rylan was strong, Kira was balanced, and Peter was fast. If he dashed through the hard parts, he didn't waste energy.

As Rylan moved into an easy section of the rock face, Kira dropped onto their blanket and tore off a chunk of bread from their stash in the picnic basket. "It's nice to have a Weekterm morning off," she said. "Those training sessions have been killing me."

"You're still practicing at the museum?" Sephiri raised her eyebrows. "It's been weeks!"

"I know. I think I've finally gotten Mother's approval. She wants to make sure my tours are perfect before I lead them alone. My last test is this afternoon."

"Wanna trade?" Peter sipped tea with his hands wrapped around the canteen. "I'll run tours at the museum if you'll work at the mason's."

"It's a miracle you still have that job after missing so much work," Sephiri said.

"Sometimes I wish he'd fired me," Peter said. "Then I could focus on training instead of making bricks."

Sephiri shot him a sideways look and opened her mouth.

Peter tensed until Kira interrupted, "How are things at the farm?"

His shoulders relaxed. "Better, now that we don't have that Viper loan hanging over our heads. My father's considering getting a tattoo to cover the old brand."

"Your father?" Sephiri's eyebrows raised. "A tattoo?"

"I know, it's crazy. But it'd be safer, so it's not obvious he used to be indebted to them."

Kira nodded. "The Vipers are a lot weaker without Razor, but they're not gone. If any of them see his brand, they might try to get in his business again."

"Better to keep our heads down."

"You've always been great at that," Sephiri teased.

Peter laughed. The twinkle in her eye sent a warm rush through his body. He knocked his shoulder against hers. "How are things at the laundry shop?"

She smiled, dropping her gaze to her lap. "Better than I expected. It's nice to make a little coin of my own. I'm thinking about adding more days, actually. Those rich people in Paratill View have no shortage of fine gowns to clean. And, you know, being able to speed up the drying with a bit of wind doesn't hurt."

"What?" Kira gawped. "You do that?"

Sephiri's playful look danced between them. "Only when there's no one around, and only a little."

Rylan cheered, pumping his fist in the air at the top of the cliff.

Peter cupped his hand around his mouth. "Nice job, Ry!"

Rylan picked his way down the sloping gully back to where the picnic blanket was spread on the grass. He grinned and shook out his arms, his short, brown hair bobbing as he approached. "See if you can beat that, Peter!"

"As in, go *faster* than you?" Peter stood and stretched his arms overhead. "Yeah, I think I can do that."

As if suddenly remembering Peter's Source power, Rylan's shoulders fell. "Oh. Right." He dropped into the seat Peter vacated.

Peter stretched his wrists, rolled his shoulders, then placed a hand on the cold rock. He gazed up the cliff. Standing at the base, it seemed to loom taller than four stories. Above, the place where he fell on his previous attempt taunted him.

No. This time, I can do it.

He gripped the large, jutting rock, then glanced back. Sephiri watched, hands spread, prepared to cushion a fall. Peter set his feet on the featured rock and surged upward.

Sparks danced over his skin as the Source power raced through him, from the center of his chest to his fingertips. He moved with catlike speed, leaping from hold to hold so rapidly he barely touched them. Halfway to the top, the route became complex. His fingertips barely fit on the jutting ledges. Wind whipped through his hair as he danced from hold to hold, hands growing numb on the cold rock. He reached for the next small, sloping ledge, with his right hand around a corner and his feet on tiny, barely visible edges.

His fingers ached. *Too cold. I can't . . . quite—*

A hand slipped.

His foot cut out, and his body swung like a barn door in the wind. He gasped and tightened his grip on the corner, barely holding on.

"Nice save!" Rylan called from below.

Peter risked a glance down. At the base of the cliff, his friends had lifted to their feet. Sephiri waited, ready.

He took a deep breath, then exhaled and re-balanced. Catching the edge of the crimp, he moved carefully upward.

Maybe I got a little overeager with my Source speed, he thought.

He tried to channel Kira's methodical nature instead. Left hand on a crimp, right hand to grasp a ledge, left hand on the same ledge, then both palms flat as he lifted himself.

"Whew!" he exclaimed. "That was—Augh!"

With a hiss, a green-and-black checkered snake lunged toward his face, fangs bared.

Peter jerked backward and to the side, avoiding the attack. His hands scrabbled at the dirt on the ledge but found no purchase. With another shout, he slipped off the cliff and plummeted toward the ground.

The wind whipped around him. He closed his eyes.

Whump.

He landed hard on a cushion of air, knocking the wind from his lungs. He glanced to the side and found himself floating half his height above the ground. When the cushion dissipated, he dropped the remaining distance, landing in the dirt.

"Are you all right?" Sephiri asked.

Peter groaned as he sat up. "Yeah." He winced. "I'm fine."

"Sorry for the hard catch. I didn't expect you to fall. What happened?"

Peter caught his breath, then pushed disheveled, sweaty hair from his forehead. "Tartis viper."

"What?" Kira frantically looked around where they sat, like another one might pop out of the grasses. "You saw one?"

"Nearly got bitten by one." Peter flopped onto his back, his heart still racing.

"Tartis vipers are . . . bad, right?" Rylan asked.

Kira scoffed. "Yeah, I'd say so. Their venom kills in seconds. He'd probably have been dead before he even hit the ground."

He gulped. "Yeah, that's bad."

"If they're nesting up there, we need to find a different crag to climb," Sephiri said. "You sure you're okay?"

Peter nodded. He sat up, then threw the others a shaky grin. "Really. I'm fine. Even with venomous snakes around, this is still better than working for Jenkins. I bet those reflexes will serve me right in the army. Right, Rylan?"

"Are they going to be throwing vipers at us in the army?" Rylan grimaced. "I changed my mind. You can join up alone."

Peter raised his eyebrows. "You want to be a bricklayer forever?"

Rylan groaned. "I'm joking, Peter. But I *do* think you're a little too obsessive about training. They'll train us when we join, that's the whole point."

"They wouldn't let you join at all if they knew you had Source power," Sephiri said.

The humor drained from the conversation.

"Seph, they won't find out," Peter said. "I've got good reflexes, and Rylan's abnormally strong. There's nothing to it."

"You can't guarantee that," Sephiri said. "Someone can, and *will*, figure it out. It just takes one slip."

"We won't slip."

"You don't know that. You can't know. But what I *do* know is what happened to my parents when they were found out." Her blazing eyes stared at him.

A breeze whipped through Peter's sweaty hair, making goosebumps rise on his nape. "And it shouldn't have," he said. "What happened to them was awful, but we know how to keep ourselves safe. It's barely a risk."

"How can you be sure of that?" Sephiri asked. "How can you trust the army?"

"It's not about trust," Peter said. "My whole life I've thought that I would be stuck on the farm. Now I have a chance to do what I want. The Source power isn't just a risk, it's an advantage. Who wouldn't want a soldier with our skills? I'll climb the ranks fast!"

"The higher you climb, the further the fall," Sephiri said, hands on her hips.

"Guys!" Rylan said. "Can we have this argument somewhere without the risk of tartis viper bites?"

Sephiri held Peter's gaze for a long moment. Her dark skin and hair matched her eyes, which glowered at him. He thought she might smack him with a powerful gust of wind, but then she sighed and cut her gaze to the side. "You're right."

Kira gazed at the sun. "I need to get back to town, anyway. It's later than I realized, and my mother will be furious if I'm not on time." Kira shooed them off the picnic blanket and packed up the basket. "We should hurry."

Peter nodded. Things were tense between him and Sephiri. No matter how many times they had the same argument, they never seemed to get anywhere with it. But a better life was so close he could taste it. And Sephiri was right. It was a risk—but he couldn't just let go of that desire.

Peter dragged his feet as the four friends hiked back toward the city. Sephiri walked alongside Kira, who set a brisk pace. Rylan dropped back to join Peter.

"You gotta stop bringing it up, man," Rylan muttered. "That argument never goes anywhere."

"I know, I know." Peter kept his gaze on his feet. "I'm sorry. I don't mean to cause tension with everyone."

"Don't worry. It will blow over."

"Every time it comes up, it seems to hurt her a little more."

I don't want to hurt her, Peter thought. *I want her to understand.*

"Don't look so depressed!" Rylan clapped him on the shoulder. "You just survived a harrowing battle with a tartis viper. I think that deserves a proper meal at the tavern, don't you?"

Peter wasn't rich, but he did have a few copper tid in his pocket. He smiled. "You might be onto something."

3

"Guys, come on!" Kira hustled through the cobbled streets of Brufec Heights toward the museum. "Hurry!" Sweat beaded at her temples. *We should have left much earlier. Mother's going to be furious.*

"Why are we coming?" Rylan asked.

A watery feeling ran through Kira's gut. *Did I forget to tell them?* She cringed. "Just come on!"

She rounded the corner, breathing hard, and found the decorative columns of the museum stretching up its impressive, white-stone edifice. Her breath caught. Her mother waited in front of the building's heavy wooden doors.

Kira leaped back around the corner before she was spotted. She patted her hair, trying to smooth down any sweaty flyaways, and then handed the picnic basket and blanket to Peter. She untied her dress from where it had been bound up around her waist. It hung to the ground and hid her trousers. She pressed against the fabric, attempting to smooth out the wrinkles. Stains of dirt marred the elbows of her plain dress, and sweat dampened her hand as she wiped her face.

I hope I look passable.

Rylan, Peter, and Sephiri all blinked at her.

"I need a favor," Kira said. "Do you have a minute?"

"I'm starving," Rylan moaned.

Peter's eyebrow lifted. "A minute for what?"

"Dinner's on me . . . soon. Please?"

Rylan frowned and then looked at the others.

Kira forced a quick smile. "Just follow my lead." Kira took a deep breath, straightened her posture, and rounded the corner. "Hello, Mother."

Rosalyn Lancaster didn't have a single hair out of place. Attired in a fine blue dress, her plaited, pale hair created an understated but elegant look. She looked wealthy, as she always did. Kira appreciated growing up in ease and comfort, but her mother's tendency to show off grated on her.

"Kira." Her mother peered down her nose. "I see you've brought your audience?"

Rylan cocked his head. "Wait . . . wha—"

A jab from Sephiri stopped him mid-sentence.

"Yes." Kira gestured at her sweaty, dirty friends. Rylan rubbed his side and put on a sudden grin. Sephiri ducked her head in greeting, looking sheepish. Peter ran a hand through his shaggy hair.

"All right, then." Her mother sighed. "Welcome, all three of you. Kira will take you through our new exhibit, Art of the Late Tarvinian Era."

"Sounds great." Rylan's dull tone indicated he'd rather head toward the stocks.

Rosalyn closed the heavy doors behind them. Inside, the museum was quiet and dimly lit, and the late afternoon sun streamed in from the skylight. She gestured for Kira to step forward.

Kira straightened her shoulders. *I can do this. Confidence. Speak clearly.*

She lifted her chin. "Welcome to the Palenting Art and

History Museum," she projected in a clear, professional voice. Peter's eyes widened with her change, and she suppressed a laugh at his expression. "If you'll follow me, I'll guide you through our latest collection."

Her three friends followed like ducklings, and Rosalyn stuck close, watching with a keen eye. While a nervous tingle did run through Kira's body, a rush of adrenaline did as well. She led them into the western wing of the museum. Inside, rare statues filled the center of the elegant room, artifacts displayed along the far end, and paintings hung from the walls. Rylan slumped, taking in the large exhibit.

"As you can see, this exhibit features a fine statue of King Caelinus, who presided over Norshewa from years 704 to 720 of the Tarvinian Era. Discovered by a fishing vessel off the western coast . . ."

The words fell off her tongue with practiced ease. She recited the history as she walked her friends through the statues of leaders, then led them to the back of the room, where a glass case held the rare artifacts.

"I don't get it," Rylan said as he peered inside. "Why display stuff like this? They're just knives, right?"

"They're more than knives." Sephiri nudged Rylan. "They're ceremonial, used in rituals but not for everyday use."

"Exactly," Kira said. "That knife was part of a coronation ritual, to be exact. Another piece of the same ritual was this, one of our rarest and most precious artifacts, the royal Tarvinian crown."

Kira had seen it dozens of times. Its dull silver surface barely reflected the sunlight shining through the window. Ten rounded points rose around the circular object.

Peter blinked at the crown in the case. Rosalyn looked disappointed at the lack of reactions, but Kira couldn't blame them. "Though it lacks the gold and gems we see on modern crowns, it's more valuable than all the treasures in the king's stores. This crown is made of pure baltham."

Sephiri gasped.

Rylan's face screwed in question. "Baltham? What's that?"

"One of the rarest materials on the continent," Kira said. "And this is the largest amount of it any of our researchers have seen."

"Whoa." Rylan's eyes widened. "That sounds . . . important."

"This crown is over one thousand years old," Kira said.

"How many?" Her mother asked.

Kira's stomach turned. She pressed her lips together and glanced at her mother. "Um . . . one thousand and . . . fifty . . . four?"

"Fifty-six."

She sighed. "This crown is one thousand and fifty-six years old." *Not that any guests will care about the exact number.*

"Whoa!" Rylan had wandered to the other side of the exhibit and stood slack-jawed in front of a large painting. "What's this?"

Rosalyn rolled her eyes.

Kira crossed the room. As tall as her, the faded painting showed a vast, golden throne room, piled with gems and weaponry. In profile, seated on a huge throne draped in green velvet, a tall, severe man gazed past the gems toward the open throne room door. A repeating pattern of circles with stacked rectangles inside was carved into the golden door frame. The man rested an elbow on his knee while his chin was propped on his fist and a bracer shaped like a golden serpent wrapped around his arm. He clenched something small and gold in his hand, but in the painting's condition, it was difficult to make out what it was.

"This guy looks serious," Rylan said.

"This is a portrait of King Xilxidor painted over seven

hundred years ago," Kira said. "That's a hundred years before the supposed disappearance of the city of Kytalia"

"Kytalia!" Rylan gasped. "The City of Gold. I've heard of that. Incredible!"

"King?" Peter stepped closer to the painting. "Were they a kingdom?"

"Norshand never had control of Kytalia," Kira said. "Nor did anyone else."

"Where's this city now?" Rylan asked. He and Sephiri drew closer, elbowing Peter for space.

"The only record we have of the city is the oral histories, and the art made about it," Kira explained. "According to legend, they built it entirely from golden bricks. It was a city of great wealth and prestige, with endless supplies of rare gems. Access to a mystical healing power kept its citizens healthy and young."

"Healing?" Sephiri asked. "From what?"

"No one knows," Kira said. "But the stories speak of people who traveled to the city to have their wounds and illnesses healed."

Peter leaned even closer, pointing at the canvas. "What's he holding?"

Sephiri squinted. "Looks like a knife."

"We're not sure," Kira said. "Some art historians have suggested it's supposed to be the Key of Kytalia."

"A key?" Rylan asked. "Key to what?"

"Not *a* key . . . *the* key. Legend says there's a key to unlock the treasures of the city. They call it the Key of Kytalia, but no one knows what or where it is. They think that's what he's holding, though."

Rosalyn tutted.

Kira's gaze snapped to the ground. "Please stay behind the line." She chided herself for getting lost in the story and forgetting the rules.

"Oh, sorry." Peter took a step back, bringing his feet behind a white line on the ground. "So what happened to it? Where's Kytalia now?"

Kira glanced back at her mother, who raised her eyebrows.

"No one knows for sure." Kira shrugged. "King Xilxidor was the last to rule before the city disappeared into the Straith Mountains."

"Disappeared? How does a city disappear into the mountains?" Peter asked.

"The stories say that in Kytalia, thievery wasn't just a crime, it was morally forbidden. As time passed, the city grew and outsiders arrived. They coveted the wealth of the city. People took gold and gems from the land for themselves, even stealing from their neighbors. As the greed spread, King Xilxidor feared the city's downfall. To protect his kingdom, he hid it deep in the mountains."

"That doesn't sound possible," Peter said. "Hiding a city?"

"Because it's a legend." Rosalyn stepped forward. "Paintings depict the stories told during that time, but we have no historical evidence that Kytalia ever existed. However, in our collection, we *do* have genuine artifacts from that era that demonstrate how the people in those times lived. Kira?"

Kira felt a flush creep up her neck. Her mother allowed the tour to go off-script sometimes—but not *too* far off-script. "Of course." She motioned away from the painting. "This way, please."

She guided them through the rest of the exhibit, noting how Peter continued to glance back toward the painting of King Xilxidor. She didn't rush, but didn't linger, and soon enough finished the tour with a curtsy. "That concludes our exhibit on Art of the Late Tarvinian Era."

Sephiri and Peter clapped, and Rylan glanced towards the door. "That was awesome, Kira," Rylan said. "Can we eat, now?"

"Adequately done, Kira," Rosalyn said. "Memorize your dates, and you can lead tours starting on Halfday."

Kira exhaled and managed a weak smile. She didn't expect glowing praise, but it would have felt nicer if her mother could be more positive. *Either way . . . it's done.*

The four friends hurried out of the museum in an overlapping chorus of growling stomachs.

"I'm starving," Rylan said. "Think the Bitter Bat will be crowded?" He led the way, moving with purpose through the streets toward the popular inn, already talking Sephiri's ear off about the meats and cheeses he planned to order since Kira was buying.

Peter lingered behind them, next to Kira. "Do you think it's real?" he asked. "The City of Gold?"

Kira sighed. "I should have known you'd latch on to that story. I don't know. Mother doesn't believe so. She thinks someone would've found proof it existed by now, an artifact or something related to Kytalia. But all we have is the art, which makes it seem like a myth."

"That's what *she* thinks," Peter said. "What do *you* think?"

"I don't know. There's a lot of art about it. Like . . . a lot. It shows up in plenty of stories around that period."

"Everyone thought the Amulet of Power was a myth, too," Peter murmured.

Kira nodded.

"So it could be out there? Somewhere in the Straith Mountains?"

"Please don't get any ideas."

"I'm not." Peter's grin suggested otherwise.

"I have *got* to stop inviting you to the museum."

4

_____

C*lang!* The sound of iron striking iron echoed off the stone walls.

Rylan grunted, holding his sword over his head to block Peter's strike. "Slow down a little, will you?"

"Doesn't that defeat the point?" Peter pivoted on the ball of his foot and thwacked Rylan in the flank with the flat of his training sword. "Killing blow!"

Rylan whined and stumbled backward. "That's gonna bruise!"

"Then block it."

They moved back into their starting positions, and Peter raised his sword. The early morning sun fell in golden stripes through the oversized windows of the Garrison, which now had glass in their frames. The renovation of the space was complete, and it was beyond anything Peter had imagined. Inside was vast and open, with a training space, a large, rough-hewn table in a functional kitchen, and lofted bedrooms for each of them. It had a roof, proper doors, actual walls—no more crumbling, soot-stained rocks everywhere.

Some of the treasure they'd found in the Fortress of the Sun had gone to the Vipers to pay off the Fairfields' loan, and some went to help Rylan's mother get back on her feet. But a sizable chunk went to buying and fixing up the Garrison. It was warm, nice, and protected from the rain. Sephiri lived there full time, and the rest of them split their time between the Garrison and their parents' homes. But more and more nights had them staying in their warm, private bedrooms.

Peter had no regrets about how they'd spent the money, but it meant he still had to work at the mason's until he could join the army next season.

Rylan scoffed and waved a hand at Peter. "You run through your sword forms. I'm going to make breakfast."

"We can grab something on the way! Come on, practice with me."

"I want oatmeal. I'll make some for Seph, too."

"We need all the training time we can get if we want to make it into the army, Rylan."

"I know, I know." Rylan set a small pot over the kitchen fire. "But we need to eat, too."

Peter ran through sword forms, practicing his footwork across the width of the training space. "I don't want to just be a foot soldier," Peter said. "I want—"

"To be great, I know."

Peter sighed and set his sword aside. "It's going to be harder to stand out if we're not using our Source power."

"Better to be a mid-level foot soldier than caught using Source." Rylan stirred the oatmeal into the pot and peered inside.

"Maybe there's something else we can do." Peter wandered to the table and dropped into a chair.

"I think we should train a reasonable bit, then have whatever skills we do when we sign up." Rylan ladled the oatmeal into bowls. "Sephiri! Wake up! I made breakfast!"

Peter propped his chin on his hand. The night before, he

had struggled to sleep as thoughts of wandering through a vast city of gleaming gold ran through his mind. "What if we found Kytalia? That would impress the commanders, right? I bet they'd send us on important missions to find other lost places."

"Are there a lot of lost places in Rynor?" Rylan asked. "Seph! Wake up!"

"Stop yelling!" Sephiri called from her loft. "I'm awake!"

Peter hummed. Rylan was right—it was a stupid idea. And Kira's mother was probably right, too. *If it were real, an artifact would've shown up at some point.*

Rylan set a bowl in front of Peter, then groaned as he sat at the table with his own. "I'm still tired from climbing. We should use the Amulet before we head to work."

Peter downed a spoonful of oatmeal—perfectly textured, with a bit of honey. Rylan had improved his cooking skills during his time at the Garrison.

A ladder led to Sephiri's loft, but instead of using it, she hopped down. Her eyes gleamed white as she softened her fall with her power and landed soundlessly on the hay-covered floor. The sudden burst of wind rustled the dust in the room and Peter's clothing. "Morning!" she chirped. Her dark hair fell loose to her shoulders, and she beamed at both of them.

Sephiri had changed a lot since she'd shared the Source. She was lighter on her feet, held her head higher, and smiled more. Keeping the ability a secret all her life had been like a millstone around her neck. After sharing it, she became a different person. Brighter. Happier. She plopped down at the table. "Thanks for making breakfast, Rylan."

"You have work today, too?" Peter asked.

Sephiri nodded. "Half-day in the shop, and the rest running deliveries."

"We might see you out and about," Rylan said. "We're on a job site today."

"Moving on up in the world, huh?" Sephiri waggled her eyebrows.

"Something like that." Peter slurped the rest of his breakfast. He wasn't looking forward to spending the day at the job site, but it was different from the monotony of molding bricks at the shop.

"We should get going," Rylan said. "The site's across town."

"Good call." Peter's mouth turned up at the corner. "You'll need the time. Some of us aren't as fast as others."

"If you run through this city, there's no way you'll go unnoticed."

Peter laughed. "Speaking of the Source . . ."

He stood and walked to the hearth, where the fire had quieted to a low flame. Wriggling a loose stone free from the corner revealed a small wooden box hidden in its cavity.

He opened the box, revealing the Amulet of Power nestled in silk. Nearly the size of his palm, the deep blue jewel faded to red at the top. Set in silver, it caught the dim light, sparkling like an ocean wave in the sunshine. The flame upon the sea. His breath still caught at the sight of it.

"All right," Rylan said. "Go."

Peter lifted the Amulet by its thin, silver chain and rested it in his palm. At the moment of contact, its power surged through him, rushing over his nerves like cool water. He took a deep breath, eyes closed, and let the sensation wash over him. He felt like he could run to the northernmost tip of Norshewa without stopping to catch his breath. The tallest peak of the Straith Mountains seemed accessible. He felt unstoppable, powerful, quick, and—

"Time's up." Rylan picked up the Amulet by its chain. "My turn."

"Whew! So much better." Peter exclaimed. "I didn't realize how depleted I was."

Rylan placed the Amulet in his palm and held it with his eyes closed.

Peter counted, watching as a smile traced Rylan's face. "Ten." Peter snatched the Amulet back. He returned it to the box, then tucked it back into its hiding place at the hearth.

Sephiri watched from the table. "How many times this week?"

"This is the first one." Rylan puffed out his chest. "See? We're making it last."

Sephiri raised an eyebrow and glanced at Peter.

He nodded. "We haven't forgotten the warning—just as it gives power, it can corrupt."

"I could hold it all day," Rylan said. "It feels amazing!"

Peter sighed. "And *that's* why Kira's making us use it in pairs."

Sephiri relaxed. "I'll clean up. You two get to work." She waved her hand, shooing them off into the cool morning.

ON THE NORTHEAST side of Palenting, the job site lay at the edge of town. A clock in the street showed it was later than Peter had realized. He picked up his pace, pushing through the morning rush.

"Ugh," Rylan said. "We're still gonna be late."

An urge to run gnawed at Peter, as if the power inside him begged to be used. *If Rylan can refrain from lifting market stalls, I can hold back, too.* They kept their powers under wraps and made their way to the north side. The fine white stone buildings of Paratill View gave way to the hardier brick of the army facilities on the northeast edge. Peter huffed as they passed them by.

A damaged guard tower loomed ahead. Rylan and Peter trudged through the surrounding mud as they joined the other contracted masons to haul rocks.

"Fairfield!" Jenkins barked. "There you are! Get over here!"

Peter sighed. "Another workday begins."

A few hours in, Peter's back hurt. His hands were rubbed raw from hauling bricks, and sweat dripped down his nape despite the wiether chill in the air. He dragged another pallet of bricks through the mud with Rylan. "You know . . . I prefer working in the shop."

Rylan wiped the back of his hand across his forehead, leaving a streak of mud. "I do too."

They labored through the day until the sun lowered to the horizon. Jenkins dismissed the crew, saying they hadn't made enough progress, but he always said that. Exhausted, sweaty, and covered in mud, Peter and Rylan headed south.

"Today sucked," Rylan said. "I'm about to go back to helping my mother at her shop."

"As a seamstress?" Peter knocked his shoulder against Rylan's. "Come on, we're joining the army. Only a season left!"

"A season of this." Rylan gestured at his muddied clothes. "I'm gonna end up spending whatever coin I make at Sephiri's laundry."

"Eh, there are worse things to spend it on."

"Why don't you just work on the farm?" Rylan asks. "Is your father still insisting you become a mason?"

Peter pressed his lips together. "Yeah, he wants me to stick with it."

"Still stuck on the danger thing?" Rylan asked.

Peter nodded. "That and he thinks the army will take me too far from Palenting."

"Isn't that the point?" Rylan raised his eyebrows.

"For me, yeah. But even though the farm is out of debt, and my father's making money, they want me to stay close."

"Just because you join the army doesn't mean you'll get posted halfway across Terrenor."

Peter shrugged then let his shoulders slump. "He still thinks I should become a craftsman."

"That'd be great," Rylan grumbled. "Too bad we're just glorified bricklayers."

Peter tugged at Rylan's shoulder. "Come on. Let's walk by the facility."

"You're unbelievable. Don't you want to get back and clean up? And eat? I'd love to eat."

"It's on the way! We'll just take a minute."

Men's shouts and clanging swords rang through the air as they approached the army training facility. Peter's mood lifted, and he picked up the pace. "They're ending soon. Hurry!"

The training facility comprised a small arena behind the barracks, built of wood and brick with a floor of hard-packed sand. It wasn't exactly open to the public, but they didn't block it off, either. Peter wove through the wood and stone columns supporting the stands with Rylan at his heels.

Dozens of soldiers scattered about the ground, armed with training swords, shields, clubs, maces, knives, and even bows. Peter's eyes widened. The soldiers were fast, focused, and precise. Their weapons clashed. Their heels dug into the sand. Every soldier wore the same thick leather armor and plain linen shirts. Peter tugged at the sweaty collar of his work clothes. In one season, he'd be in that arena too, in that polished leather armor, his blade shining in the late afternoon sun, shoulders burning with exertion, each strike of the sword one step closer to his goals. His mouth pulled into a grin.

"Can I help you boys?" a deep voice asked.

Peter jolted so hard he smacked his head on the nearest wooden post. He rubbed his temple, grimacing, while trying to bow to the man behind the deep voice: Commander Isert.

The tall, intimidating man sported a head full of silver hair falling to his chin. Intricate designs around the city seal of Palenting embossed his leather armor. He raised his eyebrows, peering under the stands at Peter and Rylan. Rylan glanced around as if considering bolting. Peter put a hand on his shoulder and squeezed.

"Sorry, sir," Peter said, his voice wavering. "We were walking home from a workday."

"Your route takes you beneath the arena stands?" Commander Isert asked.

"Um," Rylan said. "Yes?"

Peter knocked his shoulder against Rylan's. "We're working with Jenkins the mason at a nearby job site, but we'll both be joining the army next season. We want to see what you do so we can be as prepared as possible."

The commander nodded. He narrowed his eyes as he inspected the two of them. Peter prepared for an evening in the stocks when the man's face broke into a smile. "Next time, use the door." He pointed to the arched entrance at the other side of the arena. "There are stairs to a viewing area."

Peter gawped at the door. "We can come in and watch?"

"Citizens are welcome." Commander Isert's expression hardened. "Though we look down upon trespassing."

"Right," Peter said. "Sorry, sir. Next time we'll use the door. Thank you, sir!"

"Now, run along. We're wrapping up today, but you're welcome back another time."

"Yes, sir! Thank you, sir!"

Commander Isert's smile reappeared. "I look forward to your entrance into the training program next season."

Commander Isert turned, marched back into the arena, and shouted a command. The soldiers ceased their training and turned to face him with quick precision.

Rylan grabbed Peter's forearm and dragged him from under the stands and into the street. "Come on," he said, "we're not supposed to be under here!"

"Yeah, but we're not *not* allowed," Peter said. "You heard

what he said!"

"Now he's going to remember us for being the two who hid under the stands," Rylan said. "Come on, I'm about to pass out from hunger."

Peter turned back to the stands with a last gaze of longing. He sighed. "Fine, let's go. Where do you want to eat?"

"Maybe Harrison's Tavern, or Mucklungs, or the Bitter Bat, or—"

Peter chuckled.

"What?" Rylan pouted, like the laugh offended him.

"It's crazy. Before we found the Amulet, we never would have discussed where to buy dinner. I'd love something hearty. Meat, maybe some potatoes." He tugged at his shirt caked in dried mud. "The taverns will never let us in like this, though."

"I don't want to go all the way back to the Garrison to clean up. How about Palentor Bites or the Meal House?"

Peter frowned. "They'll be packed." A rich aroma of roasted garront on a spit and grilled verquash caramelizing made Peter's stomach grumble as they entered the town square. "Let's get something from one of the market stalls."

The vendors were out in force, selling boar, game birds, roasted vegetables, fresh crusty bread, and hard cheeses from their stands. The sizzle of grease dripping on a fire reached his ears. The thick smell of seasoned meat filled his nose. *Who needs a tavern?* Peter beelined to the closest stand.

"What happened to you?" a familiar voice sneered. "Did you roll around in the horse stables on your way here?"

Peter closed his eyes and groaned. "Yeah, that's exactly what I did." He paid the vendor for two roasted garront legs, then turned.

Ashton Dunn wore a fine silk shirt and his usual smarmy expression. His lips twisted into a smirk, and blond hair fell into his eyes. "I can tell. You smell terrible."

Peter took a bite of garront. The meat was tender and

perfectly spiced, melting in his mouth. "Come on, Ashton, I'm just trying to eat." Peter stepped around him and handed the other garront leg to Rylan, who traded it for a skewer of roasted verquash.

"Better enjoy it," Ashton sneered. "I know you can barely afford those little skewers. This must be a treat for you after a tough little workday."

"At least we *can* work," Rylan said. "Some people aren't handed everything on a silver platter."

"Rylan," Peter muttered. "Not now." He pushed his way past the older boy.

Ashton stepped aside with a scoff but then slapped the skewer out of Peter's hand. "Watch where you're going."

Peter stared at the cooked garront, now a feast for ants in the mud.

"You jerk," Rylan hissed. "I've had it with—"

"Rylan!" Peter grabbed him by the upper arm. "Don't."

"That's right," Ashton sneered. "Keep your dog leashed."

Rylan shrugged off Peter's hold, then made a show of stumbling. He shoved his shoulder into Ashton, smearing his fine silk shirt with dirt. "Whoops. Sorry, Mr. Dunn. I've got a great laundry shop recommendation if you need one."

Ashton's jaw dropped. "You—You—Gah!"

Peter bit back a laugh at Ashton's expression. Shaking his head, he took one last gaze at his ruined skewer, then gestured for Rylan to follow.

"This shirt cost more than you'll make in a season!" Ashton shouted as they left. "You better watch your back!"

Peter and Rylan rolled their eyes, then kept laughing as they ambled back toward the Garrison, sharing what food they still had. The weather was chilly as the sun set, but the food was warm, and Commander Isert's smile—had it been a little impressed?—was still in the forefront of his mind. He'd had worse work days.

5

Peter woke to the sound of rain thrumming on the Garrison roof. He stuck his head out of his lofted bedroom and peered at the window. It wasn't just a drizzle; it was torrential, and heavy storm clouds filled the sky.

Rylan stuck his head out of his own room, and they looked at each other. "You know what this means?" Rylan asked.

Peter grinned. In unison, they shouted, "No work today!"

The foreman had made that clear when they started—the mud would be impassable in rain like this. If Peter was dedicated to being a mason, he would go to Jenkins' shop to find other work. But with his enlistment date looming, he wasn't about to give up a surprise day off.

Kira had stayed in the Garrison the night before, which meant all four of them indulged in a leisurely breakfast as the rain pattered against the windows.

"I need to pick up a few things from the market for dinner," Sephiri said. "Anyone want to brave the rain with me?"

"I'll come," Peter said. "I've got to stop by the farm, and the market's on the way."

Kira shrugged. "I don't mind the rain."

"Well, I'm not hanging out here alone," Rylan said. "We'll all go."

They finished breakfast, then bundled into boots and waxed cloaks with oversized hoods.

Other than the rain, the streets were quiet. Water collected in shallow puddles on the uneven road. Despite the weather, the market in the square still hummed with activity, shielded from the worst of the rain by overlapping umbrellas and large canvas awnings stretched over the stalls.

"Look!" Kira gestured to a vendor with a huge wagon parked across the marketplace. "The animal wrangler is here!" She grabbed Sephiri's hand, and they raced across the square to the wagon.

The wrangler only came to town a few times a season, and they never knew when he would show up. He traveled across Terrenor, working as a veterinarian and a taxidermist, and sometimes he brought rare, exotic animals. The wealthy folks in Paratill View, with their greenhouses and gardens, loved to purchase the colorful birds and rare reptiles he brought from Feldor's Kyrd Forest.

The wrangler wore heavy canvas clothes and a loose brown hat. His black goatee was greased to a sharp point below his chin. He nodded as the friends approached the cages stacked outside the wagon.

Peter lowered his hood. In one cage, a green lizard the length of his arm flared its collar and bared its dual rows of teeth. In the cage above, a glossy black bird ruffled its feathers and blinked its beady eyes. There were toads behind glass, a slinky, ferret-looking critter with a long ruffled tail, and even a huge, motionless turtle with a glossy yellow shell.

"Look at this little guy!" Sephiri exclaimed. She knelt and cooed at a small fox with huge, flicking ears. The creature tilted its head at her, and Sephiri mimicked the motion.

Peter smiled, his eyes not on the fox. *Cute.*

"He's friendly, too," the wrangler said. "Good critter to have around if you want to get a mice infestation under control."

Sephiri's eyes widened. "I mean, we do live in a sizable space . . ."

"I don't think that's a good idea," Kira said with a smile. "We already have alley cats."

"You won't if you bring this one home," the man said.

Sephiri grimaced. "Yeah, maybe not the best idea."

"What's in there?" Rylan pointed at the back of the wagon, where heavy canvas covered one of the larger cages. He leaned closer. The cage rattled and something within growled. He stumbled backward. "Whoa!"

"Best keep your distance, boy," the man said. "That one's a special order."

Peter stepped closer, curiosity piqued. "What is it?"

"She's in a bad mood because of the rain. These critters don't like water. I've been trying to get her to sleep, but they are willful." He lifted the canvas.

The creature inside the cage growled and bared sharp, yellow fangs. It was a small, dog-like animal, with a protruding spine, spindly legs, and large, clawed paws. Its eyes were a deep red, like rotting blood. Scars pockmarked its black and wrinkly, hairless skin. It drew its lip back even further and its tongue lolled out of its mouth, foaming with saliva as it growled.

"What is that?" Rylan asked.

The creature howled, then launched its spindly body toward the front of the cage. Its jaws caught on the bars. Drool slid down the metal as it growled and thrashed, red eyes gleaming at Rylan.

"A blood panzil," the wrangler said. "Hard to catch these little suckers. They're pack animals. Dangerous, but easy to travel with. They only eat once every month, right after they shed their skin."

"Shed their skin? Like a snake?" Kira asked.

"It's a bit scarier than a snake's shedding. Bloodier, for sure. They look like they've been burned when it happens." The wrangler dropped the canvas back down over the cage. Inside it, the blood panzil snuffled and rattled the cage before quieting.

A well-dressed man strode up with a loud, cheerful greeting, grabbing the wrangler's attention. He nodded at the four friends, then turned to the potential customer to offer a firm handshake.

Rylan grimaced at the cage. "I think I've seen enough. I don't want to be here if that thing gets out."

"Too bad we can't take that little fox with us." Sephiri sighed.

"If you want it, you can clean up the cat bodies," Kira said.

Sephiri shuddered. "Fine, fine, let's go."

After a lingering gaze, the group peeled away from the wrangler.

"I'm going to the butcher," Sephiri said.

Rylan's drifting eyes lit up. "Ooh! Gammit!" He rushed toward a small table where a handful of old men sat around a game. "You know where to find me."

Peter followed Kira to the spice stand. He made casual conversation with the seller as she examined the peppercorns.

"Who's that?" Kira set down the fancy salt she had been admiring and nudged Peter's elbow. "Have you seen that vendor before?"

Tucked at the far end of the market, a small stall sat in front of a dilapidated building. The awning barely covered the goods. The vendor sat on a stool, smoking a long pipe with one shoulder exposed to the rain.

Peter handed over coins for the peppercorns and a few other jarred spices. "Maybe a traveling vendor?" He slipped the purchases into his bag. "Should we see what he's got?"

Kira nodded and smiled. "The traveling guys always have the best goods."

Sephiri joined them with cuts of paper-wrapped meat piled in her arms. She whistled at Rylan, who waved them off, already sucked into the gammit game.

The vendor barely greeted them as they approached, keeping his attention on the pipe. He was short, balding, and missing his right ear. Peter leaned over the stand and peered at the wares for sale: tiny clay pots from Tarphan, jewelry from Norshewa, and ornate knives from Feldor.

"What's this?" Kira poked around the pile of knives and withdrew a slim, unassuming dagger. Its dull blade contained rusty pockmarks, and dirt covered the hilt. Kira smoothed her thumb over the cross guard. A faded gold color glimmered under the dirt. The grip contained a divot, as if a decoration were missing.

"One argen for that," the vendor said. "It may not look like much, but it's a rare artifact. You've got a good eye, missy."

"It's beautiful," Sephiri said. She shifted the meat into one arm and brushed her fingertips over the dull blade. "It wouldn't be hard to restore."

"Do you see this?" Kira pointed. "This marking?"

"It looks like . . ." Peter squinted at the blade. A circle with stacked rectangles carved into the hilt. He lowered his voice. "Like the symbol from that painting—the one of the king."

"So you were paying attention to the tour," Kira said. "Yeah. It's the same."

The vendor's eyes flicked their direction.

"Does that mean it's from the city?" Sephiri asked.

Kira frowned. "I don't know. Anyone could've added this symbol to the hilt."

"But that's not exactly common knowledge, is it?" Peter asked. "I didn't even know there was a symbol until I saw it in that Kytalia painting."

The vendor exhaled a cloud of smoke into the rain. "What did you say, boy? What painting?"

"Uh." Peter paused, his senses heightened at the vendor's keen expression. "A painting in the museum. Of . . . Mykalia. Which is, um, an old coastal city. It's gone now. Sank into the ocean."

The vendor laughed to himself. "Right, right. I must've heard you wrong." He pointed to the scar where his ear once was. "My hearing's not as good as it once was. I thought you said something about Kytalia."

"Kytalia?" Kira asked innocently. "That old myth?"

"Ran into a guy who claimed to have the Key of Kytalia a while back," the vendor said. "I was going to, uh . . . trade with him for it, but he didn't have it. Just had that old knife. Looks Feldorian to me. Just another scammer trying to make a quick argen."

Peter's heart pounded as he glanced at Kira. She raised an eyebrow and dipped her chin.

"I think it's pretty," Sephiri said, slowly emphasizing each word. "Don't you agree, Peter?" Her eyes shone.

I'll bet this is it, Peter thought. *The Key to Kytalia.* "One argen's a lot for something so old, though." He waited, holding his breath as he avoided looking at the man."

"Fine," the man grumbled. "Five tid."

Peter forced back a grin. "I'll take it."

After exchanging coins, Peter took the knife from the stall. He turned it over in his hands, peering at the hilt, the marking, the gold gleaming through the dirt. He handed it hilt-first to Sephiri.

As they walked away, Sephiri pulled her lower lip between her teeth, then looked up with a small smile. "You think this is it?"

"I'm not sure," Kira said, "but I think it's possible."

"Guys!" Rylan called as he ran up. "I won five pintid!"

The rain let up a little. With the errands done, Kira, Rylan, and Sephiri headed back to the Garrison, and Peter split off to head south to Lowside. He walked the muddy streets with his hands stuffed in his pockets and his cloak tight around him.

Could the knife be the Key to Kytalia? Does this prove the city is real?

Could it actually unlock the city's riches?

He turned those questions over in his mind as he walked, wondering how he could find out. Even if they had the Key, they still had to find the actual city. And there was always a chance that it really was lost, never to be found again.

KNOCK, KNOCK. "MOTHER? FATHER?" Peter didn't wait for an answer before sticking his head inside his parents' cottage.

"Peter!" his father replied. Cauldrons boiled over the roaring hearth, filling the room with a toasty warmth. "Come in, come in, my hands are full."

"I got the spices you needed." Peter withdrew the jars from his bag and laid them out on the table. "How's Mother?"

"She's doing well. She stepped in the—"

"Peter!" His mother entered from the back room and broke into a broad grin. "How lovely to see you."

Things were different at the farm now that debt didn't weigh his parents down. His father didn't have to make a profit with the harvest. They grew for subsistence and used the rest of their time to do what they enjoyed. His father experimented with pickling vegetables, and his mother enjoyed growing flowers.

His mother's illness that had grown worse over the years seemed to have cleared. Ever since being in proximity to the Amulet, her mind had become sharp again. Her memory had come back, and joy returned to their family once more.

His father examined the peppercorns with a pleased grin. "These are just what the pickled radishes need. Good find, son."

"Are you staying for dinner?" His mother asked.

"Can't tonight. I've got an early start at work, so I'm heading back to the Garrison."

"That's such a nice place you've put together, but a bit drab," his mother said. "Let me send some flowers home with you. As soon as the rain lightens, I'll gather some. It'll liven up the place."

"Take some of these, too." His father pulled an unlabeled jar from the pantry and tossed it to Peter. "Let me know what you and your friends think."

"What is it?"

"It's a surprise."

"We have some fresh bread, too," his mother said. "Shall I cut you a few slices for the walk?"

Peter laughed. "I'm fine, Mother. This is plenty."

It was strange to remember how pain and stress had once defined his home. He'd never seen his parents so light, so happy. He stayed for a while, catching up, laughing, and sharing a smile. Finally, he embraced them both. With his bag laden with goodies and his heart light, he made his way back to the Garrison in the drizzling rain.

6

Sephiri leaned over the kitchen table, chopping the verquash, onions, and greens into small chunks. She snuck a glance at the cauldron. It hung over the fire, the bone broth simmering inside.

Shoot! I'm not ready yet.

She paused from chopping and wiped the sweat off her forehead. The uncut meat waited for her on a slab. It needed the longest time to cook, but she still needed to finish the onions.

"Man! I'm starving!" Rylan shouted after striking his wooden sword against a practice target. "How much longer till dinner?"

Sephiri's pulse sped. "Uhh . . . a bit, still."

He groaned.

"Hey!" Kira shouted to get his attention. "If you're not cooking, you don't get to complain. Don't forget, you're on dish duty tonight."

His shoulders fell and he nodded before raising his sword to an imaginary opponent.

"Here, let me finish that," Kira said, taking the kitchen knife out of Sephiri's hand.

Sephiri sighed and flashed a smile. "Thanks." She unwrapped the meat—a large hunk of beef, ready to be chopped into small pieces for the stew.

The girls worked side by side at the table while Rylan practiced his sword forms.

"What'd you do with the knife?" Kira asked.

"It's on the hearth." Sephiri nodded to where she'd set it on the stone above the fire. "I'll sharpen and clean it after dinner."

"That was kind of Peter to buy it for you," Kira said, a mischievous grin forming.

Sephiri's cheeks reddened. "It wasn't for me. It was for all of us."

"You're blushing." Kira's voice was quiet but teasing. "He bought it because *you* liked it."

"That's not why. He's interested in it because it might be from Kytalia. He doesn't—He doesn't think of me that much."

"Mm." Kira didn't sound convinced. "And if he did?"

Sephiri's face felt even hotter. "Well, I don't have to worry about that, do I?"

Kira knocked her hip against Sephiri's. "I know you like him."

Sephiri's heart leaped into her throat and beat rabbit-fast. "What? Of—of course, I don't!"

Kira muttered a skeptical hum. She smiled, gazing at the table as she moved the knife over the vegetables.

"Fine," Sephiri admitted. "Maybe a little."

"Just a little?"

Sephiri didn't answer. She cleared her throat and glanced over to the training area where Rylan was still absorbed in his sword forms. "Do you think Peter knows?"

"Not a chance," Kira said. "He wouldn't know a girl liked him if she slapped him upside the head."

"Should I try that?"

Kira stopped cutting and turned with her brows pinched. "Should you wh—"

Sephiri's half-smile made her stop. Both girls paused until they burst into laughter.

"It doesn't matter, anyway," Sephiri said, her laugh fading. "We're friends, and that's more than enough."

"Really?"

"Of course it is." Sephiri added the onions to the meat, then dropped both in the simmering cauldron. "I mean, we have this great space, enough food. I even have a mattress. It's more than I ever wished for when I was little."

Kira's expression softened. Finished with the vegetables, she added them to the soup, too. "That doesn't mean you can't want more, you know?"

Sephiri wrinkled her nose and gazed into the soup, focusing on its rich, enticing aroma instead of the dull ache in her heart. Kira meant well. Sephiri just didn't know how to explain it. Everything—the Garrison, the money, the comfort—still felt unreal, like it could disappear at any moment. One wrong move and she would be back on the streets again, splitting her time between the cold doorways of abandoned buildings in Schuggec Row and the tiny rooms in Yani's inn. Nothing was promised. Nothing was secure. She wished Peter understood that, too. *If anyone knew we kept the Amulet here—if anyone finds out we have Source power—this wonderful life will be a mere memory.*

She minded the soup, stirring as it cooked. Finished with the help, Kira returned to what she was reading. Sephiri enjoyed passing the time like that, side by side, tending to their own tasks.

The Garrison doors swung open. Peter called out a greeting, then shook his body like a dog, sending raindrops flying off his cloak. "Smells good in here!"

"Soup's almost up," Sephiri called back. "Don't track mud on the floors!"

Kira peered at Sephiri for a long moment but said nothing. Kira cleared the table of the cooking supplies, and the four of them sat around it as Sephiri spooned the stew into bowls. Rylan tore a loaf of crusty bread into pieces, then stuffed a bite into his mouth, grinning at Kira when she swatted at his hand.

Peter spooned the stew into his mouth. His eyes widened. "Whoa. This is fantastic."

"All Seph," Kira said. "I just chopped vegetables."

"Thanks for cooking," Peter said. He caught Sephiri's eyes.

She looked down into her bowl with a smile. The compliment felt like a touch. "Glad you like it."

"While I was training, I was thinking," Rylan said.

"Did you hurt yourself?" Kira teased.

Rylan chucked a bit of bread at her. "I was *wondering* . . . Is that knife real?"

"Well, it's certainly a real knife," Kira said.

"You know what I mean!"

Peter sipped his broth, then his brows pulled together. "How would we be able to find that out?"

All eyes turned to Kira. She sighed. "Do you want me to ask my mother? If it *is* real, there's a high probability she'll just take the knife."

Sephiri stood and pulled the knife from its place on the hearth. She'd cleaned it as best she could with a rag and some water, so the gold hilt shone in the warm firelight. Something about the knife called to her, drew her in. She ran a finger over the empty divot where a jewel should sit, and then the delicately engraved symbol beneath it. "Didn't your mother say there weren't any artifacts from Kytalia?"

Kira nodded. "So this is either fake or really, really special."

"More than special," Peter said. "Life-changing."

Rylan took another bite of bread. "If the knife is from

Kytalia, and it really is this . . . Key, that means the city is real, right?"

"Possibly," Kira said.

"Then we can find it." Rylan grinned. "If we thought the Fortress of the Sun had some gold, can you imagine what kind of money is in something actually called the *City of Gold*?"

"And the healing power," Peter said. "The power to heal any wound, any illness . . . Is that even possible?"

"In the past, I would've said no," Kira said. "But after seeing what the Amulet can do . . ."

"What do the myths say, Kira?" Sephiri set the dagger down in the center of the table. They peered at it, like they expected it to get up and tell the stories itself. "What's Kytalia supposed to be like?"

"The stories vary." Kira picked up the knife and turned it over in her hand. "The city isn't huge—they built it in a clearing in the mountains out of the store of gold the founders discovered. It's not sprawling, but it's tall."

"How much gold is there?" Rylan leaned over the table.

Kira shrugged. "It's just a myth. But the buildings are supposedly made of gold and inlaid with gems."

Rylan's eyes widened. "So you can just walk up, chisel off a hunk of gold, and be set for life?"

"That can't be true," Sephiri said. "Someone would've found it by now."

Peter took the knife and pointed to the engraving. "Maybe someone did."

"Then where'd they go?" Kira asked, but the other friends stared back with blank expressions. "If someone found the city, wouldn't they be hauling cartloads of gold and jewels into the nearest town? I haven't heard of that, so . . . what happened to them?"

Peter grimaced. "If this knife ended up in a random

vendor's stall, whatever happened to them must not have been good."

"We're getting ahead of ourselves," Sephiri said. "We don't even know if Kytalia is real. All we have are the myths."

"The myths"—Kira raised a finger while a faint smile grew on her face—"and the paintings."

Sephiri held her breath. She joined Peter and Rylan in staring at Kira.

"You think we missed something?" Peter asked. "That there might be a clue in the painting?"

Kira shrugged. "If there are any leads, they'd be there. That image is the only reason we could identify the engraving on the hilt."

"Please don't make me go through your tour again," Rylan said. "It was great, I swear, but it took forever!"

Kira rolled her eyes. "It's my mother's tour, not mine. And no, I don't mean we should go during the day. Mother would be too suspicious."

Peter grinned. "You mean . . ."

"Tonight?" Sephiri's pulse raced. "Should we go look?"

"As long as we don't take anything," Kira said. "I don't want to relive that fiasco with the sword."

"No theft," Peter agreed. A smile broke across his face. "Just some educational research." He had that gleam in his eye, the one he only got when he was excited about something, and his excitement was infectious.

If Peter believes it's real, then I can't help but believe it, too, Sephiri thought. If the city was real, and the riches, they'd be set for life. Not only that—but maybe Peter would give up his plan to join the army. With that in mind, the meal tasted even better.

7

The sun dipped beneath the horizon by the time Peter and Rylan cleaned up the dishes. The rain ceased, and the cobbled streets gleamed with puddles reflecting the light of the waxing moon. Peter tugged his cloak tighter around his shoulders against the wiether chill as they walked toward the museum. His body tingled with anticipation.

"Do you think it's real?" Sephiri asked, keeping her voice down. "The City of Gold?"

Gold.

He imagined it, like the painting in the museum: gold climbing the mountainside like vines, gold sparkling in the sunlight, gold archways dripping in gems, and gold cobblestones under his feet. Enough wealth to transform his life again —enough to transform all of Palenting. *If the army had some of those resources* . . . His mouth tugged in a smile. *Forget the leather armor and the wooden training swords! We could all wear the finest steel armor inlaid with gold, wielding sharpened blades with gems in the hilt polished to gleaming—*

"Hello? Peter?" Sephiri waved her hand in front of his face. "Are you there?"

"Sorry." He laughed and shook his head, dispelling the fantasy. "The city? I don't know. I *want* it to be real, but . . ."

Rylan turned to the others as they approached Paratill View. The moonlit facade of the museum loomed behind his silhouetted form. "So are we sneaking into the museum again?" he asked. "Same as last time?"

"Not this time," Kira said. "After that little stunt, Mother increased the security. There's no way we'd pull it off."

Peter frowned. "Then how do we get in?"

Kira smiled and issued a faint chuckle. "Through the front doors." She pulled the hood of her cloak down and hustled up the stairs to the museum, leaving Peter, Rylan, and Sephiri blinking in the street behind her.

"Kira!" Peter hissed. "What are you—"

Kira threw a grin over her shoulder, then rapped her knuckles on the museum doors. "Hello? Mr. Murray? It's Kira Lancaster!"

The doors swung open a crack, with the chained bolt still in place. A curious eye peered out. "Miss Lancaster? What are you doing here at this hour?"

"Hi," she said in a warm, cute voice. "I'm, uh, supposed to run tours in the new exhibit tomorrow, but I'm totally not prepared. My final practice runs didn't go so great." She clasped her hands behind her back and rocked on the balls of her feet. "Do you mind if I practice a little? I don't want my mother to know I'm not confident, which is why I'm—"

"Who are these folks?" The guard peered over her shoulder.

"My audience. I need them or it doesn't feel real. I promise I'll only go through it once, then I'll be out of your hair."

The man glanced over his shoulder and sighed. After a moment, he closed the door, clunked the lock, and opened the door. "Thirty minutes. Then you've got to run along."

"Thank you so much!" Kira waved everyone inside with a bright smile.

"Thanks," Peter muttered as they passed the guard, who grunted and returned to his post.

"Wow," Rylan whispered. "That was easy."

"Yeah," Sephiri agreed. "A lot easier when you're not trying to take anything home."

"Shh! We don't have long." Kira led them to the Late Tarvinian exhibit, and they beelined to the painting of King Xilxidor.

In the dimmed lights of the closed museum, the painting looked even more impressive. "There it is," Kira whispered. She leaned closer to the painting of the gold-drenched king in his throne, then pointed at the golden doorframe, with its circles and rectangles. "The symbol."

Sephiri pulled the golden dagger out of her bag and held it up. The two symbols were mirrors of each other: the circle with the stacked rectangles on the hilt, and the same symbol on the doorframe in the painting. The object in the King's hand looked the same as the hilt of the knife. Sephiri shifted the blade into her palm and closed her fingers around it. When she did so, Peter thought it looked older than the hilt in the painting, but other than that, it seemed identical.

His heart pounded. *This must be it. The Key of Kytalia.*

"Look," Rylan said. "It's here, too!" The same symbol appeared on the king's throne.

"And here, too!" Sephiri pointed to the symbol painted on the golden floor.

"Whoa." Peter stepped closer, his excitement tempered by his curiosity. Was there more to the painting than what met the eye? "It's not just on the painting."

"What?" Kira asked. "What do you see?"

He reached out to the painting's frame, not stopping when Kira hissed through her teeth. His fingers touched it. He half-expected something to happen—an alarm to blare, a guard to rush in—but the museum was silent.

Carved into the side, near the top right corner of the frame, he found a small circle with four tiny rectangles. Like a miniature version of the stacked shapes.

"Are there any others?" Sephiri asked. "On the frame?"

"I can't see the top," Kira whispered. "It's too high."

"Here, let me just—"

"Rylan!" Peter gasped and stepped forward, hands raised and heart pounding. Before he could intervene, Rylan grasped the sides of the painting, lifted it, and pulled it away from the wall.

Footsteps sounded in the main hall.

Kira sucked in air as her eyes grew wide. "Um, and over here, you'll see the ceremonial knives used by the Rynorian royalty," she projected. "Follow me this way."

Peter ignored the heavy thudding of his pulse as he trained his ear toward the hallway. The footsteps paused, then turned and ambled away.

Rylan grimaced and set the painting down with a soft *thunk.*

"We need to hurry," Kira said.

"There's another," Peter said, touching the top corner of the frame. "Near the other symbol."

"That has to mean something, right?" Sephiri held the dagger close to her chest. "Doesn't it?"

Peter ran his hand along the paper backing of the frame. "I bet it does," he whispered. "Seph, can I see the knife?"

"Peter, no," Kira hissed.

He held up a hand. "You won't be able to tell, I promise."

Sephiri handed the knife over with a trembling hand. Peter slipped the tip of the blade between the frame and the paper backing. Carefully, slowly, he pried it away from the frame. The knife tore the paper. The ripping sound echoed in the silent gallery. Kira mumbled despair and rubbed her temples. Peter cringed. He worked the knife to the side, peeling the paper away from the frame.

"Careful," Kira said. "Be really careful."

"But hurry," Rylan whispered.

Peter nodded. He glanced toward the door. The guards could come back at any moment. He worked the knife faster.

With another tearing sound, the backing paper pulled further away from the frame, leaving two hands' lengths of space. Peter leaned closer in the dim light. "There's something in here," he whispered.

"What is it?" Rylan tried to peer over the frame, which he held in place.

"Paper." Peter wriggled his hand inside, careful not to rip any more than necessary.

"It's probably documentation," Kira whispered. "From whoever donated it to the museum."

Peter pulled the paper out. It was yellow with age, fragile to the touch, and felt like it might disintegrate if he handled it too roughly. Tiny, delicate script ran across the top of the paper.

He turned it over.

No way.

Crooked lines covered the page, forming coastal lines, rivers, and mountains.

"A map," Peter whispered.

"Miss Lancaster?" the guard's voice called down the hallway.

Kira gasped. "And over here," she blurted, "the centerpiece of the exhibit is the statue of King Caelinus, who started his rule in 704." She lowered her voice to a whisper. "Rylan, put it back! You two, block the painting!"

Rylan jumped into action, grasping the painting on either end of its massive frame. Peter and Sephiri rushed to stand between the painting and the hall. Peter tried to appear like he was listening to Kira while puffing his body as large as possible to hide the view.

"King Caelinus had revolutionary agricultural policies and was the first in the land to move away from the serf system."

"Miss Lancaster!" The guard's voice was loud and firm as he stepped into the exhibit.

The room was silent. Peter held his breath, staring at the guard.

The man gestured past him. "What is he doing?"

Peter's stomach jumped. He pictured Rylan staggering with the enormous painting balanced in his arms and a torn flap of paper waving in the air. He cringed as he spun. To his shock, the painting hung on the wall, straight and undisturbed.

Rylan inspected the painting up close but jumped back at the guard's inquiry. "I'm sorry! I wanted a closer look."

The guard's eyes swept over them. His brow furrowed.

Peter's heart beat rapid-fire. Behind his back, he gripped the knife and the map.

"If you're about finished," the guard said, "It's getting late, and I think it'd be best if you headed home."

"Right," Kira said. "Thank you so much for letting me practice. I can't thank you enough!"

The four of them scurried out of the western wing, leaving the guard behind. Peter looked back as they turned down the hall. The guard gazed with his head cocked at the painting of King Xilxidor. Peter passed the corner and pushed Rylan out the front door.

"You got it?" Kira asked as they rushed away from the museum. "It's a map?"

"I think so," Peter said. "Come on, let's check it out."

Too eager to make it back to the Garrison, they cut across the square to the Bitter Bat Inn. The tavern was raucous with late-night activity, crowded with people downing flagons of ale and dense, hearty stews. It was a mix of wealthy patrons and workers, loud and full of laughter that usually grew in volume as the night progressed. Kira snagged a table near the fire in the corner, and Peter shouldered through the crowd to buy a basket of bread with a thick hunk of rich, salted butter.

The four of them squeezed around the table, and Rylan and Kira grabbed portions of bread. Peter tore off a chunk, smeared it with butter, and handed it to Sephiri. His fingers brushed hers as he handed it over, his heart fluttering at the touch. She ducked her chin. Clearing his throat, he pushed the basket aside enough to lay the map out on the table.

With their backs to the room, leaning over the map, they formed a semicircle of privacy.

"It's real," Sephiri whispered.

In the dim light of the tavern, the ink was barely visible, drawn in delicate lines. A winding path led from what looked like a coastline to the center of the page. A cliff drawn on the water's edge contained the label "Cliff of Tears," with two lines traced on it like crying eyes. Halfway up the path, "Pools of the Moon" identified a small circle. Farther along the trail, tiny script scrawled "Mountain of the Bat." The labeled mountain had two spires, a wider one on the left, and a narrower one on the right, drawn in a careful but shaky hand. Next to the mountain, a bold X marked the end of the twisting path.

"What are these places?" Rylan asked. "I've never heard of them."

"This must be the Straith Mountains," Sephiri said. "That's where the city disappeared, right?"

"But there's no range on the map," Kira said. "Except for 'the Mountain of the Bat,' whatever that is."

"What about the text on the back?" Peter asked.

Kira turned the map over and squinted at the faded writing that ran along the top of the map. "It's Tarphic."

"What does it say?" Sephiri asked.

Peter chewed on bread as Kira frowned at the script. The noise of the tavern washed over them, the laughter and fire making the atmosphere cozy and private, despite the crowd.

"Listen to this." Kira sat up straighter. "'He who visits Kytalia receives the blessing of infinite healing and all the city's sacred treasure. Only the snakes can find it, now.'"

The friends stared in silence. Peter's heart pounded.

"That's weird," Rylan said.

"The translation could be a little off," Kira admitted. "I think that's the gist, though."

"Your Tarphic's good. I'm sure it's right," Peter said. "Snakes, though?"

"It could be a reference to King Xilxidor and his bracer," Kira said. "Not literal."

"So it's real." Peter touched the edge of the map. "It's an actual city."

"I knew it was real," Rylan said, grinning. "Now we need a snake to act as a tour guide."

"It could be another part of the myth," Sephiri said. "Have any of you heard of these locations?"

Silence fell around the table.

"And this coastline doesn't look familiar. Is it even water? It hardly looks like a map at all. It's a sketch."

"But why else would it be in the painting?" Rylan asked. "And marked with the symbol?"

"Hard to say," Peter said. "This painting must have changed a lot of hands, though. It could be fake."

"It could be," Kira said.

All four stared at the map for a long moment.

"I think we should try to find it," Peter said.

"How?" Kira asked. "Where do we even start?"

"The snakes." Rylan crossed his arms over his chest and sat back in his chair. "Obviously."

Sephiri sighed. "We could try to compare it to some existing maps of the coastline. But the drawing's so old, I don't know if it will align with any real maps."

Peter folded the map and slipped it back into his bag with

the golden dagger. "We'll keep thinking on it. That's a good idea about checking maps. Who knows, maybe we'll run into someone who can help."

Someone like Commander Isert, Peter thought. He didn't dare suggest it to the group. Sephiri wanted him to stay as far away from the army as he could. But if anyone would be familiar with the places on the map, it'd be a man who had traveled all of Terrenor.

If he knew I had a lead on Kytalia . . . If I could bring proof of its existence . . .

He'd never have to worry about getting a good army placement again. *This could be my chance.*

Peter looked up. Sephiri watched him with a curious expression, her face shadowed in the dim light. The heat of the tavern had brought a flush to her skin, and the firelight danced in her dark eyes.

He swallowed a lump in his throat. "Let's get back to the Garrison. It's getting late."

They stepped out of the crowded tavern into the dark, wet streets of Palenting.

Motion in the alley beside the Bitter Bat drew Peter's eye—a flash of blond hair. He glimpsed Ashton Dunn, watching him from the shadows beside the inn. Peter furrowed his brow. Once spotted, Ashton ducked back into the alley and scurried in the other direction.

"What is it?" Sephiri asked.

"Nothing," Peter said. "Let's go home."

8

The chill of the early-morning air crisped Peter's lungs as he passed through the streets. He dodged bleary-eyed children fetching water at the cistern. Vendors opened their stalls in the market, filling the air with sweet and savory aromas. Soldiers filtered out of the barracks, forming disciplined lines as they entered the training facility. Peter swallowed around the bundle of nerves in his throat as he approached the heavy wooden doors to the army offices.

He steeled himself and grasped the knocker, shaped like a hawk's head.

"Enter," a gruff voice called through the door.

Peter pushed the door open, peering through the gap as it widened. He'd never been inside the offices, only walked past them on his commutes. He stepped over the threshold and closed the door behind him. The room was sparser than he expected. A desk sat under the large window with chairs on either side. A shelf of scrolls filled one wall, and a map of Terrenor hung on the opposite.

Behind the desk, Commander Isert sat in a finely upholstered chair, quill pen moving across a scroll unfurled on the desk. He looked up, then adjusted the glasses on his nose. "Good morning."

"Good morning." Peter bowed, unsure what else to do. "I, um—I hoped to have a minute of your time, Commander."

"You're the boy from the arena. The one who snuck in."

"Um." Peter cringed. *Not the best way to be remembered.* "Yes, that's me. I'm Peter. Peter Fairfield."

"Sit down, Peter Fairfield. I have a few minutes."

Peter smiled, then hustled to the hard-backed, wooden chair across from the desk and sat. He pushed down his nerves as he stared at the commander's massive frame and silver hair. *If I can pull this off, it could be the start of the rest of my life.*

"I found something you might be interested in." He pulled the map from his bag and held it out.

Commander Isert adjusted his glasses, then leaned closer. His brow furrowed as he peered at the paper.

"It's a map to Kytalia," Peter explained. "The City of Gold. According to my research, no one in Rynor has ever found proof of the city's existence. But I think this map proves it's real, and that it can be found."

"Son . . ." the commander said.

Peter barreled forward. "And I think I can find it. If I do, I want it to benefit the Rynorian army. I can find the city and bring back its resources. It's not just gold, Commander, there's supposed to be a powerful healing source, too. If the army had that kind of power at its disposal—"

"Peter," the commander interjected.

Peter snapped his mouth shut.

"Where did you find this map?"

"At the market," Peter lied. "From a traveling vendor. He had a lot of old maps from all over Terrenor, and this was tucked among them, hiding in plain sight."

Isert sighed and rubbed his temple. "Vendors who roam

Terrenor produce items like this all the time. They tempt buyers with rumors and tales, not history."

"But—"

"I know it's exciting to imagine places like the City of Gold are out there waiting for us. Forget about it, though. Focus on your training rather than chasing myths."

Peter felt his nostrils flaring. "How can you be sure it's a fake?"

"Son, you're not the first to find your way to my desk with a plan to find something ancient and forbidden that will change the course of history. But I can tell you this: the army doesn't need treasure hunters. We need soldiers. Dedicated, ambitious, and determined soldiers." He tapped his quill on the parchment. "I can tell you have those qualities. Just make sure you're directing that energy the right way."

Peter bit back the argument already building behind his teeth. "Right."

The commander raised his eyebrows.

"Right, sir."

Peter glanced at the map on the wall. It was huge, detailed, and drawn with a level of care he had never seen before. He stared at the coastline, looking for the same shapes on the map. But all the coast looked the same, jagged and winding. How could he ever determine what section the map illustrated? There were barely any details on it at all.

Peter dismissed the idea of showing the knife to Isert. If the commander thought the dagger was real, he might confiscate it. And if it really was the Key to Kytalia, they would need it to unlock the treasures.

If anyone is going to find the City of Gold, it's me and my friends.

"That'll be all," Isert said.

Peter stood, the wooden legs of his chair scraping across the polished floor. "Thank you for your time." He stuffed the map into his bag and slunk out of the office.

Outside, in the early morning light, the narrow streets around the barracks were alight with activity. Officers moved into their offices, and young recruits hurried back from the market, their baskets laden with supplies. Peter let the hustle and bustle wash over him, hoping it would push away the painful longing in his chest. *Soon I'll be a part of this,* he thought. *I'll prove Isert wrong.*

His shoulders slumped as he made his way back to the town square, where the morning market was in full swing. Vendors clamored over each other for the attention of the growing crowd, and customers bumped into each other as they navigated through the space. Fruit pastry would make Peter feel better. He bought a handful to take back to the Garrison, and an extra cherry one to eat on the walk.

Despite the commander's snubbing, Peter wasn't discouraged. If anything, it could be a way for him to impress the man even further. If Isert didn't think Kytalia was real, he'd be even more amazed when Peter showed up with proof. Peter and his friends had the knife. They had the map. With Kira's research skills, they could find a map with old labels like "Cliff of Tears," or get one with a better outline of the coast. All the pieces were there.

This could work.

"What's this all about?" a familiar voice called.

Peter looked up. In the center of the square, a tall, broad-shouldered man in a thick cloak had his hand snarled in a man's shirt—a familiar-looking man.

Father?

His father struggled against the brute. Both of his hands clenched the large man's wrist, but his efforts to push him away seemed unsuccessful.

"Hey!" Peter rushed toward the center of the square. "Leave him alone!"

The stranger looked up with a sneer. A long, vertical scar

ran down one eye. The rage in his eyes sent a shiver down Peter's spine.

"Peter!" his father said.

The stranger shoved his father backward and released him. Peter rushed forward and caught him as he stumbled.

"A waste of my time," the stranger snarled, baring his teeth like an animal. The gesture turned Peter's blood cold. But then the man turned and shouldered off through the crowd.

"Good timing." Peter's father clapped him on the shoulder. "Didn't know if anyone was going to help."

"Who was that guy? Did you know him?" Peter followed with his eyes as the stranger disappeared around a corner.

His father shook his head. "Never seen him. I was talking to vendors, trying to sell my jars, and he just . . . grabbed me. Started demanding information about the vendors. Who I knew. Looking for someone." His father rubbed his forehead and sighed.

Strange, Peter thought. "You're okay, though?"

His father nodded. "Just another lovely day in Palenting," he said with a sardonic grin. "I'm glad you showed up. I think I'll head home now."

"Here, take one." Peter held out a pastry.

His father accepted it with a laugh. "Thanks, Son."

His mood soured, Peter made his way back to Schuggec Row with the bag full of pastries. *Why would someone harass him like that? Because Father seemed to know all the vendors in the market? Who was that man looking for?*

As he approached the Garrison, marks in the mud caught his attention.

Hoofprints?

It wasn't often that anyone on horseback came to Schuggec Row. Horses were for the army and the wealthy, not for the kinds of people who lurked in the Row and in nearby Lowside.

His mood soured even more. Then, at the sight of their home, it went from bad to worse.

The Garrison doors stood open. Three horses waited outside, and two more hitched to a wagon marked with the seal of Palenting. Peter rushed inside, eyes wide.

"There you are, Mr. Fairfield," Constable Eastling crossed his arms over his pristine, unmarked uniform. A half-dozen guards flanked him in leather armor. Kira, Sephiri, and Rylan sat at the table, hands on the surface as a guard watched them. Their faces were pallid, and Rylan still wore his pajamas. "We'd like to ask you a few questions about the Palenting Museum." The guards spread out and looked through the Garrison.

"The museum?" Peter echoed. His chest pulled tight with anxiety.

This is bad. Did the guard see us mess with the painting? Did he discover the cut in the backing? No, it was barely visible—and how would anyone know anything was missing? Surely no one knew the map was in the painting at all.

"We have some routine questions," the constable said.

A guard lifted the lid of a clay pot in the kitchen and peered inside.

That doesn't seem routine, Peter thought.

"Were you at the museum recently?"

"Sure, on Weekterm," Peter said. "Kira led us through a tour of the new exhibit. Her mother, the owner, was there, too."

"Right." The constable narrowed his eyes. "And have you returned to the museum since then?"

Peter caught Kira's eye. She managed a faint nod—a tiny gesture that looked like a twitch. The guard watching her didn't even register it.

"Yes, we, uh, went back last night."

"To do what?"

He gestured toward Kira. "Kira works there, and we were helping her rehearse."

The constable fixed him with a stern gaze. "In the middle of the night?"

Peter swallowed. "Yeah." His voice croaked.

"And all you did was rehearse?"

A nod.

A thick silence hung tense in the room. The constable waved a hand. "Search the place."

Peter's jaw dropped. "What?"

"Have a seat." The constable grabbed Peter by the shoulder and manhandled him to the table.

"What are you looking for?" Peter asked. "We were only there to practice Kira's tour!"

"I've heard the excuses. Now, keep your mouth shut. We'll ask if we need further information."

Peter held his bag closer to his body. He had the map. Sephiri would have the knife in her bag. If they got searched . . . But the map was old and ratty, and the knife looked like a piece of junk. *Would they know what they were?*

Peter leaned toward his friends. "Did they tell you what they want?" he whispered.

"Quiet," the guard watching the table snapped. He punctuated it with a hard slap to the table.

Peter jumped. He scowled but kept silent. The guards spread out, rooting through the training supplies, the kitchen cabinets, and even the lofted bedrooms upstairs. Peter gripped the edge of the table to keep his temper under control as the guards pulled jarred goods out of the pantry and tossed them aside. The noise in the loft meant they must be going through drawers and shelves.

He sighed. *It will take ages to put this place back together.*

The guard in the kitchen frowned when he found nothing, and then moved to inspect the hearth.

Peter went still, holding his breath. He kept his eyes on the constable but tried to watch the guard out of the corner of his eye. *Don't react. Don't look suspicious.* As long as the guard didn't take an interest in the loose rock at the corner, they'd be fine.

Sephiri caught his eye. Her mouth pressed into a thin line.

If the guards found the Amulet, they could lose a lot more than the Amulet itself.

The guard trailed his hands over the hearth. Peter swallowed. The man worked his way closer, toward the corner.

"Sir!" a guard called from the training area. "Over here!"

The guard examining the hearth rushed to the training area.

Peter breathed out, then frowned as he turned. *What did they find?*

An object wrapped in canvas hid in the rack of beaten-up wooden swords and shields. The guard retrieved it and peered inside. "This is it!"

Rage burned in the constable's eyes. "I knew it."

"Wait, what?" Kira shouted. "We didn't do anything!"

"Then where did this come from?" The guard placed the canvas-wrapped item in the constable's hands.

Peter frowned. "I don't understand. What—"

The constable unwrapped the fabric.

Kira gasped.

"What?" Peter cried.

Sephiri clapped her hands over her mouth. Rylan slumped forward and rested his forehead on the table.

Held in the constable's hands, the Tarvinian Crown shone in all its gray baltham glory. "Stolen in the night," he hissed, "and then stashed here to be sold. You wretched, lying thieves. Take them away!"

"We didn't do it!" Peter shouted. The guard grasped him by the upper arm and hauled him to his feet. "We didn't steal it!" He struggled against the strong hands. He could have broken the grip and run, but he wouldn't leave his friends behind. *Plus, I can't use the Source with the constable staring me down.*

The guard tied his wrists behind his back in a quick, practiced knot, and then hauled them away from the table.

"Sure." The constable gestured for the guard to lead them to the door. "The crown that's missing from the museum just appeared, stashed in your cupboard—wrapped up and hidden? Clumsily, I might add."

"It wasn't us!" Rylan wriggled in the guard's hold and earned a smack to the back of his head for his trouble. "Someone must have put it there!"

"Stop arguing," the constable said, "or I'll gag you as well." He marched the four of them out of the Garrison and into the waiting wagon.

"I can break this," Rylan whispered, wriggling his bound hands.

"Then what?" Kira whispered back. "We'll just get in more trouble."

"How did that get there?" Sephiri slumped into the corner of the wagon.

Peter fidgeted in his bindings, the rough rope itching his skin. As the wagon pulled away, flanked by the horseback guards, a familiar face appeared at the edge of the Garrison.

Ashton leaned against the wall. He smirked and waggled his fingers as the wagons pulled away.

Peter scowled. "I think I have a good idea."

9

The icy stone floor of the jail sucked the heat from Peter's bones. He rubbed his hands over his arms, trying to draw warmth into them. The dampness of the cell didn't help. Water dripped from the crack in the ceiling, plinking on the floor.

They'd only been locked up a few hours, but it already felt like ages. How long would they be stuck there? Peter had spent his share of afternoons in the stocks, but this was worse.

This is serious.

"This sucks." Rylan leaned back against the wall.

"How are you not freezing?" Kira said around her chattering teeth. "It's colder in here than it is outside!"

"I run hot." He held his arms out and beckoned with his hands. "Come on, squeeze in."

Grumbling, Kira pressed her shoulder to Rylan's on one side. Her eyes widened, and then she wriggled a little closer. "You do run hot."

Rylan grinned. "I think it's a Source thing."

"Shh," Sephiri hissed. "Someone's coming."

The prison guard walked by on his rounds. His disinterested, piggish eyes peered through the bars.

"Can we have a small fire in here?" Kira asked. "It's cold."

The guard knocked his club against the bars. "Quiet down."

"At least we're not tied up anymore," Sephiri sighed after the guard had left, rubbing her reddened wrists.

Peter's wrists had already healed, thanks to his rapid-healing ability, but the disrespect of being bound in the first place grated on him.

Ashton is going to pay for this. Getting shoved around and beaten up was one thing. Even the time he burned the Fairfield farm—that had been impulsive. This . . . This was different. Ashton planned it. He broke into the museum. He planted the crown. He probably even told the constable where to find it.

The crown is so rare, so invaluable—A shocking truth hit him —*we may never get out of this cell.*

"Kira Lancaster!" a high-pitched voice shrieked. "Is what the constable tells us true?"

Rosalyn Lancaster stormed in, spitting like an angry cat. Dirt stained her cloak at the hem. Her hair was unstyled and her cheeks flushed. The whites of her eyes gave her a crazed look that made Peter pale.

"Mrs. Lancaster!" Constable Eastling rushed after her, passing the other guard who sat at his desk. "I must insist! Citizens are not allowed—"

"Mother!" Kira leaped to her feet. "Listen—"

"I hear the Tarvinian Crown was found in your little fort," Mrs. Lancaster said. "I knew these three were a bad influence on you, but *this?* Stealing from the museum our family built? I thought better of you, Kira."

"We didn't steal it, Mother," Kira insisted. "Someone *planted* it in the Garrison so the constable would think—"

"Don't be ridiculous," Mrs. Lancaster said.

Eastling shook his head. "I said the same thing. They always tell the same story."

Mrs. Lancaster shot the man a withering look. She exhaled and pinched the bridge of her nose. "We're pleased to have the crown back in the museum, where it belongs. I'm sure you will agree it's best we handle this family issue internally. Let Kira out so I can take her home and deal with her."

"I'm sorry, Mrs. Lancaster, I can't do that." Eastling shifted his weight. "Although displayed in your museum, the crown is city property. This is more than a 'family' matter."

Her stare could have withered a statue. "Fine, constable." She pulled a heavy pouch from her pocket and shook it. "How much will her bail cost me?"

The man swallowed. He looked at the pouch of coins in her hand the way Rylan looked at a roasted suckling pig. Through seemingly great effort, he shook his head. "I can't let any of them leave before the Lord of Justice sees them."

Mrs. Lancaster closed her eyes. She inhaled, then exhaled again. Her gaze was as cold as her voice when she turned back to Kira. "I will take care of this. Afterward, I expect you to behave like a Lancaster," she sneered at Peter, "and not like a pitiful thief from Lowside." She swept out of the jail as quickly as she'd arrived, with the constable trailing behind and calling for her attention.

Silence hung in the air. Peter's shame nauseated him. *I didn't do anything. I knew Mrs. Lancaster didn't like me, but . . .*

"Ouch," Rylan muttered.

"Tell me about it," Kira said.

If Mrs. Lancaster can't get us out of this cell, no one can. Peter swallowed the thick catch in his throat. *We'll have to do this ourselves.*

"I say we get out of here." Peter stood. He approached the bars, then peered down the darkened hall. The lone guard sat at a rickety wooden table at the end, shuffling a deck of cards and facing away. "Rylan, can you bend the bars?"

"What?" Rylan blinked. "We're breaking out?"

"You have a better idea?"

"Waiting for the Lancasters?" Sephiri asked.

Kira cringed. "They'll only get me out, Seph. Not all of us."

"We'll be stuck here unless we can prove Ashton took the crown," Peter said. "But I have no idea how we would do that."

"If we get out, won't Eastling just track us down again?" Sephiri raised her eyebrows.

"We'll have to avoid him," Peter said. "I've got an idea for that."

"Well, I don't want to be stuck in here." Rylan stood and stretched his arms over his head. "Let's get out of here."

"Shh," Sephiri hissed. "He'll hear you!"

Rylan cringed.

Peter pressed his face against the bars. The guard had abandoned his card game and spoke to a prisoner in a cell near the end of the hall. The man leaned close to the bars and thwacked his bat against the steel, the sound echoing through the jail.

"We might need to wait for him to wander off or fall asleep or something," Peter waved a hand at Rylan. "See if you can do it first."

Rylan gripped the bars and gritted his teeth. A vein in his temple popped as a few sparks danced over his bulging arms. He pulled outward, a low groan coming from his throat. The bars began to bend.

A door down the hall clattered open. Kira grabbed Rylan by his shirt and jerked him backward.

"The constable?" Sephiri asked. "What does he want now?"

Peter ran his hands down the bars. They contained a definitive bend, but the casual observer wouldn't notice.

"Niels!" a gruff voice called. "You were meant to report to my office this morning."

Kira frowned. "That's not the constable."

"Commander Isert," Peter whispered. "What is he doing down here?"

The commander strode down the narrow hallway, his expression pinched. He glanced at the cells as he walked. Peter swallowed, took a step back, and rested his hand against his face. He hoped the man would be too focused on finding the guard to see him.

No such luck.

Commander Isert paused as he was about to pass the cell. "Peter Fairfield." He crossed his arms over his chest. "It appears you didn't take my advice."

Peter lowered his hand. He turned to the commander and swallowed. "It's not that, sir. Listen to me. It's just a misunderstanding—"

The commander raised his eyebrows. "I believe it's *you* who should listen to *me.*"

Peter snapped his mouth closed. His gaze flicked to the slightly bent bars, but the commander didn't appear to notice the glance.

Isert peered down his nose at the four of them behind the bars. "It's a shame to see you boys down here. I'd hoped to see some promising new soldiers in the arena next season."

Peter's heart beat fast. "*Hoped*, sir?"

"We rarely bring on recruits with a criminal record."

"It's just a mix-up." Peter grabbed the bars of the cell. "I can fix this."

"It's best that you focus on your work if you ever get out of here. I wouldn't count on an army career anymore."

"No! You don't understand!" Peter wrapped his hand around the bars as desperation rose like bile in his throat. It was no good trying to explain what Ashton had done—no way the commander would believe it. "I can prove it, sir, if you'll just—"

"Stick to what you know and stay out of trouble." The commander turned away.

"I'll—I'll find the City of Gold!"

The other three in the cell tensed.

The commander laughed, the sound echoing on the walls as he continued walking. "If you do that, I'll promote you straight to commander myself!"

"That went well," Rylan muttered when they were alone again.

"Does he know?" Kira's brows pinched together. "Did you tell him?"

Peter's eyes flicked between his watching friends. He hung his head and nodded. "I went to him for help. I thought . . . maybe he'd know something about the city or its location. He only laughed me away, though."

He slumped against the wall and slid down until he sat on the cold floor. His heart seemed to fall until it rested in the pit of his stomach. Ashton had done worse than frame him for thievery. He'd ruined his life.

Maybe Mrs. Lancaster was right. I'll never be anything more than a lowlife thief. I'll never join the army. Never see Terrenor. Never have a life worth anything.

Sephiri sat down next to him but said nothing. She set her hand on his knee and squeezed.

He glanced up, and she caught his eye with a faint smile.

She doesn't deserve to be stuck here. None of us do.

The four of them sat in silence as Commander Isert spoke to the guard. Peter's heart pounded. There was no resolution. No announcement. The commander left as briskly as he'd arrived, not sparing a glance at the cell as he passed.

No, Peter thought, *Ashton's stupid trick won't keep me from my goals.*

"So, what do you all think?" Peter nodded to the bent bars. "Looks like Rylan can do it. You up for busting out of here?"

"If we get caught, we're in serious trouble," Kira said.

"We're already in serious trouble. Plus, we won't get caught," Peter said. *I won't let that happen.*

"You think we can make it?" Sephiri asked.

"Do you trust me?" Peter asked.

Sephiri nodded.

Peter's heart beat hard. "Now, we need to wait for the right moment."

Time dragged on for the next couple of hours. Coughs sounded from other cells, but the lone guard remained quiet, sitting at his desk at the far end of the corridor. Rylan kept his arms loose. Peter paced, antsy and eager to do something. When he pressed against the bars for the hundredth time, a smile tugged at his mouth. The guard slumped against a small table, his back growing and shrinking with rhythmic breaths. Peter turned to the others. "He's asleep."

Rylan gripped the bars of the cell. He gritted his teeth and grunted as he pulled the metal. The muscles in his forearms stood out with the force of his effort. The steel groaned. Peter peered down the hallway, heart in his throat.

The guard stirred.

Peter held his breath. The bars groaned more as they pulled apart. Rylan stopped, panting. The four friends froze.

The guard shifted but then settled back into sleep.

Peter exhaled. "Kira, go."

She nodded. The slimmest of the four, Kira was just able to squeeze through the gap in the bars. She crept down the hall toward the guard. The man remained slumped over the table, snuffling in sleep. Kira approached him and glanced back toward the cell.

Peter nodded, his nerves on edge. *Be careful, Kira.*

She kneeled. Keys hung from the guard's belt, dangling. She touched the ring. The keys rustled and jangled.

The guard shifted again.

Kira froze. Peter's hands felt clammy as he held his breath.

After giving the man a chance to settle, her fingers danced over the keyring. She opened the loop, then pulled the ring free from his belt.

Her hands wrapped around the keys, keeping them silent as she hurried back down the hallway to the cell.

"Nice!" Peter whispered as Kira returned triumphant. "Quick, let's get out of here!"

Kira slid one key into the lock. *Clunk.* Didn't fit. Peter looked down the hall. The guard still slept. Kira tried another. *Clunk.* Didn't fit.

"Hurry, hurry," Sephiri hissed.

Clink. The third key fit. Peter grinned.

Kira turned the object, and a sharp click filled the air. Eager to escape, Peter pushed the cell door open.

The hinges wailed.

He froze.

"Uh oh," Rylan muttered.

"Hey!" The guard startled awake and stumbled to his feet. "Hey, what do you think you're doing?"

"Go, go, go!" Peter shouted. Sephiri raced forward first.

She sent a powerful gust of wind roaring down the hall. It slammed into the guard and knocked him backward onto his table. He smacked into the stone wall and slumped to the ground. Playing cards fluttered around him like early wiether leaves on a windy day.

"Nice!" Peter called.

Hoots and shouts filled the jail from the other cells.

Rylan and Kira rushed down the hall toward the door, with Peter and Sephiri behind them. Rylan chuckled as he slammed his shoulder into the door. The lock snapped. The door swung open, and the four friends tumbled into the narrow alley behind the jail. They took off running, disappearing into the busy streets of Palenting.

10

"Be quick, everyone. We need to get out of here as soon as possible." Peter shoved as many provisions as he could fit into his bag. "The guards will be here any minute now."

"Peter, should we . . . ?" Kira held up the wooden box at the hearth.

Peter paused. He glanced around the room, finding Sephiri and Rylan staring at him, too.

What's more dangerous, bringing the Amulet with us, or leaving it behind?

"Leave it," Sephiri said. "It's safer here."

"She's right." Peter nodded. "We don't know what we might encounter."

"Where are we going?" Rylan heaved the backpack with their camping equipment onto his shoulders.

Kira pulled the map from its hiding place with the Amulet and waved it. "Where else?"

"Shouldn't we lie low for a little while?" Sephiri asked. "We could stay at Yani's. Or camp in the Dorthar Mountains."

"I'd rather spend our time wandering around looking for treasure than hiding out somewhere," Rylan said.

"Yeah," Peter grinned. "Where would the fun be in that? Plus, if we find Kytalia, we'll have enough artifacts to make up for the mishap with the crown."

"Did we even figure out where in Terrenor this part of the coast is?" Sephiri asked.

"We'll figure it out," Peter said. *I don't know how, but we will.*

Kira tucked the map into her bag. "Let's stop by the market on the way out. Maybe we can find an atlas."

"Exactly. Kira's always got a plan." Peter adjusted the bag on his shoulders. "What do you think, Seph?"

She nodded. "I guess getting out of Palenting is one way to lie low."

Peter grinned. "Ready to go?"

Sephiri went still, then pressed her forefinger against her lips.

Peter fell silent. He strained his ear toward the door, then heard it rumbling in the distance—hoofbeats.

"As ready as we're gonna be!" Rylan said.

They scurried to the back window. Peter pushed it open and the four friends scrambled out, one by one. As he closed the window from outside, the front door burst open. Peter ducked away at the sight of guards with drawn swords.

"HEADS UP." Peter touched Kira's shoulder and nodded toward the Bitter Bat where they drew near an idling guard.

"I doubt we're high on their list of priorities," Kira whispered as they passed. "They have the crown back, after all."

"Won't they be looking for you after the escape?" Rylan whispered.

Kira sighed. "Probably. But my mother usually gives me a

day or two to come home on my own. Better for our family's reputation that way. Of course, I did already mess that up by getting thrown in jail." She pulled her scarf tighter around her face and over her blonde hair.

"Is that all she cares about?" Sephiri asked.

"Seems so."

"We should still be careful, though," Peter said. He pulled his cloak tighter around his shoulders and raised the hood over his head. *Hopefully, we won't be recognized.* "Let's keep moving."

Kira led the way through the square. "I think there's a book vendor at the far end of the market."

It was late, and most of the vendors had gone home for the day. The night market housed the herbalists, the distillers, the loan sharks, and the vendors whose wares may or may not have been obtained legally. It wasn't quite bustling, but it wasn't empty, either. Once they found the maps they needed, they'd return to the camp where they'd dropped their gear in the woods outside Palenting.

Peter peered around the vendors, trying to look both interested and unassuming at the same time. The stand with all the Feldorian knives caught his eye. Its wares remained on display, but the one-eared vendor was nowhere to be seen.

A faint groaning sound reached his ears. *What's that?* He stopped and tilted his head, looking toward the building behind the stand.

"What is it?" Kira whispered.

"I don't know." Peter passed the stand and entered a narrow alley that ran between the market and the dilapidated building next to it. A narrow door rested open a crack. Peter creeped to the opening and peeked inside. His breath caught.

The missing vendor sat tied to a chair in the center of the small, dusty room. His arms wrapped around his chest, bound with rope behind his back. He strained at his bonds but didn't appear to make any progress. A gigantic man in a thick cloak loomed over him, sneering at the vendor. The moonlight fell in through the window in a white beam across his face, where a long vertical scar ran over his eye.

A familiar shiver ran down Peter's spine. It was the same man who threatened his father. The stranger had been looking for someone. Or *something*. Behind him, Kira, Rylan, and Sephiri pressed in as well, peeking into the crack in the door.

"Where is it?" the man growled. "I'll give you one more chance."

"I told you all I know!" The vendor pulled against his bonds again. "If you want to buy other knives, I can help you, but I can't—"

"I'm done asking." The scarred man tugged at the bonds. Behind the vendor's back, the ropes fastened to a long, narrow stick, like a lever. He turned the stick, which pulled the ropes tighter, pinning the man's arms even closer to his body. "Tell me where the dagger is, now."

The vendor groaned, but the sound caught in the back of his throat. "I don't know who they were or where they went!" he choked.

Another turn of the stick.

The tied-up man gasped and writhed. His breathing became quick and labored. "I can't help you because I already sold it!"

"Who. Were. They?"

"I said, it was kids!" He gasped again, like a fish flopping on the shore. "A boy and two girls—wait, there was another boy, too. I don't know their names. I'm not from here."

A slick sheen of sweat formed on Peter's palms. His heart raced.

"You don't let kids walk away with something like that," the man threatened. "What did they want with it?"

"I have no idea. They thought it looked nice!" The vendor shook his head. "Please, don't turn it more!"

The scarred man paused and took a step back. With a slow metallic scrape, he pulled a long, mean knife from his belt, as long as his forearm, and curved. Next, he retrieved a tiny vial from his pocket. The vendor shook, sweat pouring down his face as the man uncorked the vial and dripped a portion over the edge of the weapon. A thick green viscous liquid ran down the blade. "Do you know what this is?"

The vendor looked up at him with wide eyes, then shook his head.

"This is poison extracted from the reaper frog. You know it?"

Again, the vendor shook his head.

"It's powerful. Hard to find the frogs—even harder to extract the poison. If you touch it, your skin will burn. If you drink it, you'll vomit for days. If it enters your bloodstream . . ." He let an evil grin grow. "Let's just say it's not pretty."

"Wh-wh-what do you mean?" the vendor stammered.

"The first day or two, you'll feel achy and sore. Soon an infection will grow. It'll hurt, a burning sensation, like you're holding a flame to the wound. Then the fever starts; next, the spasms." The man lifted the knife to the moonlight and watched the poison gleam at the edge of the blade. "About a week in, when the spasms start, you're close to the end. By day eight, you're dead, killed by the intense pain of your internal organs liquifying."

The vendor swallowed, sweat dripping from his face. "What do you want?"

"The kids."

He closed his eyes and sighed while a shudder ran through his body. "I'm sorry, but I don't know anything."

The man's scar flinched as he stared. He stepped closer and pressed the blade to the vendor's throat. It didn't draw blood, but the vendor's skin turned white under the pressure. A line of green dribbled down his neck. A faint hiss bubbled in the air, mixing with the man's whimpering.

"You stole the knife from Denton. Why sell it to a group of kids?"

"It was just a dusty old knife! You heard him in that Marris bar. He said he had the Key of Kytalia! But he didn't! He was just drunk!"

The man's jaw dropped. He stepped back and scoffed, loud and clear. "You idiot. That knife *is* the Key of Kytalia."

"What?" The vendor's eyes widened. "I-I didn't know."

"You've made my job a lot harder." The man pinched the bridge of his nose.

"I never would've sold it if I had known!" the vendor said. "Believe me!"

"Oh, I believe you. I believe you're that stupid. That foolish." He slid the knife into the scabbard on his hip, poison and all.

The vendor sighed, his shoulders falling.

"And that means you're useless." He grabbed the stick attached to the ropes. "You shouldn't have sold that dagger." With a jerk of his arm, he cranked it again. And again.

Peter pressed his hand to his mouth as his eyes widened.

A cruel grin spread across the man's face.

The ropes tightened and a desperate groan ripped from the vendor's throat. "No!" he choked out, "Please!"

A sadistic look of delight covered the scarred man's face. Another crank.

The vendor's arms squeezed tighter and tighter around his own chest. He howled until a sickening *crack* of bones echoed through the room, and he slumped motionless in the chair.

Peter's stomach turned. An urge to hurl his last meal racked his body.

Kira covered her mouth with her hand, and Sephiri gasped.

Peter's sinuses cleared. The gasp was too loud.

The man looked up, peering through the gap in the door,

directly at them. Without a pause, he bared his teeth and rushed forward.

Peter stumbled backward until his back crashed into the alley's brick wall behind him. The man lunged for him, but Rylan got to him first, slamming into his shoulder and knocking him off balance with his Source strength.

Dazed, the man took a moment to steady himself, then whirled to face Peter with his eyes blazing. "You kids stumbled into the wrong room."

With fast fingers, Peter snatched the knife from Sephiri's hip scabbard, then lunged forward with his incredible speed. He slashed at the man's thigh, leaving a deep, bleeding gash. The man didn't react to the injury. His gaze was instead on the blood-drenched knife in Peter's hand—the one with the rust, the gold, and the symbols.

"You!" he growled with wide eyes.

The man lurched toward Peter like a rabid animal. Peter ducked around him, scraping against the brick wall of the alley and crashing to the ground. Dazed, he scrambled backward, grip still tight around the hilt of the knife. The man pulled his own knife from its scabbard and brandished it. Rylan shrieked and flung himself backward, leaving Kira wide-eyed and frozen in the center of the alley.

The guards will show up any second now, Peter thought as he clambered to his feet. *They can't catch us here!*

"That knife is mine!" The man swung his blade in a high arc, aiming for Kira's face.

Kira screamed.

Sephiri's eyes turned white. She raised a hand, and a gust of wind rushed through the alley as strong as a tidal wave. Peter pressed himself flat against the wall. The wind rippled the clothes on his back, but he held firm. The man took the brunt of the gale. It smashed into him, sending his body careening backward. He blasted out of the alleyway into the town square and slammed into a distiller's stall. Wood and liquor flew every-where. The man slumped into a heap as the seller shouted and cursed above him. Guards rushed over, drawn by the commotion.

Peter scanned the alley. His friends looked as stunned as he felt. "We need to go, now!"

They raced out of the alley, away from the town square and into the tiny streets surrounding it. Shouts rang out from the market area as guards converged. Sephiri led the way, guiding them into the maze of alleys. Peter kept his eyes on his three friends ahead of him, ready to use his Source speed to distract or knock aside any guards that might get in their way. His pulse pounded in his ears.

At the edge of the city, their cover disappeared. They hurried across the short cleared section to the dense forest border, and only then did Peter look back and see that they were, somehow, unfollowed. Rylan hunched over, hands on his knees as he sucked in air. Sephiri wiped her brow, and Kira stood dazed and wide-eyed next to her. Peter slumped against a tree trunk and tried to catch his breath.

"Who was that guy?" Rylan asked. "What just happened?"

"He saw the knife," Peter said. "I stabbed him in the thigh, and he didn't even flinch."

"He knows we have it?" Rylan swallowed. "That can't be good."

The sound of the vendor's ribs cracking echoed in Peter's mind. If the scarred man caught them, he'd do something just as bad—or worse—to get the knife back. That wasn't a pleasant thought. But—He jerked his head to the others. "If he wants it, it must be real, right?"

"Guys." Sephiri's voice was faint.

"It must be." Rylan's eyes widened. "Why else would someone be so determined to get it?"

"Exactly! And we know it came from Marris. We need to

find the guy he stole it from, this Denton. Maybe he'll know more about the city. We didn't get the better map we wanted, but this is a lead. A *real* lead!"

"Plus, it's not like we can stick around in Palenting," Rylan muttered.

"Guys!" Sephiri snapped.

A pallid-faced Kira slumped against a tree with her hand pressed to her upper arm. She met Peter's eyes shakily, then withdrew her hand. Her palm was red with blood.

"It's not bad." Her voice wavered. "It's just a shallow cut."

"A shallow cut," Sephiri's voice sounded hollow.

Rylan's face paled like Kira's. "The cut—was it from . . . ?"

Kira blinked rapidly, then nodded.

"His knife?" Peter asked.

She nodded again.

The reaper frog poison. Peter opened his mouth, but no words escaped. His eyes flicked to Sephiri, who brimmed with tears.

"Maybe it was a bluff," Rylan said. "Maybe it was olive oil or something. Maybe the poison had wiped off."

Kira shook her head. She held up a finger where a smear of green rimmed the red stain of the blood. "There was poison, and now it's in me. I feel it."

"Maybe it's not that bad." Rylan's voice shook.

"What he said about the reaper poison was accurate," Sephiri said in a small voice.

"It's fatal," Kira said. Her voice was flat. "Fatal and incurable."

They sat on the soft earth of the forest. In the pale moonlight, Sephiri cleaned the shallow cut, then applied a layer of barkleaf balm.

Kira blew out a long breath. "That helps. Doesn't sting so much."

"What do we do now?" Rylan asked. "Go back to Palenting?"

"I'm not spending my last two weeks in jail. Or worse, with

my parents." She pulled her cloak back around her shoulders. "And if they find out about this, you'll *all* be dead."

"You won't die," Peter said. His firm voice surprised even himself.

Kira looked up. "You can't will this away, Peter."

Determination settled in Peter's chest like a stone. "I know that." A weak smile grew on his face. "But we *can* cure it."

Sephiri's eyes widened. "In Kytalia."

"Kytalia has the power to heal anything," Peter said. "We just have to find it. You'll be fine, Kira." He put as much assurance in his voice as he could.

But if we can't, and we don't find the city, she's doomed.

"I guess we better get ready to travel." Kira managed a faint smile. "I was serious about my parents not finding out."

The tension broke. Rylan barked a laugh, then climbed to his feet. He helped Kira up. "I believed it. City of Gold, here we come!"

Peter led the way through the trees, back to their hidden gear. Kira seemed fine so far, but if what the man said about the poison was true, she'd deteriorate quickly.

We have a plan. She'll be fine. I'll make sure of it.

11

"I wish we'd snagged an atlas before we left," Kira said. She unfolded the map and peered down at it. Sephiri walked behind her, hands on her shoulders, to guide her around any obstacles on the trail. "This would be a lot easier if I could compare it to a map of Terrenor proper."

"I wish we'd snagged better bedrolls," Rylan said. "I hate sleeping in the woods. Last night was rough."

"We'll get both once we reach Marris." Peter gazed at the Dorthar Mountains looming above them. The four friends hiked south along a narrow trail tucked in the foothills. Marris was a few days' hike south, and packing in a frantic rush didn't make for a great provisions store. They'd need to do some hunting if they didn't want to live on moldy cheese.

"They must be landmarks," Kira said. "Cliff of Tears, hmm . . . The coastline on the map could be near Marris. Maybe they'll have a library where we could do some research."

"Not the library!" Rylan groaned.

The group hiked at a brisk pace as the sun traveled across the sky. The air was crisp with wiether chill. They were far enough outside of Palenting that Peter didn't fear being chased by the guards, so he allowed himself to enjoy the woods. The Dorthar foothills were quiet, save for the birdsong in the trees and the occasional rustle of a fox in the grass.

In the late afternoon, Kira slowed, and a grimace flickered across her expression. Peter dropped back, letting Sephiri and Rylan take the lead.

"Here." He gestured for Kira's bag. "Let me carry that."

"I've got it," she said. "I'm fine."

Peter tugged at its strap. With a sigh, Kira paused, then pulled it off her shoulder and handed it to him. It wasn't heavy. Peter carried it with his own load without issue. Kira blew out a long breath and managed a weak smile before brushing a few sweaty strands of hair off her face.

"How do you feel?" he asked.

"Sore." She rolled her shoulder. "Like I've been shooting too many arrows."

"Did the balm help?"

Kira nodded. "A little. I'll put on more tonight."

Peter nodded. "We've still got a lot of hiking to do. But you know, I'm sure Rylan would be happy to carry you."

"I don't need that," she blurted.

"What?" Rylan called from up the path. "Did you say something?"

"Nothing," Peter said. "Keep walking."

Kira offered a small smile, then knocked her shoulder against Peter's. "I'll be fine. Don't worry about me."

"I know you will." A cold curl of anxiety wound in his chest, despite his words of confidence. *I wish she were the one with the Source healing power, instead of me.* "Once we find Kytalia, everything will be different."

"What do you think it will be like?" Kira asked. "Do you think it will be like the paintings?"

"I bet so." His face tugged into a grin. "I bet it will be even better."

"How so?"

Peter hummed and hooked his thumbs into the straps of the bags he carried. He pictured a soaring golden city with gleaming walls and streets paved with gems. "It'll be empty," he said. "Maybe overgrown, with vines and stuff growing over the walls and the buildings."

"Sounds spooky."

"It'll be like it's waiting for us," Peter said. "We'll have as much gold as we could ever wish for. And we'll get the healing power. We'll stay there for a few days and rest up before we head back. When we return, we'll take some of the treasure to the constable. And the museum. Then we'll make Ashton fess up."

Kira laughed. "Can't wait to see how we pull off that last part."

"We'll figure it out."

She nodded. They fell into a comfortable silence as they traveled, breaking in the afternoon to snack, rest their legs, and take stock of their remaining provisions. "We don't have a lot," Sephiri said as she looked through the stash. "Some bread, some cheeses, and the jarred goods Peter's father made."

"Those are tasty," Rylan said.

"Yeah, but not enough for a few days of travel."

"I can still shoot," Kira said. "We'll hunt something."

"Or I can," Peter said, with no intention of allowing Kira to spend the energy. "Between the two of us, I'm sure we can catch something. Let's go a little further and find a good place to camp."

The sun creeped toward the horizon as they hiked. Peter scanned the foothills for a good place to settle in for the night, ideally with a water source.

"What's that?" Rylan asked.

Ahead, smoke puffed toward the sky above the tree line.

"Looks like a campfire," Kira said.

"Someone else is out here?" Sephiri asked.

"Could be bandits," Peter said. "Keep on your toes."

They walked closer, sticking to the trail. Peter's eyes danced through the underbrush, scanning for anything indicating danger.

Crash!

A woman tripped out of the tree line and flopped onto the trail. She yelped, then scrambled to her feet, dusting off her trousers and oversized, well-worn shirt. Her plain clothes looked handmade, and maybe secondhand. Her fiery red hair caught the dwindling light of the sun. Looking up, she caught sight of Peter and yelped again.

"Whoa!" Peter stopped in the middle of the trail with his friends behind him. "Are you okay?"

"You trip over that root again?" A man with the same red hair emerged from the tree line. He was tall and broad-shouldered, older than Peter, but younger than his parents. He wore the same rough-looking clothes as the woman. When he turned toward Peter, the multiple garronts hanging from a rope around his neck swung from side to side. "Hey, folks. Traveling through?"

"Um." Peter shifted the bags on his shoulder. "Yeah, just passing through."

"Nice weather for it." The woman smiled, showing off the freckles dusting across her nose.

Peter's tense shoulders relaxed. *They don't seem like bandits.*

Rylan took a few steps forward. He stared at the garronts, his mouth drooping.

"Where you headed?" the man asked.

"South," Kira said.

"Guess you're going the right way, then!" Both strangers laughed.

"What about you two?" Sephiri asked. "What are you doing out here?"

The woman looked at the man and shrugged. "Found a nice spot to stay a while, I suppose." She grinned. "Us and some friends spent a few seasons traveling between villages, but we grew tired of packing up and moving. We found a great little space here in the foothills, and we've been here half a season. We'll head south once it gets too cold. I'm Nalva, by the way, and this big lug's my brother, Naldoc."

The man raised his eyebrows. "Lug? Who's got all the garronts?"

"*I* caught them. You're just carrying them." Nalva rolled her eyes, then turned back to Peter. "Anyway, our camp's this way, and it's getting late. If you four are looking for somewhere to post up for the night, we can provide a warm belly, good drink, and a fire big enough to keep the critters at bay."

"Really?" Rylan asked, wide-eyed.

"Sure thing. We enjoy sharing and making friends when we can. No worries if you'd rather mind your own business, though. There's plenty of space in the woods, and we won't bother you a lick."

Peter turned to the others. Rylan's eager eyes and bit of drool at the mouth gave away his interest. Sephiri smiled, and Kira nodded. Peter looked closer at Kira. Her pallid face held a sheen of sweat.

She could use a hot meal and a good fire.

Peter turned back to the strangers. "That'd be great."

"Wonderful!" Naldoc clapped his hands. "What a happy surprise." He trundled toward the trees with Nalva at his heels.

Peter followed. A small, freshly worn path led deeper into the trees. They walked a few minutes, skirting the base of the mountain. Somewhere, water bubbled. The sound grew louder until the tree line opened to a clearing on the banks of a wide, fast-moving creek.

"No wonder they stopped here," Rylan said. "This is a great spot!"

"It'll be great until the snows come in mid-wiether," Naldoc said. "For now, it suits us fine. Set your things down and take a rest."

Eight tents tucked about the campsite, with about twice as many people that Peter could see. Lines hung between the branches, drying clothes and rags. A few small, stocky ponies chewed on the rough grass by the river. In the center of the clearing, a bonfire roared beneath a cauldron and a spit, stoked by a young, slim woman with short, braided hair and big brown eyes. She looked up at the sound of Naldoc's voice. Her eyes widened at the sight of the four friends, and then her face split into a charming grin.

"Whoa," Rylan said.

"Close your mouth, you're catching flies." Sephiri elbowed him in the side.

"Who is that?" Rylan whispered, awed.

"How would we know?" Kira asked.

Naldoc gestured to an open space by the river's edge. "You can set up your gear here."

"Need a hand?" The girl with braids hurried over. "I can help you with your tent. I'm Esmee."

"Yeah, that'd be—that'd be great," Rylan said. He stammered as he tugged the tent out of the bag. "Thanks. I'm Rylan."

"Where are you headed?" Esmee asked. "Nalva said you're going south?"

"Down to Marris," Rylan said. "Then wherever our map takes us."

Peter pressed his lips together and held his breath.

"It's a long day's walk from here to Marris," Esmee said. "What are you going for? Enjoying the coast?"

"Something like that." Peter joined to help with the tent, cutting off Rylan before he shared too much. Kira sat on a nearby log, and Sephiri applied another layer of barkleaf balm to Kira's wound. Esmee glanced at the two but said nothing.

"What about you?" Rylan asked. "What brings you out, um, here?"

Esmee smiled at him. Rylan's blush turned even darker as he knelt, hammering the tent spikes into the earth. "It's a perfect spot to camp," Esmee said. "Once you're here for a few weeks, you realize how much better it is than dealing with the noise and the rush of the cities. I used to work in an inn before I came out here. We have people of all backgrounds, though. Vince used to work in the history archives in Palenting. Jayla was an architect. We have a few farmers, too. We accept everyone. All fourteen of us have something in common, though. We love nature and the peace of being out here."

"That sounds nice," Rylan said.

He'd die of boredom after a week of camping in the woods, Peter thought, shaking his head. "We should refill our canteens," he said. "Wanna come, Seph?"

Sephiri glanced at Kira, who nodded.

"Sure." Sephiri stood.

They walked down the bank of the river, a short distance from the camp. Water rushed over a jutting rock formation, tumbling in a fast waterfall within arm's reach.

Sephiri uncapped a canteen and held it under the gurgling water, gasping when the icy mountain water splashed over her hand.

Peter glanced back at the camp, where Esmee and Rylan continued to talk. With the sun tucked behind the trees, the light faded quickly. The campers gathered around the fire. Garronts turned on the spit, and a woman chopped vegetables into the cauldron beneath it. Peter's mouth watered. *I hope it tastes as good as it smells.*

The breeze shifted. A faint odor turned Peter's nose and

replaced the pleasant aroma of the cooking meal. He grimaced at the nauseating change. "Do you smell that?"

Sephiri stood. Her nose wrinkled like a displeased bunny. "Ugh. Smells like something rotting."

Peter squinted deeper into the woods at a rise where the river curved. "There's a bunch of flies over there, too."

"Gross. No wonder no tents are over here." Sephiri sealed the canteens. "Let's get back."

Peter lingered while she headed back toward the campsite. He stared at the faint specs of circling flies. *There must be something dead over there. Well, it's the wilderness, after all.*

"Come on, Peter!" Sephiri called. "I don't want to miss out on freshly roasted garront."

"Neither do I." Peter turned and hurried to follow her.

Darkness fell like a blanket over the landscape. The rest of the campers emerged from their tents and pulled logs and stumps up to the crackling fire. All wore similar clothes, hand-sewn and overlarge, and a few cast glances at the four friends as they took their seats. Conversations were low, and the food smelled incredible. Peter and Sephiri joined Kira and Rylan, seated with Esmee. She smiled and gestured for them to sit on two open stumps.

"Join us, join us!" Naldoc grinned as Peter sat. "Dinner will be ready shortly."

"Smells great." Sephiri extended her hands toward the fire, warming her palms.

Next to Esmee, another man joined them. He was older with a warm smile and dark hair he wore loose, nearly to his shoulders. "It's always a treat to have guests," he said. His gaze flickered to Sephiri, to her hip. "Looks like you've got similar taste to me."

Esmee laughed. "This is Vince, the archivist I told you about."

"That's the only thing I miss about life in the city," Vince said. "Nothing like a long day in the archives to get the blood flowing. Mind if I look at that knife?"

Sephiri swallowed. She glanced at Peter, and Peter ducked his chin. Better to stay friendly with the hosts.

"Sure," she breathed. She pulled the knife from her belt, then handed it over.

Vince held it close to the firelight and turned it over in his hands. "This is an old piece. Lovely work of craftsmanship," he said. "Too bad it's in such terrible shape. Would be a fun restoration project, though." He handed it back with a smile.

"I hope to do just that one day." Sephiri's posture eased as she returned the knife to her hip.

Better keep the Key in a bag from now on, Peter thought. *The last thing we need is more interest in it.*

"I trust you've gotten what you need to be comfortable?" Naldoc stood and turned the spit, rotating the roasting birds.

"I think we're good," Peter said, prompting a thought. "We caught a whiff of something rotting when we were at the stream."

Naldoc's gaze cut to Peter with a flicker of concern. After a second, his expression softened, and he returned to the spit. "Oh?"

"I didn't see what it was," Peter said, "but since it's close to the water, I thought you might want to know."

"It's probably that deer," Nalva said.

"Weren't you supposed to take care of that?" Naldoc's eyebrow arched.

"Sorry." Nalva shrank back. "I'll take care of it tomorrow."

Naldoc turned back to Peter. "A wolf killed one upstream the other day. We prefer to let nature run its course and leave its remains for the scavengers, but we noticed it was a bit close to camp. Nothing to worry about though. For now, let's celebrate! Shall we, Dirteaters?"

The campers shouted in agreement and a few raised wooden mugs.

"Dirteaters?" Kira asked.

Nalva pulled a large wineskin out of her bag and uncorked it to more hoots and cheers.

Esmee leaned closer, her braids falling into her dark eyes. "That's what we call ourselves. Or that's what people in the villages started calling us. Because . . . well, we don't prioritize the fine clothing and big banquets and such that people in cities have. People joked we ate dirt to survive. Obviously"—she nodded toward the fire—"that's not true, but the name stuck. Now, we like it."

Rylan smiled. "It's memorable."

"And for our guests!" Nalva handed Peter and his friends carved wooden mugs filled halfway with a viscous, dark, sweet-smelling liquid. "Valcor blood! Cheers!"

"Valcor blood?" Sephiri peered into the glass with wide eyes.

"It's what we call our special wine." Esmee clarified. "We ferment it ourselves. It's strong, but it's good."

"Our guests last week sure loved it," Nalva said with a chuckle.

Esmee nodded and matched her grin. "Remember how that old man showed us his bird tattoos? What a hoot!"

Nalva burst into laughter. "He had been so demure before. Valcor blood makes you crazy!"

"Crazy in a good way," Esmee added with a wink.

Kira and Sephiri both nodded in gratitude, but neither took a sip. Peter held his mug close to his face. The strong, acrid scent of the wine pummeled his senses and turned his stomach.

The Dirteaters filled their cups with the liquid from the wineskin. Shouts of, "Cheers!" echoed around the fire ring. Esmee drank, staining her lips dark.

Rylan hooted, then gulped from his glass.

"Go ahead, girls!" Naldoc said. "Drink!"

Kira shook her head. "Thank you, but I'm slightly ill—I shouldn't."

"And I don't generally drink," Sephiri said with a smile. "But I'm sure it's wonderful."

"Do us the honor," Nalva said. "Then you'll be an honorary Dirteater!"

Peter pressed the rim of the mug to his lips but didn't take a drink.

"It's fantastic!" Rylan scooted closer to Esmee, who took the wineskin and refilled his mug. "You should sell this. You'd make a killing!"

An older woman climbed to her feet and carved the garronts right on the spit. They passed out food: steaming vegetable stew in a thin broth, with hunks of garront cut right into the bowls. Peter's mouth watered at the dense, rich aroma, the tender meat, the hunks of carrot and verquash. His stomach growled.

Naldoc watched him from across the fire, shadows dancing across his rugged face.

The hair on the back of Peter's neck prickled. A whisper of caution teased his mind. Despite his hesitations, he put on a smile and raised his bowl in thanks. Naldoc nodded, then his attention turned to the Dirteater next to him.

Peter leaned closer to Kira. "Don't eat," he whispered.

Kira nodded. Sephiri caught Peter's eye and pressed her lips together. *She's got the same feeling as me,* he thought. *Something's off.*

Rylan did not get the message. Halfway through slurping his stew, he laughed with Esmee between bites. Peter poured bits out when no one was looking. As the Dirteaters ate and drank, they directed less attention toward the four friends. The valcor blood flowed and the laughter grew.

When the eating slowed, the campers pulled out large, handmade drums. Three Dirteaters pounded on the drums in a fun, fast-paced rhythm. Esmee leaped up with a delighted shout and offered her hand to Rylan. A dopey grin covered his face. He took her hand and jumped to his feet, stumbling and crashing into the fire. Esmee laughed, then led him in a high-energy dance. Other Dirteaters paired off and joined them.

A young man approached Sephiri and offered a hand. He was tall and lean, with dark hair and flushed cheeks. She swallowed. Her eyes flicked toward Peter, then back, but then nodded and accepted. The young man guided her into the fray.

Peter's stomach twisted. He eyed the hand on her hip as the two bounced and turned to the music. Sephiri's dancing was less chaotic than the other Dirteaters, but her smile grew the longer she moved.

Peter glanced down at the mug she had set down. *At least it's still full.*

Kira remained seated, watching the dancing while biting at her lip. Her face drooped, pale in the firelight, with her knees pulled to her chest.

Peter leaned toward her. "Stay here. I'll be right back."

With the Dirteaters distracted, Peter crept away from the fire and returned to the banks of the babbling creek, his senses on full alert. He glanced over his shoulder. No one seemed to have noticed him sneak off. He moved quickly and as close to the shadows as he could, avoiding the beams of white moon-light dappling the ground. The shouts of the party continued behind him, laughter and music ringing through the air.

A breeze rustled through the leaves, bringing the stench with it.

A gagging sensation racked his body. *A deer? I don't think so.* The smell was too strong, too nauseating. He'd been around dead animals before. What he smelled was different.

Peter climbed the hill, keeping his body low. The rancid

smell worsened. Fat flies buzzed through the air, knocking against his arms and head as he walked. He pulled the collar of his shirt over his nose. It was better to smell his own sweat, rank from travel, than the unfiltered stench coming from the hill.

The drums pounded louder, faster, driving him forward. With his heart in his throat, he crested the hill and looked down. His breath caught.

It wasn't a deer.

A shallow, sloppily dug pit hidden on the other side of the hill with a half-dozen bodies thrown inside. Human bodies. Limbs were bloated and rotting, picked at by scavengers and flies. The colorless skin shone pale in the moonlight. One man's body had gray hair matted with dirt and blood. His ripped shirt revealed a slew of tattoos across his back. Bird tattoos.

Peter retched. Bile burned in the back of his throat. His empty stomach threatened to expel whatever it held. His foot slipped on the bank of the creek and he fell, foot in the mud and hands in the dirt as he barely kept out of the icy-cold water. He gasped for air, his chest heaving, then spit a wad of acrid bile into the dirt.

His thoughts raced. *Who were these people? What happened to them?* He tried to ignore his fears but couldn't shake the horrific conclusion. *The Dirteaters killed them, and we're likely next.*

He spun to look toward the fire and dancers in the distance, resolved in what they must do.

We have to get out of here.

12

P eter returned to the campfire with a forced smile and his gait purposefully unsteady.

"Where were you, Peter?" Naldoc called from the dance circle. "Come dance!"

Peter laughed, then pressed his palm to his temple. "That valcor blood is potent!"

Naldoc roared with laughter, then took Nalva by the hands and led her in a frantic, wild circle.

"Where's Rylan?" Peter whispered.

Kira remained by the fire, warming her hands. She looked at him through heavy eyelids. "Huh? I don't know. Last I saw, he was dancing with that girl."

"We need to find him. Now." He scanned the dancing crowd, looking for Rylan's bulky form. The crowd of people turning and bouncing in the flickering light made it a challenge. "We need Seph, too."

"What's going on?"

Sephiri's bright laugh caught his ear. In the center of the dancing crowd, the young man she was with spun her around, then pulled her close. Her dark hair waved, gleaming in the firelight. The young man held a mug in one hand while the other remained on Sephiri's waist. He leaned closer and spoke in her ear. She shook her head and pulled away. He laughed, unperturbed, then sipped from his mug. When he held it out to Sephiri, she peered at it, her brow furrowed.

Peter rushed forward, his fear sending a faint surge of Source power to his muscles. He took Sephiri by the arm and smiled at the young man. "Mind if I cut in?"

The young man glowered, but Peter didn't back down. He pulled Sephiri away, then took her by the hands, joining the dance as well as he could. "Is something wrong?" Sephiri asked over the pounding drums. "You look shaken."

"Did you drink any of that?"

"No." Sephiri's eyes widened. "Why?"

"Go get Kira," Peter said as quietly as he could, "and get our stuff—whatever you can carry without anyone noticing. Leave the tent. We have to get out of here, *now.*"

"What happened?"

"Did you see where Rylan went?"

The lines on her forehead deepened. "He and Esmee went down toward the creek." She pointed past the tents. "Said they were going to jump in the water, that there's a pool."

The drums changed pace again, and the young man with dark hair lingered nearby. Peter let go of Sephiri. "I'm going to find him. Get Kira and head south." She nodded. Peter didn't want to leave her on her own amid all the Dirteaters, but he had to trust her. *She can take care of herself.*

Peter darted into the trees. He stuck to the darkness and headed to where Sephiri had pointed. As he rounded the creek's bend, the gurgling quieted. The pounding drums remained, but they were fainter, like a thunderstorm in the distance instead of over his head. A splash and a trill of laughter sent him ducking behind a tree.

Rylan slumped against a boulder at the edge of the pool. He

leaned to one side, dazed but conscious. A dopey smile covered his face as Esmee climbed out of the pool, wearing only a thin undershirt and her trousers. She pushed her wet braids off her face and smiled at Rylan. "Don't you want to join me? The water feels great."

"Yeah," Rylan said, his head lolling to the side. He shifted but couldn't seem to move. "I do."

Then Peter saw him. Naldoc.

The red-haired man crept toward Rylan from behind the boulder, holding a long, thin knife. His eyes blazed, and he bared his teeth like a wolf. He raised the knife over his head, the mean silver blade gleaming in the moonlight.

Source power surged through Peter, crackling in his veins like lightning. The world slowed. Naldoc's knife froze in the air, poised to plunge into Rylan's neck. Peter exploded off the balls of his feet, raced forward, and crashed into Naldoc with all his weight. He wasn't strong like Rylan. He couldn't hit a target from a distance like Kira. But he could still save his friend.

Naldoc went down hard, slamming into the muddy earth on the banks of the pool. He yelped. His head cracked against a rock, and the knife slipped out of his hand and into the water. Esmee shrieked and stumbled backward into the pool.

"Come on!" Peter grabbed Rylan by the wrist. "Let's go!"

"Huh?" Rylan blinked at Peter with blown pupils and a slack mouth. He didn't seem to notice any of the commotion behind him. "Where we goin'?" he slurred.

Naldoc groaned and rubbed his head.

"Get up!" Peter hauled Rylan to his feet.

Esmee rooted around in the water until she stopped and grinned. She straightened with the knife in her hand. "I don't think so," she hissed.

Naldoc rose to his feet. Rage burned in his eyes as blood trickled from the gash in his forehead. "You'll pay for that."

A shout rang out behind Peter. More Dirteaters emerged

from the trees, all armed and grinning with the same wild expression Naldoc wore.

Peter spun, looking for a way out. His breath was heavy, and his eyes flicked in each direction. Surrounded. All sides. *There are too many of them!* With Rylan's weight pressing against him, he couldn't run for it. He swallowed hard, steeled himself, and readied for an impossible fight.

Whoosh!

An arrow sang through the air, flying over Peter's shoulder to bury itself in a Dirteater's shoulder. The man howled and staggered backward. Naldoc roared and whirled toward the source of the attack as three more arrows sang through the air. Two hit Dirteaters, and Esmee dodged the third.

Chaos broke out. Naldoc lunged toward the source of the arrows while two Dirteaters surged toward Peter. He kicked one in the gut and the other in the shin. A gust of wind rustled the canopy as frantic splashing turned his head toward the pool. Esmee rushed at him, waving her knife. Peter backpedaled. The wind intensified. He paused, his head cocked. *Wait. Is that—*

A torrent of air blasted into Esmee. She screeched as she flew backward, landing on her back with a massive splash.

"What was that?" a dark-haired Dirteater asked. "It's the girl with the knife!"

Peter spun as Sephiri emerged from the trees.

Her eyes blazed white. Deep lines furrowed into her forehead while another gust of wind raced through the clearing. It surged toward the earth, digging a ditch in the shore, and picking up mud like a tornado. Sephiri raised her hand, and the mud slammed into the Dirteaters' faces.

"Go!" Kira called to him. "Go, go!"

Peter hauled Rylan onto his back. His large friend managed a grunt and hung on. Peter took off through the trees, running behind Sephiri and Kira. Rylan's weight slowed him. His muscles burned and his breathing strained, but a blend of

Source power and adrenaline kept him moving. He pounded the dirt as he ran, lit by the light of the moon.

Thwock! Thwock! Darts landed in the nearby trees. Another sailed past Peter's ear.

"Watch it!" Sephiri called. She pushed Peter ahead, and then blasted a gust of wind behind them, knocking aside the trailing Dirteaters.

"This way!" Kira led them deeper into the foothills, darting around trees, until they reached a small outcropping of rocks. "In here!" she urged.

Peter crouched and followed Sephiri under a rock. He dropped to his knees and dragged Rylan behind him. After a moment, the narrow space opened into a tiny cave, hidden from the trail and invisible from the rest of the woods. The chamber was barely large enough for the four of them. They crouched in silence, and Kira peered out of the entrance.

Heavy footsteps tromped through the woods nearby. "How could you be so foolish?" Naldoc's faint voice snarled. "You let her get away!"

"We'll find her. Don't worry!" The other voice sounded like Vince, the historian.

"Are you sure that was it? There wasn't much light."

"I know what I saw. It was *the* knife," Vince said. "The Key of Kytalia. You know how many hours I spent staring at that painting when it was in the archives?"

"How could a bunch of kids have it?" Naldoc said.

"They must not know what it is. And they brought it straight to our hands. What luck. Usually we only get a few coins and some dried food."

Nalva's voice chimed in, "I wonder if they're looking for the city."

Peter barely breathed until the voices faded along with the footsteps.

After a few minutes, Kira sat back with a sigh. "I think we lost them."

Sephiri slumped against the wall of the cave. "That was too close."

Rylan sprawled across the ground, taking up most of the limited space. A sliver of moonlight fell across his face. "Heeyyyy," he slurred. "What happened?"

Sephiri grimaced. She touched his forehead, then checked the pulse at his neck. "He's feverish, but not too bad. He seems either drugged or drunk."

"From that crazy wine?" Kira pulled out the provisions. She'd snagged their bags, but the run had taken a toll on her. Light purple circles hung under her eyes, and sweat dotted her face. She tore off a chunk of bread and passed pieces to the others.

"There was something in it," Peter said. "I'm sure of it."

Sephiri nodded. "Probably some drug. Either they're immune to it, or they put it in our cups."

"You think they've done that before?" Kira asked.

Peter nodded. "You know that group they said came by not long ago?" Peter raised his eyebrows.

"What about them?"

"Dead. The Dirteaters killed them."

"What?" Sephiri asked, wide-eyed. "How do you know?"

"Naldoc said it was a dead deer over the hill, remember?"

Sephiri covered her mouth with her hand.

"Bodies," Peter said. "Human bodies."

Kira swallowed hard, her face pale.

"I'm guessing they intercept people traveling, then kill them to take whatever supplies they have. Out here, no one will be missed."

"And now they know about the knife," Sephiri said.

"I heard that," Kira said. "That man recognized it from the painting, same as we did."

If they know what we have, they won't stop looking for it, Peter thought. "Let's sleep here tonight," he said. "Give them time to give up the search, then we'll move out tomorrow."

"It's not like we have a choice." Kira gestured to Rylan, who already snored.

Peter chuckled and shook his head. "Poor guy. He sure was out of it."

Sephiri and Kira settled down in the small cave, lying on the small floor and leaning against the packs. Before long, their breathing evened out into the slow rhythms of sleep.

Rest didn't come as easily to Peter. Leaning against the wall, he gazed at the dark ceiling, with only the dimmest moonlight able to find its way in. The Dirteaters bothered him. *How many travelers have they killed? Have they done this all over Terrenor?*

An idea came to him. *Maybe we should go back to Palenting and tell Commander Isert! That'd be something real I could give him —something we could fix, right now.*

Kira snuffled in her sleep and rolled over. Peter's heart sank. *We can't. Not yet.*

We have to find Kytalia.

The Dirteaters could wait. Isert could wait. Kira couldn't.

THE NEXT MORNING, Peter woke to the sun shining into the cave and birds chirping outside. His back was sore, but his body itched to move.

Rylan lifted himself onto his elbows. He blinked, then groaned and rubbed his temples. "What happened last night?"

"Your girlfriend tried to murder us." Sephiri offered a canteen to Rylan.

"Esmee?" Rylan chuckled, then raised the canteen to his lips and took a greedy gulp.

No one else laughed. Peter raised his eyebrows and pressed his lips together.

Rylan's eyes grew, and he choked on his water. "Are you serious?" He wiped water off his chin with the back of his hand. "The nice girl from the camp?"

Peter cringed. "Yeah . . . she's not as nice as you think."

They caught Rylan up on the Dirteaters' attempted murder and their narrow escape in the night.

"Argh!" Rylan groaned, flopping onto his back with a whine of despair. "This always happens! I think a girl likes me and then she tries to kill me."

"This *always* happens?" Kira echoed.

"I thought we had something special," Rylan lamented.

Sephiri pulled some bread out of a pack and passed around small hunks to each of them.

The bread only served as a tease, and Peter's stomach ached with hunger. "We should get moving. We'll stick to the woods until we're further away from their camp. They could be looking for us still."

"This sucks," Rylan said. "They seemed so nice."

"We need to be more careful," Sephiri said, tucking the knife into a bag. "We don't need more people figuring out where we're going or what we're after."

"We'll keep to ourselves," Peter agreed. "Don't trust anyone."

"All right, Rylan." Kira waggled her hands at him, then held out the heaviest pack. "Let's go. Time to hike."

Rylan moaned and groaned, looking green around the gills until Peter reached out to take it.

"I'll carry that one for a while," Peter said.

The four friends creeped out of the cave, shuffling on their knees until they could stand. After determining there weren't any Dirteaters around, they headed south again.

"What about you?" Peter asked Kira, as Sephiri and Rylan made their way ahead. "You feeling all right?"

"Yeah, I'll put on some more barkleaf balm when we take a break." She ran a hand through her hair, then busied herself tying it back. "My joints are sore, but I'm okay to travel."

Peter nodded. There was nothing else he could do about the reaper poison—nothing except get to Kytalia before it was too late.

13

They reached Marris in the late afternoon. The bustling port city was bigger than Peter had envisioned. Fishermen pulled their boats in and out of the docks, shouting greetings and commands as they cast off lines or hauled in nets of fish off the decks. Gulls swooped in from the pale stone buildings down to the docks, floating on the ocean breeze. The sea glittered on the horizon. Cobbled white stone filled the town square, where merchants ran stands beneath brightly colored umbrellas or floppy straw hats. The air was warmer than it was near Palenting, and the salty breeze put a skip in Peter's step.

"This place is beautiful." Sephiri gazed around the market, awed.

"It's so colorful!" Kira led the way to the stall of a clothing merchant, who had a spread of fabrics dyed in bright blues, reds, and indigos. "Look at this teal! I think I need a new cloak! And these fasteners—is this gold?"

The sun-weathered old merchant smiled. "Looks like it, doesn't it? It's sunsbeite—harder than gold and has a self-healing quality."

"I've heard of it, but I've never seen it in person," Kira said. "Self-healing?"

The woman drew her thumbnail over the fastener on the cloak. Her nail left a dark line on the metal, like she'd scratched it. Kira gasped. But then, the woman drew the pad of her thumb over the scratch and it disappeared, leaving the sunsbeite flawless. "I use it in clothes for its resiliency."

"Is it valuable?" Rylan asked, eyes wide.

"Not as valuable as gold if that's what you're asking," the woman said with a laugh. "It leaves a residue, so it can't imitate actual gold. It's pretty common in southern Rynor." She lifted her hand and showed a black streak on her thumb where she'd smoothed out the scratch. "Quite neat, isn't it?"

"Still, it's beautiful." Kira bought a few handkerchiefs from the woman but left the sunsbeite cloak untouched.

The friends wandered through the market while the sun shone down and the sea breeze tousled Peter's hair. The shops differed from the familiar ones in Palenting, louder and brighter. Brave gulls swooped down toward the food stalls, looking to steal bites.

"I need a proper meal." Rylan rubbed his forehead. "I still feel like a horse kicked me."

"Well, you shouldn't have accepted strange drinks from strange ladies," Sephiri said.

"Fresh fish!" a bright voice called over the hubbub. "Fresh, grilled fish!"

"Oh, that sounds good!" Peter's mouth watered at the aroma coming from a stall at the edge of the docks. *They must take the day's catch off the boat and put it on the grill.* He led the way through the market, heading toward the voice.

"I'll bet it's not even poisoned," Rylan joked.

The fish vendor smiled as they approached. The woman was young, not much older than Peter, plain-looking but with warm eyes. "You four look hungry." Her gaze lingered on

Sephiri, but then flickered back to Peter. "What can I get you?"

"Skewers, please," Peter said. "Four to start."

The woman smiled and plucked the skewers off the grill. "Two tid."

"That's it?" Peter mumbled around a bite in his mouth as he fished out the coins. The flesh was tender and flaky, perfectly cooked with a sweet tang of citrus drizzle. "Wow! It's good."

"Get four more," Rylan insisted.

Peter grinned at the merchant and fished out two more tid.

She handed them the skewers, clearing off the grill. "Good choice." She took the tid Peter offered, then reached into a small crate at her side. "Here, you look hungry. On the house." She handed Peter a bag of oysters with a smile that made his stomach somersault.

"Come on," Rylan said, chewing a mouthful of fish and pulling at Peter's shoulder. "I want to watch the ships."

"Thanks," Peter murmured to the young woman. Reluctantly tearing his gaze from her warm smile, he followed his friends down to the dock, where they sat on a bench near the railing and dug into their meal.

Sephiri pulled the dagger off her hip and held it out to Peter. "For the oysters?"

"Stash that away." Kira glanced over her shoulder. "We don't need a repeat of the Dirteaters."

"Plus, we probably shouldn't use a priceless artifact to open food." Peter pulled out his own small knife and popped an oyster open.

With a chuckle, Sephiri stuffed the dagger into her bag. "Good point."

"So what's next?" Rylan asked. "We made it here. Now what?"

Kira raised an eyebrow. "You seem to feel better."

"It's amazing what good food will do."

"Let's start by asking around," Peter said. "The vendor in Palenting said he stole the dagger from a guy named Denton. Maybe he's got a shop in the market, or maybe someone else knows him."

"We better get a move on before the sun goes down." Kira finished her fish, then stood and smoothed out her travel trousers as if she wore a fine gown. "And we should find somewhere to stay tonight. Sleeping in that cave was not the most comfortable."

The group split up, each of them taking a different direction to search and inquire. Peter asked around the docks, but the fishermen were not keen to talk to him. In the market square, the merchants were friendly at first. When they heard the name "Denton," they grew cagey and tight-lipped, insisting Peter buy something or be on his way. Discouraged, he approached another stall in the square, where an old woman sold sweet-smelling hand pies.

"I'll take a cherry one, please," he said.

"Of course, son." Her eye twinkled as she looked him over. "You don't live around Marris, do you? Passing through?" The old woman wrapped the pie in wax paper before handing it to him.

Peter dropped a coin in her palm. "Looking for someone. A man called Denton."

"The old baker?"

Peter looked up, eyes wide. "You know him?"

"Of course. Us bakers stick together." She smiled, pointing over her shoulder. "His shop's just off the square. He closes at sundown, though, so you'll have to hurry."

"Thank you!" Peter said. "Seriously, thank you!"

Peter rushed back toward the dock where their group had agreed to meet. Rylan's, Sephiri's, and Kira's glum faces showed they had little success. Sephiri lit up at Peter's approach.

"You got something?" she asked.

His smile grew larger. "I think so. Come on, we gotta hurry!"

Peter led them through the quieting square and into the narrow alley the old woman pointed out. He peered at the storefronts and signs, passing a tailor, a grocer, and a net repair shop, until finally . . . "There!"

Outside the bakery, an older man in a flour-dusted apron carried chairs inside. "Sir!" Peter called, hurrying forward. "Are you the baker?"

"We're closing up for the day," the man said. "If you want anything, now's the time."

"Denton?" Kira asked breathlessly.

"Close." The man pointed at the sign in the window. *Benton's Bakery.*

Peter deflated.

"You need some bread?"

"Yes," Rylan said after a brief pause. "We do." He followed the baker inside. Kira rolled her eyes and went with him.

"Close," Sephiri echoed with a smile. "At least we'll get some bread."

"Benton." Peter raked a hand through his hair, then leaned against the brick wall of the bakery. "I thought we had a lead here."

"Admit it, it's a little funny." Sephiri knocked her shoulder against his. "We'll find our lead. Give it time."

"Time is the one thing we don't have." Peter peered over his shoulder, through the glass window of the bakery. Inside, the baker stuffed pastries into a paper bag as Rylan grinned. Kira held a muffin and smiled as she broke off a piece.

"We'll have enough time," Sephiri said. "We'll get her the healing she needs."

Peter nodded. *I have to believe that. We have to try.*

Sephiri took a breath like she wanted to say something else, but then the bakery door clattered open, and out walked Rylan, laden with goodies.

"Might not be the guy we were looking for," Rylan said, "but this guy can bake!"

"And he gave us a recommendation for an inn," Kira added. "Come on, let's get a room before it gets dark."

They found the modest inn near the coast, a block west of the town square. The wooden and brick building contained a thatched roof with smoke puffing from a small chimney. Stained glass windows framed the door. Sephiri held the door open, and Peter nodded in thanks as he entered.

Groups of people packed the common room, talking and laughing around the roaring hearth. The innkeeper welcomed Peter and his friends with a cheerful wave, despite appearing buried with orders. Unlike most inns, the room wasn't dingy and dark. The windows facing the ocean hung open to welcome the sea breeze.

"Why don't you ask around about Denton, then grab a table," Peter said. "I'll talk with the owner."

Peter made his way to the bar, where he squeezed between two broad-shouldered men. The innkeeper still had rooms available, he was glad to say, two on the top floor with their names on it. Peter happily paid for them, with a little extra for heaping servings of vegetable stew from the cauldron on the hearth.

"I'm looking for someone," he asked. He kept his voice low, just loud enough to be heard over the noise.

"Lots of folks come through Marris," the innkeeper said as he dried a glass, "so I see a lot of faces. Happy to help if I can, though."

"A merchant," Peter said. "Or trader. Someone who came through here a few weeks ago. Denton?"

The innkeeper's hands stilled before he resumed drying the glass. "I can't say the name's familiar."

Like everyone else in the town square. "You're sure? He was in Marris, I'm positive. If you could—"

"Son, I don't know the name." His voice had turned harsh. "I suggest you take a seat and enjoy your meal."

"We've come a long way. We—"

A man at the end of the bar caught the innkeeper's attention, drawing him away.

Peter's shoulders fell. Leaving the bar, he huffed as he sat at a table in the corner, interrupting his friends' idle conversation. A waitress deposited four steaming bowls of soup on the table.

"Any luck?" Kira asked.

"Got two rooms for the night," Peter said.

"What about Denton?"

Peter pulled his chair closer. "Something weird is going on. I think people know more about this guy than they're letting on."

"Was the innkeeper cagey?" Sephiri asked. "No one I spoke to would say anything—like just hearing the name scared them."

"Same here," Rylan said. "Their mouths shut after I brought the name up."

Peter took a sip of his thin, salty soup while his mind grasped for ideas.

"I'll find the library tomorrow," Kira said.

"How will the library give us information about merchants passing through?" Rylan asked.

Kira raised her chin. "Don't doubt the power of the library."

Sephiri snorted. "If anyone could figure it out, it's you, Kira."

"At least we get an actual bed tonight," Rylan said.

"You didn't seem to have any trouble sleeping on the ground yesterday." Sephiri grinned.

Rylan leaned in, his mischievous eyes flitting between the others. "You think the innkeeper has some of that valcor blood on tap?"

"No!" Peter laughed. "Please, no."

After the soup, they broke into the pastries and bread from

the bakery. It was nice, after a few days of hard travel and low stores, to have a good meal and treats. The inn quieted as patrons left the tavern or headed to their rooms, leaving the low, rhythmic roar of crashing waves through the open windows. Peter's eyes grew heavy from the rest and the meal. The four friends retired to the third floor, to the two rooms at the end of the hall.

Kira and Sephiri waved as they slipped into their room. Peter led Rylan to the next door.

Denton. Kytalia. Man at the market. Peter worked the key in the lock and paused as the hair on his nape prickled.

"What is it?" Rylan asked.

Peter glanced in both directions down the empty hall. He shook his head to clear it. "Nothing." The innkeeper had gotten under his skin. *I'll feel better after a good night's sleep, in a proper bed. We'll figure out who this Denton guy is first thing.*

The room was small and dark, with the shutters drawn and twin beds on either side. Peter stumbled in, drawn to the soft mattress and crisp sheets.

Halfway across the room, the hair on the back of his neck stood up again. *Something's wrong.*

From behind the armoire, a shadowy figure rushed out of the dark corner. Peter couldn't even scream before rough canvas pulled over his head and a rag tied over it, around his mouth. An acrid smell leeched into his nostrils. His head spun. He pulled against powerful arms and moaned into the gag, but it was useless. The dizzy blackness faded to nothing as he passed out.

14

The canvas hood ripped off in one rough motion, and Peter blinked in the dim torchlight. Cold stone leeched the heat from his body. Water dripped from the rafters and landed in shallow puddles. A musty smell turned his nose, as if he'd wandered into a crypt. His three friends slumped against the wall near him, blinking and looking around as he did. With a vaulted ceiling and dark doorways on either side, the small room gave no sign of where they were.

Peter eyed their bags, chucked in a corner. His stomach turned. *Did they root through them? What about the knife or the map?*

Five men stood in front of them. Four of them hung back, glowering. Scars and tattoos covered their muscled arms, and stains dirtied their dark clothes. In the center, a man sneered at Peter. Stringy blond hair pushed off his face. Rough hems lined his unstained silk shirt. His black boots were polished to a shine. Gleaming silver jewelry adorned his fingers, and a necklace with a black oval pendant hung around his neck. Behind him lay a long wooden box in the shape of a coffin. Peter gulped.

"What's going on?" Rylan slurred. "Where are we?"

"Quiet," the blond-haired man snapped. "We'll do the talking."

Rylan flopped on the ground, tugging at his bound wrists. "Who are you? You can't bind me with these!"

"Shh!" Sephiri hissed.

Rylan staggered to his feet. He made it halfway up, slumping against the back wall before a goon stepped forward and socked him in the stomach.

"Hey!" Peter shouted. "Leave him alone."

The goon laughed as Rylan groaned and fell back to his knees.

"Rylan," Peter muttered. "You can't bust us out of here. Give it up."

Rylan attempted to stagger up again.

"Watch it," the goon growled. Instead of going for Rylan, he grabbed Kira by the hair.

Kira sucked in a breath. Her face contorted, straining, but she didn't make a sound.

"All right, all right!" Rylan said, holding up his bound hands. He sat back down, and the goon released Kira.

Peter shoved down the flare of anger burning in his chest and turned to Kira. She nodded, face pale, as if to say *I'm fine.*

"You four aren't exactly subtle, you know," the leader said. He took a step forward. "Asking nosy questions all around the town square. Even badgering the innkeeper. Who are you?"

"We're travelers," Peter said. His head throbbed from whatever they'd used to knock him out. "No one special."

"Innocent travelers don't ask so many questions," the leader snarled. "What are you doing in Marris?"

Peter narrowed his eyes. "Asking questions."

The heavy boot from a man slammed into his gut. He

groaned, closing his eyes and bending over. Pain throbbed all the way to his skull.

"Marris is Norivonne territory," the leader said. "And I run the Norivonne. My name is Renaud Denton."

Peter's eyes widened. *Denton!*

"I believe my brother Louis is the guy you're after. He's a trader of sorts with a hobby of pursuing legends—things lost and forgotten by time." He paused and raised an eyebrow. "Why did you want to find him?"

Peter pressed his lips together and remained silent.

"Would you like to speak with him?"

His eyes flicked between the men. "Um . . . sure."

"Well, you can't because he's dead."

Sephiri breathed in sharply.

"Killed."

"We didn't know," Kira said.

Dead. Peter's heart sank. *There goes our lead.*

"There's something you're not telling me," Renaud said. "What is it?"

Peter gulped, his heart rate speeding. Neither he nor the others spoke.

"Nothing, huh?" Renaud stared hard at Kira, leaning toward her. His eyes narrowed.

Peter's pulse thudded, his eyes flicking between Kira and Renaud.

After a tense pause, the leader took a step back. His hard gaze softened, then he tapped his foot against the wooden box behind him. "Show our friends what's inside."

A man picked up a wooden stick with a net on the end from beside the box. He pushed the lid on the box aside with his foot. The net slid through the gap, then made a scooping motion before withdrawing. The goon held the net far away from his body, while a tiny black scorpion wriggled in the fabric.

"Paratill scorpions." Renaud leaned close to the net, smiling at the bug like one might at a beloved pet. "Hard to find. Lucky for us all, they live only on the Isle of Paratill, but unlucky for you, we have several here. One sting and you're dead in under a minute." He tapped the edge of the net.

The scorpion lifted its tail in a threatening arch. Peter shuddered.

Renaud grinned. "I quite like the little fellows. Even named our organization after them."

Norivonne? Peter thought. *How is that named after them?*

"If you won't talk, one of you will spend some quality time in this box with about two dozen of our little friends." He straightened, and the goon dumped the scorpion back into the box and closed it.

Peter swallowed hard. "What happened to your brother?"

Renaud blinked, looking thrown for a moment. "What?"

"We're sorry to hear about his death," Sephiri said. "What happened to him?"

"He was murdered," Renaud said. "Bound with rope, arms pulled around his chest like a vice. Someone tightened the rope until he suffocated, his lungs crushed by his own broken ribs."

Peter breathed in quickly. *Like the vendor in Palenting!* His eyes met Sephiri's. A ring of white circled her pupils. *The man with the scarred face!* The killer tracked the vendor to find the Kytalian knife while they'd been working in reverse to find the source.

"You wouldn't know anything about that, would you?" Renaud stepped closer until he loomed over Peter. "Seems you might."

"I don't." Peter's voice sounded weak. "Haven't heard anything about it."

Renaud kicked him hard in the side.

Peter groaned and leaned over. Bile burned in the back of his throat.

"You're hiding something!"

"We're not!" Kira said.

"Then why were you asking every merchant in town about him?"

"We, uh . . ." Peter cast his eyes around the tiny room.

"Answer me!" Renaud roared.

"We don't know anything!" Rylan shouted back. "Let us go!"

"Let me offer you a little encouragement." Renaud waved a hand at the goons. "Prepare the box."

Peter clenched his teeth as the goons pushed the lid off the box. A foul smell permeated the room, thick in the still air. Peter's stomach turned. One goon pulled on a thick pair of gloves and then reached into the box with a grimace. He didn't retrieve more scorpions. Instead, he hauled out a bloated, limp body.

Kira gasped. Sephiri covered her mouth, her body retching.

The goon shook lingering scorpions off the body, then dropped the corpse to the floor, its limbs slapping the cold stone. Black veins streaked from the dead man's temples down his neck, which turned at a sharp, obscene angle. Dried blood coated his mouth. The dead man's eyes were black. No white. Like a pool of ink.

"Norivonne," Kira whispered. "Tarphic for Black Eyes."

"Who is that?" Rylan asked.

"No one of importance." Renaud nudged the limp body with his foot, then grinned at Rylan. "Ran into me at the tavern and made me spill my drink. Treated him to the scorpions for his trouble."

The goons chuckled.

"Their poison puts on a good show. It shuts down your nervous system. This man bit off his tongue, then broke his neck from the spasms."

Kira folded her hands over her mouth, eyes wide.

"I'll give you some time to think it over. Consider what you know about my brother's death, and I'll be back to ask you one more time before you end up like this." He flicked a hand at his men. "Take them away."

A man grabbed Peter by his upper arm and hauled him to his feet. They dragged the four friends out of the dark room and into a larger, drafty space next door. Overhead, the stone walls reached to the high rafters, where rats scuttled and moonlight peeked through gaps in the thatched roof. A few crates were stacked around the edge of the room, but what held Peter's attention was the dark gap in the middle of the floor. One man grabbed a plank of wood and lowered it into the pit.

"Hey!" Rylan shouted. "What do you think you're doing?" He broke out of the man's hold. "You can't keep us here!"

"I think we can," Renaud said.

Rylan grimaced and pulled at his bindings. The muscles in his forearms flexed, and the rope dug into his flesh, reddening his skin.

"Ry!" Peter scolded. "It's not the time."

The rope groaned and frayed.

Renaud's eyes widened. "Handle this," he said to the guards.

The guards grabbed Rylan and tugged him backward. He shouted again and pulled harder at his bindings, but before he could break them, the guards wrestled a dark rag over his face.

"Rylan!" Peter cried.

The larger boy struggled and then slumped, rendered unconscious by whatever chemical soaked the rag.

The guard dropped Rylan onto the ramp, then gave him a nudge. He tumbled into the pit like a kid rolling down a hill.

One by one, the men shoved Peter and his friends down the plank like a ramp, until they all huddled together at the bottom. Peter peered up at the oval of dim light above them and at Renaud's scowling face.

"Remember what I told you," Renaud said. "I'll return tomorrow for your answer."

Kira exhaled through her nose and leaned against the earthen wall.

The goons removed the plank. Peter lunged for it, trying to hang on, but the men laughed and wrenched it out of his grip. A latticed metal gate swung closed over the pit and clunked as it locked.

"Rylan!" Sephiri said. She went to Rylan's side and shook his shoulder. Rylan groaned but didn't rouse into consciousness.

"It must be what they used to kidnap us," Peter said. "He's out cold."

Sephiri sat back. "He'll be okay?"

"I think so," Peter said. "We all were good last time. Hopefully it wears off soon."

"Kira, are you okay?" Sephiri asked.

Kira's eyes pinched shut. She thunked her head against the wall and nodded. "I'm fine. Just hurts a little."

Sephiri pointed at her shoulder where the reddened skin swelled. "The gash . . . it's oozing."

Kira glanced down and grimaced. "What did that man say about infection?"

Peter swallowed, wishing to avoid having to answer. "He said intense pain would follow."

Her jaw tightened. After a long moment, she nodded.

Every moment in the pit was another moment the reaper poison had to work through her. They still had no leads on Kytalia, and Kira had barely a week to live.

15

_____

A skittering overhead woke Peter from a restless half-sleep. He blinked up at the darkness, anticipating seeing one of the Norivonne. He half-expected them to dump scorpions into the pit. At least that would be a quick death for Kira, instead of the slow, unstoppable march of the reaper poison.

Peter rubbed his eyes. Sephiri slumped against his shoulder. Her expression was soft in sleep, and a strand of dark hair fell across her cheek. A weak smile pulled at Peter's lips. None of them had slept much, and they could use whatever snatches they could get.

There was no further noise overhead. *Did I imagine it?* It was hard to see in the darkness, with only slivers of moonlight cutting across the rafters above.

As he peered at the underside of the thatched roof, a shadow moved.

It was too big to be a rat or any creature that crept through run-down places like this. The shadow moved elegantly. Peter made out the slope of a shoulder and tied-back, long hair in a beam of moonlight—a girl. The figure made her way across the rafters until she stopped above them. A coil of rope adjusted on her shoulder, then she peered into the pit.

Peter squinted up, trying to make out the girl's face, but it was too dark. *If she is a Norivonne, what's she doing sneaking around the rafters?*

"You tied up?" the girl whisper-yelled.

"Yes," Peter replied as loud as he dared.

"Watch out, I'm dropping something!"

A small, sheathed knife dropped through the metal lattice and landed in the center of the pit.

Sephiri jerked awake, eyes wide.

"It's okay," Peter whispered. He placed a hand on her knee and squeezed. "I think we're getting out of here."

Sephiri glanced down at his hand, then back up at him.

Peter jerked his hand back, his face flushing. "Um . . . Can you grab the knife and cut these?"

Was Sephiri embarrassed? Peter couldn't tell in the dim light, but she nodded.

Peter held his hands up while Sephiri worked at them. She sawed the knife back and forth while the blade bit through the fibers of the rope. Finally, the strand snapped and the coil loosened. Peter sloughed off the rest of the coil, then rubbed his raw, sore wrists with a groan.

Overhead, the girl fastened the rope around the rafters and then dropped the coil to land with a *whump* in the center of the latticed metal door.

Peter cut Sephiri's bonds as quickly as he could.

Rylan groaned as he roused. "Wh-what's happening?"

"We're getting out of here," Peter whispered.

"My head hurts," Rylan groaned. Peter cut his bindings, and Rylan rubbed his wrists. "Thanks."

"Someone's helping us," Peter whispered.

Overhead, the figure slid down the rope and landed on the gate. Before Peter could get a look at her face, she jumped off and crouched by the lock. Her hands moved deftly, and in a moment, it clunked open. She heaved the gate up. It creaked and then thunked against the floor. The rest of the rope trickled down through the new opening.

Kira blinked awake more slowly. She peered at the rope, then up toward the opening in the grate. "What's happening?"

"We're escaping," Peter whispered.

The girl above gripped the rope and crawled back up it, moving with ease. Peter cut Kira's bonds, then stuffed the knife into his pocket.

"Climb up!" the girl whispered from the rafters. "Hurry!"

"Who is that?" Sephiri asked.

"I don't know." Peter stood. "But this looks like our way out so we better take it."

"Let's go." Sephiri nodded. "Kira?"

Kira swallowed. She hauled herself to her feet, using the wall for balance. "I don't think I can."

"What?" Peter asked. "What do you mean?"

She gave him a small smile and nodded toward her shoulder. "I don't think I can climb."

The gash on her shoulder looked worse than it had. It wasn't healing—it was *rotting*. The skin was more swollen than it had been a few hours before, and dried, bloody pus encircled the wound. Peter cringed. His own shoulder throbbed at the sight.

"Can you try?" Sephiri asked. "We have to get out of here."

Kira took the rope in her bad hand, tried to grip it, and then yelped in pain. She dropped it and staggered back. She cupped her good hand over the wound and exhaled a few times through her nose as she regained her composure. "I can't," she whispered. "I'm too weak."

"Can you hold on?" Rylan asked.

Sephiri looked up. "What?"

"To me," Rylan said. "If you can hold on, I can climb."

"You can do that? Even after being knocked out?"

Rylan nodded, then bent over.

Overhead, the girl rattled the rope. "Hurry!"

"Go first," Peter said to Rylan. "We're right behind you."

"I'll catch you if you fall," Sephiri promised.

"No one's falling," Rylan said. "Kira's not *that* heavy."

Kira wound her good arm around Rylan's shoulder and hopped onto his back. "Hang on tight," Rylan said with a grin. Source power danced like sparks down his arms. He gripped the rope and then pulled himself up, hand over hand. The strain was obvious—not as easy as usual. But he hauled them up.

"Lucky we have a strongman with us," Sephiri muttered, her tension easing as Rylan and Kira made it to the rafters.

"Come on, move!" the girl above insisted.

"You go next," Peter said, pushing the rope toward Sephiri.

She nodded, then sighted up the dangling line. After taking in a breath, she jumped, pulling her legs up and wrapping her feet before she stood. She moved well, pull after pull, like they practiced in the Garrison.

After Sephiri disappeared, Peter scurried up, making sure not to show off his ability too much with the stranger watching. The girl waited on the beam, along with Rylan, Kira, and Sephiri. Rylan grinned, looking like he'd barely broken a sweat, but Kira knelt, her hand braced against the rafter as if she didn't trust her balance.

The girl grabbed the rope and pulled it up, hand over hand, until it coiled back on her shoulder.

She finally looked up and smiled at the four friends. In the dim moonlight, Peter could make out her features: brown hair, warm eyes, and a nose that slanted to one side like it'd been broken in the past. She looked a little older than Peter and strangely familiar.

"You were at the docks," Peter whispered. "The girl selling fish."

"That's me." She winked. "I can get you out of here, but we need to move."

"Who are you?" Sephiri asked. "How did you know we were here?"

"I'm Mirelle," she said. "I like to mess up the Norivonne's plans whenever I can."

A door clanked in the distance, and low, gruff voices and laughter filtered up to the rafters. Mirelle swore under her breath. Despite being rough around the edges, Peter liked her friendly face and confidence.

"We need to get out of here before they realize you're gone," she said.

"I have to get my bag," Peter whispered.

Mirelle gaped at him. "Your *bag?*"

"It's important," Kira said.

Mirelle turned her gawking expression to Kira. "Are you all right? You look like you're about to pass out."

"I'm fine."

"If you say so." Mirelle hiked the rope higher onto her shoulder and turned back to Peter. "We can replace your stuff in town."

"I can't leave without that bag," Peter whispered. "If you all want to leave, that's fine."

"Didn't you hear?" Mirelle whispered. "The Norivonne are here. And if they catch you attempting to escape, we're *all* facing the scorpions."

"Lead the rest of them out. I'll be there soon."

Despite the danger, Peter wasn't concerned. *I'll drop, grab it, and run out before they can catch me. It'll be fine.* A wince from Kira caught his attention. His jaw clenched. *We're not leaving here without that map.*

"I'm going with you," Sephiri said.

"Me too," Rylan said.

"If you think we're splitting up now, you're crazy," Kira said.

Mirelle sucked her teeth, then sighed. "I didn't realize I was getting a bunch of lunatics." She tossed her hands up. "If you insist, we'll get it."

"We?" Peter raised his eyebrows.

"If that bag's important, let's make sure these Norivonne jerks don't get to keep it." She smirked, catlike. "This way."

Mirelle led the way, creeping across the rafters. Peter moved behind her, trying to keep each step silent on the wood. The moonlight leaking through the roof lit his way as he followed Mirelle, crossing over the brick wall that separated the two rooms.

There it is!

Their bags sat in the same corner behind the wooden box. Even from above the rafters, the rancid, rotting smell coming from the box burrowed into his sinuses. His stomach lurched at the terrible stench, and he struggled not to gag. The laughter from the Norivonne grew.

Where are they?

The heavy wooden door to the small room clanged open. One of the big goons ambled in and scooped their bags up like they were nothing but sacks of flour. "I'm coming, I'm coming!" he shouted over his shoulder toward the other voices. "I've gotta take these to the sorting room at the warehouse!"

Peter groaned. All he could do was watch as the man left with their supplies, the map, and the Key in his arms. *If they search them . . .*

"The warehouse?" Rylan whispered. "Do you know where that is?"

Mirelle nodded. "It's not far. I can take you there." She waved her hand, shooing them in the other direction, then led them back the way they'd come. She glanced over her shoulder with another catlike smirk, then moved effortlessly, even with the thick coil of rope over her shoulder.

Who is this girl?

Voices picked up behind them again. "Let me check on our prisoners first," a man boomed.

Mirelle hissed again, "Hurry!" She rushed forward and stopped at the roof. She worked her hands into the thatching and pulled it apart—a gap that appeared to have been used before. It was just wide enough to slide her body through. "Be careful, the ledge is narrow!"

Peter squeezed through the gap behind her. She wasn't joking—the roof offered only a narrow gutter, barely the width of his foot, that wrapped around the roof and creaked under his weight. He leaned against the thatching with his heart pounding, then followed Mirelle as she crept toward the far edge. The wiether night was chilly, sharp, and salty. Ocean waves crashed somewhere in the distance.

"Move fast," Mirelle hissed. "I'm not sure how long this gutter will hold."

Mirelle rushed to the corner, then slid down the drain spout, landing on the ground with a soft thump. Peter hurried to follow. He slid down, followed by Kira and Sephiri.

"Where's Rylan?" Peter whispered when Sephiri arrived on the ground.

She looked up. "He had trouble with the opening, but I think he—"

Rylan emerged through the gap in the roof. The gutter groaned when he rested his weight on it. Peter's breath caught at the sight of the gutter pulling away from the roof. Rylan's fingers grew frantic, grasping at the straw. Peter met Sephiri's eyes, and she nodded.

Peter spun to Mirelle. "Which way?" He grabbed her shoulder and stepped away from Rylan, drawing her eyes. "They're gonna hear all this noise! We need to hide!"

"Right," Mirelle said. Her face scrunched up as if deep in thought.

Peter's eyes flicked over Mirelle's shoulder. Rylan lurched backward, high above, and Sephiri's eyes blazed white. With flailing arms, Rylan dropped from the rooftop into a cushion of air. Mirelle's hair blew in a puff of wind, wrapping her face.

She pried her hair away and held up a finger. "The tunnels!" Rylan scrambled to his feet as Mirelle turned around. "That was fast," she said, having missed the true nature of his rapid descent.

"Where are we?" Sephiri asked.

They had seen little of Marris—just the port, the square, and the docks. Wherever they were was nowhere near as beautiful as the square. There was no color. Plain stone formed the squat buildings with crumbling roofs and muddy alleys between. The faint smell of the salty sea air thickened with the scent of mud and rot.

"Where'd they go?" someone shouted from inside the building.

"Boss'll kill us," another voice whined. "We gotta find them."

Mirelle's eyes widened. "Follow me!"

Rylan scooped up Kira without asking.

Mirelle took off, footsteps loud in the mud. Peter and the others followed as she darted across the road and in between two crumbling stone buildings. Around the back, she threw open two wooden cellar doors and hurried inside.

Down a short flight of steps, water dripped from the narrow, sloping hall's ceiling. The floor was wet and muddy, fading into a dense wall of darkness. *Where is she leading us?!*

Rylan paused beside Peter. "Should we . . . ?"

A voice roared from the other side of the road, "Spread out and find them!"

"What choice do we have?" Peter said. He plugged his nose

against the stench of rot emitting from the hall and then rushed down the steps into the gloom.

It was dark. Wet. Musty. The doors clattered closed, and darkness descended like a blanket over him. "Put your hand on the wall," Mirelle whispered from ahead. "Follow it."

"I don't know about this," Sephiri muttered.

"We're going under the warehouses," Mirelle said.

"You can put me down," Kira said. "I can walk."

A set of feet hit the tunnel floor with a splash.

Peter could barely see ahead. "Everyone okay?" he called over his shoulder as he stepped forward.

"We're good," Kira said.

"Keep moving," Mirelle said. "These tunnels aren't secret. They could search down here."

Peter followed the wall and the sound of Mirelle's steps, feet sloshing through shallow, stagnant water. Not knowing how long they'd be walking, he startled after a few minutes when he collided with Mirelle's back. Overhead, dim light leaked through what looked like a trap door. Mirelle smiled at him over her shoulder.

They were close. Very close.

Peter swallowed and took a step back.

Mirelle pulled her lower lip between her teeth, almost shy. "We made it."

She grasped a ladder built into the wall and climbed. The trapdoor above flung open with a *thunk* and Mirelle exited.

Peter followed, eager to return to the light. He stumbled onto the street with his friends just behind. A familiar building loomed before them.

"Hey, Benton's Bakery." Rylan poked his head in the dumpster next to him. After a second, he grinned and pulled out a loaf of bread still wrapped in wax paper. "Think this is still good?"

Kira cringed. "If you like your food with rat feet all over it."

Rylan shrugged. "I've eaten worse." He unwrapped it.

Peter leaned forward, hands on his knees, and exhaled. His clothes were muddied and torn, and his wrists rubbed raw from the bonds. He reached into his pocket and withdrew the small knife. He offered it hilt-first back to Mirelle. "Thanks."

She flashed her playful smile as she took it back. Her fingertips brushed over his. "Sure." She ducked her chin, then slipped the knife back into her pocket.

Sephiri cleared her throat. "We need to get to the warehouse."

"Right." Peter straightened, hoping his ears weren't red. Kira's pale face and trembling hands caught his eye.

"It's not far," Mirelle said. "But I don't think it's a good idea—"

"You don't have to come with us," Sephiri said. "But we must get that bag."

"If we're lucky," Rylan spoke around a mouthful of bread, "maybe the Norgiphon or whoever will be busy looking for us elsewhere."

"Norivonne," Kira said.

"That's what I said."

Mirelle glanced around at the four of them. Rylan and Sephiri squared their shoulders, and Peter did the same. *We can't leave Marris without that map,* he thought.

"All right. You are serious." The teasing grin returned to her face. "Let's have fun, then."

16

M irelle led the four friends through muddy alleys, avoiding any illuminated paths or late-night wanderers. The moon lit the way, and a few taverns had glowing windows, but most of Marris was quiet in the depths of the night.

Back near where they'd escaped from, Mirelle led them up a rickety ladder, onto the roof of a three-story building. The wind needled at Peter's face, sharper the higher they climbed.

"That's it." Mirelle pointed at the squat two-story stone building next to them. It wasn't tall, but it was large—longer and wider than the Garrison. Wooden planks boarded the windows shut, and the doors sported heavy-looking chains and a lock.

"Is anyone in there?" Kira asked.

"How do we get in?" Rylan added.

"I wouldn't even try." Mirelle gestured at the doors. "Dogs watch the doors on the inside, along with an armed patrol. That's where they keep everything—not just what they steal, but their treasury, too. No one gets in unnoticed."

"So, our bags are in there?"

"Probably, yeah, but it's a sizable space. You'd be lucky to find them even if you aren't avoiding attack dogs."

"Look at that window." Kira pointed at a window on the far side of the second floor. "The wood is rotting. We can pry it off."

"Good eye."

"If we get in on the second floor, we might avoid the dogs," Rylan said.

Mirelle shrugged. "That could work."

"Let's do this," Peter said, then turned to Mirelle. "Thanks for everything."

She looked sidelong at him. "What do you mean? I'm coming with you."

"What?" Peter asked as Kira said, "Why?"

She raised her eyebrows. "Do you know how much money they keep in there? If you four think you can get in without getting caught . . . Well, I could use some of it."

"Enough money to risk getting mauled by dogs?" Rylan asked.

Mirelle undid her tied-up hair, shook it out, and then retied it into a high ponytail. "I already risked getting caught and stung by scorpions. Might as well keep going."

"Sounds great." Peter grinned. She seemed feisty, determined, and a troublemaker, just like they were. "We need all the help we can get."

Sephiri pursed her lips. Her eyebrows furrowed, but she said nothing.

"Let's grab the ladder," Peter said. "That should be long enough to get us over to the other roof if we're careful."

"I'll help." Sephiri motioned for Peter to follow her. "The rest of you wait here and keep watch."

"Don't you remember what we talked about in the woods?" she whispered when they were out of earshot. "About getting involved with strangers."

"She got us out of that pit," Peter whispered back. "If she

hadn't come for us, we'd be there waiting to get stuffed in the scorpion box."

"We would've found a way out."

"Maybe," Peter said. "Look, Seph, I get it, but we're being careful. We'll get our stuff, we'll figure out where to go next, then we'll leave Marris. If she can help us do those things, that's great."

Sephiri hauled up the ladder. "Fine. We need to be cautious, though. It's bad enough the Dirteaters found out what we're looking for."

Peter took the ladder and carried it over his head. "We'll play our cards close to the chest. But we don't have a lot of time. If her knowledge can get us back on the road faster, we need to take advantage of it. Kira needs it."

Sephiri didn't look convinced, but she said nothing further. They walked the ladder back over to the roof.

"I don't see any guards," Mirelle whispered. "This is our chance."

Peter placed the ladder on the edge of the roof. It reached across, sloping down to the flat roof of the warehouse. Peter went first, creeping across the ladder while Rylan held the end. The wood creaked under his weight and bent. He swallowed and looked down: nothing but the hard dirt road below him. A fall would break a leg at best. He moved on hands and knees, as swiftly as he dared, focusing on the edge of the roof ahead of him instead of the fall below. A tease of wind ruffled his hair, forcing his hands to clench the ladder harder. Only once his feet reached the opposite roof did he exhale.

He grasped the end to keep it in place. Kira crossed over next, then Sephiri, then Mirelle.

Rylan went last, climbing onto the ladder with his legs shaking. The wood creaked under his weight. "Guys," he whispered, "I don't know about this . . ." He continued forward, step after step. Near the middle of the ladder, a deep groan of old lumber filled the air.

"Hurry!" Peter called.

Rylan surged forward. The shifting of his weight turned the groans into cracks until the ladder splintered like a rotten log down the middle. He jumped for the edge of the roof, his hand stretching forward. The breaking support under his legs killed his momentum. His eyes formed wide circles. He extended his arm as far as it would go, but the distance was too great.

With a loud clap, Mirelle's hand grasped his. "Oof," she moaned, sliding toward the edge.

Peter lunged and wrapped his arms around Mirelle's waist.

"What was that?" a distant voice called.

"Pull," Mirelle hissed.

Peter didn't have time to worry about the unseen alerted guard. He heaved against Mirelle's narrow middle and pulled backward while she braced her foot on the edge of the roof. Together, they hauled Rylan up and onto the warehouse roof, just in time for all five of them to drop flat to their bellies as shuffling feet rounded the corner into the alley.

"See anything?" a voice asked.

"Ladder broke," another said. "Check the roof."

Mirelle wriggled closer to the edge of the roof on her belly, then peered over. "They're gone. We need to move. They'll check up here."

"In and out," Peter said. "Let's get our bags and get out of here."

Sephiri crept to the edge and peered over. "I'll get the window." She climbed over the edge of the roof, then lowered herself down to the narrow sill.

Mirelle peered over her shoulder and glanced around the rooftop. "Any guards inside?"

Sephiri peered through a gap in the boards. "Not that I can

see. It's pretty dark." She tugged at the rotted plank until it popped off the window. "Got it!"

Peter had prepared to wince, but the decayed wood made little noise. He reached down and took the board from her. After removing two more planks, the gap looked wide enough.

"I'm going in." Sephiri slid through the opening.

Peter dropped onto the windowsill next and followed her inside.

The window opened to a second level that looked down on a vast and dark warehouse space. A wraparound balcony stored dusty crates. Peter crept forward and peered over the railing. Stocks of goods filled the main floor: crates, bags, swords, furniture, even a few statues. Lit torches flickered from the stone walls, casting everything in a dim orange glow. A handful of guards in ratty leather armor sat around a wooden table near the front doors. They played a game of gammit with a stack of coins in the center of the table. Three dogs snoozed at their feet.

"This place is huge," Sephiri whispered after the other three arrived. "Any idea where this sorting room they mentioned is?"

Mirelle shook her head. "No idea."

"Maybe something like that." Kira pointed across the warehouse to a thick wooden door that stood half-open between the stacked crates.

"Nice," Mirelle said. "I'll bet you're right. How do we get in there without the guards noticing, though?"

"We need to make sure they're noticing something else," Peter whispered. He caught Sephiri's eye. "I felt the wind picking up outside. That might give us a distraction."

Sephiri nodded.

"That's it?" Mirelle glanced around at the four of them. "Just hope for wind?"

"I'll get the bags," Peter said. "But it's a long way back to the stairs to return up here. I'm not sure—"

"I'll open the front doors," Rylan said. "It'll be easier to lose them in the streets."

"Anything on the rooftops?" a voice called from outside.

Peter tensed.

"Nothing that I saw," someone called back.

"We need to get going," Mirelle whispered. "If they catch us, they won't put us in the pit. It'll be straight to the scorpions."

"I'll stick close to you, Rylan," Kira said, her determined face pale.

Sephiri nodded, her face pinched with concern as she watched Kira. "I'll stay here as a lookout."

"All right. Let's go, Mirelle." Peter creeped further down the narrow balcony, closer to the far end of the warehouse. Behind him, Rylan and Kira slipped out of the window the same way they'd come in. Sephiri waited on the balcony.

The warehouse was quiet, save for the low voices of the guards slurping ale and muttering over their game. Mirelle moved light-footed as a rabbit, and together they made their way to the far end of the warehouse, above the open door to the sorting room.

"What now?" Mirelle peeked over the railing, her shoulder pressed in a long, warm line against Peter's. "How do we get down without being noticed?"

"We wait for the right moment," Peter whispered.

Mirelle opened her mouth as if to ask a question, but nothing came out.

Peter grinned. *Sephiri has it under control.*

"Anything good in those packs you found?" a guard around the table asked.

Peter stiffened.

"Dunno," someone replied. "Haven't checked."

"You mean you brought in four new bags but hadn't gone through them yet?"

"It's Renaud's loot. I'm not gonna—"

"You have to go through it to let him know what we've found, idiot." A chair scraped. "I'll do it."

Peter tensed.

"Should we go?" Mirelle asked.

He shook his head. "Just wait." *Come on, Seph!*

A delicate breeze blew through the cracks in the boarded-up windows. The standing guard stopped and turned, and the others glanced up. One rubbed his upper arms, and another poured another drink.

Here it comes.

A gust of wind slammed into the warehouse. Air ripped the planks off the window, snapping them in two and scattering the pieces across the stone floor. Guards shouted. Wind caught the table and sent it flying. Ale and cards went everywhere, and the guards stumbled as they tried to stay standing under its force. Crates tumbled and clattered, and the dogs went wild, barking at the commotion.

Peter didn't have to say a word. He and Mirelle hopped over the railing, dropping to the ground amid the cacophony of shouts, cracking wood, and barking dogs. Mirelle grinned, then darted to the edge of the room to root through the Norivonne stash.

With Mirelle's back turned, Peter could finally use his power, too.

He took in a breath. Source power flowed from the center of his chest through his veins, all to the tips of his fingertips and the soles of his feet. The world slowed around him as he raced into the sorting room. He grinned at the sensation.

Just as Kira had guessed, it was a holding room for stuff. Bags and boxes scattered through the room, some of them still bloodstained from whatever ill fate had befallen the owners. A loud crash in the main area reminded him of their urgency. He glanced around, wild-eyed. *It has to be here.* He rushed to one side of the room and dug through the piles.

The noise escalated in the warehouse. "Who's that girl?" a guard shouted. "Grab her!"

They see Mirelle. The guards know we're here!

A burly, red-faced guard appeared in the doorway. "Hey! There's someone in here!" He rushed toward Peter and drew his sword. Peter gasped and dodged as the weapon swung down in an arc.

Something outside the room slammed. A loud crash reverberated through the building. Shouts filled the air along with the unmistakable sound of unsheathing swords.

Peter stumbled backward as the guard lunged at him again. He attempted to both look for their bags and avoid the man at the same time.

Mirelle screamed.

"I'm coming!" Peter called. Source power danced down his arms as he charged forward, low, and shoved his shoulder into the guard's gut. The man doubled over and dropped his sword. Peter scooped it up. He gripped the hilt and jabbed it into the man's leg. As the guard fell to the ground, howling and clutching his thigh, Peter saw his bag. All four of their bags, in fact, tossed in a corner and half hidden behind a wooden crate.

He raced to the bags, bouncing off the wall from the momentum. Grabbing the straps of all four, he slung them over his shoulder and ran with the sword tucked under his arm.

The warehouse outside the sorting room was in complete chaos. The front door rested wide open. Rylan stood amidst broken chain links, ducking punches from a guard. Peter darted through the warehouse.

"Peter!" Mirelle called.

She was on her back near the door. An immense guard dog

barked and snapped at her face. She writhed on the floor, barely keeping its jaws away from her face.

"Help her!" Rylan shouted as he socked the guard in the jaw.

Peter sped forward and dropped his gear. He grabbed the animal by its back haunches and spun, using his Source speed to fling the dog behind him. It slid across the smooth floor, only stopping when it bumped into the far wall. When it regained traction, the animal bared its teeth at Peter, growling as it pumped its feet to race back.

"Run!" Peter shouted. He hauled Mirelle to her feet, and they ran as fast as they could out the front doors, splitting the load of the bags.

"Go, go, go!" Rylan shouted, hot on their tails, carrying the last pack.

"Follow me!" Mirelle shouted.

Another gust of wind rushed past them. Peter snuck a glance back as the doors to the warehouse slammed shut. A dog yipped in surprise, and the guards shouted again, crashing into the closed doors.

Sephiri and Kira emerged from the shadows in the street. Rylan tucked an arm around Kira as the four friends hurried after Mirelle. The Marris local took a hard left, threw open a set of cellar doors, and dropped back down into the darkened tunnels.

Peter went last and shut the storm cellar doors behind him. The five of them stood still in the darkness as footsteps and barks thundered past in the alley above. He barely dared to breathe until the footsteps faded to silence.

Rylan chuckled first. His snicker soon broke into a genuine laugh, muffled behind his hand, which set Kira off, and then Peter and Mirelle. Finally, Sephiri ended up giggling as well.

"Come on," Mirelle said. She exhaled and wiped the sweat from her forehead. "My place isn't far."

Mirelle led them through the tunnels again, shuffling, stumbling, and following her voice. They exited at the town square, near the docks. She led them up a rickety staircase on the backside of a bait shop, and through a narrow door to the attic level of the building.

The attic room was less a home than it was a squatter's room. She seemed to have made it as welcoming as she could, but the sea breeze sneaking through the gaps in the wooden walls and thatched roof left the space cold and drafty. A straw-stuffed mattress sat in the corner with a thin blanket. Mirelle's belongings were stacked up in repurposed wooden crates from the docks, and a faint smell of fish permeated the room.

"It's not much." Mirelle shrugged. "But it works."

Space was tight with all five crammed inside, but Peter's relief at getting away from the Norivonne overcame any discomfort. The wooden floorboards creaked as he sat and leaned against the wall, setting the stolen sword beside him. He opened the clasp on his bag and rooted inside. His heart felt in his throat until his fingers found the rough edges of the map to Kytalia. Further rummaging located the hilt of the knife.

Mirelle sat on her thin mattress and worked on the laces of her boots. "Whatever's in that bag must be important."

Peter hummed in response. Sephiri's gaze flickered to his. He wouldn't say anything—she was right that they needed to be careful. "Thank you for helping us." He pulled out their canteen of water and handed it to Sephiri.

Despite the risks, he itched to tell Mirelle what they sought, to show her the map, and to see if she knew anything about the lost city. Even if she knew nothing about the dead merchant, Denton, maybe she'd heard of the city. Maybe she knew the landmarks. Even rumors might help. And she seemed like the type that kept an ear out for rumors.

But Peter didn't share, and Mirelle didn't press. Even though they hid in her drafty room, she seemed to respect their privacy.

"You said you liked to mess up the Norivonne's plans." Rylan sprawled across the floor, propped up on his elbows. He was as dirty as the others, with mud caked up the legs of his pants and his arms covered in dirt and sweat. "What's the story there?"

"Their gang runs Marris." She sighed. "They messed up my life, and I like to return the favor."

"What'd they do?"

Her hands stilled on the laces of her boots.

"Rylan." Kira turned to Mirelle. "Ignore him. He's nosy." She sat cross-legged next to Sephiri, who poured a small stream of water over the gash on her shoulder. Kira grimaced, sucking air through her teeth.

"Sorry," Sephiri whispered. The water ran pink with blood as it trickled over the gash and down Kira's arm.

"No, it's okay." Mirelle stared at the floor for a moment before speaking. "They, um . . . killed my parents when I was a kid."

Rylan paled. "Oh, wow. I'm sorry."

"It's all right." Mirelle laid back on her bed, leaving her bare feet hanging off the edge. "I was young. It was always us three, me and my folks. I've been on my own since then. I enjoy Marris, but it's hard to get a leg up in this city with the Norivonne running everything. So I have my fun getting back at them." She patted her pocket, the impact making a jangling sound. "I got a pretty good sack of coins from their warehouse. Might rent a proper room for a few weeks."

"Thanks for getting us out of there." Sephiri's words sounded like a struggle to speak. "I don't know what we would've done without you."

"Ended up in a coffin full of scorpions, probably." Rylan

made a circle with the thumb and fingers on both hands and held them over his eyes. "Black eyes. That's where we'd be."

Mirelle laughed. "I don't know. I think you four might've figured something out."

"We're lucky you showed up," Peter said. "Really."

She rolled onto her side and smiled at Peter, a softer, more open smile that made the butterflies in his stomach beat their wings again. "Worked out for me, too."

17

D espite the short length, it was far from the worst night of sleep Peter had had. Mirelle had extra blankets, which already made it better than the night they'd spent squashed in the cave. Peter woke to the sun slanting through the gaps in the wooden walls, falling in golden beams across his snoring friends. Outside, the docks were alive with activity. Shouting voices of fishermen carried on the breeze, overlapping with the breaking waves of a restless sea and vendors preparing for market.

Mirelle was gone.

Peter sat up. He peered around the room like she might pop out from behind a crate.

He stood, careful not to disturb the others. They might as well get a bit more sleep—they all needed it, especially Kira. *Maybe Mirelle went into the market? Maybe she had work to do at the docks? Or maybe the Norivonne found her.* He slipped out the door and onto the staircase.

"Oh!" Mirelle stood before him, frozen mid-step. "Sorry, I was just—"

"Oh! I just woke up—" Peter said at the same time.

"You first." Mirelle tucked a loose lock behind her ear. Her hair was down and damp at the ends. She wore a clean set of clothes, patched and threadbare like the ones from the day before.

"I just woke up and was curious about where you were," Peter said.

"Bathhouse. Having a few coins, I figured it was well past time for it. I was coming back to see if you were awake."

"I am." He flashed a small smile.

She returned it. "The others?"

"Not yet."

"Want to come with me to set up my stall?"

"What about the Norivonne? Won't they be looking for us?"

"Not this early," she said. "They're all drunks. They never come out before noon."

Peter followed down the rickety stairs and back into the marketplace. The excitement he had felt the day before had been replaced with a tense gnawing in his gut. The market still contained the bright umbrellas, the delicious-smelling treats, and the unique vendors. But now, he checked every dark corner and narrow alley for Norivonne goons lurking in the shadows.

"This way." Mirelle smiled over her shoulder. Her loose brown hair fell around her shoulders and gleamed in the early morning sun. The sunlight brought out hints of auburn. The teasing smile under her crooked nose made his heart skip a beat—not in the way it did when he looked at Sephiri, but in an exotic, forbidden way.

Mirelle led the way to a tiny stall tucked at the edge of the marketplace beneath a yellow awning. An old woman worked in front of dozens of tea tins: green, black, white, floral, fragrant, nutty, earthy, fermented. Mirelle bought two steaming cups of hot black tea with a heavy splash of fresh milk and handed one to Peter. He held the mug in both hands, and the warmth chased away the wiether chill.

He gazed across the docks, and his eyes widened. "Whoa!" An enormous three-masted ship with dozens of sails floated in the harbor, near to shore. Its veritable army of sailors lowered rowboats and hauled cargo. "Where's that ship from?"

"I dunno. Searis. Kandis. Lorranis. Even from across the Westfale. Probably here to trade goods, take shore leave, or pick up labor." She sipped her tea. "Wanna watch?"

"We can do that?"

She chuckled. "Of course!"

They strolled back to the docks and weaved between the sailors and the fishermen. The boardwalk narrowed to a pier that jutted into the undulating sea, quieter the farther they walked. Peter leaned over the rail. The white frothing caps of the waves threw small droplets of water onto his face. The ship looked massive up close: its gleaming wooden sides, the busy activity on the deck, the white sails tied tight against the masts. Sailors in uniform sang a distant shanty in unison as they scrubbed the deck.

"They're probably resupplying," Mirelle said. She sipped her tea and leaned against the rail next to him. "Fresh water. Citrus. All of that."

"Rynorian navy," Peter said.

"Yep. I wonder how long they've been out at sea."

"Wow." Peter couldn't take his eyes off the beautiful ship.

"Is that what you want to do? Be a sailor? See the world?" Mirelle quirked an eyebrow.

"No, no. Or I mean . . . I don't know. I've never thought about it."

"You haven't thought about what you want to do?"

He hesitated before responding. "At the moment, I'm just thinking about the next day. Maybe the next week, if things go well."

She hummed in understanding. The breeze tousled her hair as she faced the ship.

I want to tell her everything, he thought. Not just about the wild quest for a lost city, but all the events that led him there. His hopes of joining the army. Past troubles with the farm. How he fought and crawled his way out of poverty to a somewhat-comfortable life with his friends. He could envision Mirelle with them, in the Garrison, training together, sharing meals, laughing around the hearth.

Sephiri's warning lingered in his mind, as did the stench of the bodies the Dirteaters had cast aside.

First, we find Kytalia. Then . . . maybe I can come back to Marris. A twinge of guilt pulled at his gut. *What about Sephiri?* He imagined her laughing in the Garrison, tucking her hair behind her ear as she smiled at him. *I haven't promised anything to her. Plus . . . Mirelle and her spirit of adventure would fit with us well . . . as a friend. Yeah . . . just a friend.*

Two sailors rowed a small boat through the choppy waters. "Morning!" one called as they approached the pier. "How's the market today?"

"Just getting started, sir!" Mirelle called back. "Plenty of coffee. And Benton's Bakery has the finest bread you'll taste this side of the Straith Mountains."

"Wonderful!" The sailors rowed past to pull into the dock proper, and Mirelle threw them a jaunty wave. The sleeve of her shirt slid down to her elbow, and a bright red mark on her forearm caught Peter's eye.

"Are you okay?" He nodded to the mark. "Did you get burned?"

"What?" Mirelle asked. She grasped the hem of her sleeve and readjusted it. "No, it's—it's old."

An awkward, silent moment followed. "I'm sorry," Peter said. "I don't mean to pry."

"It's okay. It's just—It's not something I like to remember." She smiled again, but it was flat and unsure. "Before they passed away, my parents had a . . . particular method of punishing me."

"Oh." Peter's stomach turned. *They burned her? As punishment?* "I'm sorry."

"It's okay. It's in the past."

Silence hung between them, and Mirelle turned her attention back to the ship.

"Should we get breakfast?" Peter asked.

"I've got to get my stall ready," Mirelle said. "Gotta keep my relationship with the fishermen, you know."

"Sure." Peter sipped his tea but hardly tasted it. "Well . . . I guess I'll head back to the others."

"Hang out up there for as long as you need."

He smiled. "Thanks. I'll see you after a bit, I guess."

She tucked a strand of hair behind her ear. "Yeah. See you."

Peter left the dock with an unfamiliar, strange emotion heavy in his chest. He picked up a few things in the square: hard-boiled eggs, fresh bread, and a large container of hot tea from the kind old lady. He hauled everything back up the narrow staircase to Mirelle's room, where Rylan continued to doze, but Sephiri and Kira were awake and talking.

"Ooh, that smells good," Sephiri said.

"Where's Mirelle?" Kira asked.

Peter motioned over his shoulder. "Down at the docks."

She raised a curious eyebrow. "You were with her?"

"For a bit. She's setting up her stall. I got us breakfast."

"Breakfast?" Rylan groaned and sat up. "You're my hero."

Peter spread out the food and shared sips of tea.

Kira swallowed some bread, then sighed. "So, what now? Where do we go from here?"

"The Denton lead is gone," Rylan said. "Without him, what are we doing in Marris? We've got nothing."

"Let's not forget, Denton died the same way as the man who

sold us the knife," Sephiri said. "It sounds like that man with the scarred face was here before, and he's hunting this knife."

"So we need to keep moving," Peter said, remembering the Dirteater who recognized the knife. "We need to stay ahead of whoever else is trying to find the city."

"And we need to avoid having our eyes turned black from those scorpions." Rylan's body shook in an exaggerated shudder.

"Where do we go?" Kira asked.

Peter rifled through his bag and pulled out the map. He smoothed it out on the floor in between them. "There must be something here. Some kind of clue that will point us in the right direction."

Peter leaned over the map, like the ink might reveal new secrets instead of the same confusing labels he'd memorized. The mountains. The Cliff of Tears. The Pools of the Moon. The Mountain of the Bat with its two spires, waiting near the marking that had to be the city.

"It's still just a lousy map," Rylan opined. He reached into the bag, pulled out the small golden knife, and tossed it between each of his hands. "With labels for places no one has heard of."

"We know it's in the mountains," Kira said. "Probably the Straith Mountains."

"Don't say 'probably,'" Peter said. "If it's not in the Straiths, we're *really* screwed."

"If this water is the ocean, then the Cliffs of Tears must be on the coast, right?" Sephiri tapped the map.

"So if the city is in the Straith Mountains, and these cliffs are on the coast . . . should we start there?" Kira suggested.

Peter raised an eyebrow. "Where the Straiths meet the coast?"

"Yeah. It doesn't draw it that way on the map, but it doesn't mean it's *not* it."

"Go all the way to the Straith Mountains?" Rylan tapped his thumb against the hilt of the knife. "From here?"

"Careful with that." Sephiri's eyes flickered down to the knife.

Peter gulped. It'd be more hiking, days of it, across the hills and into the forests, trekking through the wilderness with just the sea on the horizon to guide them. "We don't have that kind of time," he said.

Kira pressed her lips into a thin line. A fresh bandage wrapped around the gash on her shoulder, but the swelling had worsened. The rest of her arm was pale, and her hand trembled.

"Let's get a boat," Rylan said. "There's plenty of them here. Surely, we can find someone willing to sail us to the mountains."

"That's actually . . . not a bad idea," Sephiri said.

Rylan huffed. "Don't sound so surprised. I can have good ideas." He spun the knife in his hand, then his thumb hit the bottom of the hilt hard.

The blade detached from the hilt and dropped to the floor, banging against the wood.

"What just happened?" Sephiri asked. Her hand darted forward, and she snatched the blade from the floor. "Did you break it?"

"I don't think so," Kira said.

Rylan raised the hilt. The blade had slid off, revealing a long, narrow metal piece with delicately carved teeth. The dull gray object contained engravings of stacked rectangles along the side.

"It's a key," Sephiri whispered.

Peter's eyes grew, and his heart beat faster.

"So the legend was literal. It's an *actual* key." Kira leaned closer. "How'd you do that, Rylan?"

"This bottom piece is like a switch, I think," Rylan said.

"Can I see?" Peter accepted it from Rylan. He turned the hilt over in his hand. At the bottom, a plain metal ring capped the end. Peter ran his thumb over it. It didn't move. He pushed at it from the side, and it shifted. With the right pressure, he turned it and then pressed down with a click.

Sephiri handed him the blade. He slid it back down onto the hilt. It clicked into place around the key. Then, when he turned the ring and then pressed down, it clicked again, and the blade slid off.

"Whoa," Rylan said.

"Nice find," Peter said. Excitement raced through him. "I'm guessing we'll need that key for something. We need to keep this close. I mean, if there was ever proof that the city is real, this is it!"

"We better get that boat," Sephiri said, her eyes glimmering.

The four friends finished their food in a hurry, packed their things, and headed down the narrow stairs into the Marris marketplace. With the sword from the warehouse tucked into his belt, Peter led through the square, straight to the docks where Mirelle lingered by her stall. She smiled and motioned them over to her grill, where fish already sizzled.

"You look all packed up," she said. "Heading out?"

"Onward." Rylan grinned. "Adventures await. Gotta get a boat."

"Where to?" Mirelle asked.

"West," Kira said in a non-specific manner before anyone else could answer.

Mirelle's gaze flicked to Peter.

"But we'll come back to Marris," he said, his heart fluttering.

"You will?" she asked.

"Maybe." Sephiri pulled at Peter's arm. "Come on, we should find a boat to charter."

"Be careful," Mirelle said as she turned the fish on the grill. "Make sure you don't get on a Norivonne boat."

Peter paused. "What?"

She glanced up. "Yeah, they own a lot. Smuggling runs. Transporting passengers. Stuff like that. As long as you don't get on one of theirs, you'll be fine."

"How will we know?" Kira blinked at Mirelle. "Are they marked?"

Mirelle chuckled and shook her head. "Use common sense, you know? If the captain looks seedy, maybe try another."

The four friends glanced at each other, and Peter hiked his bag higher on his shoulder. "Do you know captains? Anyone who's not involved with them?"

"Umm . . ." Mirelle raked her hand through her hair. "I'm not sure who's at the docks today."

"It'll just take a minute," Peter said. "Could you help us? Just once more?"

Mirelle pulled the fish off the grill, skewered it, and took a bite. Then she shut the grill and grinned. "All right. Once more."

The four friends walked down the dock with their hoods up. Mirelle led the way, ambling down the docks with a skip in her step. She passed fishermen working on their boats, sailors, cargo boats, and small local operations, too. She led them to the far end of the dock, where a small white, single-masted boat bobbed in the waves. A white-haired old man with a creased face and a gold tooth looked up as they approached.

"Mirelle," the old man said. "Fancy seeing you here."

"Hi, Cap. I've got a few friends here looking for a ride."

"Friends, huh?" the old man said. "I'm Captain Hughes. I was about to cast off. Where are you kids looking to go?"

Peter glanced around, hesitating a moment. "The, uh, southern end of the Straith Mountains."

"What are you looking for in Barrentis?" the captain

grunted as he hauled a crate from the dock onto the rickety boat and tied it down to the deck.

"Barrentis?" Kira asked.

"That's the village at the southern end," the captain said. "You're, what . . . trekking into the mountains?"

"Something like that," Peter muttered.

"Mm." Captain Hughes straightened and crossed his sun-weathered arms across his chest. "Well, you're in luck. I'm heading to Portris, in Tarphan—just past Barrentis. I can drop you off there if that's where you're looking to go."

"How long would it take?" Sephiri leaned forward. "We're kind of in a hurry."

"Well, the sea doesn't care about your schedule," Captain Hughes said with a toothy grin. "Usually takes about a day, day and a half, but I can't make any promises."

"Better than going on foot," Rylan said.

Peter snuck a glance at Kira, who steadied herself with a hand on the side of the boat.

"Can't do it for free, though," the Captain said. "You kids would take up cargo space, you know."

"How much?" Peter reached into his bag.

"Typically I'd charge two argen, but for friends of Mirelle, I'll take one." He winked at Mirelle, and she responded with a curtsy. "But I don't provide any food or water. You're on your own for provisions."

Beyond the boat, the ocean waves rolled in, white-capped and glittering in the morning sun. *Barrentis. There has to be something there*, Peter thought. *Something that will lead us to the Cliff of Tears, and then to Kytalia.*

But if we're wrong . . .

It'd been three nights since Kira'd been poisoned. That meant they had three more to go. If they were wrong, she was doomed.

This is the only lead we have.

"You've got a deal." Peter handed the argen to Captain Hughes. "We'll gather our supplies."

"Don't take long. I cast off in half an hour, and I won't wait for you. I'm on a schedule, too. And you're not gonna find another boat heading that way this late in the morning."

"Ahoy!" someone shouted from down the dock. "Excuse me! Oops—sorry!" A man in a plain, dark suit knocked into a few sailors as he rushed toward the boat. A canvas bag slung over his shoulder, and a floppy hat shaded his eyes from the sun. He looked like he'd come from the library of Palenting, not the colorful Marris marketplace.

Peter stepped backward to avoid the man. The stranger came to a stop, red-faced and breathing heavily. "Sorry," he said, "Whew! Woke up late. Had too much to drink at the tavern last night. Sorry." He wiped his forehead. "Someone at the bar said to look for the Seacutter. That you were headed to —" His eyes turned up, and he snapped his fingers. "What was the name of that city?"

The captain leaned forward with his eyebrows raised. "Portris?"

The man pointed. "That was it!"

"With a stop in Barrentis?"

"Exactly! I'm looking for a ride to . . ." The man's eyes shifted to the others. "Barrentis." A pause followed. "Are you taking on passengers?"

"Crazy," Rylan said with a grin. "That's where we're going."

Peter covertly nudged Rylan in the side.

The new arrival smiled.

"More passengers? Well, that depends," Captain Hughes said. "The boat's a little crowded now, but if you have the funds . . ."

The stranger and the captain stepped aside and continued the conversation in lowered voices.

Peter leaned close to Mirelle's ear. "Do you know him?" he whispered.

She shook her head. "Never seen him."

Peter bit his lip, his body awash with nervous energy. Is this man trouble? What waited for them in Barrentis and in the mountains? What if the Norivonne were still chasing them?

Rylan glanced between Mirelle and Peter, then up to the boat. "Hey Mirelle, you want to come with us? Or are you busy with your work?"

Mirelle started. "What?"

Rylan shrugged, then offered a smile. "You've been a great help. I'm sure we could use the extra hands as we travel, huh, Peter?"

Peter hoped his face wasn't flushed. *Have I been that obvious?* He felt drawn to her, but this search was for him and his friends. Still . . . he didn't want to leave her behind, and Rylan noticed. "He's right. You have helped a lot."

Mirelle rubbed the back of her neck. "I don't know if that's a great idea."

Sephiri balked. "It's really not necessary, Mirelle, you've done enough for us."

"But . . . if you wanted to come—" Peter began.

"She's got stuff to do here in Marris," Kira said. "You have a life, Mirelle."

"Not much of one," Mirelle said. "I mean, this is the most excitement I've had in a while. I don't really get along much with people in Marris."

Kira's expression softened.

"The Norivonne aren't fond of me either," Mirelle continued, then laughed. "As I'm sure you can imagine."

"Let's let things cool off with them," Peter said. "Come with us. Captain Hughes seems to like you, right?"

She nodded.

Peter glanced at his friends. Sephiri looked unconvinced.

Kira's expression was still soft, and Rylan watched the vendors at the dock laying out fresh pastries and savory hand pies.

"We'll need your eyes in case there're any Norivonne in Barrentis," Peter said. "It makes sense. And it'll only be a day."

"Day and a half." Sephiri crossed her arms. "And then the return trip."

Mirelle gave a little one-armed shrug. "I don't want to overstep."

Peter glanced at Sephiri, his eyebrows raised in a hopeful plea.

She pressed her lips together. After a tense pause, she finally sighed. "It's not overstepping." Her voice was strained. "You're welcome to join us."

That charming catlike smile reappeared on Mirelle's face. "All right. I'm in." She glanced back at the boat, where the stranger in the suit clambered awkwardly onto the deck. Captain Hughes ushered the man into a corner, looking fed up already.

"I'll stay here," Rylan thumbed over his shoulder. "Help the captain situate the cargo—get him on our good side."

"I'll stay, too," Kira said.

Peter placed a hand on her forearm. "You okay?"

"Just tired." She managed a weak smile. "I'm all right. Really. Make sure you get enough drinking water. And some more medical supplies, if you can."

He nodded.

"I'll get us the best provisions Marris has to offer," Mirelle said. "Follow me."

18

C aptain Hughes had said thirty minutes, which meant they had to hurry. Peter and Sephiri raised their hoods as they followed Mirelle back to the marketplace to restock their provisions and get water.

"So, what are we thinking?" Mirelle chirped. "Pies? Pastries? Cured meats? Fish?"

Peter wove through the busy square. They filled up their canteens with fresh water at the cistern. The next stop was at a booth selling cured meats. Unsure of how long they'd be out in the wilderness, Peter bought several days' worth.

While keeping a wary eye on the clock mounted in the square, they made their way to a vendor selling small, savory hand pies. Peter bought some for the journey and one for them to split.

"What are these?" Peter asked the elderly woman manning the vendor stand. He leaned closer to the stall, peering at a glass jar full of small golden candies.

"Candied ginger," the woman said with a smile. "Good for seasickness."

He nodded. "I'll take some."

She spooned a handful of candies into a scrap of canvas, tied it off, then handed it to Peter alongside their hand pies.

Mirelle tried to pay with some money she'd taken from the warehouse, but he waved her off. When he pulled out his coin purse, a knot formed in his stomach at its lightness. It was enough, but not by much. *We'll have a lot more once we find Kytalia,* he told himself.

"We should move." Peter checked the clock again. "Only a few minutes left, and we still need to find some bandages for Kira."

Sephiri took a bite of her share of the hand pie.

"How is it?" Peter asked.

Her eyes widened, and she fell still.

"What?" Peter asked.

She grabbed him by the shoulder, then tugged him against the wall, in the shadow of the awning. "Do you see them? By the tavern?"

"What?" Peter craned his neck toward the tavern. "Who?"

His breath caught as he saw them. Two redheads, dressed in well-worn, dark clothes and scouring the market.

"It's Naldoc and Nalva," she whispered.

"You think they're looking for us?"

"Who?" Mirelle asked. "More people are looking for you?"

"I don't know," Peter whispered. "Maybe they're just here for supplies."

"I doubt that," Sephiri whispered. "You remember what they said in the woods?"

"What?" Mirelle asked. "What did they say? Who are these people?"

Peter's heart pounded. If the Dirteaters saw them, it wouldn't go well. "Let's get back to the boat."

"Act casual." Sephiri pulled her hood lower over her face.

They made their way through the market, sticking to the crowds. Peter hunched his shoulders, making himself smaller, while Mirelle craned her neck around.

"Stop that." Sephiri swatted at her shoulder. "I said to act casual."

"I would, if someone would tell me what's going on."

"First, let's get back to the boat," Peter said.

He stopped before they reached the docks. Esmee lingered by Mirelle's fish grill, panning the crowd with her eyes. The friendly expression she'd worn by the campfire was gone. With her braids tied back, she looked furious. Her brow furrowed, and a nasty scowl had replaced her smile. She wore the same plain clothes as the young man next to her—someone Peter remembered from the Dirteaters' campsite.

"We have to hide," Sephiri whispered.

"What if they find the boat?" Peter whispered. "We can't let them see Kira and Rylan."

Sephiri paused. "That's our way out of here."

And they might kill them, Peter thought.

Esmee muttered something to her companion. They both spun to face the docks and stepped toward the boats.

"They're gonna find them," Peter breathed. His pulse thudded as the Dirteaters drew nearer to the boats.

"We've gotta do something," Sephiri said.

Peter turned to Mirelle. "Sorry about this." He shoved her to the side. She swore and stumbled into the crowd, knocking a passing fisherman off his feet and sending his basket of bait across the ground. She whirled toward Peter, eyes wide.

Peter dropped his hood. "Hey! Esmee!" He stepped farther from Mirelle.

The braided Dirteater turned. She found him, and a wicked smile spread across her face.

"Solve one problem and create another," Sephiri muttered. "Run!"

Peter grabbed Sephiri's wrist, and they took off running.

They shouldered past vendors, knocking baskets and sending a shopper tumbling to the ground. "Sorry!" he called.

"Hey!" a vendor shouted at him. "Watch it—whoa!"

Peter checked over his shoulder as Esmee knocked the yelling vendor to the ground. "Get back here!" Esmee shrieked in hot pursuit.

They ran toward the closest alley, but as they approached, a man crossed the entrance, hauling a wooden cart full of chickens. Peter jumped onto the edge of the cart, and it rocked on its wheels. The chickens clucked and flapped their wings, sending white feathers flying. Peter hauled Sephiri onto the cart.

"Get down!" the chicken vendor shouted. "What do you think you're doing?"

"Come on!" Peter pulled Sephiri and scrambled atop the chicken cages. Esmee and the other man struggled to make their way through the crowd as people stopped to peer at Peter and Sephiri towering over the square. From the cages, Peter reached for the wall of the alley. He grasped the edge and hauled himself up onto the roof, then reached down to help Sephiri. Wind blew her hair upward as she rolled onto the roof next to him. "Run!"

They raced across the flat roof of the building by the square. Peter checked behind them and blanched to see Esmee and the young man reaching from the chicken cart to the roof. They huffed and puffed but continued pursuit.

At the edge of the roof, Peter leaped across the narrow alley and clung to the angled thatched roof on the other side. Sephiri landed a second later. Peter grasped the roof, heart in his throat as his feet scrabbled on the slick thatching. Through much effort, he hauled himself up to the narrow top of the roof then slid down the other side. His feet caught on the gutter at the edge, and he launched himself forward, over the alley to the next flat roof. Sephiri landed a moment later. Peter checked behind while they continued running.

Esmee and her companion slid down the roof behind them. The young man shouted as he careened over the edge and crashed into the alley below. Esmee kept her feet and then leaped across the gap. She cursed at the fallen man but continued running toward Peter without pause.

"We've got to lose her," Sephiri said through her heavy breaths.

"How?" They approached the edge of the roof.

"Follow my lead!"

Sephiri's eyes blazed white as she swept a hand forward. Wind followed the motion, blowing off the roof and clattering open a window across the wide alley. Behind them, Esmee closed fast, her eyes blazing, and sweat running in rivulets down her face.

"Go first!" Sephiri shouted.

Blood drained from his face. "I can't make that!"

"I got you!" Sephiri said. She reached out.

It was like climbing. He had to trust her. With the wind at their back, he took her hand and jumped.

They hurtled toward the stone wall of the building. Peter was about to smash into it when a gust of wind rushed beneath them, giving him just enough of a boost.

"Reach!" Sephiri cried.

Peter stretched as high as he could, just enough to get his hand on the windowsill as their bodies hit the building. He pressed his toes against the stone hard, like he did when climbing. Sephiri dangled beneath him, gripped tight with his opposite hand.

He groaned. His shoulder burned. His muscles screamed in protest. Wind buffeted them from below. They scrabbled their feet against the wall until he lifted her high enough to grab the windowsill. One hand, then the other. Finally, the two of them clawed through the window.

He grunted as he landed on the wooden floor and rolled onto his back.

"Scoot over," Sephiri said.

Peter shifted to the side. The wind blew again, and a large shelf against the wall teetered and then crashed to the ground. Its bulk blocked the window.

"You can't hide from us!" Esmee shrieked.

Peter struggled to his feet, limbs aching and lungs pumping. They were in the attic of an old building. Rotting furniture covered in dust filled the space. Peter sneezed. "The tunnels," he said. He wiped the dust from his eyes and shook it from his hair. "We need to get to the tunnels, then back to the docks."

Sephiri nodded. They crossed the attic and shouldered open the opposite window. The alley was empty below. They were close to the warehouse district—where Peter knew there would be an entrance to the tunnels. He scrambled out of the window and dropped to the alley below, using the Source to roll as he hit. Sephiri dropped next to him, quieter, lighter on her feet. Peter never knew if she was using the Source, or if it was just a part of her now, making her move as delicate as a bird.

They took off again, running further from the marketplace, looking for the familiar cellar doors that led to the tunnels. "This way! I remember!" Sephiri called.

He followed her through the narrow alleys. They squeezed around dumpsters and crates, scrambled around the abandoned buildings, and . . .

Skidded to a stop. Peter's lungs burned, even with the Source flowing through him.

They found the cellar doors to the tunnels by the warehouse. They were just as Peter remembered, except that Naldoc and Nalva now stood in front of them, grinning. The demeanors that had convinced the friends to join them at the campsite were long gone. The siblings looked murderous —hungry.

Naldoc raised a crossbow. "Fancy seeing you here. What a treat."

He launched a bolt from the weapon. Peter ducked fast enough to feel the bolt whoosh over his shoulder and hear the *thunk* of the tip embedding into something.

Sephiri cried out.

Peter whirled toward her—*was she hit?* Sephiri cowered, the bolt embedded in the stone wall just past her. A hand wrapped around Peter's forearm and yanked him forward. Nalva's rancid breath rushed over his face as she pinned him to her body. She pressed the tip of another crossbow to the underside of his jaw. The sharp tip of the bolt stung his flesh. Nalva's hold tightened on his forearm.

"Where's the knife?" Naldoc demanded. He pointed his reloaded crossbow at Sephiri. "Tell us, or you both die."

"What are you talking about?" Peter snarled. "Let us go!"

"We saw it in the woods," Nalva hissed. "The Key of Kytalia. Do you think we're stupid? Give us the knife, and that map we heard you talking about."

"I don't know—agh!" The tip of the bolt dug into his flesh, and a hot bead of blood rolled down his throat.

"Stop!" Sephiri cried. "Don't hurt him!"

"Seph, don't!"

Sephiri held her hands out to the Dirteaters in acquiescence. "We have it! We have both!"

"Don't tell them, Seph!" Peter struggled in Nalva's hold, even as the trickle of blood rolled down his neck. "What about Kira? We can't let them have it! Just run, go, now!"

Sephiri shook her head. "I'm not leaving you."

Peter thought of the sword in his belt and his incredible speed. *I could pull it and strike these two down.* His stomach turned. *But could I do it before their trigger fingers loosed one of their bolts?*

"Tell us, now," Naldoc growled.

"Both are in his bag," Sephiri said. "Just please, don't hurt us."

The bag pressed between Peter and Nalva. Naldoc grinned as Nalva dropped her hold on Peter's forearm and shoved him forward. "Get it out," she demanded. "Now."

Both Nalva and Naldoc trained their weapons on Peter. "You're lucky we didn't gut you first," he sneered. "For what you did to our camp, after all the hospitality we showed you."

Peter opened his bag and looked at Sephiri. *We can't let them do this,* he thought.

Sephiri met his eyes. With Naldoc's and Nalva's attention on Peter, she pointed a finger toward the ground and mouthed the word '*cover.*'

Peter's eyes widened.

He dropped and covered the bag, then looked up as Sephiri's eyes turned white.

Sephiri swept her hand forward, and a blast of wind ripped up the alley. It split in two around Peter, like a river breaking on a rock, and rushed past him in both directions. The air slammed into Naldoc and Nalva and sent them both flying like a tornado caught them. They shouted and flailed their arms, tossed like pebbles.

"Let's go!" Peter said. He jumped back to standing. "Get on my back and hold on!"

"Can you run with us both?" Sephiri asked.

"We don't have a choice."

She hopped on his back and wrapped her arms around his neck. Peter exhaled, ignoring the rush of warmth rushing through his body at her touch. *Can't think about that, now.* He let the Source travel through him then exploded off the balls of his feet.

Weaving through the narrow alleys, they left the redheaded Dirteaters mired in the gale-force winds. Peter raced toward the marketplace.

"Hurry!" Sephiri shouted into his ear. "Let's get to the boat!"

At the edge of the square, Peter skidded to a stop and dropped Sephiri off his back. "Keep an eye out for the others." He took her wrist and led her through the bustling crowd. They moved with their heads low and shoulders curled inward. His stomach turned when he glanced at the clock. *Ten minutes late. Let's hope the boat's still here.*

"There they are!" Esmee's voice rang out through the square. "By the cistern!"

Peter spun. Esmee stood atop the flat roof of the nearest building, her dark eyes boring into his. The sound of her voice drew the attention of the vendors and shoppers in the square.

The other young man stepped out from a shadowed space under the tea vendor's awning. He snarled, then rushed forward with a drawn sword. The people near him gasped and hurried out of his way.

"Ugh." Sephiri groaned. "We can't catch a break, huh?"

"Keeps things interesting," Peter said. "Go!"

They shoved through the crowd again, running as fast as they could.

"Grab them!" Esmee crowed. "They're headed to the docks!"

The young man cut them off and lunged at Sephiri, grasping at her cloak. She cried out and stumbled. Source power surged through Peter, and he charged, landing a punch in the man's side. The Dirteater grunted and released his hold on the cloak. Sephiri gasped and ran forward again, leaving the man doubled over behind them.

The wood of the dock thundered under their pounding feet. Peter's breath burned in his lungs. His shoulder ached, and blood rushed in his ears.

"There they are," Sephiri panted, pointing ahead. At the

end of the dock, the untied Seacutter was pushing off into the sea.

"Wait!" Peter cried out. "Wait for us!"

"Come on!" Rylan shouted from the deck. "Run!"

Captain Hughes adjusted the sails, seemingly uncaring of Peter and Sephiri racing toward the boat. On the deck, Mirelle, Kira, Rylan, and the stranger watched—Mirelle and Rylan jumping up and down and waving their hands like it could make them run faster. The gap of water between the dock and the boat grew wider by the second.

"Go, Seph!" Peter shouted. "Jump for it!"

They reached the end of the dock at the same time and jumped.

The wind picked up behind them. It shoved at Peter like a hand pushing him. His arms windmilled as the air hurled him forward, and he landed with his torso on the deck and his legs flailing behind him. Mirelle grasped his wrist and hauled him up. Rylan did the same with Sephiri.

At the end of the dock, Esmee and the other Dirteater skidded to a halt and glowered at them. Esmee's eyes burned with rage, and the young man leaned over with his hands on his knees, his chest heaving.

"That was close," Rylan said. "Nice jump."

Kira angled her thumb toward the captain on the far side of the deck. "We tried to get him to wait, but . . ."

"It's all right," Peter said between breaths. "It . . . worked out . . . this way." He rolled onto his back, sucking in a lungful of air. Around him, everyone kept speaking, but he couldn't make out the words over the rapid beating of his heart. Sephiri's fingers wrapped around his forearm and squeezed. The touch grounded him. He caught his breath and his heart rate evened out as he looked up at the cloud-less morning sky.

"Are you okay?" Mirelle asked. "Who were those people?"

"Some thieves we ran into on the way to Marris," Peter said. "I don't think they like that we got away."

"That much is obvious," Mirelle muttered.

"Sorry, I pushed you."

She waved the apology away.

"Did you get any medical supplies?" Rylan asked.

Peter shook his head and pushed his bag toward Rylan. "Got some food and water, but that's it. I'm sorry, Kira."

Kira shrugged but didn't meet his eyes. Her skin had grown paler, and she looked exhausted, like she hadn't slept in days. "Not like it would do anything."

"Is it infected?" Mirelle's gaze zeroed in on the bandage on Kira's shoulder.

"Something like that."

On the other side of the deck, the stranger in the suit talked to Captain Hughes, who appeared to be moments from shoving the guy off the boat himself.

Peter sat up. "The captain doesn't seem concerned about our, um, arrival."

"Just a normal day in town." Mirelle chuckled. Brawls in the square are common. "You can see why I'm not too keen on sticking around."

Kira gasped. Her body turned rigid.

Frowning, Peter pressed himself up onto his elbows. "What is it, Kira?"

Her arm trembled as she held it out. Her weak voice was barely audible. "Look."

The Seacutter traveled west, passing the rest of the boats and the people from the square. On the last dock, standing stock-still among the bustling fisherman, stood the tall, grizzled man with the vertical scar on his eye. The man from the Palenting market—the one who poisoned Kira.

A shiver ran down Peter's spine, but he held the man's stare. The gulls cried overhead as their boat sluiced through the quiet waves. Posts of the pier drifted by. He didn't know who the man was or how he had found them, but he wouldn't cow to his piercing gaze.

We make it to Barrentis. We head into the mountains. And then we'll find the city.

19

The day progressed with the boat cutting its way through the deep blue waters along the southern coast of Rynor. The port city of Marris faded in the distance behind them. Its pale buildings and bright awnings disappeared into the rocky coast. Ahead, the Straith Mountains rose like sharp teeth reaching for the sky. Peter's heart swelled at the sight of the great rocky barrier between Rynor and Tarphan. The Dorthar Mountains around Palenting paled in comparison to the jagged peaks.

Kytalia waited somewhere out there.

Time passed leisurely on the boat. With nothing to do but wait, they lounged on the deck and stayed out of the captain's way. Rylan helped a bit, hauling ropes and shifting crates when necessary, more out of his inability to sit still than any desire to assist.

Peter stood and stretched his arms over his head. He'd dozed for the past few hours, recovering from his escape through the alleyways of Marris. Kira remained asleep, her chest rising and falling in a reassuring fashion. She and Sephiri lay beneath a makeshift shade where a cloak strung like an awning between two of the crates. Peter leaned on the railing of the ship, gazing toward the mountains.

"So, son!" the stranger ambled next to Peter. The man looked out of place in his city slacks and fine white shirt with the sleeves rolled up to his elbows. The floppy hat remained, but he'd lost the suit jacket. The man had dark eyes and high cheekbones, and his narrow nose already turned pink in the sun. "That was quite an entrance on the boat earlier."

Peter huffed a laugh. "Not the way I like to start a trip."

"I'd hope not," the man said with a laugh. "I've had some interesting experiences myself, but nothing like that! What happened?"

"I'm sorry . . ." Peter said. "Who are you?"

The man hit himself on the forehead. "How rude of me. I'm Adrian." He offered a sweaty and limp hand to shake.

Peter cringed as he took it. "Peter."

Adrian raised his eyebrow as if waiting for an answer.

Peter cleared his throat. "Those folks? Um . . ." His eyes shifted around the boat. "We had a disagreement in town. It was nothing."

"What's taking you to Barrentis, Peter?"

"Had to leave Marris."

"Well, that much was obvious." Adrian barked a laugh, loud enough to send a seagull flapping off the top of the mast. "So just going to Barrentis to see the sights?"

"There's always something to be found at the ports," Peter said. Adrian's sharp gaze and tense posture kept him tight-lipped. "What about you? What takes you there?"

"I'm, um . . . meeting with a business contact." Adrian gazed toward the horizon. "A, uh, colleague."

It was Peter's turn to raise his eyebrows.

The Seacutter crested a big swell, swayed, and then rocked

down to the other side. Adrian gripped the railing and grimaced. His face went pallid.

"You all right?" Peter asked.

"I'm fine. Not the best at sea travel, though. It makes me nauseous."

"Oh, here." Peter reached into his pocket and pulled out the canvas bag he'd purchased in town before the chaos began. He opened it and held it out to Adrian. "Ginger candies. It should help with the nausea."

Adrian blinked, surprised, then took one. "Thank you."

"Take another," Peter said. "There are plenty."

Adrian chuckled, then took another. "Thank you. That's . . . quite kind of you."

"Hey, Peter!" Mirelle perched on the boom, straddling it, and kicking her legs in the breeze. "Look at this!"

Peter nodded at Adrian, grateful for the excuse to step away from the conversation. He clambered up the mast, then crawled onto the boom, careful not to disturb the ropes around the sail. He scooted up behind her. "What is it?"

She looked over her shoulder and smiled at him. Her skin glowed in the midday sun. "Dolphins!"

Peter tore his gaze away from the curve of her lips and looked to where she pointed at the sea. Close to the boat, a pod of dolphins leaped out of the waves, sending sprays of white sea foam into the sky with each jump.

"Wow," Peter said. "I've only ever heard about them."

"Aren't they beautiful? It's like they're escorting us."

He gripped a dangling rope as the boom wavered in the wind. The motion of the sea made his legs shake and his knuckles turn white. "You seem pretty comfortable up here. You travel around by boat a lot?"

"Here and there." Mirelle swung her legs back and forth, like she sat on a bench in the town square, instead of on a boom above the swaying deck. "Thanks for letting me come with you."

"Hey, it was only fair. Your connection got us the discount."

"Comes from spending too much time on the streets of Marris," she muttered.

Peter smiled. "I think it comes from being friendly."

She turned away, a faint blush coming to her cheeks. "You know . . . for all the time I've spent in the city, I've never seen those folks who chased you. Who were they?"

"No one important," Peter said. "They call themselves the Dirteaters. They're not from Marris."

Once I get back to Palenting and get in with the commander, we'll take care of them.

"Is that why you kept that sword?"

"One of many reasons." He tapped the hilt of the sword hanging from his belt. "You ever use one?"

"Ha! No way. My favorite weapon is called *not getting involved.*"

"Want to learn a few moves?" Peter ignored the unexpected coil of nerves building in his chest. "Give the dolphins a show?"

"You'd show me?"

"Sure!" Peter hopped off the boom and landed with a thunk on the deck. Mirelle laughed and dropped next to him, landing gracefully on the wood. Adrian glanced over from where he chattered away to the captain.

Peter pulled his sword out of its sheath and handed it to Mirelle, hilt-first.

Her eyes widened as he took it in hand. "It's lighter than I expected."

"Yep, smithed that way—to strike faster rather than swing harder."

"Makes sense," Mirelle said. "Easier for you to move around."

"Exactly."

She lifted the sword, and Peter took a step back, laughing. "Whoa!" He raised both hands in surrender. "I give up!"

She laughed, flushing.

"Here, I'll show you some basics." He moved to her side. "First, it's all about balance, so make sure your feet are beneath you."

Kira caught his eye, watching as she sat under her makeshift shade.

Walking in the opposite direction, Sephiri headed toward the far rail, looking out to the sea. Peter's stomach sank at the sight of her tense shoulders.

Blinking, he turned his attention back to Mirelle. "So . . . front foot forward, rear foot back. Knees loose." From her side, he tapped against the back of her knee, his heart swooping. "A bit, um . . . farther."

"Like this?" Her leg slid forward, and she flashed an enthusiastic smile. She held the weapon with both hands.

"That's it. You want to be light on your feet. And with a sword this weight, you'll want to wield it one-handed."

"That seems a little advanced," Mirelle said. She kept both hands tight around the hilt.

"Trust me, it's better. Try it!" Peter reached over and grasped her wrist, then peeled her other hand away from the hilt.

"Like this?" Her pulse thrummed under his fingertips.

"Now bring it up, then down at an angle, like you're slashing someone in front of you. An angle is better than straight up or down, or even a stab, because you cover more distance and can step out of the way of a counterattack. So . . ." He set his hand at her elbow, guiding her to raise the sword. "Up here, then down."

"Ha!" Mirelle squawked, then brought the sword down on a hard diagonal, a little too hard. The sword slipped out of her fingers and clattered across the deck. It bounced against a crate and came to a skittering stop near the mast.

"Um." She drew her hands together under her chin. "Oops."

Peter snorted. "Well, at least you didn't fling it into the ocean."

"Sorry! I got a little excited."

"Throwing knives is a thing, too." Peter chuckled. "Maybe that'd suit you better."

"I'm not throwing any knives! I'll probably hit one of you, knowing my luck."

"I'm no good at them either," Peter said. "Kira's the one with the good aim. Knives or arrows."

"The bow is more my style," Mirelle said. "My brother was an excellent shot, too. I used to shoot with him."

Kira looked their way, head cocked, "We'll have to try some throwing. If you can shoot a bow, you can throw knives."

"Hopefully better than I threw this one." She grabbed the sword from where it rested beside the mast and returned it to Peter with a sheepish smile.

Peter tucked it into his belt with a grin. "Maybe we'll try again on solid land."

"Yeah, I'll blame the boat," Mirelle said. "That'll make me feel better."

"I'm starving!" Rylan ambled over and dropped onto the deck next to them.

Sephiri snorted. "What else is new?"

"Hey!" Rylan put his hands on his hips. "I'm the only one doing any work around here."

"That was your choice."

"Yeah, but it still made me hungry. Let's eat!"

With the sun drifting toward the horizon, the five of them unpacked the hand pies Peter snagged in the marketplace before the morning devolved into chaos. While some pies had received a few crushed edges during the action, they remained mostly intact. The group shared the different flavors, so Peter got a mouthful of roasted garront, another with verquash, and his favorite contained a rich, soft cheese. It was almost luxurious to relax on the deck, eating as the waves lapped against the sides of the boat. Peter stood and leaned against the rail, gazing out at the mountains in the distance, marvelling at how their silhouettes jutted from the earth. A moment later, Sephiri joined him.

"I knew the Straith Mountains were big," she said, "but I didn't think they'd be *that* big."

Her hair blew in the salty sea breeze, brushing across her face that glowed in the warm sun. She tucked a loose strand behind her ear. A soft crease marked the edge of a smile. Despite her insistence on staying around Palenting, she seemed to enjoy the chance to see the world. Comfortable warmth built in Peter's gut as he took in the sight of her face.

"It's intimidating," he said. "How are we going to find anything through all of that?"

"Simple!" Rylan said around a mouthful of pie. "We look for the Cliff of Tears!"

"Cliff of Tears?" Mirelle asked. "What's that?"

Peter glanced at Sephiri, who kept her gaze fixed on the swells of the ocean. They intended to keep their plans secret, but Peter was a little relieved Rylan had let a bit slip. There was always a chance Mirelle might know something. "We're not sure," he said. "Just that we have to find it."

"That's not a great lead," Mirelle said. "The Straith range is huge. You're going to hike in there and look for a single cliff?"

"Maybe." Kira stood and moved toward the railing. "Peter, you have a second?" After a couple of steps, a pain-filled grimace covered her face. Her hand jerked up, like she wanted to grab the bandage on her arm. Her palm hovered over it, and a tremble wracked her body. With an exhale, she lowered her hand and straightened up. Dark blood stained the bandage.

"We should change that," Peter said.

"With what bandages?" she muttered. "It doesn't matter. It won't do any good."

"Bandages?" Adrian looked up from where he leaned against a crate with a book open on his lap. "Someone hurt?"

"It's nothing. I'm fine."

"I've got some in my pack." He stood and grabbed his bag. "Can I look?"

Kira balked and took a step back like a spooked animal.

Adrian stopped, bag in hand, and raised his other in a gesture of surrender. "Sorry. I'll leave you alone. I have experience with injuries and some supplies, so I thought I'd offer."

Silence hung over the boat, interrupted by the whipping of the sails. The deck rocked beneath Peter's feet, rolling on the waves.

Kira sighed. "If you have supplies, I guess that would help."

Peter narrowed his eyes, staring at Adrian. *Who is this guy who travels around with a bunch of medical supplies? And what is he looking for in Barrentis?*

Kira sat back against the railing, and Adrian knelt next to her. She hissed as he peeled off the old bandage. The gash beneath it looked worse than ever: swollen, angry red, oozing dark blood and green pus. Kira sucked her teeth and turned her gaze to the sky.

"What did you want to talk about, Kira?" Peter asked.

Kira's eyes flicked to Adrian then back to Peter. "It's nothing. Maybe later."

"What happened here?" Adrian asked.

"Just a cut," Kira said.

"It looks infected. *Worse* than infected."

"It'll be fine. I'm fine."

"Really, you need to see a—"

"She said she's fine." Peter's words cut across the deck, silencing the man.

Adrian didn't ask more questions. He cleaned the worst of

the dried blood and the pus, then wrapped it in a fresh bandage. "I have painkillers, too, and some anti-inflammatories. Those will help."

"Sure," Kira said.

Peter and Sephiri glanced at each other and then toward the mountains.

Three more nights, Peter thought. *That's not much time.*

20

The dawn sun glowed through Peter's closed eyelids. He woke to gulls calling from their perches atop the masts.

"Ahoy!" Captain Hughes called. "We'll be docking soon!"

Peter stood from his bedroll and stretched. Mirelle groaned and pulled her blanket over her head, matching Rylan. Sephiri was already awake, as was Adrian. Kira sighed and sat up.

"Rest as long as you can," Peter said.

"Thanks," Kira murmured. She looked like she hadn't slept at all. Her face was ghostly white, and the light purple ringing her eyes had turned deep violet. Sweaty blonde hair stuck to her temples. She needed all the rest she could get. There was no telling what awaited them once they left the boat.

Peter scarfed down some food, then he and Rylan followed Captain Hughes' instructions as they managed the sails. Captain Hughes moved with ease, guiding the small boat toward the town growing in the distance.

"Is that it?" Rylan asked. "Is that Barrentis?"

"The one and only," Captain Hughes said. "We've made good time, despite all of your extra weight." He chuckled.

The port in the distance looked more like a village than a town. It was tiny but pretty, with white stone buildings and orange and yellow awnings. The dock stretched into the calm ocean, where sailboats and fishing boats loaded up with people. Past the town, the mountains loomed larger than ever. The surrounding landscape looked lush and green, and the brisk salty breeze carried a wiether chill.

Tall, dark cliffs lined the coast at the edge of town. The captain kept his distance, taking a wide berth around the eroded and jagged cliffs to slide into the bay where Barrentis nestled.

Kira packed up her things. She and Sephiri stayed close, speaking in low voices. Adrian had his book open again, scratching notes in the pages. Mirelle finished packing then leaned against the deck rail with a bit of breakfast pie in hand.

"Whoa!" Rylan pointed at the cliffs, his eyes wide. "How does the rock do that?"

A wave crashed against the dark rock at the base of a cliff. Moments later, water spilled out of two holes in the cliff face and back into the sea. The sight sent a strange shiver down Peter's spine.

"It's a trick of the tides," the captain said. "When it's high tide like this, the water in the cove is deep enough to spill out of those gaps in the rock. The folks in Barrentis say it's a curse."

"A curse?" Kira stood next to Peter, gazing at the cliffs with a furrow on her brow. "What do you mean?"

"It's just an old myth. A lord's daughter fell in love with a fisherman here in Barrentis, but her parents refused to let them marry. Instead, she was to be shipped off to Norshewa to marry a lord there. When she learned this, she kissed her beloved goodbye, then threw herself off this cliff here, choosing to be with him forever in the sea rather than live without him in Norshewa. So now, the cliffs remember her sadness, and they cry."

"That's sad," Rylan said. "Poor girl."

"They call it Trisiote dula Rochelo."

Kira cocked her head and frowned, staring at the rocks. "Tarphic," she whispered.

"What is it?" Peter breathed. "What does it mean?"

Her eyes grew, and she inhaled sharply. "If I'm right, it means . . . 'Sadness of the Rocks.'"

His brows pinched. "Sadness . . . ?" It clicked. "'Tears?'" He forced his voice quieter. "Could this be the Cliff of Tears?"

Kira's mouth curled up. "It sure looks like it."

He glanced at Sephiri. Her eyes slanted toward his with a sparkle in them.

"Hey, Captain?" Kira asked. "Do you know a lot about the old myths from around here?"

"As many as any old sea dog would, I suppose."

"Have you heard of the Pools of the Moon?"

Captain Hughes raised his eyebrows at Kira. "Where are you hearing about these old stories?"

"I study a lot of history," Kira said.

He shook his head. "That's another myth. Years ago, sailors used to travel into the Straith Mountains looking for the fabled Pools of the Moon. The story was that if one traveled to the Pools and left a gift, the tides would be in your favor for long trips."

"So they're in the Straiths?" Peter asked.

"I don't know that they exist at all." The captain smiled. "It was a way for sailors to get lost in the mountains and disappear. We're not supposed to be on land like that, you know." He laughed.

If there are stories, they might be real, Peter thought. A tingle ran through his body. *We're close. I know it.*

"Do you know where the pools are supposed to be?" Peter asked.

The captain waved his hand toward Barrentis. "Somewhere

up the valley from the town. I don't think anyone really knows, though."

Sephiri bounced on the balls of her feet, staring toward the town. "We can do this," she whispered so only Peter could hear.

Captain Hughes guided the boat into the bay, and the passengers made their way to the front of the bow. Peter leaned over the rail and gazed out at the town as they approached. The dock was busy and crowded. People hauled fishing gear into boats, and workers started their mornings in the town square. Barrentis didn't have the energy of Marris, but there was a warmth that drew Peter in.

"Guys?" Kira's voice wavered. "Do you see that?"

Peter tensed at the tremble in her voice. "See what?"

He leaned forward and squinted. Tiny shapes stood at the end of the docks. *Could that be*— His eyes grew as he gasped.

"Dirteaters," Kira said. "Waiting for us."

NALDOC LEAPED OFF HIS HORSE, rage burning through him like a flame. When he got his hands on the kids, they were going to pay. He had planned to just kill them and take whatever goodies they had stashed in their bags. But now it was personal.

Dirteaters didn't let their guests *get away*. No one had escaped their clutches since he had ascended to the leader of the group. If those *kids* got away, it wasn't just riches that were on the line. It was his reputation.

But if he got the Key of Kytalia, and then the city's treasures, his role as leader of the Dirteaters would be permanent.

Kytalia.

How did these kids get the Key?

That didn't matter. Soon it would be his, and they would be dead.

"Come on," he said when Esmee, Nalva, and the others

joined him. They stalked down the dock, shoving past fishermen.

The boat approached. The captain looked unperturbed at the helm as he docked.

"Hughes!" Naldoc shouted. "Captain of the Seacutter!"

"What?" the captain shouted. "I'm not taking any commissions right now."

Naldoc shoved past the worker on the dock tying the boat up. He jumped onto the deck with a thump, rocking it under his weight.

"Hey! What do you think you're doing?"

Esmee clambered onto the deck behind him. She looked around, eyes wide and furious. They'd both only grown angrier as their horses thundered along the coast to Barrentis, arriving just ahead of the Seacutter.

"Where are they?" Naldoc roared. He kicked a crate. "Where are those kids?"

The Captain stared wide-eyed at them. A brown-haired girl stood against the rail along with a confused-looking man in fine slacks. The rest of the deck was empty.

"Search it!" Naldoc shouted. "Find them!"

The Dirteaters knocked things around, kicking crates to the side and overturning them. They opened the trapdoor into the body of the ship and rooted around inside. Naldoc's anger grew with each passing moment.

"Where are they?" Naldoc roared. He stormed across the deck and grabbed the brown-haired girl by the arm. She pulled against him, yelling and thrashing until a yank on her hair calmed her down. He hauled her close, pulling her head back to expose the throat. His knife felt heavy on his belt, still sheathed, but itching for blood. "I saw those four kids leave on this boat in Marris. They have something I need. Tell me where they are, and I'll let the girl live."

"Relax." The captain looked unperturbed, which only made

Naldoc more furious. "That girl's just a passenger. She doesn't know anything. The four kids you're talking about? They asked to be dropped off at a beach yesterday, only a few hours out of Marris, so I did. You won't find them here."

Naldoc narrowed his eyes.

Nalva climbed up from beneath the boat and shook her head. "No sign of them."

"Search the city." Naldoc shoved the girl down.

She hit the deck with a yelp and landed in a heap. She scooted away, rubbing her cheek where it had cracked against the wood.

"Search the docks and the beaches, just in case."

"Good luck," the captain said with a cheeky smile.

Naldoc resisted the urge to backhand the smile off his face. He sneered, then led his crew off the boat and back down to the docks. The fishermen gave them a wide berth. Naldoc and Nalva stalked off the dock to search the square, while Esmee and the other young men split off to search the beaches along the edge of town.

They found no trace of the kids, neither in the square nor along the beaches or docks. It was as if the four of them had disappeared off the boat into thin air. "We'll have to head east," Naldoc growled. "If the captain dropped them off near Marris, maybe we'll find tracks crossing the trail. Back to the horses."

Nalva nodded and left to gather the men. Naldoc scowled as he watched the Seacutter bobbing at the end of the dock.

Those kids won't slip away again.

~

"LOOKS LIKE THEY GAVE UP." Kira squinted, leaning forward on the rock she perched atop. "They're on their horses, and it seems they're heading out of town."

"Let's make sure they're headed away from us," Peter said.

The four of them hid in a cove just east of the city, sopping wet and cold. They'd scrambled onto the rocks at the edge of the cove, the seawater lapping at their feet. Peter's shoulder burned with exhaustion from the swim to their hiding spot, far enough away from the docks that the Dirteaters' search hadn't found them.

Rylan tugged his shirt off and wrung the seawater out. "Good thing you saw them when you did, Kira."

"And good thing the captain and Mirelle agreed to cover for us," Peter said. "Hopefully, the Dirteaters didn't damage his cargo." His stomach clenched. *Or Mirelle.*

"I can't see the boat," Kira said. "Yeah, hopefully they're all right."

"Add it to the list of people we'll pay back after we find the city," Sephiri said. "Kira, how are you?"

"Been better." Her arms trembled.

Peter's heart sank. If she admitted to not being well, she must be in terrible shape. He swallowed. *Two more nights.*

It hadn't been a long swim, but she barely made it using her one good arm. Rylan had to help her out of the sea and into the cove. If the tide had been going out, she wouldn't have made it at all.

"Let's head into town," Peter said. "We'll feel better after we dry off and get our stuff."

"If it's there," Sephiri added.

"It will be," Peter breathed, trying to convince himself it would be true and push away the knot in his stomach. *She's got to be there. She hasn't let us down yet.*

The four of them clambered out of the cove and onto the narrow strip of beach. Sephiri summoned a breeze, and they shook off and wrung out the worst of the water while the wind dried them off. Peter worked his hands through his hair, teeth chattering as the cold wind ran through it.

"I need a hot tea," Kira said.

"And a change of clothes." Rylan grimaced. "My shirt smells like kelp."

"Everything in these port towns smells like kelp. You'll fit right in." Sephiri steadied Kira by the elbow as they finished drying off.

Peter nodded. Kira was paler than she'd ever been, and she trembled. They needed to warm up, and soon.

Barrentis wasn't far. They arrived at the docks after only a short walk from their cove. Rylan insisted Kira hop onto his back, and then, despite his complaints about being wet and kelp-smelling, he stomped around in the surf as they traveled. Peter and Sephiri walked along the hard-packed sand, avoiding the lapping waves. They hurried, keeping an eye out for any Dirteaters who may have stayed in the city.

They crept up the stairs from the beach to the docks, which were still busy with fishermen and a few vendors.

"No Dirteaters," Rylan said. "Looks clear to me."

"No Seacutter either," Sephiri said, her inflection dropping.

Rylan audibly winced.

"Mirelle must have, um, already offloaded our gear." A waver tickled Peter's words as his stomach tightened. "The captain wasn't staying here, remember?"

"You think she unloaded and moved everything that quickly?" Sephiri asked. "That was a lot of stuff to carry. If she's run off with the map and the knife, we're—"

"She'll be here," Peter interrupted, his words sounding more forceful than he intended.

"Where's she supposed to wait for us?" Rylan asked.

"Not sure. Somewhere in the square, I hope. We didn't have much time to plan."

Smaller than Marris, Barrentis held a quiet marketplace built around a dolphin-shaped fountain gurgling in the center of the square. The buildings nearby were short and squat, built of pale stone with their shudders open to the sea breeze.

A few wooden tables sat outside a building, with a sign marked 'TAVERN' swinging over the door. Vendors dotted the square, selling nets, grilled fish, and jarred goods. The aroma of grilled meat wafted along the breeze and made Peter's stomach growl.

The door to the tavern swung open, and a girl with brown hair poked her head out.

Peter grinned, a flood of relief washing over him. "Told you."

Mirelle smiled back and waved the four of them over. Kira slid off Rylan's back, and they all crossed the square to enter the tavern.

"You made it!" Mirelle led them to a table in the back. "You four can really swim. How'd you dry off so fast? I've got some hot drinks already ordered. I assumed you'd be miserable."

The tavern was plain, with an earthen floor, a few lanterns, and a rickety staircase leading up. An ancient woman stood behind a low bar, tending a cauldron. In a corner near the hearth, Mirelle had commandeered one of the bigger tables. Peter sighed, his shoulders relaxing at the sight of their bags. But then—

"What's he doing here?" Rylan asked.

Adrian waved jauntily from the table. "Quite an exciting journey, wouldn't you agree?" he called. "Sit, sit, the fire feels wonderful."

Mirelle shrugged. "I needed his help to carry everything."

"My colleague's not here—the one I was meeting. Can you believe that? The lady at the inn said he left town yesterday. It seems I traveled all the way here for nothing."

The four of them sat down with Mirelle and Adrian. The old tavern keeper hobbled over with mugs on a tray and a kettle of tea. Adrian thanked her profusely—a little too enthusiastically, Peter thought—and then busied himself pouring tea and passing the mugs out.

"I'll be right back." Peter jumped to his feet and followed the tavernkeeper to the bar. "Excuse me."

She glanced his way over an armload of dirty dishes.

"I was wondering . . . I'm trying to find the Pools of the Moon. Have you heard of it?"

The tavern keeper sighed. "Are those old dogs at the docks telling tales again?"

"What do you mean?"

"You won't find anything in the Straiths. We've been losing young sailors to that silly quest for too long. Mind the tides yourself. There's nothing in the mountains for you."

"So they're real?"

She laughed. "How would I know? I learned long ago to stay out of those mountains."

Peter frowned and nodded before scurrying back to the table.

Mirelle tilted her head. "What did you need?"

"Nothing. Just asking about the town."

As if something tweaked in her jaw, Mirelle cupped her cheek and grimaced.

A red and swollen bump on her chin caught Peter's eye. After closer inspection, he spotted bruises along her arms, too. "What happened? Are you all right?"

Mirelle shrank back as the rest of the table turned her way. "There was trouble when we docked."

"Dirteaters?" Rylan asked in a low voice.

She nodded. "They ransacked the boat."

"Looking for you four," Adrian added. "Same group from Marris. I don't envy you, being on those guys' bad side."

Peter gave Adrian a sidelong glance. *What is this guy even doing here?*

Mirelle caught Peter's eye and gave him an apologetic half-shrug. "I got knocked around by the Dirteaters. Adrian patched me up afterward."

"Then I remembered about that nasty gash on your shoulder," he said to Kira. "Especially after you jumped into the ocean. You'll need to change that bandage again."

"It's fine," Kira said.

"I've got my stuff with me. Let me change it for you."

Kira pressed her lips together, but then relented and scooted her chair closer.

Adrian frowned. "How are you feeling? You're sweating. Have you been trembling?"

"It was cold," Rylan said. "We swam a lot."

"This isn't normal exertion," Adrian said. "You might have a fever coming on. I have a tincture that should help with that."

Kira stared glassy eyed as Adrian rooted around in his bag. Occasional tremors made her twitch.

Peter's eyes flicked to Sephiri, who carried deep lines over her brows.

"So where are you going now?" Mirelle asked. "Looking for your Pools of the Moon?"

Peter's breath caught. He glanced at his friends, who stared back. He swallowed the catch in his throat and nodded. "I'm sure the Dirteaters will be back to look for us. Can't stay here, so we'll head into the mountains."

"Mm." Mirelle took a sip of her tea. "Probably best if I lie low for a while, too. I wouldn't want to run into them on my way back to Marris. You think they'll come back here?"

Peter's stomach dropped. She was right. They got away once, but that wasn't a guarantee the Dirteaters would leave them alone for good. *She helped us so much. We can't just leave her to fend for herself.*

"I wonder if—" Peter glanced around the table.

Rylan and Kira wore similar expressions of concern. Sephiri looked at Kira, and she shrugged. Rylan's brow furrowed.

"They wouldn't let you off easy," Peter said.

Mirelle shrugged. "I'm used to dealing with the Norivonne. How bad could these Dirteaters be? I'll be okay."

Kira pressed her lips together, and Sephiri sighed.

"Maybe you should stick with us," Rylan said.

Mirelle's eyes widened. "Really?"

Peter nodded. "I think that might be a good idea. The Straith Mountains won't be safe, but at least we'll have each other's backs."

Sephiri glared, her eyebrows shooting up. "I'm sure Mirelle has her own business to attend to. And we don't know how long we will be gone—or how safe it will be."

Mirelle wrapped her hands around her mug. "No, no, I shouldn't. Whatever you guys are after . . . it's not my place to interfere."

Tension tugged at Peter's chest, like he was being pulled in too many directions at once.

"I only wanted to cause a little trouble for the Norivonne." Mirelle smiled, but there was a tinge of sadness in it—a haunted touch. "I did that. I don't need to bother you further."

"It's not a bother," Peter said. "Come with us."

Rylan glanced between Peter and Sephiri. He looked over his shoulder at the door to the tavern, like he expected one of their pursuers to burst in behind them. "I mean, it might not be a bad idea. Traveling to the Pools of the Moon and back would kill a few days if the Dirteaters came back sniffing around. You don't have to come all the way, Mirelle."

"All the way where?" Adrian asked. He was half-listening as he focused on Kira's bandage.

Peter snapped his mouth shut.

But then his gaze traveled to the man's bag of supplies and to Kira's exhausted expression.

Adrian's gaze followed his own. "I'll need to find a place to lie low as well. My connection didn't show up, so I'll hole up here for a few days. But . . ." He looked at Kira's wound. "It might not be a good idea to leave her without medical care, especially if you're in the Straiths. If you want my help . . ."

"I'll be okay," Kira said.

Will she?

We might need all the help we can get. If her condition gets worse, he might get us a little more time.

"Maybe it's best if we stick together for a few days, if you're up for it?" Peter said. "They'll be looking for all of us, and we don't have time to wait around."

"Peter," Sephiri hissed under her breath. Across the table, her eyes narrowed at him. It wasn't ideal, dragging the strange man along. But his medical skills might give them a little more time.

"Just until we reach the Pools of the Moon," Peter clarified. "Everyone, finish your drinks. We leave now."

21

The wilderness north of town grew thick with vegetation. Mountains loomed high overhead, their jagged peaks soaring into the clouds. The ridges blocked the worst of the wind and funneled the rain into the spongy soil. As a result, a dense mountain jungle covered the land. The trees had thick, sturdy trunks and grew so tall and broad that their leafy canopies blocked out much of the sky.

The lack of trail indicated few people from Barrentis made their way into the mountains. Peter peered at the map as they hiked, careful to keep it hidden from Adrian and Mirelle. But the map wouldn't do them any good—not until they reached the Pools of the Moon. Captain Hughes and the woman at the bar both said it might be real, but Peter had no solid leads on how to find it other than walking up the valley from town into the mountains. All he could do was trust it was real and hope his instincts took them in the right direction.

At the same time, mountains surrounded them. Even determining which direction they traveled was a challenge. Peter sighed. There wasn't much he could do but hope.

Hope, and try not to punch Adrian. The man was an irritating travel companion, whistling and scratching in his note-book when they passed interesting trees and plants. Peter couldn't figure out what kinds of things made him pause, and he stopped worrying about it after a few hours of hiking. They took frequent breaks for Kira, and Adrian changed her bandages when needed. Still, she ended up on Rylan's back, worn out from hiking over the uneven terrain. Sweat beaded on her nape and stained the underarms of her shirt, even when she was doing nothing more than hanging on to Rylan.

"Tracks!" Adrian said to no one in particular. "And so pristine. This earth is marvelous for tracks." He knelt and leaned closer to the paw print in the dirt, then pulled out his notebook.

While their traveling companion was distracted, Peter hurried to Mirelle's side. She was just as sweaty as the rest of them, huffing and puffing as she traversed the roots and exposed rocks. She smiled when Peter approached. "I'm guessing those Dirteaters won't follow us out here," she said. "This was a good way to stay off their radar."

Peter nodded, then glanced over his shoulder. Adrian was still a ways behind them, inspecting the dirt. "What do you think of Adrian?" he whispered.

She blinked, slow like a cat, as she pondered the question. "I'm not sure," she admitted. "It's weird he showed up out of nowhere and stuck with us, isn't it?"

"Did the Dirteaters push him around, too?"

She shook her head. "Just me. He kept out of the way. I don't know if they even acknowledged him."

"But he still wanted to come with us. It's strange."

"He's been friendly, though," Mirelle said. "I'll keep an eye on him."

"He is helping Kira, I think."

She nodded. "I hope her fever clears soon."

"It's getting worse," Peter admitted.

"What is it?" she asked. "What happened?"

Up ahead, Rylan hiked Kira higher on his back and then picked his way over a fallen log.

"Reaper poison," Peter said. "A fever tincture won't do anything."

They hiked in silence for a few moments. "I'm sorry." Her soft, steady voice made it clear she knew what that meant. There was no solution. Nothing a strange man with a medical kit could fix. They could only try to delay the inevitable. "What are you doing, then? Why bring her into the mountains?"

BOOM!

Thunder cracked in the distance. The sound jolted Peter, and he stumbled over an exposed root. Mirelle caught his arm and steadied his balance. Her touch felt warm and tender. Somewhere deep in the trees, an animal yelped, and another responded.

"Did you hear that?" Mirelle asked. "What was that?"

Peter found his feet. "Sounded like a fox."

Sephiri looked back over her shoulder. "You okay?"

"Just surprised," Peter replied. He looked up toward the canopy and the darkening sky. "I didn't see the clouds roll in."

"Can't see a thing through these leaves!" Adrian said. "Storms gather over these mountains often, though. The peaks block the winds from blowing them across—quite a phenomenon. It's why these trees get so big."

"We should find somewhere to wait out the storm," Sephiri said. "If Kira gets wet, her fever will worsen."

Another crack of distant thunder split the quiet. A few colored birds exploded from the branches of the trees and soared into the sky.

"Agreed," Peter said. "It's nearly nighttime, anyway. Keep an eye out for a shelter, everyone."

They trekked on. Long minutes came and went with nothing to show for it. The sky past the canopy darkened, and the thunder grew steadily louder. Peter grew frantic, even considering how much shelter some of the larger leaves might provide.

"Here!" Rylan shouted from the front of the line.

Peter jogged forward to where a rocky hill formed one side of the trail. A small overhang tucked low to the ground, halfway hidden behind a large tree. It seemed to burrow into the rocks.

Kira dropped from Rylan's back. Her legs wobbled, and she braced a hand against the tree. She dipped her chin at Peter, like she said, *I'm fine.*

Even if she wasn't.

Rylan ducked into the opening. "Check this out!" he shouted back. "It's way bigger inside!"

Sephiri sighed. "Good. I wasn't looking forward to another night like our *last* emergency cave-dwelling."

"This happens a lot, huh?" Mirelle teased, ducking into the cave after Rylan. The rest of the group squeezed in; Peter went last.

After shuffling in a crouch, the room opened up, and he stood to his full height. He blinked in the blackness as his eyes adjusted to the dim light leaking in from the narrow entrance. The cave was spacious, with a high ceiling and darkness that seemed to ooze backward without end, as if the mountain itself were hollow. It smelled earthy, musty, with a sharp, rotten tang. Peter grimaced. The scent stung the back of his throat and turned his stomach.

"What is that?" Kira asked. "Do you smell that?"

Sephiri pulled a small torch from her bag and lit it with flint. The flickering firelight danced along the cave walls. She gasped and dropped the torch. It rolled across the hard-packed earth and cast its light and shadows up in a frenetic dance.

The cave wasn't empty.

The sharp, acrid smell came from the rot. A deer decayed at the far end of the cave. The bulk of the meat on the carcass had been devoured, if the jagged shapes of its wounds were anything to go by. There were smaller dead animals too, squirrels and garronts, as well as—

"Is that . . . ?" Kira whispered.

"We need to get out of here," Peter hissed.

Bones. Not animal bones—*human* bones. The empty eyes of a human skull stared through Peter from its place in the dirt. There was a traveler's pack, too, frayed and rotting.

"Ah," Adrian's voice quivered. "This must be where the tracks I found led to." He nodded toward the ground where large paw prints pressed into the earth.

"What kind of animal leaves those prints?" Rylan asked. "Six toes? And claws?"

"Guys?" Sephiri picked up a thin membrane. Translucent in parts, the long, clear film folded over itself, stained with portions of a reddish-black substance. "What is this?"

"Looks like animal skin," Kira muttered.

Sephiri dropped the membrane and rubbed her fingers as if trying to free them of an unpleasant substance.

"Um, that's not the only one." Rylan pointed to where a dozen clear sheetlike objects jumbled in a disordered pile.

"Let's get out of here," Peter said. "*Now.* We'll find somewhere else to wait out the storm." He bent to duck back through the cave entrance until his feet stopped. His legs felt stuck in place as his heart dropped.

A guttural rumble filled the air as he met the eyes of a blood panzil. Larger than the one he'd seen in Palenting, it had the same dark, hairless body and ragged ears. It dug its six-toed paws into the ground and lowered its head enough to see into the cave—its *den*. Two more animals approached from behind the other, adding their growls in a chorus.

Peter gulped. He'd found a blood panzil pack's den, and he was trespassing.

The beast's red eyes flashed. It pulled its lip back, baring its fangs. Behind it, fox-like barks rang out in quick succession.

More panzils appeared, snarling, pawing at the ground. There were too many of them. Half a dozen at least, with more emerging from the tree line. Drool dripped from their teeth as they stepped closer.

Peter checked side to side, his heart pounding. *There's no way to get past them!* He took a step backward. The wrangler's words about them feeding after shedding their skin came to him in a rush.

The panzils yelped. A low and long growl rumbled from the one in the front.

Peter picked up the torch.

The cave continued behind them, narrowing into an unknown dark tunnel. "We've got to find another way out," he shouted to the others. "Come on!"

The tunnel wound into the darkness, narrowing as he raced deeper into the mountain. Light from the torch scattered shadows. The earth hardened to stone under his feet, and the tunnel angled upward. Behind him, Kira gasped for breath. Peter held the hand of her good arm as he ran, hauling her forward. The others were hot on their heels, rushing forward, stomping, and shouting. The ceiling felt lower, like the tunnel shrank as they went.

Behind them, yelps bounced off the stone of the cave, along with wet, nasty snarls that sounded too close for comfort.

Ahead, a sliver of grayish light appeared, bleeding through a crack in the tunnel. Peter shouted triumphantly. He dropped Kira's hand, gave the torch to Sephiri, and then raced ahead.

The crack curved down the wall at the end of the tunnel. Dim light sneaking through provided a glimmer of hope. The rocks were different textures on either side. This wasn't just a crack in the rock. This was *two* rocks. A boulder blocking an entrance. Peter squeezed his fingers into the crack and pulled, but he wasn't strong enough to move it.

"Rylan!" he called. "Help!"

Rylan rushed forward. "Move!" He shouldered Peter out of the way with such urgency Peter stumbled into the tunnel wall. "Sorry! Watch out!"

The wet, angry snarls of the panzils grew closer.

Rylan dug his heels into the dirt and grunted. The veins in his arms bulged as he pushed. Sparks danced along his skin.

Peter glanced back—Mirelle and Adrian faced the hideous sounds coming from the other direction, oblivious to Rylan's twinkling body.

"Get back!" Sephiri brandished the torch at the panzils. The beasts pressed against each other, shoulder-to-shoulder in the narrow tunnel. They gnashed their teeth at Sephiri. She thrust the torch in their faces, making them snarl and step back, only to push forward to her again. "Back!"

Peter pulled the sword from his belt and squeezed past the others. Standing beside Sephiri, he lunged forward with the blade, striking at the animals. They pawed and snarled at the new threat, knocking it into the wall. The sharp tip found the neck of one. It yelped and howled, flashing sharp teeth in his direction. The wound didn't appear to faze it.

Rylan's grunts grew louder, and the grating of stone filled the passage. Dim gray light flooded the tunnel. "Come on!" Rylan shouted.

Peter checked. A gap had formed—wide enough for them to squeeze through.

Rylan led Kira out first, then Mirelle wriggled through. Peter took the torch from Sephiri and bared both his sword and the fire at the panzils. "Get outside!" he shouted. "Run!"

"You're coming with me!" Sephiri grabbed him by the back of the shirt and tugged. With each step backward, the panzils moved closer. Hunger gleamed in their blood-red eyes.

Sephiri reached over his shoulder and thrust her palm forward. Wind swept down the tunnel, hurling the panzils back. They yelped, stumbling backward from the sudden assault. One snarled from where it had crouched low, unaffected by the wind. Peter hurled the torch at it, then slid through the gap, following Sephiri.

Rain fell in sheets. Peter hardly felt the cold even as it needled at his skin. His breath heaved in bursts as he took unsteady steps back, keeping the sword up.

The panzil appeared in the gap at the boulder. It shoved its head through, snapped its jaws, and snarled. Drool dripped from its teeth as it pushed forward, trying to squeeze its body through, eyes wild.

"Back up!" Peter gripped the hilt of his sword, the only weapon they had to fight it off.

The panzil stilled as rain landed on its snout. It flattened its ears and whined, jerking its head back. The animal remained close, staring through the gap. It tossed its head and pawed at the ground again. Behind it, the other animals yelped anew, a high, frustrated sound.

"They don't like water." Kira wrapped her arms around her own shivering body. The rain plastered her hair to the sides of her face. "They won't come out in the rain."

"Are you sure about that?" Adrian asked, voice shaking. He kept his gaze fixed on the panzils snapping their teeth in the cave.

Thunder cracked across the sky. In the tunnel, the panzils whined and retreated. Peter stepped closer, catching sight of the pack turning tail and trotting back toward the heart of their den, looking more like regular street dogs than the bloodthirsty creatures they were moments before. He sighed, then pushed his wet hair off his forehead. Between the storm and the rapidly approaching night, visibility was limited. "Let's get out of here and find a place to sleep."

As the rain pummeled them, the six travelers slogged through the dark jungle and the mud until they found a passable shelter: a rock cropping beneath an overhang, shielded from the worst of the rain and the wind. It was too wet for a fire. All they could do was wring out the worst of the rain from their clothes and huddle together under the rock, staying close to conserve warmth.

"We'll try to get a fire going as soon as it stops raining," Peter said. *If we can even find any wood dry enough.* "That'll help."

Kira nodded. There was a distance to her demeanor, though, like she only half-listened.

"I'll take the first watch. Try to get some sleep."

As the other five settled down as best as they could, Peter crept to the edge of the outcropping and gazed into the dark, rainy trees.

Where did the tunnel spit us out? How are we supposed to find the Pools of the Moon? Are we going to wander the Straith Mountains until Kira dies?

He looked over his shoulder. Sephiri shivered with her eyes closed, pressed against Kira for warmth.

That's what happened to her parents. Soldiers lost in the mountains—swallowed by the unforgiving landscape. When they'd found their way out of the mountains, the army rejected them—feared the powers they'd found. *The same power sparking in my veins now.*

We won't get lost. We know the pools are around here somewhere. But water isn't magical—if we can find a stream, we can follow it. Maybe we'll get lucky.

Peter swallowed hard and turned his gaze back to the foliage. He kept his hand on the hilt of his sword in case any other creatures emerged from the tree line to turn them into a meal. Tomorrow, in the light of day, they'd keep moving. *We'll find Kytalia. Kira will be healed. And when I bring proof of the city home, Commander Isert will respect me.*

He couldn't waste energy worrying. Too much was at stake.

22

———————

Sephiri had always been a light sleeper. It was a skill she developed as a young girl sleeping in the nooks and crannies of Palenting, to ensure her few belongings didn't get stolen. It was that attention which alerted her of steps crunching in the distance.

She blinked her eyes open, taking care to not move. Was it a panzil? Or a harmless creature looking for its own meal in the deep night?

Crunch. Crunch. It didn't sound like an animal. It sounded like something with two legs.

No—she must've been imagining things. They were the only people out there in the Straiths. No one came that deep into the mountains. It was too dangerous.

She thought she heard a voice, faint on the wind. A whisper. Almost inaudible.

She sat up. Around her, the others were still asleep—including Rylan, who was supposed to be on watch.

She strained. Was it a voice?

The sound never came again. It was gone. Or had she ever

heard it in the first place? *It was probably just the wind, rustling through the canopy overhead. Playing tricks on me.*

She shivered and laid back down on her bedroll. The Straith Mountains were dangerous like that. It was too easy to get confused, turned around . . . Lost.

THE RAIN BROKE in the night. When Peter awoke to the birdsong overhead, Sephiri had a fire going.

"Morning," she whispered.

He blinked several times, his mouth hanging ajar as he stared at the burning wood. "How did you—"

"You think this wind power is only good for blowing people over?" She grinned. "It's pretty helpful for drying out wood as well. Also, check your clothes."

Peter touched his shirt that he'd laid across a branch. *Nearly dry.* "That will never get old. Thanks."

"We'll need more water today," Sephiri said. "Running low. I'm heating some now just to give us something warm to drink."

Peter nodded. "You get any sleep?"

She shrugged. "Enough. I kept waking, though. I heard weird noises in the jungle."

"Noises? Panzils?"

"Didn't sound like animals. I thought I heard voices, but it could have been nothing." She shivered. "I don't know. It was unnerving. Being all the way out here is strange, you know?"

His heart sank. "Does it . . . make you think of your parents?"

"In a weird way. It's not like I was with them when they were here, but it's . . . It's strange. It feels like they're still nearby." She sighed and poured hot water into a mug.

"What were you hearing?" Peter asked. "What kinds of voices?"

"I couldn't place it," Sephiri said. "Whispers. Rustling. It could've been the wind. I was likely just imagining things."

The wind, a figment . . . or someone coming after them. They'd let their guard down in the mountains, talking and laughing as they went. If they were being tracked, they were making it too easy. "We need to move soon, anyway. The panzils will come out looking for a meal sooner rather than later."

"Which way are we going?" Sephiri asked. "Should we try to walk around the mountain back to whatever path we were on?"

Peter shook his head. "Not sure I would call that a path. If we go back to that cave, we'll pass the panzils again. I think we'll need to go from here and bushwhack a little."

"Won't that increase our chances of getting lost?" Sephiri asked. "How do you know we're going the right way?"

Peter shrugged. "I don't." He pointed the direction the valley ran. "That is my best guess."

Sephiri shuddered. She pulled her knees close to her chest and gazed into the fire.

Peter sat on the log next to her. It was still damp, and the chill bled through his pants. He extended his hands toward the flames and savored the radiant warmth while he tried to gather his thoughts. "Are you okay?"

"I'm fine," she said. "Just tired. My imagination made me anxious. And things are complicated, you know?" She glanced toward Adrian's bedroll, where he snored, still bundled up.

"I know having outsiders with us isn't ideal."

She sighed. "I understand. I mean, if Adrian weren't tending Kira's shoulder, who knows how bad it would be? I can clean it, but I don't have all the fancy stuff he does. He's a bit—" She lowered her voice, "off, I guess, and I still don't know why he's sticking with us. It makes me nervous."

"Me, too," Peter said. "I'm keeping an eye on him, you know."

"I know."

"And about—"

"Morning," Mirelle greeted. She stretched her arms over her head and shook out her messy hair. "Do we still have any of those hand pies?"

Whatever Peter was about to say about Mirelle sputtered and died on his tongue.

She plopped down next to the fire and rooted through the provisions. Sephiri returned her attention to her small mug of hot water.

Mirelle found a hand pie and pulled it out. With a grin, she raised it in question. Sephiri shook her head. Mirelle shrugged, then tore it in two and reached over the fire to hand half of it to Peter. The sleeve of her shirt rode up her forearm, and the scarred flesh of the brand on her forearm was visible. Sephiri's eyes darted to it. Mirelle sat and tugged the sleeve down. "We should get more water today," she said.

"We will," Sephiri said. "We already discussed it."

"Great," Mirelle said.

An awkward silence hung in the air. It crawled over Peter's skin like ants. He chewed on the cold meat pie, with one hand extended toward the fire.

"Let's catch some more food before we keep going," Mirelle said. "We don't have too much left."

Sephiri raised her eyebrows. "I imagine we need to keep moving. What do you think, Peter?"

"It won't take long." Mirelle stood and stretched her arms overhead. "After the rain is the perfect time. Come on, Peter."

He glanced at the others as he stood. "They're all still asleep, so I guess it wouldn't hurt to hunt a bit. What comes out after the rain?"

Sephiri's expression soured as she gazed into the fire, but she said nothing.

"Garront," Mirelle said. "I heard them rustling around this morning. Come on, we'll be quick."

"Maybe that was the voice you heard this morning, Seph."

Mirelle raised an eyebrow. "A voice?"

"It was nothing," Sephiri said. "Wind in the trees. I'll wake Rylan, and we'll pack the campsite." Sephiri glanced at Kira's sleeping form before turning back to Peter. "Don't take long."

He grabbed Kira's small bow and a few arrows, careful not to wake her.

"Garronts love weather like this," Mirelle whispered as they crept away from the campsite and into the trees along the base of the surrounding mountains. "It should be easy to nab a few."

The mud squelched under their feet, and rain dripped from the canopy. Fat droplets landed on Peter's shoulders and the crown of his head. He suppressed a shiver. He considered himself a decent hunter, but in the unfamiliar terrain, he followed Mirelle's lead. She seemed to track signs he could hardly see: disturbed leaves, traces of droppings, bits of nests near tree roots. They moved through the vegetation in comfortable silence until, after a few minutes, Peter heard the rustling.

They stopped moving, half-hidden behind a tree. Mirelle grinned, then nodded towards a thorny bush growing a few small, dark berries. The leaves of the bush quivered, and a fat, brown bird emerged. Mirelle gestured for the bow.

Peter handed it to her.

She handled the bow with familiar ease. Nocking an arrow in the bowstring, she aimed and let it fly. The arrow sailed through the air and pinned the unsuspecting garront to the ground. The *thunk* stirred another bird from the brush. It rushed out, squawking, and flapped its wings as it tried to take off into the air. Mirelle nocked another arrow and released it in the space of a breath. It struck the garront out of the air and sent it tumbling to the ground. "That's a female," she said. "I bet there are eggs!"

It was a victorious hunt: two birds and a half-dozen eggs.

"You're good with the bow." Peter grinned as he tied up the birds and hung them around his neck.

Mirelle packed the eggs into her cloak and carried it like a basket. "These will be great. If we boil them before we go, they'll keep for a while. I hunt a lot of garront outside of Marris."

"There are a lot of them in Marris?" Peter wasn't concerned about the garront population density, but he wanted Mirelle to keep talking. He wanted to know more about the day-to-day rhythms of her life up in that tiny squat above the docks.

"Enough," she said.

"What keeps you there?" he asked as they made their way back toward the campsite. "In Marris?"

Another question weighed on his mind. *Why don't you come back to Palenting?* It was easy to imagine Mirelle slotting into their lives back home, lazing in the lofted bedrooms of the Garrison and laughing on the cobbled streets of the city.

Mirelle sighed. "I don't know. Habit, I guess? It's where I've always lived." She paused and cradled the eggs close to her chest and stared at her feet as she shuffled through the wet leaves. "I guess I'm still hoping I'll figure out some way to avenge my parents. Don't want the Norivonne to win, you know? I don't want to give them the satisfaction of running me out of the city."

"But don't they run the entire city?" Peter asked. "How would you get back at them?"

Mirelle huffed a laugh. "I guess that's the problem. Maybe I'm waiting for something that will never happen. It'd be easier if I had—" She stopped.

"Had what?" Peter asked.

"If I had some money," Mirelle admitted. "Even if I wanted to leave Marris, I couldn't. I only have that place to stay because some guys at the docks take pity on me. Maybe I could imagine a new start if it felt realistic. But right now, it's out of reach. So I focus on what makes me happy." She grinned, but there wasn't much humor in it. "Messing with the Norivonne."

"You know . . ." Peter paused, weighing his words. "There might be a way for you to make some money."

"What do you mean?" Mirelle asked.

The campsite peeked through the trees ahead. Rylan, Kira, Adrian, and Sephiri were all awake. Rylan and Kira packed up their things as Adrian changed Kira's bandages.

"Don't tell anyone else," he whispered, "but we're looking for Kytalia."

Her eyes widened. "Kytalia? The City of Gold?"

"It's real," Peter whispered. "We found a map. We'll find the city, and there will be enough money for all of us to do whatever we want."

"You think it's real?" Mirelle asked. "I thought that was just an old story."

"Stories are often rooted in truth." Peter thought about the Amulet tucked away in Palenting. He thought about the Source running through his body, and the spring Sephiri's parents found in those same Mountains. "But we have leads. Good leads. I can't give you the details, but—Trust me. It's real."

"I trust you." Her words were barely audible. Crinkles formed at the corners of her eyes.

Peter's heart fluttered. Kytalia wouldn't be just a new start for him—it'd be a new start for all of them. He pulled the two garronts off where they hung around his neck and held them overhead. "Keep the fire going, Seph. We have some cooking to do!"

Back in camp, they dressed and roasted the garronts over the fire. Kira ate some of the meat, but not much. Peter watched her, but she wouldn't meet his eyes. She stood up as they put out the fire, then leaned against Rylan's side.

"She's struggling." Adrian appeared at Peter's side, his sudden presence jolting him. "She's upright. Eating. That's all good, but—" He furrowed his brow. "That cut is getting worse. It doesn't look like any infection I've seen. What happened? What did you kids get into?"

"I don't know." Peter tried to avoid the question. "We need to move before the panzils come back, though."

"Peter's right," Kira said, her words bleary. "Let's get going."

"It looks like some animals go through here." Peter nodded toward a narrow, worn animal trail winding through the trees. "We can follow this. I bet it leads to a water source. Then we can follow the water . . ."

"Upstream," Rylan said. "North. We sort of know what we're looking for."

"What's that?" Adrian asked. "What are you looking for?"

Kira sighed. "Maybe it'd be best if you went back to Barrentis, Adrian. I'm—I'm grateful for all the help, but there's not much else you can do."

"That'd be a treat for me," Adrian said, "but I must admit, I'm not sure where I would go."

"It's south," Peter said, pointing downhill.

"South, so . . . past all the panzils. On my own."

Peter frowned, his eyes flicking to the others. He let out a loud sigh. "You should probably stay with us until we can make it back."

It wasn't perfect, but it'd have to do. With light from the sun peeking through the trees in the east, he turned north, faced the thick vegetation, and led the way. As they left the campsite behind, the distant yelping of the panzils echoed through the trees.

"Good timing," Rylan muttered.

Hiking through the jungle was not as easy as it had been the day before. The rising sun brought heat, and the thick vegetation blocked any hope of a breeze. Humidity hung in the air, trapped by the canopy above.

Sweat poured off Peter's body as he trudged up the incline. His feet slipped in the mud, and he pulled on tree trunks and bushes as he passed. Behind him, the five others scrambled as well, huffing and puffing as they made their way north. Kira returned to Rylan's back, making cringing sounds as he jostled her.

Atop a ridge, the terrain flattened out into a path. Whether it was an actual trail or an animal's path, Peter didn't know, but it was good enough to be away from the panzils' cave and back on steady ground. By the sun's placement, it had to be around noon. Peter's throat ached, but the canteens were empty.

"Peter." Sephiri wiped the sweat from her forehead. "You hear that?"

He tilted his head, listening. Wind rustled through the trees overhead. Birds chirped in the branches, and hawks cried.

Then he heard it. The soft gurgle of water. He breathed a deep sigh of relief and shot her a smile. "This way!"

The narrow path wound around a corner, and the terrain narrowed. A cliff rose high overhead, and from it fell a narrow, sparkling waterfall. It tumbled first onto a ledge on the cliff, and then spilled to the right, onto another ledge, and then down to a pond in front of them.

Kira slid off Rylan's back with a huff and made her way to a flat boulder near the edge of the water. She plopped down atop it and gazed out over the rippling surface.

"Do you think this is the right way?" Rylan asked as he and Peter made their way to the waterfall.

The cold water splashed over Peter's hand and wrist as he held the canteen under the rushing torrent. He looked up toward the few peaks they could see, but there was nothing bat-like about them. It was just mountains. Mountains and trees, as far as the eye could see. "It's north, isn't it?"

"Maybe we got turned around," Rylan said.

"Hard to get turned around when we don't know where we're going." Peter filled the first canteen, and Sephiri brought over the rest of the containers.

"We don't have much time," Sephiri whispered, her eyes flicking to Kira. "She's struggling."

"One more night," Peter said. "According to that man with the scar, by the day after tomorrow, she'll be dead."

"Peter." Kira waved a listless hand, beckoning him to her.

"Here, I'll help." Mirelle took Peter's place at the waterfall, assisting in filling up the rest of the canteens.

Adrian leaned over the pool and peered into its depths. When Peter approached, he took a few steps further away.

Peter knelt on the flat boulder near the pond's edge. At his side, Kira sat with her knees to her chest, her chin hooked over as she gazed out over the water. Her eyes were glassy, and sweat stuck her blonde hair to her temples.

Peter's stomach turned. The danger was always *real*, but seeing Kira deteriorate made her doom feel inevitable.

Peter shoved the thought down. *She's not doomed—not if we find the city, which we will.* There was no other choice.

"What's up?" Peter asked. "Are you hurting?"

She managed a weak chuckle. "Always. But . . . I've been wanting to say something." She paused while her face screwed up as if gritting through a wave of pain. When the instant passed, she blew out a breath. "I have a bad feeling."

"Don't worry," Peter said. "We're moving in the right direction. We'll get there soon."

She shook her head. "No . . . I—" She stopped, staring across the surface.

"What is it?" Peter asked. "Something in the water?"

"No," Kira said. She waved a design in the air. "The shape of the pond."

Peter stood. The flat boulder sat on the bank of the pond,

and the bank curved around it in a C-shape. The middle was the widest part, and the shape tapered to points on either side of them. Just like—

"A crescent," Kira said. "A crescent moon."

Peter straightened, his eyes growing. "You think . . . ?"

"It could be." She nodded towards the cliff, where the waterfall spilled over the ledges before it splashed into the pool below.

Peter raced back to the others.

"What is it?" Rylan asked.

"Give me a boost," he said. He tugged Rylan to the side of the waterfall. "Sephiri?"

She raised her eyebrows.

"Watch my back?"

A smile grew on her face. "Of course."

Rylan folded his hands together and boosted him up to a narrow ledge. Peter gripped the slippery edge, set his feet on the rock, and scrambled upward. The waterfall spat cold droplets onto his skin as he hauled himself up. He stood above his friends, gazing down at the crescent-shaped pond. Farther up the trail, another pond peeked through the trees, then another past it. He leaned to the side to get a better view of their shapes but then frowned. *I need to get higher.*

He turned back to the cliff and scoped out handholds on the wet cliff face, as far away from the waterfall as he could. He clambered upward. His feet slipped on the rock, but his tight grip kept him from falling. He continued, higher and higher. His arms ached. His legs grew weak and shook. He planted his hands over the top of the cliff and heaved himself over the final ledge. He wheezed and panted, resting on his knees, and leaning into a tree with its roots digging through the rock. After a moment to catch his breath, he stood, holding onto the tree, and leaning toward the edge.

A laugh escaped his throat, and his mouth pulled up at the

side. Far below, three pools lined up in a perfect row. A crescent, a half circle, and a full circle stacked atop each other, like a drawing of the moon's phases.

"We found it," he whispered. "The Pools of the Moon."

23

R enewed with energy, Peter led the group, pushing north. The Cliff of Tears was real. The Pools of the Moon were real. Every clue on the map had proven true. Each step took them closer to the City of Gold. Even their mishaps had brought them closer to the goal. It was like the city *wanted* to be found, like it called to Peter.

It was the kind of mission Peter could see himself going on for the rest of his life. With the army's resources to support him, he could travel all of Terrenor, seeking lost artifacts, ruined cities, and all the pieces of Terrenor's rich history lost to the sands of time. With real funding, and real support—armor, weapons, and maybe even some soldiers at his command, anything was possible!

Sephiri hurried up to walk at Peter's side, snapping him out of his fantasy. "I get we don't want to send them off to their deaths, but I wish those two weren't with us," she whispered. "Weren't they buying time to avoid the Dirteaters? Weren't they meant to go back to Barrentis after the pools?"

Peter checked over his shoulder. Adrian brought up the rear, behind Kira and Rylan. Mirelle walked in the middle with a new determination. After learning about their goal, she seemed as focused as the rest of them.

She fit right in.

"Yeah, I know," Peter said. "We're pretty far from Barrentis, though. I'm not sure either would make it back on their own. I'm a little creeped out by Adrian. At least he's helping with Kira, though."

Sephiri sighed. "I wish I knew what he wanted. It's weird."

"He's probably a doctor or a medic. He sees Kira as his responsibility."

"But she's not. She's *our* responsibility."

"I know." Peter squeezed Sephiri's hand. "She is, and we're going to get what she needs."

Sephiri nodded, then stood straighter. "We know we're on the right path. We need to find the Mountain of the Bat, now."

"What do you think we're looking for?" Rylan called.

Peter glanced behind.

Rylan hiked Kira higher on his back and then craned his neck up toward the peaks. "How will we know?"

"The others were pretty obvious," Peter said. "I bet the mountain will be, too."

"Hope you're right," Rylan muttered.

They trekked onward.

KIRA KEPT her arms wrapped around Rylan's neck as he hiked over the rough terrain. Pain lanced through her body with each of his steps. It was a dull throb, incessant, like the infection grew through her bones. Her sluggish brain drifted in and out of alertness.

Until recently, the poison had been bearable. The wound ached and burned, but keeping it clean and smearing the barkleaf balm had kept the worst of the pain at bay. Even with the poison-induced aches, she could still travel and wasn't useless.

Then the fever started, and with it came exhaustion, shakes, and terrible, ceaseless pain.

I hate being a burden like this, she thought, feeling the jolt of Rylan's steps as he walked. *I can't even drag my weight over the trail.* Her body was breaking down. Each beat of her heart pushed the poison deeper into her system. She could feel it.

She forced a smile and kept a brave face for her friends, not wanting them to know how deep the pain went. How each breath was a struggle. How every night she wondered if she'd wake up the next morning.

As THE MORNING faded into midday, the terrain grew rougher. Gnarled roots wound from tree trunks like veins, cracking through the soil and catching Peter's toes. The path formed a series of long switchbacks, winding up a never-ending hill. He paused to catch his breath.

Behind him, Sephiri sweated buckets—pouring off her face in rivulets. Red-faced, Rylan huffed and puffed with Kira on his back. Mirelle was as spry as ever with her hair tied atop her head, while Adrian looked like he was one strong wind away from falling down the mountain.

"I wish we knew if . . . this was even the . . . right way." Sephiri said around breaths.

Peter nodded, then resumed the uphill slog. A few steps later, his foot caught on an unsteady rock half-buried in the dirt. He grunted, falling forward onto his palms. The rock skittered down the steep hill of the mountain, bouncing over roots and into the muck below. They had climbed high enough that he could see the trail they'd been following, stretching back toward the coast. He even spotted the top of the cliff where the Pools of the Moon lay hidden below.

Is this the right way? He set his hands on his hips and frowned.

"Peter," Rylan said.

Maybe there's another path that leads from the Pools of the Moon —something easier to navigate. He squinted at the cliff in the distance, trying to find the shape of a trail in the dirt, something that would suggest a different path.

"Peter, look."

Two small mountain tops peaked over the hill.

"More mountains," Peter said. "Great."

The map flashed in his mind—the illustration of the peaks. Two spires, like the ones in the drawing. *Could that be . . . ?*

He scrambled up the slope, forgoing the switchbacks. Digging his heels and hands into the earth, he hauled himself straight up the incline, using roots and rocks to help. He climbed higher, keeping his gaze toward the peaks as they rose over the horizon. Rocks tumbled down the slope, pulled loose by his hands. His legs ached as he hauled himself up, higher, higher, until he crested the ridge.

Mountains spread out to the east and the west, jutting towards the sky like teeth. But Peter only had his eyes on one.

Across a valley, a mountain rose ahead of the others. It projected stark against the afternoon sky: two sharp peaks like ears and a flat ridge between them—like a bat's head. Peter's heart leaped into his throat. He grabbed onto a tree trunk, whipped around, and hung off it as he shouted down to his friends. "This is it!" he called. "The Mountain of the Bat!"

"I'm not following your path," Mirelle called back. "Wait!"

Peter kept one hand on the tree trunk, swinging back and forth as he gazed up at the two twin ears peeking over the ridge.

We really made it. Kytalia must be nearby.

He closed his eyes, tipped his face to the sky, and took a

slow, deep breath, letting the smell of wet earth and cool mountain air overtake his senses. He imagined he could even smell Kytalia, too. Something cold, metallic, dusty, promising. It waited for them. It was old, forgotten, left to become nothing more than a myth, but Peter knew it was real. He was about to show all of Palenting—and Commander Isert—that he was right.

Sephiri drew close, wiping her forehead with the back of her hand. "Let's see what's over this hill." The rest of the party followed her.

"Are you okay?" Peter asked Adrian with a raised brow.

"Just fine," he said through heaving breaths, glancing up. "A bit out of shape, it appears."

"Not used to traveling over terrain like this?" Rylan asked.

"Something like that." Adrian adjusted his bag and nodded. "Onward, I suppose."

"Why don't you let me down, Rylan," Kira said. "I can walk a bit."

"Right, so we can crest this hill and you can immediately slip and fall down it?" Rylan joked. "I don't think so."

Peter beamed as the others joined him on the ridge.

"Whoa!" Rylan exclaimed. "We found it!"

The Mountain of the Bat soared across from them. It looked immense. Dark stone and white peaks jutted up against the blue sky rich with puffy clouds. Emerald-dark trees dotted the stone halfway below the peaks and then cascaded down like waves. More mountains surrounded the valley below, dark, jagged, and dense with trees.

"We're almost there," Peter said. "I knew we'd find it. Hang on a bit longer, Kira."

Sephiri squinted toward the structure. "One peak looks shorter than the other. Do you see that?"

"Eroded, probably," Kira said. "Who knows how old that map is?"

Something new caught Peter's eye. Dotted through the valley, rough objects blended into the wilderness. Objects that looked like buildings. Old buildings. There was a square, a smattering of structures around it, and a small lake at the far north side behind the largest one.

Ruins.

"There it is!" Peter shouted. "We made it! Come on!"

He leaped off the ridge, racing down the steep hill with his heart pounding in his chest. His feet dug into the dirt as he ran, which became a skid. He leaned back against the dirt as he half-tumbled into the valley. He nearly crashed into a tree and then tumbled to a stop at the edge of the valley.

"Come on!" he hollered. "Through here!"

His friends' shouts behind him urged him forward. Peter rushed through the trees, shoving aside branches and brush. Birds exploded off branches in a cacophony of titters. He smelled it again in the air—the promise of wealth, of a discovery, of a *future*—

He burst through the tree line, eyes wide and a grin tugging at his face.

The valley was quiet.

The first thing he noticed was the color—or lack of it. There was no gold in sight. No glistening walls. No gleaming gems glinting under the sun. A layer of dust and dirt covered the ruins, with creeping vines winding from their foundations to their soaring pinnacles.

Despite the initial letdown, he refused to feel discouraged.

The ruins spread through the valley, barely larger than the land of Peter's family farm. Collapsing stone buildings stood on either side of Peter, flanking a wide town square paved with cracked and weedy gray stone. Across the square, the buildings seemed larger. Some were several stories tall, with collapsed, rotted wooden beams. The largest of the buildings stood a few stories above the rest. Coated with dirt and vines, the pyramid-shaped structure contained a narrow, steep staircase that led to its peak. From where Peter stood, the stairs seemed to go nowhere. Yet the building had an imposing aura, like it was from another world, planted deep in the Straith Mountains and then forgotten.

"We made it!" Rylan threw a victorious fist in the air as he stumbled down the slope to the edge of the city.

Kira slid off his back. Even though she hadn't done the brutal hiking the rest of them had done, sweat still coated her, and her pallid skin contained splotchy red marks. She wavered on her feet, but then regained her balance and peered around the ruins. "This place looks like no one's touched it in centuries," she said.

Mirelle knelt by the crumbling building closest to them and ran her hand over the edge of the low stone wall. She pulled it back, then dusted it against her clothes.

"All right!" Rylan clapped his hands. "So, where's the gold?"

"I'm sure it's here somewhere," Peter said. "Let's split up and search, all right?"

"Gold?" Adrian looked up from his sketchbook, a light seeming to turn on in his head. "Ah, I see. It all makes sense." He pointed at them. "You seek the lost City of Gold! I hate to break it to you all, but it's just a myth."

"A myth? Where are we now, then?" Peter gestured around. "A lost city!"

"The Straith Mountains are full of these," Adrian said. "People constructed settlements and trading posts throughout the range, but the humid air, the rain, the constant flooding—" He nudged his foot against a large crack in the stone square. "It does things like this, you see? The dirt below is so full of water and mud it disrupts the foundations and breaks the stone. It becomes impossible to keep up, making it dangerous and unlivable. Hence, abandoned."

Something sour twisted in Peter's gut, but he ignored the

sensation. *We followed the map and found all the landmarks—this must be the place.*

"Let's split up," he said. "We'll search the ruins and see if there are any traces of what we're looking for. Adrian, Mirelle, you two wait here for us."

"Wait?" Mirelle balked. "I can help! This is a lot of territory to cover!"

"There's something specific we seek," Kira said. "Trust me."

If this isn't Kytalia, Peter thought, *then we have no way of saving Kira. She only has one day left.*

"I'm fine with that." Adrian sat on one of the low stone walls. With a crumbling crash, it disintegrated beneath him. He hooted as he fell onto the cracked stone beneath him. With a huff, he made himself comfortable on the ground and pulled out his sketchpad.

"I'll look around here," Mirelle muttered. "See if I can find anything."

Peter nodded at his friends. The four of them split up. Freshly motivated, Kira tottered through the nearby low buildings. Rylan explored the west side, and Sephiri the east. Peter crossed the square, heading toward the largest structure. As he approached, it seemed to grow in height, huge and imposing, like someone carved it from the mountain itself.

He approached the base with a hand extended, half-expecting it to react—like the ground might collapse under him if he dared touch it. But when he ran his hand over the stone base of the structure, nothing happened. The stone was cold to the touch and dirty. He pulled off handfuls of weeds and vines and tossed them to the ground. The more detritus he removed, the more stone he uncovered. Just stone. Cold and rough. No glinting gold, no jewels. No carvings that suggested where the city came from or who built it.

Plain stone.

He proceeded up the external steps. The staircase was wide,

but the steps were shallow and steep. He walked on the balls of his feet to keep his balance as he moved up and up and up. Soon his calves burned, and his heart pounded. It was worse than the hiking, more intense, and soon he used his hands, too, to haul himself up the last quarter of the steps.

Eventually, he made it to the top. Free from vines and weeds, lichen encrusted the stone. It was pale green and papery under his feet and crunched when he crossed it. The staircase ended at the flat top of the structure, square stone, with a small stone table. No gold. No jewels. Nothing.

Peter circled the table. He tapped the stones with his toes, looking for something loose or cracked. He shoved at the table, putting his weight into it. He peered at the edges, looking for markings or symbols.

Nothing. It was just a table on a platform.

With hands on his hips, he gazed up at the Mountain of the Bat. It loomed like a ruler looking down on the small table. *Maybe this was something ceremonial,* he thought. *Sacrifices while the mountain looked down.*

A dark lake stretched out on the opposite side of the pyramid. Reflecting the mountain, no motion rippled across the glassy surface.

Peter sighed and returned to poking at stones atop the structure. No trapdoors opened. No secrets were to be found. If there was a healing potion in this city, it was bound to be in the tallest building. Surely there would be a bit of gold, a fancy jewel—*something.*

The others gathered in the square below. "Anything?" he shouted.

His voice echoed through the mountains and off the other buildings.

"Nothing here!" Rylan called. "Rocks and dirt!"

"Rocks and dirt," Sephiri echoed.

Peter made his way back down the pyramid. He met his

friends in the center of the unevenly paved square. "Nothing at all?"

"I got chased by a rat," Kira said. "That's the extent of my excitement."

"I found some old, rusted pots and pans," Sephiri said. "That's it."

"Where even are we, then?" Rylan picked up a random bit of stone from the detritus and hurled it at nothing. "We hiked all the way here! We found the places on the map! If this isn't Kytalia . . ." His words faded.

"Maybe this is it." Kira looked up at the Mountain of the Bat, her somber words heavy in the air. "But maybe this is all there is. Maybe the treasure really is just a myth."

"It's not a myth," Peter said. "We *know* it's not."

The four friends glanced at each other. They had the dagger still—proof that the city existed and a key that would open something. Peter hadn't seen any markings on the surrounding buildings, nothing that even resembled the symbols on the hilt of the dagger or in the painting of King Xilxidor.

"You've made it this far," Mirelle said. "I mean . . . I don't know what you're looking for, but you can't give up now. If the landmarks are real, the city has to be, too. Doesn't it?"

Peter met Mirelle's eyes. She gave him a nod.

Her trust in him coursed through him like a flame. "It has to be here," Peter said. He scanned the ruins like his gaze could uncover something they missed. The symbol of Kytalia had to be there somewhere. Secret doors, hidden passages—things weren't always what they seemed. "Maybe the gold is underground, or there's a door to that pyramid somewhere."

"We must be missing something," Rylan said. "This can't be a dead end." He looked at Kira. "It can't."

Peter nodded. "I saw a lake on the other side of the pyramid. Let's check it out—see if there's something there."

There were nods all around, but no one looked convinced. The possibility of failure weighed on Peter's shoulders. There was a real chance the city contained nothing.

Kira and Rylan led the way across the square, around the vast pyramid, where the lake they had seen from high on the ridge hid behind a small hill. "Oh, it's gorgeous," Kira said as they topped the hill. "I'm desperate to rinse off." She made her way down the backside and stumbled down to the banks of the lake.

Peter sighed. It would be a pleasant break. They'd refill their canteens, wash off the worst of the sweat and dirt, and figure out where to check next. The sun fell low on the horizon; they'd need to find a campsite soon.

A few steps from the lake, the ground under Kira's feet shifted and moved like a wave. She screamed and flailed her arms as she lost her balance, but she didn't fall—it was as if the ground gripped her feet and heaved her to the side like a predator shaking its prey.

"The sand!" Adrian shouted. "It's not safe!"

Peter raced forward without thinking. Time slowed down around him as Source power propelled him. He saw everything in slow motion. Kira's mouth locked open in a scream as her arms grasped at nothing. The dark sand sucked at her feet, pulling her deeper with each breath. It was fast, drawing her in like a whirlpool. Her eyes widened as she reached out toward Peter. He skidded to a stop at the edge of the sand and reached for her.

"Peter!" She reached back. Their fingers touched.

He leaned further over the sand as it pulled her deeper, deeper. Kira lurched forward, and they locked their hands around each other's wrists.

He wrapped his fingers around her, feeling her finger around his wrist. "Hold on!" Source power rushed through him again, electric in his veins as he pulled. Their grip remained intact as he hauled her backward, freeing her from the grip of the sand.

They collapsed into the dirt at the edge, chests heaving. The sand settled back into stillness, looking like nothing more than a normal bank.

"That was close," Kira muttered. "Thank you."

Peter huffed a shocked laugh. He sprawled on the dirt, staring up at the sky and the peaks of the Mountain of the Bat overhead. A third peak stuck up from the new angle, appearing similar to the other two.

"Kira!" Sephiri called from atop the small hill. "Are you okay?"

She waved an arm. "I'm okay!"

"So much for your rinse-off." Peter helped her to her feet, then looped her arm around his shoulder to stagger back up the hill. "Let's regroup on solid ground."

"Wow, you sure are fast," Adrian said with a tilt of his head as he arrived.

Peter froze.

The man kneeled next to the sand and poked at it with a finger. "This mountain must have been volcanic at one time. That sand looks like ash blended with silt. That's what gives that sucking quality. If it's gathered in a deep pit, you'll be hard-pressed to find a way out." He nodded at Kira. "You're lucky."

Peter exhaled and nodded. "We'll keep our distance."

"I need to rest," Kira said. Her knees wobbled as she leaned against Peter. She barely felt heavy at all. Only then did Peter notice how gaunt she appeared. The poison drained her of her vitality, and it seemed to be picking up speed.

They made their way back around into the ruins. Kira sat on the lowest steps of the pyramid with a sigh.

"Should we camp here?" Mirelle asked. She wandered into the square, near the center, and stared into an old well. "Are there more parts of the city we need to look around, or more quicksand to fall into?"

"I still think we're missing something." Peter rubbed his temples. "We have to be."

"How will we know?" Mirelle asked. "Is there something we should be looking for? A marking? A symbol? If there is, then you should—*ah!*"

Her words cut off, and her hand flew to her neck. Her eyes lost focus. She swayed on her feet, then collapsed to the ground.

"Mirelle!" Peter leaped to his feet. The five of them shouted over each other and look around. Adrian hit the ground next, then Kira slumped back against the steps.

"What's happening?" Rylan shouted from Peter's side. "Where are they—" He stammered, swayed, and slumped to the ground.

Peter gasped as he stared. A small red dart stuck in the side of Rylan's neck.

"Peter, move!" Sephiri grasped his arm and hauled him aside just as a dart whizzed past his face. White washed over her eyes as the wind picked up, diverting another dart Peter hadn't seen. *Where are these coming from?*

A dart whistled through the air and hit him in the shoulder.

He took a stumbling step back, then ripped the dart from his shoulder and hurled it to the ground like an offending wasp. The wound stung. Pain radiated from the wound throughout his nervous system. Sephiri called his name, but it sounded like cotton stuffed his ears. His knees gave out. As darkness crept into the corners of his eyes, Sephiri fell. He tried to reach for her, but his arms wouldn't cooperate. He gasped. Pain shot through him, and then darkness took over.

24

Peter's head hurt—a dull, relentless throb, like someone tapped the inside of his skull with a small, sharp hammer. He blinked his eyes open.

To his surprise, he was in the same location. The same hard stairs of the ruins lay beneath him, and overhead, the sun had barely moved. He exhaled hard, and moved to stand, but then found both his hands and feet were bound. *Well, that's not good.* Around him, his friends, including Mirelle and Adrian, were bound in the same way, and all of them remained unconscious.

"He's awake," a man's voice said.

Peter spun. His body shook as he tipped his chin down to find the source. He gasped. *Naldoc!*

The Dirteater sneered at him. His red hair was greasy and matted, and dust smeared his face. Nalva had a wild look in her dark eyes as she rooted through one of the Dirteaters' bags. Esmee looked no better, and the fury in her eyes made her look nothing like the nice girl they'd met around the campfire. Two other young men stood with them.

"Must've gotten a dud dart," Naldoc said. "Check the dose next time."

"I checked them a dozen times," Nalva spat.

Peter would have laughed if their situation weren't so dire. He felt the weakened effect in his body. The Source had worked hard to push the foreign substance through him in the same way that its power healed his wounds and increased his speed.

"We'll start with him," Naldoc said. "He seems to be their leader, anyway. Bring him here."

Esmee grabbed Peter by the front of his shirt and hauled him away from the stairs. Peter staggered forward, still weakened from the effect of the dart. She shoved him to his knees.

"All right, boy." Naldoc stood straight. He rolled his shoulders and cracked his knuckles. "I'll give you one chance to tell me the truth. You're seeking Kytalia, correct?"

Peter swallowed. He tried to glance at his friends, but Esmee gripped his hair and forced him to keep his eyes on Naldoc. Nalva pulled a long dagger from her bag and unsheathed it. It was a mean-looking, narrow blade, with a chipped edge and dark stains at the hilt. She caught Peter's eyes and grinned. Her teeth were as damaged as the blade.

"We are," he said.

"What do you know?"

Peter said nothing.

Naldoc pounded him across the face, a sharp collision of the man's fist against his cheek. The pain crackled through his skull and rang in his ears.

"Is this the city?" he shouted. "Where is the treasure?"

A metallic taste bloomed on Peter's tongue where he'd bitten it.

Rylan's foot twitched where he lay on the stone.

"Search their stuff!" Naldoc shouted.

Peter's breath caught. *The dagger. The map.* "I know where it is!" he called.

Naldoc grinned. "You do, do you?"

The young men stopped before they opened their bags.

"This is it," Peter said. "We're in the ruins of Kytalia. The treasure is here, but it's hidden. I found the first symbol. There's —we have to follow them. They form a trail."

"Show me!" Naldoc said.

Nalva sliced the bonds around his ankles, then sheathed the blade. "Get up! Go!"

Peter clambered to his feet. He walked back to the pyramid steps, trying to keep his arm from shaking. "I found the symbol at the top—just a moment ago. It pointed . . ." *Think, Peter, think.* "To the east. So I need to go look there and find the symbol that will direct me to the next one, and then to the treasure."

"Do it!" Naldoc shouted.

Peter made his way east, his mind turning over. *Just need to stall for time. Once the others are awake, we'll outnumber them.*

He circled the eastern ruins, then made a big show of finding a random marking on the stones—a curved line from a randomly shaped natural crack.

Naldoc grunted and nodded, seeming to accept his expertise.

Peter took his time shuffling to the western side of the ruins to continue the hunt. The others still looked knocked out as he passed, but he thought he noticed another twitch from Rylan. When he arrived at the building on the western side, he creeped along, peering at cracks and taking his time.

"Hurry it up!" Naldoc said. "You said you knew what you were doing."

"I do, I do," Peter insisted. "I just have to find this symbol." Moments later, he made a show of finding the next sign. "Here! It's pointing north!"

"Toward that tall structure?" Esmee asked. "We were just there!"

"Sure, but there's—there's, uh, a pattern to these things," Peter said. "Find them in order, and then there will be, um, a certain number to get, and, um, the pyramid should open, and then—"

"You're lying!" Naldoc kicked the back of Peter's knees.

Peter stumbled forward. He caught himself with his bound hands, grimacing as the pebbles bit into his palms.

"You're making this up!"

"I'm not! I'll show you." He scrambled to his feet and whirled to face them.

Nalva unsheathed her chipped blade again and brandished it at him. "No more games, Peter. We're going to search your bags until we find that dagger of yours, and then we're going to pick off your friends one by one until you tell us what you *really* know."

The blade gleamed in the sunlight.

I won't let them get the dagger. I won't let them hurt anyone else.

Peter inhaled, then zipped forward, quick as a lightning bolt, and slashed his bonds against the blade. He darted back into place, then grinned at the three of them, hands free.

"How did you do that?" Esmee asked.

Naldoc and Nalva stared at him with twin wide-eyed stares.

"Oops," Peter said with a smirk.

"Get him!" Naldoc bellowed.

Peter took off running. He let the Source flow through him —just enough to keep him just out of reach of his chasers. He flew over the uneven terrain, dodging rubble as he went. Naldoc roared in anger, steps behind.

An idea bubbled into his mind.

Then he grinned.

He scrambled up the hill, cresting it quickly. The Dirteaters stumbled behind him. Before they could ascend, he skidded down the hill and then ran to the far side of the dark, sucking sand. He stayed close at the edge, the sand licking at the edges of his feet. The pit widened, and he picked up speed, keeping to the edge until it ended when the lake curved inward. He stood on a narrow strip of earth, toes at the edge of the sand.

Naldoc, Nalva, and Esmee stumbled down the hill. "How did he get over there so fast?"

"You want the treasure? You'll have to get me!" Peter held his breath, waiting to see if they would take the bait.

Without hesitation, the three Dirteaters raced onto the sand.

They made it a few steps, into the center of the pit, just as Kira had. The dark sand sucked at their ankles.

"Gah!" Esmee shouted. "What's happening?"

"Keep moving!" Naldoc wrestled one foot out of the sand, and then another. He lifted his knees high and grimaced.

"Naldoc?" Nalva stumbled forward. The sand climbed up to her knees, and she shrieked in terror as she sank deeper. Naldoc turned to face her, his face painted white. He lunged for Nalva, moving through the sand like thick mud. He grasped her forearm. The sand climbed to his thighs, then his waist. Esmee shrieked and fought toward the shore, but the sand was thick and sticky around her—she was trapped.

The three of them thrashed in the quicksand until it was up to their chests. They tried to swim, arms flailing, but it was impossible. The sand overtook them.

The screams that echoed through the mountains went silent, punctuated by the disturbing gurgle of mud.

Peter stared at the dark sand, half-expecting a hand to shoot back out. None did. His heart pounded. There was only silence. He let out a heavy breath, then his mind turned to his friends.

With the pyramid in his sights, Peter raced back around the sandpit, giving it a wider berth than before. He made his way back up the hill and over it, to the cracked stone of the square.

The two teenage young men had their swords drawn. They stared with wide eyes at Peter as he stalked back toward the square alone. Their weapons quivered, raised in their trembling hands.

Peter darted forward with his Source power and snatched both swords, taking one in each hand. He stood in front of them and held both swords out. "Do you want to fight?"

"I'm awake," Rylan mumbled. He pushed himself onto one elbow. "I can fight." He flopped back onto his side and fell back asleep.

The two young men glanced at each other, pale-faced. "I never wanted to come out here anyway," one of them muttered. They both glanced at each other, then took off running away from the ruins, heading south without looking back.

Peter flopped down on the stone pavers and raked his hand through his sweaty hair.

Now what?

Rylan began to snore.

BY THE TIME everyone had roused from the drugs, the sun was gone, and darkness was nearly complete. Peter sat up and rubbed his temples. "Guys?" he asked. "Is everyone okay?"

The sound of his voice rustled Kira into wakefulness. She groaned and lifted herself onto her good elbow. Her face was flushed, and sweat beaded on her forehead. "What happened?"

"Dirteaters followed us," Peter said.

Sephiri stirred. The aftereffects of the darts didn't seem to have any ill repercussions besides grogginess and a mild headache. Peter considered them lucky. Even Kira seemed to be no worse than she had been earlier that day.

"Dirteaters? Again?" Rylan cringed as he sat up. "What happened to them?"

"Same thing that almost happened to Kira."

"The sand?" Sephiri's eyes widened.

Peter nodded. "Swallowed them right up. Naldoc, Nalva, and Esmee—sorry Rylan."

Rylan scoffed. "Good riddance! I'm over her."

"Two young guys I didn't recognize ran off, scared. I don't think they'll bother us anymore."

"What now?" Mirelle asked. "If this isn't Kytalia, where do we find it?"

"There are more resources in Barrentis," Adrian said. "It might serve you well to find a cartographer who can provide help. Perhaps someone in Barrentis knows what this place here is. And your friend here needs a proper doctor."

"I'm fine," Kira said.

The gash oozed through the bandage. The wraps needed to be changed more and more frequently, and the pain showed on her face when she moved the arm at all. *One more day. She'd be dead before we made it halfway there.*

"We can't give up." Peter heard the desperation in his voice. "We're close. I know it!"

"But this city here is where Kytalia is supposed to be," Rylan said.

Kira shook her head. "It was too easy to find."

Everyone's gaze shifted to her. "What do you mean?" Sephiri asked.

"It doesn't fit the myth. King Xilxidor *hid* the city. It wouldn't be here, over a hill where anyone could find it. There's nothing here. People have ransacked this place over the years. I bet it was an outpost for the army or something. Remember that weird part of the myth—that 'only the snakes' could find the City of Gold?"

"Snakes?" Adrian asked. "What do you mean?"

"There are all kinds of myths," Kira said, dismissing his question.

Adrian tilted his head.

"We must've missed something," she said, attention back on

her friends. "It's not that Kytalia isn't real. We're just in the wrong place. We need to keep looking."

Faint panzil yelps sang through the air, echoing off the mountains and leaving no clue where they came from.

Peter stood, hand on the hilt of his sword. He spun, but nothing moved except the faint rustle of leaves. He glanced up, noting the dark sky. "We'll keep looking. At first light, we'll tear this place up. We'll search all day until we find it. For now, since we can't see anything, we should rest. I suggest we spend the night by the lake—close to the water."

The crew nodded.

"As long as we stay far away from that sand," Rylan said.

They gathered their gear and made their way down the hill to the lake, circling to get to the far side where the banks were rocky instead of sandy. Hills rolled through the surrounding area, filled with trees and denser vegetation. They found a flat area to make camp, nestled in the trees, and Peter gathered wood to build a fire.

Rylan dropped the bags he carried with a groan and stretched his arms overhead. "I'm going to rinse off in the lake. The cold will be good for me." He rolled his shoulders, then cringed.

He must hurt from carrying her, Peter realized. *Even with the Source, we're not invincible.*

"Kira?" Rylan pointed toward the lake. "You wanted to rinse off. Do you want help walking down?"

She shook her head and offered a mirthless laugh. "I'll pass. I find myself less motivated to be near the lake than I was before."

Minutes later, a fire roared to life. Peter sighed, noticing the aches and soreness in his limbs. The journey wore on all of them. He pulled a log close to the fire, then waved Kira over. "Here, I'll change your bandage."

She nodded and joined him with the now-familiar supplies

in her lap. The bandage on her shoulder soaked through with blood and pus, and it smelled foul, like a rotting corpse. He peeled it off and tossed it into the fire. Kira exhaled. "How's it look?"

The once-shallow gash had deepened. Edges appeared wider, as if the wound chewed away at her flesh. The surrounding skin was red and swollen to her elbow, and thick, mucus-like pus oozed from the edges. Peter tried not to grimace as he wiped the worst of the grime from around the wound. Kira hissed at his touch.

"Is it that bad?" Peter asked.

She nodded and cringed. "Getting worse. Which, I guess, is to be expected." She pushed strands of sweaty blonde hair off her forehead. "It'd be much, much worse if Rylan hadn't been my pack mule, though."

"Knew he was good for something." Peter chuckled, smearing balm on a fresh bandage, and then applied it over the gash. "Now, all we have to do is figure out where those snakes are hiding, and we'll find the city."

She huffed a laugh. "I hope I'm right about that." She nodded toward the darkening silhouette of the pyramid. "If this old city is it—"

"I think you're right," Peter said firmly. "It doesn't match the story. We're missing something."

"I'll figure it out in the morning." Kira gazed into the fire. "I just need some rest. I'll be sharper tomorrow."

Peter finished bandaging her arm, then squeezed her hand. "We'll figure it out together. We'll find the city."

She nodded, but her eyes didn't agree. There was nothing Peter could say to convince her, though—not when the poison already stampeded through her system.

"Whew!" Rylan called as he rounded a boulder and clambered back up through the trees to their campsite. "There's a great bathing pool down there. *And* it's lined by rock, so no quicksand." He shook his hair out like a dog, then plopped down by the fire. He looked alert, and he certainly smelled better.

"That sounds like a good idea. I'm going to clean up, too," Mirelle said. She had just finished clearing out an area for their bedrolls. She stood with shadows of exhaustion ringing her eyes. After flashing a smile at Peter, she headed to the outcropping of boulders at the edge of the lake.

The rest gathered by the fire, checking their bags to put together whatever small dinner they could manage.

Adrian closed his notebook, set it aside, and then headed toward the lake.

"Where are you going?" Peter asked.

"Nature calls," Adrian replied over his shoulder. "I'll be right back."

Sephiri glanced at Kira, and then they both turned to Peter. Kira raised her eyebrows and nodded in the direction that Adrian had gone.

"What?" Peter whispered.

"I think he's looking for something," she replied. "We should check it out."

"Really?" Peter balked. The man *had* been strange. Maybe it was a good idea to keep a closer eye on him. Peter stood and followed.

After passing a few trees, the lake came into view. The glassy surface of the dark water reflected the pale moon. Boulders surrounding the small bathing pool concealed it from Peter's direction, casting shadows on the shore.

Where did Adrian go? He turned in each direction, but the man was nowhere to be seen. The strange quiet of the wilderness, combined with the cool night air, made the hair on Peter's nape stand on end.

He crept closer to the boulders, where a small gap revealed the moonlit bathing pool. Facing away and mostly submerged,

Mirelle held her bare arm along the surface of the water, scrubbing at it with her other palm. Peter's heart skipped as she pulled her brown hair over her shoulder, exposing the pale skin of her upper back. His face flushed with heat, and he turned away, trying to stomp out the fluttering butterflies in his stomach.

Adrian wasn't there. He must've gone in the other direction. Peter shook his head. *Why am I following him like this? The stress is making me paranoid.*

A stick cracked underfoot somewhere in the darkness. Peter froze, straining to hear another sound. Was it Adrian, or was it a panzil? He stepped closer to the boulder.

Mirelle hummed in the pool.

Another crunch of twigs sounded along with a scraping noise. A shadow fell over the bathing pool as a man climbed atop the boulder. A knife in his hand glinted in the moonlight.

"Adrian!" Peter shouted. "What are you doing?"

Mirelle squawked in surprise. She wrapped her arms around herself and stumbled into the water.

Adrian's head jerked toward Peter. He held the knife, then leaped into the pool, splashing water in all directions. Mirelle shrieked and fell backward, her brown eyes wide as she looked up at Adrian's looming figure. He lifted the knife—an unfamiliar blade, as long as a panzil's fang, shiny like it'd been well cared for. His grip looked steady.

"No!" Peter squeezed through the gap in the boulders and then hurtled himself into the water. He slammed his shoulder into Adrian, and they both splashed into the water in a heap of limbs. "Move, Mirelle!" he sputtered through a mouth full of water. "Get out of here!"

Adrian shouted, then drove his knee into Peter's stomach, knocking the wind out of him. He gasped. Adrian wrestled himself to his feet, but then Peter slammed his fist into the man's forearm. Adrian grunted, and the knife fell from his hand

and into the pool. His face creased, but before he could react, Peter lunged again. He wrapped his arms around Adrian's waist and drove them both under the surface.

They struggled against each other, Peter's speed against Adrian's strength, throwing elbows and knees as they wrestled in the water. Peter only needed to gain the upper hand for a moment. Soon the others would be there, drawn by the commotion. They'd overpower him and figure out what he was doing there.

Peter's feet found purchase, and both their heads lifted out of the water. Adrian landed a punch on Peter's ribs, then followed it with another sharp hit on his chin. Peter's teeth clacked, and blood pooled in his mouth.

"What do you want?" Peter snarled, shoving at Adrian's face.

Adrian said nothing. He grunted and leaned his weight forward, pressing Peter down.

Water covered Peter, flooding his nostrils and stinging. His lungs clenched in terror. He lurched upward and took a gasping breath. Adrian grabbed his hair and hurled him to the side. Peter stumbled until his head cracked against the rocky banks of the bathing pool. His vision turned blurry, and then dark at the edges.

"Wait," he groaned, but Adrian was already gone. The rhythmic sound of splashing faded in the distance as Peter struggled to open his eyes.

25

"Peter! Peter, are you all right?"

Sephiri's voice sounded far away, ringing down from a great height.

"Peter, wake up!"

He groaned, then dragged his eyes open. Sephiri's face filled his field of vision. Her dark hair was backlit by the moon, still high overhead, giving her a glowing look. A small furrow marked her brow, and even in the darkness, Peter could see the small blemishes on her skin and along her hairline.

Pretty, Peter thought, dazed.

"Get him out of the water," Kira said.

Rylan's hands materialized under his shoulders, heaving him up and hauling him onto the rocky banks. Only then did Peter notice the cold water still lapping at his feet, and how his clothes soaked through. He grimaced and sat up.

A terrified thought ran through his head. "Mirelle? Is she okay?"

"I'm fine." Mirelle's voice wavered. Her face was pallid and her eyes wide. "What about you?"

"Fine," Peter said. "Just sick of getting knocked out." His

head ached, a low thrum and not a ceaseless pounding. The Source did its work, healing the bruises and the bumps from his tousle with Adrian.

Adrian, he thought with a jolt.

"Where is he?" Peter clambered to his feet, steadied by Rylan and Sephiri. "Where'd he go?"

"Mirelle said he attacked her," Rylan said. "Why would he do that? What did he want?"

"He didn't say anything," Peter said. "Just lunged at Mirelle like an animal. And then me. Did he return to the campsite?"

"No," Sephiri said. "We heard the shouts, then Mirelle called for us."

"How long was I out?"

"Only a minute."

Peter craned his neck. He looked toward the jungle, then back at the ruins. *He could be hiding in the ruins or heading back to Barrentis . . .*

"There!" Kira pointed to the far side of the lake. "That's him!"

Peter remembered the splashing. Adrian hadn't run. He'd swam.

Across the lake, Adrian climbed out of the water and onto the far bank, where he ran into the dense vegetation.

"Wait here," Peter said. He stumbled out of Rylan and Sephiri's hold. "I'll get him."

"Peter, are you sure you're okay?"

He wasn't sure. His head hurt, his body ached, and his vision was fuzzy around the edges. But he wouldn't let Adrian get away—not when they'd been nothing but kind to him and they didn't know his motivations. They didn't have time to worry about being stalked.

No more loose ends.

He took a breath and focused on the Source in the center of his chest. It glowed with each beat of his heart, a resting, idle power. He let the power flow from his chest down his arms, then his legs, all the way to the soles of his feet. Even as his friends still protested, he took off running.

Peter sprinted around the lake. His legs pounded the ground. Wind blasted against his face from the speed. The world blurred past him as he ran.

Moments later, he made it to the other side of the lake, where dense and thorny vegetation surrounded the bank. Thick vines covered the trees, and bushes and ferns grew as tall as him. He paced the edge of the lake until he spotted recently crushed plants.

Peter followed the sparse path, shoving his way through the grasping vegetation. Thorns caught on his trousers and slashed at his forearms. Trees grew close together, and vines hung like thick snakes from the branches. He grunted and pushed further. He followed the trail of trampled undergrowth deeper into the vegetation. Adrian pushed through here. It looked like he'd fallen once or twice. Peter followed the trail, footsteps and blood on the thorns reaching for him.

The further he went, the fewer signs he saw. The plants were so dense around him, swallowing him whole. Brambles clung to his legs as he pushed through, shoving vines out of his face.

His desperate run slowed to a jog. The trail was gone. There was no sign of Adrian.

Peter paused to catch his breath. He bent over and placed his hands on his knees. His lungs heaved to bring oxygen to his body. The Source felt depleted and weak. He needed rest.

The surrounding jungle was still and quiet. Small creatures rustled in the undergrowth, but he heard nothing larger than a rat. His arms stung from the thorns, and his head still ached from where he'd slammed into the rocks. The older man was gone, as if the mountains had swallowed him up.

Peter laced his hands together behind his head and tipped his head toward the sky, releasing a groan.

Then he saw it, glowing in the moonlight.

The third mountain peak—narrower than the other two on the Mountain of the Bat. It was sharp and jagged, reaching to the sky like a knife's blade. It was the same spire he'd seen by the lake, but from his new angle, it looked different.

It lined up with the peak in the center. The left peak was narrower and slightly taller, and had a jagged, smaller peak jutting out from the side.

He thought about the map.

The drawing wasn't a rough representation—it was exact. On the map, the spire on the right was narrower, with a jagged, smaller peak jutting from its right side. It wasn't drawn in a shaky hand. It was drawn in an *exact* hand. What Peter had thought were wobbly lines were accurate illustrations of the peak's jaggedness.

"We were on the wrong side of the mountain," Peter whispered. His eyes widened. "We were on the wrong side of the mountain!"

He rushed back to camp, dodging trees and vines, moving as quickly as he could without using his supplemental power. He made it back to the lake, skirted the edge, then arrived at the campsite tucked into the trees. The fire roared while Rylan tended a pot of stew. Sephiri and Mirelle sat on opposite sides of the fire. A blanket wrapped around Mirelle, her hair still wet from the bathing pool. The bedrolls were laid out, and Kira sat on hers, thumbing through Adrian's notebook.

Sephiri perked up when Peter passed through the trees. "Peter! You look terrible! What happened? Did you find him?"

Peter shook his head. "He got away. Disappeared." Groans echoed around the fire, but a smile pulled at Peter's face. "But I got something better."

"Better?" Sephiri stood. "You should get out of those wet clothes. You don't want to catch a cold."

Peter struggled out of his wet shirt and hung it over a makeshift clothesline strung between two trees, where Mirelle's clothes hung as well. "I figured out what we're missing," he said as he pulled on dry, clean-ish items from his pack.

"What?" Kira asked. "To find the city?"

Peter nodded, grinning as he approached the fire. He shook out his wet hair and laid his boots by the fire. "You know the illustration on the map."

"Of course."

"It's not a rough drawing. It's exact. I saw the other bat ear—the jagged one."

"There's another one?" Rylan asked. "What do you mean? Is this not the right mountain?"

"Not exactly. We're at the right mountain, just facing the wrong way." Peter grinned.

"What are you talking about?" Mirelle asked. "You have a map?"

Sephiri's eyes widened. "The city's on the other side of the mountain."

"Exactly!" Peter said. "We just need to get to the other side. Then we should be able to find Kytalia."

"That's amazing!" Rylan shouted, leaping to his feet. "We're almost there! Let's get moving!"

"How about we eat, first," Peter said, calming Rylan's eagerness. "And we could afford an hour or so of sleep. It won't be easy to travel through the night, but we can do it. Some food and a bit of rest will help us with the long day ahead."

"Sounds like a plan." Kira lay on her bedroll, facing the fire. Her face was still flushed with fever, and her body trembled. The trembles made her face contort with pain, but she made no complaints.

The nerve pain, Peter thought. *Not much time left.*

He settled by the fire, and Sephiri spooned out a bowl of stew for him, made from the rest of their garront meat.

"I should head back to Barrentis," Mirelle said.

Peter jerked his head up from his stew. "What? Why?"

"Right now?" Rylan asked. "In the middle of the night? You'll get lost!"

Mirelle sat on a log by the fire, with a thin blanket around her shoulders and a bowl of stew balanced on her knees. She kept her gaze low, focused on the heart of the fire, and her mouth turned down in a small frown. "No sign of Adrian, huh?"

Peter shook his head. "It was like the jungle swallowed him."

"It's my fault. He came after me." She rubbed her forearm under the blanket, at the site of her old brand. "The Dirteaters may have been following you, but the Norivonne are always following me. He was probably with them and followed us to get to me."

"He's definitely not who he said he was." Kira held up the journal. "He wasn't making notes of the wildlife and the plants. He was mapping our route. He wasn't a medic who had nothing better to do. He was interested in where we're going."

"If the Norivonne know Kytalia is real, they'll want a piece," Mirelle said. "Maybe he thought we came to a dead end, and he was going to kill me to make up for not finding the city."

"If that's the case, then you definitely can't leave tonight. He could still be out looking for you." Peter took a sip of the stew. The warmth traveled down into his bones. "It's safer to stick with us. We'll protect each other."

Mirelle seemed to draw even further into herself. "You're sure?"

"We've come this far," Peter said. "And we're almost there. One more day of trekking and we'll be there."

"You all get some sleep," Rylan said. "I'll stay on guard and wake you in an hour."

Peter nodded gratefully. He squeezed Mirelle's shoulder as he made his way to his bedroll.

He hadn't been wrong when he'd felt the city calling him. It *was* close. Close enough to smell it in the air, the scent of gold—the scent of his future.

26

P eter felt like he had just fallen asleep when Rylan's hand jostled him.

"Wake up," Rylan said. "We need to move."

Peter pressed his eyes together, then opened them again. The heaviness remained.

The group doused the remnants of the fire and left anything not essential at the campsite. Peter insisted they travel light and fast, hoping he was right about the distance not being far.

Kira deteriorated rapidly. Her fever raged, her skin hot to the touch. Her cheeks looked sunken, and her eyes held a glassy, distant look. She drifted in and out of coherency as the group scrambled to leave. It would be her last day unless they could find the city.

"Let's move," Peter said.

The trek began. Peter led the way around the lake with a torch to light the way. Rylan carried Kira on his back, while Peter, Sephiri, and Mirelle carried the gear they brought. Once they arrived at the dense vegetation, Peter drew his sword and handed the torch to Sephiri. She held the light as Peter hacked his way through the foliage.

It was tough going, and progress was slow. Thorns reached for them. Vines grabbed their arms, and the wet earth sucked at their feet. Sweat built on the back of Peter's neck. The deeper they went into the jungle, the more humid it became. The air grew thick, and the darkness rustled in the branches and underfoot.

"How far do we have to go?" Rylan asked through heaving breaths.

"I don't know," Peter grunted. "Just gotta get around to the other side. Keep moving."

A drizzle fell from the sky. Peter tipped his face up toward the sky. A dark cloud rolled across the full moon as a distant roll of thunder sounded.

"Great," Rylan muttered.

Sephiri shifted the torch to her other hand. "Rain means no panzils."

"And maybe no light if it rains hard enough. You good back there, Kira?" Rylan hiked her higher on his back.

"Mm-hmm," Kira murmured.

Peter didn't look back. He couldn't spare any time to worry about Kira—the best thing he could do for her was move faster.

After hours of journeying through the dense foliage, the jungle thinned, and the drizzling rain cleared. Peter stuck close to the steep edge of the mountain as the valley shrank. It narrowed, as if the mountains creeped closer to each other. The vegetation grew lower, sparser, and the jungle melted away. His feet slid on the muddy ground, threatening his balance. The surrounding walls grew steep and rocky.

"We made it," Peter said. "You see?"

They stood in a narrow canyon between two mountains. The slope was rough and overgrown with thick, crawling ivy. Peaks loomed high overhead. The two bat ears matched the map exactly, the right one narrower with an extra peak, the left wider and rounded.

"Is that a cave?" Mirelle pointed. "Can you see?"

The storm cloud drifted to the side, enough to allow the moonlight to shine down on the Mountain of the Bat. The mouth of a cave yawned wide, with visible stalactites hanging like teeth.

"Whoa," Peter said. "This must be it."

"Yes!" Rylan shouted. "We did it! We made it!"

His voice boomed through the ravine, bouncing up and echoing through the night. The sound was like a thunderclap in the quiet evening; Peter whirled on him and pressed his finger to his lips. Rylan grimaced in apology.

Something rustled high overhead. A series of loud, high-pitched squeaks rang out, just a few, then a dozen, then so many the sounds folded over each other into a cacophony. A cloud of bats coursed out of the cave overhead and then dove into the ravine like a tidal wave.

Peter squawked as the bats slammed into them. Their bodies crashed into his, their wings beating against his skin and hair, and their squeaking cries ringing in his ears. The friends knocked into each other, and all of them flailed to get the animals out of their hair and clothes as the bats rushed by. Fear swooped through Peter as he screwed his eyes shut, knelt into a ball, and covered the back of his neck. The bats pelted him like hail.

Then, the wind picked up. It swirled around his ankles and lifted the hem of his shirt. He squinted his eyes open. The dust around his feet hovered, caught in the wind's movement. Their torch snuffed, and darkness grew.

A tremendous gust of air howled through the ravine like a tornado, then shoved Peter into the dirt. Wind caught the bats and sent them careening backward and upwards, like leaves in a tornado, spiraling up into the night sky. The bats flapped around high overhead. They gathered into a cloud above and took off toward the trees in the opposite direction.

Peter uncovered the back of his neck and stood. He looked around, blinking.

Mirelle looked especially windswept. Her brown hair formed a wild mess around her face, and her mouth gaped. "What . . . was . . . that?" she whispered.

Sephiri stood with both hands outstretched. Her eyes blazed pure white, and her hair floated like she was underwater. The dust settled. The bats were gone.

Mirelle stared. "What's she doing?"

The white sheen swirled and then dissipated from Sephiri's eyes. She stumbled to the side and leaned against the rock wall. Peter rushed to her side and gripped her shoulder. "Seph, you okay?"

She blinked her dark eyes open. Her gaze lingered on Peter, and her cheeks flushed. "Yeah. Yeah, I'm okay."

"How did you do that?" Mirelle asked, still slack-jawed. "You blew them all away!"

"Whoa," Rylan said, staring ahead. "Guys, you're going to want to see this."

The wind hadn't just blown away the bats. It stripped the mountainside of its vines, vegetation, and lichen, leaving the bare textured rock behind. Rylan stood against the wall of the ravine, gazing up with his hand on the rock. A narrow, shallow staircase carved into the mountainside, leading to a narrow ledge then all the way to the mouth of the cave.

Peter grabbed the torch where it had fallen, then re-lit it with a flint starter. The flame burst into existence, and orange light flickered through the darkness of the ravine. The light bounced off the angles of Mirelle's face, framed the width of Rylan's shoulders, and enhanced the deep shadows under Kira's eyes. Peter approached the staircase, eyes wide.

When Rylan stepped aside, Peter saw it. A symbol—carved into the rock where Rylan's hand had been.

A circle. The stacked rectangles.

Kytalia.

"This is it," Peter whispered. He traced the circle. "This is the way."

"We made it," Sephiri whispered.

Peter's nerves tingled in anticipation. He held the torch high. "You all wait here. I'll see what's on the ledge."

He ascended the stairs, though it was more like climbing a ladder. With the torch held sideways in his mouth, he moved hand over hand, foot over foot, gripping the narrow edges of the stairs like he did the tiny features on the bare rock when he climbed for fun in Palenting. His hand reached the ledge. He hauled himself up onto it until he froze at the sound of a quiet hiss.

He took the torch with his free hand and extended it.

The light cast shadows over the featured rock. The cliff and the ledge created a small, covered area, like a shallow alcove, and the light gleamed in dozens of tiny, dark eyes.

Snakes.

Their slender bodies coiled over each other, knotted in piles of twisted serpents. A snake slithered to the side. Its tongue flicked in the air.

Peter kept still. They weren't just any snakes—they were vipers, with green-and-black checkered backs. Tartis vipers.

A viper slithered out from the alcove onto the ledge. It followed the edge to where a long, narrow crack split the rock. It slipped inside and disappeared.

To climb the stairs, they'd have to pass dozens of deadly vipers—hissing, rattling, and showing their fangs in threat.

He slowly retreated down the stairs.

"What is it?" Rylan asked. "You look pale. What did you see?"

"Tartis vipers," Peter breathed. "Loads of them. They're blocking the stairs."

Rylan tensed.

"Snakes," Kira murmured.

"Huh?" Peter turned to face her.

Kira slumped against the mountainside, looking up the stairs. Her brow furrowed. She wrung her hands, then pushed her sweaty hair off her forehead. "Snakes," she murmured again. "Are the snakes going up?"

"Up?" Peter asked. "Up the stairs, to the cave? No, they're not."

"If they're not going up, don't go up." Her voice strained to fill the air, her words distant. "Follow the snakes."

Peter's eyes widened. *Only the snakes can find the city now.* "There's a crack in the mountain. I saw one enter it."

Kira nodded. "That's where we should go."

"I think we're forgetting how deadly these things are," Rylan said. "How exactly are we supposed to keep ourselves from getting killed?"

"Tartis vipers don't like sudden moves," Mirelle said. "If you move slowly and don't surprise them, they'll leave you alone."

"You're sure about that?" Rylan asked.

She shrugged. "I've run into them here and there. They only strike if they feel threatened. If you mind your business, they mind theirs."

Kira gasped. She folded her hands over her belly and slumped, shoulders curled forward. A shudder wracked her body.

Rylan knelt beside her, his hands hovering in the air as she grimaced in pain.

"I'm okay," she mumbled. "It'll pass."

"What other choice do we have?" Peter returned to the stairs. "I'll go first."

"Peter," Sephiri said. "I'm not so sure about this."

"What else can we do?" Peter brandished the torch at the symbol carved into the rock. "This is the way we have to go. It's the path we've searched for this whole time. And Kira—" He stopped himself.

Kira laughed, but there was no humor in it. It devolved into a cough. "What about me?"

"When we get to the city, we'll fix all this. Let's go. It's just snakes."

"Just snakes," Rylan muttered. "*Just* snakes."

Peter crept back up the stairs. At the ledge, he lifted the torch. The flame was bright against the gray sky that lightened with the threat of dawn. The snakes hissed and rattled, pulled back into their alcove. "Don't mind us," Peter said in his most soothing voice. "We'll just be moving around you."

He stepped onto the ledge, staying as close to the edge as possible, so his heels hung off. Mirelle came next, then Sephiri. They crept down the ledge, eyes on the snakes.

"Hold," Mirelle whispered as a viper slithered out of the alcove.

Rylan paused where he was on the stairs, his hands on Kira's waist, guiding her up.

The serpent was silent—no hissing, no rattling. It slithered up to Peter and raised its small head. The torchlight made its small eyes gleam like gems.

Peter went still. His breath froze in his lungs. *Don't startle it. Don't move.*

The snake swayed its small head, side-to-side, like it was considering him. Its tongue flicked out of its mouth.

Inhale. Exhale.

The snake slithered over his foot. Even through his boot, he felt the weight of the snake's body and its small muscles rippling. When it slid off his foot, the serpent traveled the ledge to the crack in the mountain. It disappeared inside the narrow gap.

Peter exhaled, the tension in his shoulders easing.

"That must be the way," Sephiri whispered.

Mirelle flashed a nervous grin. "Ready to move?"

"Ready as I'll ever be." Peter's heart still pounded from the harrowing moment.

He shuffled down the ledge, with the torch low to light the vipers. As Mirelle had predicted, none of the snakes lunged at them. Their beady eyes stayed focused on the five humans, but the animals remained in their alcove.

Peter creeped down the ledge until he reached the gap that ran up the mountain's face. It wasn't just a crack, though. It was a chimney—wide enough for Peter to step inside, sideways, at least.

From where he stood, the crack looked endless. It was pitch black inside, like tar, like he would step through a veil into another world. He would be surrounded by darkness, pressed in by the rock on all sides, not knowing where it might lead.

He swallowed.

"This is where the snakes went," Peter said.

"You're kidding me." Rylan arrived on the ledge. "Don't tell me we're supposed to go in there."

"Are you sure we shouldn't go up the stairs?" Sephiri pointed up toward the large cave above them. "Wouldn't that make more sense?"

"Why else would the map say to follow the snakes?" Peter asked. "I know climbing through this crack doesn't seem to make sense, but is crawling into a cave any better?"

Sephiri said nothing.

"It's just . . . I know this is the right way."

I can feel it. How could he explain it to the others? *We have to follow the map and the clues, and the snakes are going this way.*

"But it won't be fun."

Rylan snorted. "Understatement. I don't even know if I'm going to fit."

"You are. We've done stuff like this before. It'll be a piece of cake."

They'd squeezed into strange places in their rock climbing, and run through the tunnel in the panzil's den, but nothing like this. Above them, the sky was gray with oncoming dawn, but none of the growing light made it into the tunnel. There was no light at the other end—assuming there even was another end.

Peter extinguished the torch. There was no space to carry it, and nowhere for the smoke to go—the flame would burn up the oxygen. His eyes adjusted to the darkness but still saw nothing. The snakes remained silent, tucked out of sight.

The tunnel was deep and dark. Were there more vipers in there waiting to strike if he stepped on them? What if it narrowed too much? What if the passage ended? What if they ended up trapped deep in the Straiths, swallowed by the mountains just like the City of Gold had been?

Peter inhaled, then blew out his breath to calm his fears. "Let's go."

He stepped closer to the crack, turned sideways, then slipped inside.

The mountain pressed against his back. He placed his hands against the rock in front of him. Then he shuffled his way into the tunnel. "Move slowly," he whispered behind him. "One at a time."

"Oh, I hate this," Mirelle muttered.

Darkness fell on Peter like a weight. The rock pressed in from both sides, rough against his back and hard against his palms as he scooted forward. He could only manage small breaths. Oxygen felt thin in his lungs. He heard nothing but his heartbeat pounding like a drum in his ears. The mountain was enormous, pushing at him from every side, sucking him deeper into its depths. He felt swallowed. Erased.

Another step. Another. Was the tunnel growing narrower?

He couldn't turn his head to look behind. He could only move forward.

Anxiety crawled into his throat, squirming like the vipers had across his foot.

Another step. He shuffled his feet, hoping he wouldn't hit a snake. His head bumped the ceiling—when had it lowered? He bent his knees what little they could and sidled farther. Rock dragged against his back, threatening to tear his clothes.

How long did it take? He didn't know. Never had he heard such deep silence or felt such heavy darkness. He imagined himself in the center of the mountain. Its weight loomed over him, threatening to crush him, swallow him.

Just keep moving.

His back ached. His legs screamed from their awkward angle. The ceiling lowered again, forcing him to bend his knees lower. The gap tightened. His breath grew shallower.

This is it, he thought. *We will die here.*

Maybe the stairs were right. Maybe it was that simple. Maybe I led them into this tunnel for no good reason. He wanted to call out to his friends behind him to make sure they were alive, to apologize—

And then he saw a light.

A thin line of daylight called him forward. He fixed his eyes on it and moved. He shifted his feet and ignored the drag of the rock against his back. He blocked out the pain in his legs. He wriggled his shoulders as he squeezed into the tightest part of the tunnel. It was rough against his back, his chest. He barely had enough space to move his head. He tried to shuffle forward. The rock pressed so close he could barely move. He exhaled. It was so tight he had to fight for a small breath.

Terror lanced through him.

He shifted his shoulders as much as he could.

Was the rock getting tighter? Was he imagining it?

Keep moving. Move. Move.

The light is so close. I'm almost there.

He exhaled as much as he could. He shifted his feet beneath him and pushed forward with all his might.

His shoulders popped out from the rock. The light blinded him, and he stumbled forward onto the widened path.

He stood straight. His muscles protested at the sudden change of position, and he stumbled forward.

"I made it!" Peter called over his shoulder. "Guys, I'm at the end!"

The tunnel opened to another narrow ravine. Tall, rocky walls stretched toward the dawn sky overhead. Peter took a deep breath, crisp morning air filling his lungs.

Behind him, Mirelle stumbled out of the tunnel, pale and staggering. She leaned against the mountain. "Let's never do that again."

"I agree," Sephiri said, squeezing through the final narrow section on her heels.

Kira came out next and collapsed to her knees.

Peter rushed to her side. "Kira!"

Her lips moved, but the words came out garbled. Her skin was hot with fever and scraped from the rock. Her body trembled.

"Breathe," Peter said. "Catch your breath."

Rylan squeezed through the crack a moment later.

It took a few minutes, but Kira's breath evened out. With Rylan and Peter's help, she climbed to her feet. Her legs still shook, but her eyes were clear, and she nodded. "I'm okay."

"Just a little further," Peter said.

"And no more walking." Rylan scooped Kira up, letting her limbs dangle over his sizable arms.

"We must be deep in the mountain," Sephiri said. Her voice was small, almost reverent. "It's so quiet."

Peter led them down the smooth and narrow path, winding

between the towering cliffs. The clear sky above was rosy with dawn.

After turning a sharp corner, Peter froze. His eyes widened, and his breath caught in his chest. Sephiri gasped behind him. The others crowded around, their jaws hanging loose.

The path ended at a ledge perched over a valley. A valley filled with ancient buildings.

Peter grinned. *And golden walls.*

The entire valley glowed. Sunlight reflected off the shimmering walls of the building and radiated against the stone sides of the surrounding mountains. It was a city in a lost valley, with buildings built of gold and streets paved with it. Lush vegetation crawled up the sides of the structures as if the jungle tried to reclaim the city for its own.

"We made it," Sephiri whispered. "It's really real. Kytalia, the City of Gold."

27

P eter blinked several times. The sight seemed unreal, like something out of a fairy tale.

He spent their entire journey clinging to the hope that Kytalia was real. But hoping was nothing like actually seeing the city nestled in the valley below. Glowing in the sunlight, it was even more beautiful than he'd imagined. It was beautiful because it was *real*.

Peter chuckled. "I can't believe it."

Commander Isert could never doubt him again. Not after he returned from Kytalia with a pack full of gold, gems, and an all-healing power. Kira would tell the story of how she survived the fatal reaper poison. Peter could lead a team of Palenting soldiers back into the mountains and guide them straight to the lost city. He imagined what kinds of missions the commander would send him on after that. What other treasures hid in the old cities of Terrenor? Maybe the army would commission the four of them to seek them out.

He could imagine it clear as day: Kira deep in the library archives, finding records of lost artifacts; Rylan and Sephiri preparing their camping kits for long journeys; Mirelle bringing her knowledge of southern Terrenor to their searches. The Garrison would be more than their home, it'd be the base of operations. Peter pictured himself seated at the long table in the Garrison's kitchen, inviting Commander Isert to join him and discuss his funding needs for the next exploratory mission.

They made their way down a set of steep, rough stairs carved into the side of the mountain that led to the valley floor. By the time they reached the bottom, Peter's quads ached. But he hardly felt his muscles' soreness, not with the anticipation racing through him.

The trees in the valley packed together, with narrow trunks and tall, far-reaching branches creating a thick canopy, heavy with leafy vines. Knee-high grasses climbed up Peter's thighs, and tall, bright flowers dazzled in shades of purple and gold. While the journey had been wet and miserable, full of thorns and thick brush, the valley was different. There was a softness to it, a quietness. Wind whispered through the canopy, and flowers seemed to turn their colorful faces toward them as they passed. Glimpses of the tallest golden buildings peeked through the trees.

Behind him, his friends walked in awe. Only their steps were audible on the soft earth.

After a few minutes of walking, the vegetation opened, and two golden pillars reached toward the sky, inscribed with the familiar symbol of the stacked rectangles. He smiled as he walked between them, leading the others onto the empty streets of Kytalia.

The city was even more glorious up close. Thick vegetation sprung from cracks in the narrow, cobbled streets. Vines crawled up the golden-walled buildings, blooming with white flowers. Colorful birds nested atop the roofs and in empty buildings, and they chirped and cried out as the five walked. The beating of huge wings broke the silence as the birds took flight, soaring up toward the mountain peaks high overhead.

"This place is huge," Sephiri whispered.

Peter nodded. His eyes were wide as he drank in the city. He felt as if he couldn't say anything—if he spoke too loudly or moved too quickly, he might disturb it, and it'd slip through his fingers.

The city formed two concentric circles. The outer ring, where they stood looking, comprised low, crumbling buildings, all coated in a sheen of gold beneath a dusting of dirt and crawling vegetation. The circle crawled up the mountainside across the valley, with buildings built into the rock face, half-hidden by dense ivy. Past the outer circle, another ring of buildings stood, still half-crumbling, but soaring taller than the surrounding trees.

In the center of the city, an enormous building loomed like a mountain, towering over the rest of Kytalia. It was a magnificent many-layered building of white stone and shimmering gold. A long staircase thick with moss led under a gleaming arch up to massive doors in the center of a pyramid. Half-crumbled spires and huge, open windows dotted the various levels of the structure. Vines and trees grew up and around the building as if the mountain attempted to swallow it back into itself. *I guess that's what King Xilxidor wanted,* Peter thought.

A flock of small white birds nested in a spire of the building. Their pearlescent bodies gleamed in the sunlight as they took flight, circling the pyramid and swooping in long, gorgeous lines before settling back onto its rooftops and in its arched windows.

"Wow," Rylan said. "I don't know what I imagined, but I didn't think it would be so ... so ..."

"Huge." Kira motioned for Rylan to set her down, but she continued to lean against his side. "It's even bigger than the paintings make it look."

"This is in the paintings?" Peter asked.

"Some of them. Not the one we saw." She closed her eyes as

if she tried to remember. "Kytalia was supposed to be built around a central structure. The outer buildings were for common people, but the royal family lived in the palace."

"So that's where the treasure will be, right?" Rylan asked. "That's where it was in that big painting, at least. The king in his throne room."

Peter nodded. "That's our best bet."

Mirelle stared around the valley, her mouth open with awe. "I can't believe this is real."

"Most myths have a grain of truth in them," Peter said. "At least—" He snuck a wink at Sephiri. "That's what I've learned."

"Is this all gold?" Sephiri knelt by the nearest building and ran her hand over the gleaming surface of the wall. "Everything?"

"We need to carry some blocks home," Rylan said. "We'll be set for life!"

Sephiri looked a little closer. "Hang on, is this . . . ?" She drew the small golden dagger from her pack and set the tip against the wall. She scraped the blade against the surface, and a dark line scratched in the path.

"It's plated?" Mirelle says. "Not solid gold?"

Sephiri smoothed her thumb over the mark, and the dark line disappeared.

Mirelle leans closer. "Dirt from your knife?"

She shakes her head. "It's not gold."

"What?" Rylan's eyes widened. "What do you mean, it's not gold? The point of this place is that it's a city made of gold!"

"I mean, it looks like gold," Sephiri said. She straightened and peered at the knife. "This is gold."

"What is that?" Mirelle asked.

Sephiri stuffed it back into her bag and continued as if Mirelle hadn't spoken. "The buildings are made of sunsbeite, like we saw in the market. But just because the walls aren't gold doesn't mean there's not still gold around."

Rylan sighed. "There better be gold around. That's why we came all this way!"

Kira huffed a laugh. "Right."

"Well, and obviously—"

Mirelle glanced between them, her brow furrowed.

"Okay, fine." Rylan rubbed his hands together. "So the walls aren't actual gold. There was still a lot of treasure in those paintings, right? We just need to find it."

"Pretty obvious where we need to start, then." Peter nodded toward the pyramid in the center of the city.

The five of them made their way through the empty city. The buildings had crumbled, devoid of any signs of life: no furniture, no cookware, no remains of human activity. The only life was the animals roosting in the rubble and the vegetation overtaking the structures.

Kira wobbled as they walked. She refused to let Rylan carry her, though, and instead, they picked slowly through the rubble together. Peter kept a hand on Kira's good arm, helping her balance. Her breathing grew increasingly heavy and labored. She stared at her feet, despite the jaw-dropping surroundings.

The five of them made their way through the crumbling buildings to the enormous structure in the center of the city. Up close, the mossy stairs looked even steeper, longer, narrower. Rubble surrounded the base.

The eastern side of the towering palace looked damaged from an earthquake or a landslide long before. Boulders sunk into the ground, overgrown with vegetation.

"That's a lot of stairs," Sephiri muttered, craning her neck upward. "I'm tired of climbing stairs."

"Watch where you're stepping!" Rylan grabbed Sephiri by the shirt and tugged her back before she stepped on a small nest tucked against the stairs.

"Good save," Sephiri said. "Are those eggs?" She looked up

toward the spires, where the white birds roosted. "Why would they be down here?"

"I . . . *think* they're moving!" Rylan kneeled down and peered at the eggs. Each was about the size of a fist, gray, with brown speckling. "Do you see that?"

"They're hatching," Kira said, leaning against Peter. "Keep your distance."

"Why? Aren't they birds?"

"They're tartis viper eggs," she said with a half-smile. "We must be deep in their territory. Keep an eye out for their parents."

Rylan squawked and leaped back. "I'm getting sick of these snakes!"

"Mind your business, and they'll mind theirs," Kira said. "Don't worry, it could still be up to twenty-four hours before they hatch." With a violent spasm, she gasped and doubled over.

"Whoa!" Peter grasped her by the waist and kept her from tumbling forward. "Kira! Are you all right?"

She groaned low in the back of her throat. The others gathered around, and their voices overlapped in questions of concern, loud enough to disturb the nearby birds. Peter kept his arm around her waist while Sephiri grasped her shoulder and Rylan stood ready to catch her if she fell forward.

Kira took a few slow, heaving breaths. "I'm okay." She straightened. Her face was deathly pale. "Just pain."

Just pain.

The reaper poison ran deep inside her, wreaking havoc on her nervous system. They could do nothing for the pain. The spasms and spikes of pain would continue unless they could cure the poison itself. "Not much longer, Kira," Peter said. "Once we get inside, we'll find it."

"Find what?" Mirelle asked.

"Come on," Rylan said. "I'll carry you."

Kira shook her head. She peeled out of Peter's hold and then maneuvered to the stairs, where she collapsed onto the mossy surface. She flopped back. "I need to rest. Give me a little while, then I can go."

"Let me look at your arm." Sephiri sat down next to her. "Maybe some barkleaf balm will help."

"It won't do anything, Seph. We both know that," Kira said. "I just need to rest. You go look around."

"You sure you're okay?" Peter handed a canteen to Kira.

She unscrewed it and took a slow, careful sip, then nodded. "I'll slow you down. Go. Find it."

"It won't take long," Peter promised. "This will be over soon."

"Yeah, one way or another." Kira waved a hand at Peter. "Go."

Rylan set his bag next to Kira and nodded toward her. "In case you need anything." She returned a weak smile.

"Let's find this throne room." Peter set his foot on the bottom step and began to climb. "Quickly."

Sephiri jogged to climb next to him, then Rylan and Mirelle followed behind. The tall, mossy steps made Peter's legs complain after only a short bit. His heart rate rose. He glanced up, his sights on an arch midway up the stairs and a pair of golden palace doors past them.

"I feel weird leaving her behind," Rylan said, his breath heavy. "You're sure she'll be okay?"

"She needs the rest," Sephiri said. "No sleep and getting through that tunnel were hard on her. Letting her sit while we explore is a good idea."

"We just need to move fast," Peter added.

The rest of the sentence was unspoken. *This day is all we have.*

"Hopefully there's more gold in that throne room than there

is in the rest of the city," Mirelle said. An odd sour note filled her voice.

Peter looked up at the arch as he passed under it.

"Is this giving anyone else a strange feeling?" Rylan said, adding an audible shudder. "Something about this place seems weird."

"Ruins will do that," Sephiri said.

"You know a lot about ruins?" Peter teased, stopping to inspect the arch. Glyphs were carved into the gold-colored stone, icons of snakes, birds, and other animals, but they appeared to be nothing more than decoration. He squinted, as if the shapes might reveal a deeper meaning.

Sephiri scoffed as she joined him in inspecting the symbols carved into the stone and sunsbeite. "This place was very important, if they took the time to decorate everything like this."

Past the arch and a flat, moss-covered landing, Peter led them up another flight of steps until they arrived at the great doors of the palace. Gleaming with the same sunsbeite plating, a door hung halfway wrenched open, but the floors were dusty, like it'd been open for an age.

The temperature dropped when Peter passed the doors to enter the dimly lit, empty palace. The entrance chamber was vast, with two staircases on either side leading to a wraparound internal balcony. The ceiling soared. Birds' nests and cobwebs as thick as snow filled the rafters, with white birds fluttering in and out. Immense open windows covered the far wall. Even with the vast windows, the sun barely reached into the entrance chamber. The windows opened to the mountain behind the palace, so the view was nothing but dark rock. On the second level, two huge, dark stone doors stood closed between the windows.

"Is this the throne room?" Mirelle asked. "I don't see a throne."

"Where would you put a throne?" Peter asked as he looked up at the doors. "Down low or up high to look out over the city?"

"I have no idea." Rylan gazed around the room, wide-eyed. "I've never thought about it."

"Come on." Peter rushed up the stairs to the wraparound balcony, feet slipping on the dirt and dust with his friends right behind him. The balcony was narrow and crumbling in places, but intact. Excitement built inside him like a storm as he approached the immense doors.

The doors were made of dark stone, illustrated with the same glyphs he had seen on the golden arch. Two huge cylindrical handles jutted out. Peter grasped one and pulled.

It didn't budge.

"Is it locked?" Mirelle asked.

"I don't think so," Peter said. "Just heavy."

"Step aside," Rylan said with a huge grin. "I've got this."

Peter made space for Rylan. "Don't overdo it," he whispered. "Try to conserve your energy."

Rylan nodded. Peter stepped away, and Rylan gripped the handles of the door. His knees bent and his stance widened as he pressed his heels into the floor. The muscles in his arms flexed, and sparks danced down his arms as he pulled.

"Whoa," Mirelle said.

Rylan gritted his teeth. He took one step back, then another. The stone doors groaned as they scraped along the floor. Slowly, slowly, Rylan pulled them open. Once there was a gap big enough to step through, Peter grabbed his shoulder. "That's good."

Rylan nodded. Sweat beaded on his forehead.

"How'd you do that?" Mirelle asked.

"I train hard," Rylan said with a grin.

"But—" Her mouth hung open, frozen.

"Let's check this out!" Peter interrupted. He squeezed through the gap in the door, heart pounding with anticipation.

The room had a lower ceiling, but the walls and the rafters were painted in gold. Even the floors shined with it, the gleaming only dirtied by the nests and the droppings of birds. And there, in the center of the room, an enormous golden chair rested, tipped onto its side.

Xilxidor's throne.

28

"This is it!" Peter said. Behind him, Mirelle, Rylan, and Sephiri rushed inside.

Rylan gazed wide-eyed around at the floor-to-ceiling sunsbeite. "Whoa. Some of this has to be gold, right?"

"The chair, maybe?" Mirelle approached the throne and rapped her knuckles against the armrest. "Maybe we can get some hunks off this thing."

Peter ran his hand over the back of the throne, where it lay abandoned on its side like it'd been pushed over. Cool to the touch, a layer of grime covered its surface. "I don't think this is genuine gold either." It was the same throne as the one in the painting, though it lacked the green velvet King Xilxidor had sat on, and the throne room lacked the piles of gold and gems from the painting.

Was this place ransacked? Peter wondered. *Where did everything go?*

But if someone else had made it to Kytalia first, wouldn't that be written somewhere? Wouldn't everyone know the lost City of Gold had been discovered?

Across the room, behind the overturned throne, an open

archway led to a balcony that looked out to the sheer mountainside. Peter walked out to the balcony, testing the integrity of
the stone floor as he went. He leaned against the railing. The
mountainside was a stone's throw away, dark and immense. Its
size made him dizzy, like he faced an oncoming tidal wave. He
glanced down, and his dizziness increased. A deep chasm
yawned below, so deep the daylight couldn't penetrate the
bottom.

He shivered and reentered the throne room. They were in
the right place—they just had to find the treasure. "There must
be something," he said, peering around the room. "If there's no
gold here, it has to be somewhere else."

"Where?" Mirelle asked.

"The key," Sephiri said. "The key is supposed to unlock the
treasure, right?"

Peter looked around. There were only two doorways in the
room: the doorway to the rest of the palace, and the one to the
balcony. "These are just archways. There's no door to put a key
into!"

The four of them separated and searched the walls. Mirelle
crept along the floor, peering at the bottom of the wall. Sephiri
and Rylan examined the archway leading to the great hall, each
taking one side.

Peter examined the opening leading to the balcony. He ran
his fingers over the border, which was textured with sunsbeite.

If I hid a keyhole, where would it be?

He peered closer at the sunsbeite stone on the right side of
the archway, then knelt. There, stamped into the sunsbeite, the
stacked rectangles stared back—the symbol of Kytalia, so faint
it was almost invisible.

His heart sped. *This must be it.*

He pulled the knife out of the bag. *But where's the keyhole?*

He unsheathed it and dragged the tip of the blade over the
sunsbeite. The blade left dark marks where he dragged it, until,

right in the center, the sunsbeite gave under the blade like paper.

He gasped. He pushed the blade through the soft sunsbeite, shimmied it in the space he found, and then revealed ...

A keyhole.

"I found it!"

The others rushed to his side. "Really?" Rylan asked, leaning over his shoulder.

"This should do it. This should unlock the treasure." He pulled the blade from the knife's hilt, revealing the key beneath it. The four of them paused, staring at the key in awe.

This is it. We really found it.

"Hurry," Sephiri whispered. "Time's still running out."

Peter nodded. He slid the key into place. It clunked as it settled, a perfect fit.

He turned the key.

A loud clank rang over their heads. They stumbled back. Peter watched, eyes wide, as all the sunsbeite blocks in the archway rotated, one by one. They revealed plain, dark stone backs, with sunsbeite detailing. On the left side of the archway, sunsbeite labels marked the stones: one had a zero, one had a vertical line, then two vertical lines, then three.

Across the top of the archway, new words gleamed in delicate lettering.

Sephiri gazed up at the letters, then read them aloud. "'The City of Gold can take or give. You may find death, or you may live. Take three from five or six from eight. What is left that remains great?'"

"It's a math problem?" Mirelle frowned. "We just choose two, right?"

"Five minus three is two, eight minus six is two," Rylan agreed, then stepped forward to the archway. "Even I can solve that."

His hand hovered over the stone with two marks. He peered at Peter and Sephiri for confirmation. "Press this block, right?"

Something doesn't feel right. Peter frowned at the words over the arch.

"Could it be that easy?" Sephiri asked.

"The clue asks what is left," Rylan said. "Correct?"

"Not just what is left," Peter said. "What is left that *remains great.*"

"Should I go get Kira?" Rylan asked. "This is her thing, isn't it?"

"'Take,'" Sephiri said. She tapped her forefinger on her chin. "Do you remember what Kira told us about Kytalia?"

"That it's full of actual gold and gems and riches, and if we found it, we'd never want for anything again," Rylan grumbled. "So far . . . she was *wrong.*"

"Thievery," Sephiri said. "Thievery was the ultimate crime, right? So if you *take* something, there's nothing left that's *great.*"

Peter's eyes widened. "That's it. That has to be it."

"So, the answer is nothing?" Rylan asked. "It's zero?"

"What happens if we choose the wrong number?" Mirelle asked.

You may find death, or you may live . . .

"Can't be good." Peter walked the perimeter of the throne room, inspecting the golden walls for any signs of traps.

"Could be like the old watchtower," Rylan said. "When the whole thing collapsed on us."

Mirelle cringed. "I'm not sure what that means, but it doesn't inspire a lot of confidence."

"Or maybe that's what happened," Sephiri said. "Someone picked the wrong option."

"It's got to be zero," Peter said. "I think Sephiri's right."

"You're sure?" Rylan's hand hovered over the block.

"As sure as I can be," Peter said. "Push it."

Rylan took a deep breath and then pressed the block. It slid forward and then settled into place with a loud *clunk*. Beneath them, the floor rumbled and vibrated. Peter's heart shot up into his throat. He darted a few steps back and pressed himself flat against the wall. He expected a crack to form in the golden floor below them, or for the walls to rumble and shake as the palace imploded. The rumbling grew more powerful, louder, shaking the palace from its very base. Dust and abandoned birds' nests fell to the ground. The quaking rattled Peter's feet, traveling through his bones. He took a breath and prepared himself to run from whatever calamity was about to ensue.

Clunk.

Something shifted beneath his feet and clanked into place.

Whoosh.

On the other side of the door, something flew through the air and then landed with a thunk.

"What was that?" Rylan asked. "What did it do?

Peter passed through the archway to the small balcony. Where there was clear, empty air a moment ago, a rope bridge stretched from the balcony to the sheer mountainside. The rope looked worn in places, like it'd been rotting for years. It made for a steep bridge, more like a climb than a crossing. At the far end, a ledge stuck out of the sheer wall that looked large enough for a few people to stand on.

"Whoa," Rylan whispered. He leaned over the balcony rail and poked at the rope bridge. "Was this here before?"

Peter shook his head.

"Something in the archway must've set off a mechanism to shoot arrows attached to the ropes," Sephiri said. "That must be where the healing power is."

Peter pulled Rylan by the back of his shirt. "Don't fall off the balcony."

Rylan issued a nervous laugh. "Yeah, that's a serious drop."

Birds glided on outstretched wings beneath the bridge, contrasting against the endless pit. A breeze made the rope sway like a hammock. Peter swallowed. "I'll cross and see what's up there. Rylan, go get Kira."

"I should cross," Sephiri said. "If it breaks—"

"If it breaks," Peter interrupted, "I'll need you to catch me."

Mirelle's brow wrinkled. "What do you mean? You'll catch the rope?"

Peter and Sephiri caught eyes. "Something like that," he said.

Mirelle held up her hands and shook her head. "I can't watch this." She pointed over her shoulder. "I'm going to finish searching the palace. Be careful, all right?"

Before Peter could say anything, Mirelle was hot on Rylan's footsteps, hurrying across the throne room floor. Then it was just him and Sephiri, looking out over the chasm and at the fraying rope bridge across it. Stillness fell over the palace again.

Peter swallowed. "Well . . . if something goes wrong, catch me."

"Be careful," Seph whispered.

"Always am." Peter shoved his nerves down. *I've done crazier things than this.* He'd climbed cliff faces, scaled buildings, and ascended the rotten stairs of the old Palenting Watchtower.

This was nothing. It was just a bridge.

He climbed over the balcony railing and gripped the rope. The bridge was not like any he'd seen. It was more like a net, made up of two rope railings that led from the balcony to the mountainside across the chasm. A crisscross of ropes served as the bridge's floor. Parts of the rope looked frayed and rotted, but the knots that made up the basket looked sturdy enough. Peter kept his feet spread wide as he stepped out.

The rope groaned and swayed under his weight.

"Move quickly." Sephiri's voice shook. "But don't strain it too much."

When Peter shifted his weight, the whole bridge moved—a nauseating sensation. The rope creaked and whined. He moved faster, his feet light and quickened with Source power. He grasped either side of the bridge and hauled himself up the steep angle. He watched the arrows that were sunk into the far side of the mountain, hoping they would hold. His legs pumped, stepping rapidly, barely placing any weight on a rung.

In the space of a few breaths, he reached the far ledge. Peter planted his hands on the firm rock and heaved himself up. His heart pounded.

I don't know how many times I can do that, he thought. The Source power felt weaker—diminishing fast. *I need time to recover.*

The arrows at the end of the rope were buried deep into the mountainside, made from metal and driven into the rock like bolts. Peter touched the end of one and whistled. *This system is serious.*

Across the chasm, Sephiri stood on the balcony, grinning as she waved at Peter. "What's up there?" she called. "What do you see? Watch for vipers!"

Peter turned around.

Thankfully, he saw no vipers. The small rocky ledge was barren, containing nothing but an alcove dug into the sheer mountain face. He stepped forward, touching the rock as he entered the covered space. A small table tucked against the far end of the recess. Above it, words spelled out in golden suns-beite lettering marked the wall.

"'Greed will be your downfall,'" he read. "'You may have wealth, or you may have health. Your choice is sealed by the archway.'" He stepped closer and mused aloud, "Choice?"

His eyes widened. Two things rested on opposite ends of the table. One was a small wooden chest. The other was a basin with a dusty cup beside it. The basin contained clear water, completely still. He sucked in a breath. *This must be the healing power.*

He didn't touch the basin or the cup. Instead, he opened the chest, and his heart leaped.

"No way," he whispered.

Jewels filled the box to the brim. Gems and treasures of all colors mixed in with gray coins. He ran his fingers through the contents, chuckling to himself at the tinkling of rubies, diamonds, sapphires, emeralds, and topaz.

What are these coins?

He picked one up. It was cold to the touch and hard. As he stared at the symbol of stacked rectangles, his eyes grew. *This is baltham! Like the Tarvinian Crown!*

He set the coin down and stared at the bounty. *With just a handful of all this, I'd be set for life.*

A glimpse of gold caught his eye. *More sunsbeite?* He pushed the jewels aside and uncovered a tiny golden snake head.

He drew his thumbnail over the object. No mark scarred the surface. *Actual gold.*

He pulled the golden snake from the gems. The colorful jewels clicked together as they filled in the void behind it. Peter held the golden object in front of him. The snake's body coiled, like it was meant to wrap around something.

The bracer!

It was the very bracer from the painting of King Xilxidor.

If I bring this back, Commander Isert won't be able to deny us. This is proof of Kytalia—more than the dagger, more than the map. This proves we were here.

He held the bracer in one hand. It was heavy and cool to the touch. He slid his hand into the coil with his heart pounding. The snake's body fit over his forearm, loose and too large for his lean body. He shuddered at the significance.

The King wore this.

So if this was the treasure . . . the basin had to be the healing power.

And he had to choose.

He looked up at the writing again.

I can't take both. It hit him like a bucket of cold water dumped over his head. He could cross the bridge with the jewels or with the healing water.

But not both.

The archway . . .

Peter turned around. The ledge gave him a view of Kytalia. He spied Rylan carrying Kira up the long, mossy steps. The half-destroyed side of the palace loomed over the stairs. Enormous boulders appeared to be held up only by the vines wrapped around them like grasping hands. From the ground, it hadn't looked so precarious, but from his perch, the boulders looked to fall and crush the stairs at any moment. He squinted down at the archway as Rylan walked under it. *That must be the archway.*

Our choice is sealed by the archway. What happens then? Did the palace collapse? Did it close? Did the ground open beneath them?

Peter gulped. *You may find death, or you may live.*

He slid the bracer off his arm and set it on the pile of jewels. His hand paused, resting on the gems for a long moment. Finally, he closed the chest with a sigh and turned away from the basin.

I need to talk with the others.

Peter climbed down the bridge. As much as he wanted to rush across, he didn't want to use more of his dwindling Source power. He moved carefully, holding his breath as he crossed the chasm.

Is there another way? he wondered. There had to be a way to get both. If he brought Kira to the basin, she could drink from it, and then they could take the jewels past the arch. If they had nothing to take back to Palenting, how could Peter prove to Commander Isert that they found the city?

His foot slipped, jolting him back to the present. He grasped the sides of the bridge as he regained his footing. Adrenaline spiked through his body. He stared past the ropes, feeling lost in the yawning nothingness of the chasm. He continued forward, slower.

Once he made it across, Sephiri grabbed his arm and helped him climb back over the balcony. "What's up there? What did you find?"

"It's water," Peter breathed. "I think the water is the healing power. And then there's a chest with jewels, and baltham, and the golden bracer from the painting."

Her eyes lit up. "Amazing! Why didn't you bring it?" Her face turned down. "Why do you not look excited?"

"It's complicated." Peter stepped back into the throne room as Rylan entered with a pack on his back and Kira draped across his arms.

"She's worse," Rylan said.

Kira slumped in his arms, half-conscious, her arms dangling. Sweat beaded on her pale face. Her eyes were barely open.

"Set her down." Sephiri rushed forward and helped Rylan lower her to the floor. "She needs water, and we need to cool her down. This fever is getting terrible."

"She kept spasming and groaning on the walk up," Rylan said. "Did you find the healing?"

"I think so," Peter said, "but getting her to it is going to be tricky. Where's Mirelle? Did you see her as you walked up?"

"I thought she was with you."

A shrill scream filled the palace.

"Mirelle!" Peter raced to the doors of the throne room. *Adrian!* he thought. *He must have followed us!* He skidded to a halt after a brief spurt of energy.

A massive, broad-shouldered man stood framed in the doorway. A sneer marked his face, and a vertical scar ran across his eye.

Peter jumped and backpedaled to the others. It was the man from Palenting—the one who killed the vendor, the one who stared from the dock in Marris. Peter ground his teeth —*the one who poisoned Kira.*

The scarred man haunted them for the last week—always a step behind—seeking whatever they sought. Peter had worried about the Dirteaters, and then the Norivonne, but he'd forgotten about the scarred man.

There he was, covered in dirt and sweat, with his gnarled hand on Mirelle's throat. He passed through the doorway and manhandled her into the center of the room. She thrashed against his hold and tugged against his arm. Her hands looked small and pale against his sun-damaged, callused limb. Her mouth opened and closed like that of a fish.

"Let her go!" Peter shouted. He withdrew his sword from his belt. "Drop her!"

"It won't be that easy," the scarred man said with a sneering grin, keeping his hold on Mirelle's throat. With his other hand, he pulled a long, thin knife from his belt and drew the tip up her side. "I've sought this city for a long time. And now you are going to get me the King's bracer, or I'm going to slit this girl's throat in front of you."

"No!" Rylan shouted.

"Weapons down," the scarred man hissed. "Now!"

"Do it," Sephiri whispered.

From where she leaned against the wall, Kira groaned low and blinked her eyes open. With some effort, she focused her gaze on the scarred man and Mirelle, and a frown turned the corners of her lips down.

I could slit his throat first, Peter thought. *I still have enough power. I could be fast enough.*

But the man's knife pressed against Mirelle's skin. One wrong move and his blade would slash into her throat.

Peter dropped his sword to the golden floor.

29

"**G**ood," the man said. He grinned over Mirelle's shoulder and slid the knife up to her chin, right above his hand where it still gripped her throat. "Get the Kytalian jewels and bring them here. I know you found them."

"It's not that simple," Peter said. "There's more than jewels up there."

The man raised his eyebrows. "Something better than Kytalian riches?"

"It's a healing elixir. We need it." Sephiri gestured to Kira, who stared at the scarred man with glassy eyes. "We need it for our friend. She's about to die."

"We can only take one," Peter added. "The treasure or the elixir."

The man barked a laugh, then turned his cruel gaze to Kira. "She's the one who felt the bite of my blade. Tough girl to last so long. You'd do better to put her out of her misery before the poison does. Bring me the jewels, or you'll have two dead friends instead of one."

"Please," Mirelle whispered, her lips trembling. "Peter,

please."

The scarred man pressed the tip of the knife harder. The sharp blade drew a bead of blood, and Mirelle whimpered. A tear dripped down her face as blood rolled down the blade to the knife's hilt.

"Okay." Peter's heart sank at his own words. "I'll get them."

"What?" Sephiri hissed. "Peter, what are you thinking?"

"All three of you!" the scarred man snarled. "Leave the sick one. Go!"

Rylan cringed. "All three of us?"

The scarred man stomped forward, dragging Mirelle. Peter, Rylan, and Sephiri stumbled backward through the open door to the balcony. Peter's back hit the railing, and then he looked over his shoulder at the steep rope bridge to the ledge.

"All three of you," the man repeated.

Rylan adjusted the bag on his shoulder and peered into the chasm. "Great."

"Just move smoothly," Peter said. "You can make it, Rylan. Light on your feet."

"Easy for you two to say."

Peter led the way. He climbed over the railing and grasped the two rope rails of the bridge.

"Don't worry, Rylan," Sephiri whispered. "I'll catch you if anything happens."

"That doesn't make me feel better," Rylan grumbled.

They crept up the rope bridge. It groaned under their combined weight, the rope stretching and straining. The darkness of the chasm below seemed to reach up toward Peter, calling for him to sink into it.

"What are we doing?" Sephiri muttered as they moved out of earshot. "If we give the jewels to that guy, how are we supposed to heal Kira?"

"I'll figure something out," Peter promised. "We'll take the jewels to him to free Mirelle, and then we'll get them back, bring them up here, bring Kira so she can drink the healing elixir, and then leave with the jewels."

"How exactly are we going to pull that off?" Rylan asked. "That guy looks ready to kill us."

Peter checked over his shoulder to the balcony. The man had dragged Mirelle back into the throne room. "We'll have to strike first," he said. "Once he lets Mirelle go, we attack together."

"You don't think he'll expect that?" Sephiri asked.

"Maybe," Peter said, "but he doesn't know what we can do. Seph, if you knock him down with a blast of wind, I can get the jewels back with my speed."

It wasn't a brilliant plan, and Rylan's and Sephiri's reactions confirmed it. But what other options did they have? He couldn't let Kira die. And he couldn't let Mirelle die, either.

They made it to the ledge and scrambled off the bridge.

"Whoa," Rylan whispered. "So this is it?"

Sephiri gazed at the sunsbeite writing over the alcove. "You're right. It is a choice."

"We can take the jewels down, but I think we can bring them back," Peter said. "We don't lose the choice until the jewels pass under the arch."

"You're sure about that?" Sephiri asked.

Peter shrugged. "No. But, we have to try, don't we? We can't just let Mirelle die. Without her, we'd be dead with black eyes in the Norivonne's pit."

"I don't want her to die either," Sephiri said, "but what about Kira? What if we save Mirelle and that's it? What if Kira dies because we chose Mirelle? What if we give him the jewels, and he kills her anyway?"

"That won't happen," Peter said fiercely. "It's *not.*"

"You can't tell the future," Sephiri said. "It might."

Peter stomped up to the alcove. "What else do we do? If we bring down the elixir, that man won't let us give it to Kira.

They'll both die. I don't know what we can do other than this."

And we need these jewels for ourselves. We need to prove we were here to people back home.

Rylan raised a hand. "Or we might give the jewels to the man and *all* of us still end up dead."

Silence hovered between them.

Sephiri took a slow breath. "Okay," she said. "We'll take the jewels. Once that man lets go of Mirelle, we'll strike."

Peter opened the chest, revealing the glittering gems, the baltham coins, and the bracer.

"Whoa." Rylan's eyes widened. "Who needs buildings of gold when you have this?"

The box was too awkward to carry across the bridge and too bulky to stuff in his pack. Peter pulled a cloak from his bag, then laid it out on the ledge. He pulled the jewels out of the box and set them on the cloak, then tied the four corners together, creating a makeshift bag. He stuffed the bag into his pack, then stepped away from the alcove.

Something deep in the mountain rumbled, and the ledge under their feet quivered. Rylan swore and clung to Peter's arm, like the mountain might quake to pieces beneath them.

A thick stone slab slid out from a gap in the alcove, covering the basin and making the elixir inside inaccessible.

"Great," Sephiri said sarcastically. "That bodes well."

"We haven't crossed the arch," Peter said. "When we put the jewels back, I'm sure we'll be able to get to it again."

"I hope you're right," she murmured.

Peter's stomach twisted. "Yeah . . . me too."

"Bring it now, or your friend dies!" The scarred man's rough voice echoed across the chasm from the recesses of the throne room.

Sephiri and Rylan stepped toward the bridge.

"Just you! The one with the pack! The other two stay there!"

"Peter . . ." Sephiri whispered.

"I can handle this." Peter kept his voice steady even as doubt took root in his heart.

"You can't go alone!" Rylan said.

Peter heaved his bag onto his shoulder. "It'll be fine. I can do this. Just wait here. I'll return with Kira and the jewels. Then we'll give her the elixir."

He releases Mirelle. I hand him the jewels. Then I use the Source to kill him before he even realizes what's happened.

Before they could protest further, Peter climbed onto the rope bridge and started his way across. The ropes creaked under his increased weight. He checked the arrows holding the bridge in place—they still looked secure, but there was more give to the bridge than there had been before. Traversing back and forth was wearing the ropes out. The netting groaned under his feet. A few threads in the center snapped, like a whip cracking through the silence.

Peter froze. He stared at the hole in the netting.

"Move!" the scarred man shouted. "If you want her to live!"

More threads snapped.

Peter froze. He took shallow breaths as he gave the bridge time to stop swaying. A bird soaring under the bridge cried out, its call echoing through the chasm.

The swaying stopped. No more ropes broke.

Peter glanced ahead. The netting looked sturdy at the edge of the bridge. He gripped the rope and scurried across the broken section with his feet wide and weight distributed. No more threads snapped, and the bridge held.

Sweating, and with his heart pounding, he climbed over the balcony railing. Through the throne room opening, the scarred man sat perched on the side of the overturned throne. He kept Mirelle's arm twisted around her back, and the knife remained at the vulnerable flesh of her throat.

"Peter," Kira mumbled. She still leaned against the golden

wall of the room. Her eyes only formed narrow slits. The pus and blood from the wound on her shoulder had soaked through the bandage and dripped in a dark mess down her pale arm to her wrist. "Don't ... Don't give him ..."

"Quiet, you!" the scarred man snarled.

Kira groaned. "She's not—"

"I said quiet!" The man's voice echoed through the chamber.

Cowed, Kira cringed and pulled back from the sound like a frightened animal.

"Leave her alone!" Peter shouted.

The man whipped around to face Peter. "The jewels. Give them here."

Peter pulled his pack off his shoulders and held it before him. "Let Mirelle go."

"Jewels first." The man pressed the blade against Mirelle's throat.

"Do what he says," Mirelle gasped. "Peter, please."

Kira groaned and tipped her head back, fighting to keep her eyes open. Her mouth moved as if she struggled to speak.

We don't have much time. I need to get her the elixir.

He stepped forward and tossed the pack. The scarred man showed his yellow teeth in a sneering grin. "Now, back up!" The dagger pressed against Mirelle's pale skin, and Peter stepped back.

Using one hand, the man opened the top of the pack and rooted around inside until a broad grin grew on his face. "So it's real." He pulled the golden snake out. "And you found the bracer of King Xilxidor."

"Peter!" Sephiri called in the distance. The sound made his stomach twist.

"Let her go." Peter picked up his sword. "We had a deal."

"Did we?" The man kept the knife at Mirelle's throat. "I don't remember agreeing to that."

Kira groaned. Peter's mind raced as his plans melted out from under him like snow in the suether sun.

Could I kill him before he cuts Mirelle's throat? Should I race to Kira's side and try to take her across the bridge? No—he couldn't get the elixir if the man still had the jewels. Could he get the jewels back? Surely the man would kill Mirelle if he even tried. His only chance was to strike the man down, but how could he do that without endangering Mirelle? Time was short. Each breath Kira took was one closer to the reaper poison's final act.

Behind the man, a slamming sound echoed from somewhere in the palace. A faint voice shouted, "Hello? Anybody home?"

The scarred man's pleased grin became predatory. "Listen to that. Sounds like we have company."

"Norivonne . . ." Kira groaned.

Peter stood frozen in place. *Norivonne? How is that possible?*

"You better tell your friends to stay put." The man pointed toward the doorway to the balcony. "Unless you want me to cut the rope as they cross."

Peter whipped around. Sephiri approached the opposite side of the bridge, about to climb on.

"Seph, don't!" Peter called. "Wait there!"

"People are coming!" Sephiri shouted back.

"Just wait!"

"Smart boy." The scarred man stood up off the throne, the pack of jewels at his feet, and Mirelle's arm in his hand. "Shall we see who's here?"

A man with stringy, sweaty blond hair rounded the corner and stepped through the open doors to the throne room. Sweat and dirt stained his fine silk shirt. His knee-high leather boots looked like they had gleamed at one point. A dark opal pendant hung around his neck. Four other men flanked him—tall, tattooed, and dressed in dark canvas.

"What a pleasant surprise," Renaud Denton said in a lilting voice. "A friendly reunion."

"You're late," the scarred man said. He released Mirelle from his hold and shoved her forward. She stumbled, and Renaud caught her with two hands on her upper arms.

"Mirelle!" Terror sliced through Peter like an icy blade. "Don't hurt her!"

"Hurt her?" Renaud squeezed her arms a little harder. "I could never."

"Peter," Kira whispered. Her voice was barely audible. "She's ... She's ..."

The scarred man burst into laughter. The cruel, deep sound resonated through the room. Goosebumps rose on Peter's skin.

Mirelle looked over her shoulder at Peter. Her dark eyes flashed, and a strand of her brown hair fell across her face. She tucked it behind her ear and smiled at him, but it didn't look like the smiles he'd grown used to seeing over their travels. There was neither sweetness to it, nor mischief. It was a different smile—cold, like the predatory grin he'd seen on the scarred man's face.

She turned to face Renaud, and then she kissed him.

30

P eter's heart froze, then plummeted.

Mirelle wound her arms around Renaud's neck as he held her by the waist and kissed her. He even dipped her back, a showy demonstration that made Peter's stomach turn. Mirelle giggled when they broke apart, then brushed Renaud's blond hair off his forehead. "Hi, honey."

"Hi, gorgeous," he said. "It's been a while."

"Mirelle," Peter whispered, his voice cracking. "What— How'd—" His jaw quivered. "This whole time?"

She rolled her eyes as she straightened, then stood next to Renaud. "Yes, you buffoon, this whole time. Gault, did you have to go so hard on the choking?" She rubbed her neck. "Ugh! That was a bit much. And you *cut* me!"

"Had to make it look real, sis," Gault—the scarred man— said. "You said you wanted it to be believable."

"I think you enjoyed it a little too much." She huffed. "We wouldn't have even started this charade if you hadn't let them get away in the first place."

"Charade?" Peter said. "But—But you rescued us *from* the Norivonne. You're with them?"

He glanced at Kira, whose shoulders slumped. Her weak eyes reflected sadness, and she nodded.

She knew it. She was trying to warn me.

"I'm not just *with* them." Her catlike, predatory smile returned. "I *run* them—not that anyone in Marris knows. I guessed you might know more about the Kytalian knife than you let on. Taking it back wasn't enough."

"Taking it back?" Peter asked. "It was never yours!"

"Well," Renaud shrugged. "Technically, it was my brother's. He found it, somehow, but we weren't on the best of terms. We would have gotten it from him except some idiot—who had no idea what it was—stole it before we could."

"The vendor in Palenting," Peter said.

"Initially, I just wanted to retrieve it, to get it for the Norivonne, so we had Gault here track it down." Renaud chuckled. "It seems you all gave him more trouble than he was ready for."

Gault scowled at Renaud.

"Even though he let you get away," Mirelle added, "it benefited us. Once I figured out you might know something, I decided to let this whole thing play out. I thought . . . maybe you'll lead us right to the city." She flashed a crooked grin. "Which you did."

Peter's throat tightened. He felt dazed and cold. "I trusted you." His voice was thin. "I wanted you to come back to Palenting with us. I thought you had nothing in Marris. I thought we were friends."

"It's sweet how trusting you are." Mirelle's voice dripped with condescension. "All I had to do was create a sad little story." She put on a pouty face and folded her hands. "Poor me, I'm just a lost little orphan who wants to get back at a gang for killing my parents."

"That part is true." A wicked grin crossed Gault's face. "The Norivonne *did* kill our parents."

"With our help," Mirelle added with a smirk. "To be fair, they were awful parents. We found our way out of that mess and made a new family with the Norivonne." She extended her arm in Gault's direction, pushed her sleeve up, and revealed the brand on her forearm.

It was a small oval mark, with a line through the middle—like an eye. The same marking showed on Gault's forearm as well.

No one forced her to take a brand. She'd chosen to. It was a mark of loyalty—the mark of the Norivonne.

"The gang is doing quite well in Marris," Mirelle continued. "But with the wealth of Kytalia, we can control much more. Our power could expand—Palenting, Kandis, maybe even all of Rynor. And you four were more than happy to lead us here. I can't thank you enough."

"But—but . . ." A hopeless tear threatened to fall from Peter's eye. "I thought we had something."

"If you'd lived a life like mine, you wouldn't trust so easily. You'd stick with the ones you know." She planted a kiss on Renaud's cheek. "It pays off in the end. With the riches of Kytalia, the Norivonne are going to become the most powerful gang in all of Rynor." She waved a hand at the others. "Deal with them. Let's get out of here."

Gault and three other Norivonne goons stepped forward and grabbed Peter by the arm. His eyes wouldn't focus. His mouth hung with an open gap. He didn't even think about struggling.

"Grab your little friend," Gault said, "unless you want to let her die here." He pushed Peter in Kira's direction.

In a stupor, Peter wrapped an arm around Kira's waist, then pulled her to her feet. She chuckled as he did so, delirious dead weight in his arms.

"I'm sorry," he whispered. "You tried to warn me about her."

"Uh-huh," she said, dazed.

"I'm going to fix this," Peter said. "Just . . . give me a minute."

"Get moving!" Backed up by the other Norivonne, Gault brandished his knife at Peter and herded him like a rogue sheep back to the balcony. "Join your friends on the mountain."

Peter swallowed hard. "Get on my back, Kira. I'll carry you across."

Kira swung her arms around Peter's neck. He leaned forward, taking her weight, then held on to her limp legs. It wasn't easy to maneuver with her on his back, but he climbed over the balcony rail and back onto the rope bridge.

"Hang on tight," he whispered. *And don't look down.*

Again he crossed the bridge, moving as fast as he could with his feet wide on the netting. The rope swayed and groaned, and he barely dared breathe until they reached the other side.

"Kira!" Sephiri waited at the far end. She and Rylan helped Peter climb onto the ledge and then deposit Kira onto the ground.

"Enjoy the view!" Gault shouted from the balcony. He waved a large machete over his head.

"No!" Peter shouted. He rushed to the bridge, but it was too late. Gault swung the machete down in a sweeping arc, and the blade sliced through the rope like it was butter. The rope bridge fluttered down and hung limply from the two bolts beneath their ledge.

Peter stared across the chasm as Gault laughed. Mirelle stuck her head out of the doors of the throne room and waggled her fingers in a teasing wave before they both disappeared.

There has to be a way out of this. A way to climb; a place to run.

He spun, his neck craning and eyes searching the face of the mountain.

There was nothing.

No way up. No way down. Just the chasm below them, the

alcove behind them, and the sheer, featureless rock. Even if they could climb, there was nowhere to go—the peak towered too high, and the chasm looked endless below.

Trapped. We're trapped.

The Norivonne had the jewels, the baltham, the bracer. The healing elixir was inaccessible. Kira's breaths were shallow and labored.

"I'm so sorry," Peter whispered.

The scope of his failure made his lungs tighten. It spread around him like the abyss, endless and dark. The Norivonne had everything—including the only way out. They were leaving Kytalia—leaving Peter and his friends to die.

"Where's Mirelle?" Rylan asked. "What happened?"

Peter wiped his sweaty brow. He glanced between Rylan and Sephiri, the weight of guilt pressing on him. "She betrayed us. She's—she's with the Norivonne."

Sephiri's eyes widened. She took a deep breath, then sighed. "I knew I didn't like something about her, but . . . This whole time?"

Peter nodded. "It's my fault. We can't give up yet, though. Let's see if we can get to this healing power."

"How?" Sephiri asked. "Did you get the jewels back?"

"Maybe it's just a weight trigger," Rylan suggested, rushing to the alcove. He stacked loose rocks into the empty chest and then pushed at the stone block over the basin. It didn't budge. "We just have to get the weight right. There has to be a way to trick it, right?"

"Seph?" Kira's weak voice turned their heads.

"Yeah, it's me," Sephiri said. "You're okay. We're going to take care of you."

Again Kira laughed a dark, quiet laugh. "I don't know, Seph . . ."

"Don't say that. Just hang on a little longer."

"They're going down the steps, almost to the arch," Peter said.

"This thing isn't moving!" Rylan shouted. He swore, then gripped the stone block in both hands. Source power danced over his body in tiny white sparks. Veins bulged in his forearms and his temple. He gritted his teeth as he pushed, but even with the Source flowing through him, the stone block wouldn't budge.

"If they cross under the arch, the choice is sealed," Peter said. An idea flickered into his mind. It was crazy, it was dangerous . . . but it was better than standing on the ledge and watching the Norivonne doom Kira.

Sephiri stepped toward the edge. "We have to stop them!"

"Seph, can you raise the bridge?" Peter asked. "With the wind?"

Her eyes widened. "You can't be serious."

"If I move fast, I can run across. You only have to hold it up for a moment."

"It won't be steady," Sephiri said. "If you miss a foothold or get off balance, there would be nothing to grab hold of. You'd tumble and fall. It's insane!"

"We don't have time! They're heading to the arch now! You hold it up, and I'll run across and tie it on the other side. Then the three of you can cross."

"Rylan," Kira murmured. Her hand rooted around in a bag they tossed onto the ledge.

Rylan knelt by her side. He blinked rapidly when she looped an arm over his shoulder, then he helped her up. In her other hand, she held the golden dagger. "What are you doing?" he asked.

"Walk to the edge," she breathed. "And stand still."

"You better not jump," Rylan muttered.

"Kira, what are you . . . ?" Peter asked.

Kira exhaled. Her trembling ceased, and for a moment she

looked like her old self, with her shoulders squared and her head held high. She raised the dagger and closed one eye, sighting something in the distance. Sparks danced along her skin.

Peter's heart pounded. Helpless and out of hope, he watched with a desperate desire for something impossible to happen.

Kira stepped forward, then threw the knife.

The golden blade soared through the air like one of the white birds. It flew over the destroyed side of the palace, toward the doors. The glittering gold caught the sunlight as it dived.

Peter stared. *What is she doing? How could she hope to—*

He gasped when he saw the target. Boulders perched above the stairs balanced precariously, held in place by a network of vines.

Peter held his breath. *That would be impossible.*

The blade tumbled end over end until it sliced through one of the vines.

"No way," Rylan said.

The boulders groaned as they scraped against each other. A vine snapped. Then another.

An abrupt laugh exploded from Peter's throat.

Gravity did the rest of the work. The largest of the boulders rolled off the rubble and crashed onto the landing, in front of the arch. More followed behind it in a rumbling rockslide.

Shouts filled the air. A rock crushed one of the Norivonne goons. Mirelle and the others stumbled backward up the stairs, avoiding being crushed, themselves.

Boulders blocked the arch.

"Yes!" Peter shouted. He pumped a fist in the air. *That buys some time.* "Seph, the bridge!"

Sephiri's eyes widened. "I guess we're doing this. Please don't fall."

Peter positioned himself at the brink of the ledge, where the rope bridge dangled below.

Source power thrummed in his chest, fainter than usual, but present.

I have enough power. I can make it. I have to.

Wind picked up, deep in the chasm, and then soared upward like a wave. It caught the bridge like the sails of a boat. The network of ropes hovered across the chasm, swaying in the steady, ceaseless wind. "Go!" Sephiri shouted.

The Source rushed through him with as much ferocity as the wind. Before he could doubt himself, he sped forward onto the quivering bridge.

The ropes undulated like they floated atop a churning river. The world moved slowly, his mind processing it in an instant. Birds soared in the chasm, each flap of their wings seemed to take an age. Peter kept his steps as light as he could as he moved over the bridge. The rope sank under his feet like the dark sucking sand on the banks of the lake. He sprang off the balls of his feet, bouncing from side to side. The ropes dipped and flowed, sinking, then rising. *She only has to hold it up a moment longer,* he thought. *Stay strong, Seph.*

A few more steps. The bridge trembled as if he ran across water. It dipped further, suddenly, and he pitched forward. He gasped as he lost his balance and staggered forward. It felt like the chasm rushed forward to meet him.

The wind surged anew beneath him and pitched him upward like a wave. He reached out, grasped the stone railing, and scrambled onto the balcony. Source power still raced through him as he whipped around.

He'd made it, but there was no time to celebrate his successful crossing.

The rope bridge whipped through the air like a flag in a thunderstorm. "Steady it!" he shouted.

"I'm trying!" Sephiri called back.

He gripped the railing with one hand and leaned forward, reaching for the cut rope of the bridge as it writhed like a snake. It brushed against his fingertips, just out of reach—he stretched further.

"I can't hold it much longer!" Sephiri shouted.

Farther. The chasm yawned beneath him.

He caught the rope in his hand. "Yes!"

He clutched the rope, then hauled it backward with all his might. The wind lessened, and the weight of the rope sagged. He braced his feet on the railing and pulled hard, wrapping one end of the bridge around the railing and tying it off.

His shoulders burned, and the skin on his palms stung.

The wind stilled. Peter ignored the pain in his limbs and reached to grasp the other rope. He hauled it up then tied it.

Across the ledge, Sephiri slumped back, exhausted.

She did it. I just hope she's okay.

Panting, he stood and waved at his friends. "Come on!"

He had no time to wait for them. *They'll make it. They'll be all right.* He needed to get the jewels back before the Norivonne passed the arch. His lungs burned, his shoulders ached, and the Source power was a low, faint hum in his chest.

He paused with his hands on his knees and took a slow, determined breath with his eyes closed. *No time.*

He reached deep into his well of energy. The remaining power trickled through his veins, and with a burst of energy, he barreled through the throne room, down the stairs, through the entrance hall, and out of the enormous doors.

31

D own the mossy, steep stairs, on the small landing area, the Norivonne attempted to shove the boulder out of the way of the arch. They were trapped. Half-destroyed rubble of the palace formed one side of the stairs, and a sheer drop would break anyone's legs on the other side. The Norivonne goons pushed against the boulder. The massive rock shifted a little, edging toward the drop.

"Mirelle!" Peter shouted, his chest heaving. He'd never felt like this after using the Source—never so exhausted, so weak.

Mirelle paused in her direction of the boulder operation. Her eyes widened, but then that predatory grin returned to her face. "This is unexpected," she said.

Peter drew his sword as he descended the steps. The feel of the hilt in his hand settled his nerves. The weight was familiar, and the steel blade gleamed in the sunlight, mixing with the sunsbeite surrounding him. He pressed his free hand against his legs, fighting to keep them from wobbling.

Mirelle laughed. She extended a hand to Gault, and he handed her the long, curved machete he used to chop the rope.

She spun it, then pointed it up the stairs at Peter. "You think you can beat me?"

This wasn't the girl who'd fumbled his sword on the deck of the Seacutter. That girl didn't exist. It had all been an act. She'd played him, pretending to be sweet and harmless so she could take the riches of Kytalia for her gang—the riches she held in the crook of her arm. She grinned and tossed the pack with the treasure to the side.

"Come on," she said. "Show me what you've got."

Peter arrived at the mossy landing between the steps and the arch, sword in hand. He stood straight, despite the exhaustion weighing him down. Every breath burned in his lungs. The hilt of his sword made the raw skin on his palms sting. The well of Source power in his chest felt like a yawning void: empty.

The Norivonne turned to face him, but Mirelle waved them off. "I'll handle this." She moved toward him with a smirk.

Mirelle brought the machete down in a diagonal arc, just out of striking distance. She did it again, a few sharp, elegant slashes. Her movements were graceful, and so ferocious they forced Peter back to avoid taking a machete slice to the arm. He thrust his own blade out and parried the weapon—the clang of steel ringing in the air. He gripped the hilt hard and twisted his arm, forcing Mirelle's blade down. His palms screamed in pain, and his shoulders burned with every motion.

She narrowed her dark eyes, and a determined furrow creased her brow. Before she could strike again, Peter lunged a step, blade stretched forward, and stabbed at Mirelle. She danced backward, just out of reach of the blade. Peter thrust forward again and again with more force, grunting each time. His attacks were sloppy; she avoided them with ease. She was *fast*—and Peter wasn't. Not anymore.

Peter drove his sword forward again, but Mirelle dodged and swung her machete in a wide arc at his side. He leaned away, nearly losing his balance, but parried the attack by the skin of his teeth. His foot slipped on the mossy stone, close to the edge of the landing. One wrong move and he would take a long dive to the hard ground far below.

He kept his grip tight on the hilt, even as sweat filled his palms and worsened the pain. He stayed low to the ground and lunged forward, slashing at her thighs. The tip of his sword nicked her, drawing a thin line of blood. She looked down, then exhaled hard through her nostrils.

Baring her teeth like an animal, Mirelle lurched forward with a wordless cry.

Peter grimaced as he parried her strike. The force reverberated into his bones. His blade trembled as his hands did the same. The clang of steel-on-steel rang through the city, echoing up into the mountains. They moved like that for what felt like an age, sweat building on his temple as their blades met again and again.

"You can barely hold your sword," Mirelle hissed as she swung again. "You've already lost."

With their blades locked, she pushed back hard. Peter dug his heels into the moss on the stairs to keep his balance. He gritted his teeth and strained, keeping the sharp edge of her blade off his face.

"Give up," Mirelle snarled. "And maybe I'll let you and your friends live."

A tingling sensation deep in his chest caught his attention. It was faint but present—the depleted Source power had begun to replenish.

It's not much ... but I don't need much. Just one opening.

"You think beating me will be that easy?" Peter gritted out.

He exhaled and let the trickle of Source power rush through him. Darting backward, he freed himself of their locked blades. Mirelle's eyes widened in slow motion. He rushed forward and slapped the flat of his blade against her wrist. She gasped, the machete flying from her hand and clattering to the ground.

Peter pressed the tip of his sword under her chin. "Told you."

The Norivonne men surged a step forward, then stopped, wavering as they stared.

"How did you do that?" Mirelle's voice shook.

Peter exhaled. "Give back the treasure."

Mirelle grasped the blade of his sword with her bare hand, wincing as a cruel grin formed on her face. "Go ahead, Peter. Kill me. Slit my throat."

"Give us the treasure," he repeated, "and you can leave alive."

"You don't have the guts to do it," Mirelle said. "You're a scared little boy. You can't kill me. You're not strong enough." She kept her hand on the steel, her eyes sparkling with madness. Blood trickled down her arm in sharp contrast to her pale skin.

Peter wanted to prove her wrong, to show all the Norivonne what he was capable of. His hand shook. Fear and disgust turned his stomach. As much as he willed his body forward, his arm wouldn't deliver the blow because of one horrifying truth.

She's right. I don't want to kill her.

Despite how she betrayed them, Peter remembered the girl who snuck them out of the pit in the Norivonne headquarters. She wasn't real, but the memory persisted, and he couldn't kill that girl. *Not like this.*

Mirelle shoved his sword aside and barreled forward. She drove her shoulder into his gut and knocked the wind out of him. Peter fell backward, his shoulder hitting the steps hard. Mirelle snatched his sword from his hand and turned the tip under his chin in a mirror of what he'd just done to her. Her bloody handprint still marked the steel.

Peter looked up. Mirelle loomed over him, her grip steady, the blade pressing against his flesh. "I'm not so hesitant."

"You don't have to do this." Peter searched inside for a wisp of Source power, but he found nothing. A cold shudder ran through him.

"I know I don't have to." She pushed the tip against his chin, forcing his head up. "I want to."

"Peter!" Sephiri shouted.

Mirelle looked up.

Peter sprang into action, wrapping his hands around Mirelle's wrist and jerking her to the side. She stumbled, and the sword slipped out of her hand. Peter shoved her with all the strength he could muster. She stumbled back across the landing, stepping wildly until her head crashed into the boulder under the arch. She collapsed to the ground and lay still. Renaud shouted and rushed to her side.

Peter turned and spotted his sword. It lay at the edge of the landing, leaning against the steps. Above him, Sephiri and Rylan ran down the steep staircase. Rylan removed his pack in a smooth motion and tossed it to the side, barreling forward with a rumbling fury. Peter lunged for his weapon. As he wrapped his hand around the hilt, a searing pain ripped across his lower back. He whirled around with his sword in hand, dizzy with exertion, and blood pounding in his ears. Gault, the huge, scarred man, stood with a sharp, narrow knife in hand, now wet with Peter's blood.

Chaos exploded around him. The Norivonne goons shouted as they rushed across the landing, and Rylan and Sephiri thundered down the last steps.

The Norivonne still outnumbered them two-to-one, but the sound of his friends rushing forward filled Peter with renewed energy. He shouted and thrust his sword toward Gault. The man was strong and good with a knife, but he was slower than Mirelle.

I can do this.

A gust of wind rushed past Peter, whipping over his shoulders like a passing torrent. It split around him, then slammed into the Norivonne like a wave. Their bodies flew across the landing, thumping against the boulders blocking the arch.

Rylan rushed across the landing, following the wind like a boat in the wake of the waves, and launched himself at the men. Peter trusted Rylan and Sephiri to handle the others. He would handle Gault.

The scarred man shook off his surprise at the gust of wind. He flipped his knife into an overhand grip. He raised it high, then slashed it toward Peter's face. Peter darted to the left, dodging the strike, and lunged at Gault's side. The steel edge of his blade sliced Gault's shirt open, revealing fine steel chain mail underneath. He'd have to do more than hope for a lucky strike.

Gault slammed his fist into Peter's shoulder, knocking him back. His foot caught on the edge of the stairs, and he scrambled to regain his balance. As he did, Gault stepped forward, his knife still raised. Peter withdrew up the stairs, his sword outstretched. Exhaustion burned through him. His muscles ached, and his chest heaved.

Gault swung the knife in a massive blow. Peter parried it. *Clang.* Again. *Clang.* Each immense strike made Gault's grin grow bigger. He was like a stray cat batting around an injured mouse. The man tossed the knife to his other hand and then slashed from the other direction. Peter knocked it away with his sword. He glanced at the man's chest, taunted by the faint ringing of chain mail.

I've got to do something! he thought. *I can't keep this up.*

He gulped in a heaving breath. His hand shook, the blade quivering as he parried the never-ending strikes.

Come on, Peter, find an opening!

Around Peter, the clang of steel-on-steel and the shouts of

battle filled the air. His back stung. His arms grew weak. His legs tired. A step tripped against his heel, and Peter fell backward, hard against the steps.

Gault continued forward. "It's a pity I couldn't have poisoned you when I first ran into you," he sneered. "Now, I'll have to kill you the old-fashioned way." He adjusted his hold on the knife and dove forward with sudden, sharp speed. The blade aimed for the center of Peter's chest.

Peter rolled forward, curling his shoulder inward so Gault's blade passed over him. He pressed into the massive man's body, sweat and blood stinging his nose.

Pain exploded through his upper back, far worse than the shallow gash Gault first slashed him with. It was intense, throbbing and radiating outward. Dark spots danced across his vision. Gault shoved the knife deeper. Peter shouted, then gritted his teeth against the pain as he heaved his sword up. The edge of his blade sliced into the bare flesh of Gault's neck.

The man made a gurgling sound as he stumbled backward. He clapped both hands against the gash on his neck, but it did nothing to stem the flow of blood gushing from the wound.

Fighting through the pain, Peter jumped up and shoved the center of Gault's chest. The man stumbled, his foot tripping against the side of the stairs. His legs kicked into the air as his body tumbled over the side. Wide eyes stared at nothing while the massive body fell off the edge of the building, dropping until it crashed to the sunsbeite rooftops far below.

Peter sheathed his sword with a shaking hand, then stumbled down the few steps to the landing. His body wavered on unsteady legs until he fell to his knees, the jostle sending a fresh pain shooting through his shoulder.

Across the landing, Rylan grappled with one of the Norivonne goons, pinning him down, while Sephiri blew another back a step with the force of her wind. Peter reached over his shoulder and grasped the hilt of Gault's knife. Buried deep in the muscle, the barest touch to the hilt sent pain throbbing through him. He gritted his teeth, tightened his grip, and wrenched the blade out.

The pain of the blade's removal was worse than the actual stabbing. He clamped his jaw to keep from howling as the agony lanced through him. Spots danced in his vision as he struggled to stay conscious. He dropped the knife, and it clattered to the stones, leaving splatters of blood on the moss.

He took a few deep, heaving breaths. A hint of Source power bubbled in his chest, replenished from the short time since its last use. It sparked through him, weak but present, and concentrated on the deep wound in his shoulder.

With each beat of his heart, the wound stitched itself a little more. The muscles and tendons came together, deep in his shoulder, as a healing process that should've taken weeks compressed into the space of a few moments. His head spun from the speed. His eyes lost focus, and his breath grew shallow while his body's resources focused on the recovery.

His vision cleared. He stood and pressed a hand against a nearby boulder for support as his vision spun. Next to the arch, Rylan wrestled the final Norivonne goon to the ground, then shoved him off the stairs like an unwanted sack of potatoes. Peter's shoulder ached, but the worst of the throbbing pain had subsided. He reached back and touched the wound. It was tender and still oozing, but it had become nothing more than a shallow flesh wound. The other gash Gault left across his lower back felt healed as well. Only the blood soaking his shirt was proof of how bad it had been.

They're taking care of the Norivonne. Now we need to get the treasure back up to the alcove. His eyes scanned the landing, looking for his discarded pack. He frowned. *Mirelle tossed it there. Where is it?*

"Don't let her get away!" Renaud staggered forward, pointing up the stairs. "She has the jewels!"

Peter spun, glanced up, and jerked his head back. Nearly to the palace doors, Kira climbed the stairs with the pack of treasure slung over her shoulder. "Go, Kira!" A grin tugged at his lips as he moved toward the bottom step. His legs wobbled, and he paused to catch his balance. *I can help her up. Once she gets back to the ledge—*

A sharp yank of his hair wrenched him backward.

What in the—

Cold steel pressed to his throat, cutting off his thoughts. Mirelle tightened her grip on his hair, and his scalp stung with sudden, sharp pain. He gasped and pulled at her forearm. She didn't budge. Despite her slight frame, she was strong. She hissed in his ear. "Don't struggle."

Exhaustion flattened him. He attempted to thrash, but he was too weak. His knees shook—he had nothing left to give. He swallowed and felt the edge of the blade against his skin.

"Peter!" Sephiri cried. She looked pallid, her hair stuck to her temples with sweat. She wavered on her feet as she watched Mirelle wrestle Peter into her hold.

Across the landing, Rylan stood in front of the boulders, menacing Renaud with a borrowed sword.

"Bring me the bag, or he dies," Mirelle shouted.

Up the steps, Kira froze, wavering on her feet.

"Go!" Peter shouted. "Get the elixir, Kira!"

She had the jewels. They outnumbered the remaining Norivonne. This was her chance—if Kira had the strength to get back into the palace, she could save herself.

But she didn't continue up the steps. She turned, holding the bag in both hands, and her gaze flickered to Peter.

"I won't ask again," Mirelle snarled.

Peter's neck stung as the blade bit into his skin. A hot bead of liquid rolled down to the neckline of his shirt.

Kira took a wavering step lower.

"No!" Peter shouted. "Go back!"

Kira shook her head. She continued down the mossy stairs, pausing as needed to catch her balance. When she reached the landing, she extended the bag with a trembling hand.

Mirelle snatched it with a cackle. "Renaud! We got it!"

Peter shoved her arm off him and stumbled forward. He crashed into Kira but caught himself before he knocked her down.

Mirelle tucked the bag into the crook of her arm and then tightened her grip on her knife. She stared with narrowed eyes at Peter and Kira.

To the side, Sephiri and Rylan stood watching. Rylan's chest heaved, his face flushed, and Sephiri's eyes fogged over with the white haze of her power. She panted as heavily as he did.

Peter caught their attention. "Rylan? Sephiri? Are you able to—" He stopped at their dismayed looks. Sephiri shook her head, and Rylan bent over to rest his hands on his knees.

Peter pulled his sword from its sheath and barely held it up. "I'll take you myself," he managed in a faint voice.

"Peter," Kira whispered, stopping him as he readied to lunge forward.

He turned to see Kira shaking her head.

"Let her go."

"Come on, Mirelle," Renaud called from the other side of the landing. He rested a hand on a boulder with his body squeezed through a tight space between them. "Let's go!"

Mirelle threw one last withering gaze toward Peter, then turned away to follow Renaud.

Rage burned in Peter's chest, and he lurched forward, holding his sword up, angry enough to stab her in the back.

Kira held him by the wrist. She squeezed hard—not strong enough to hold him back, but the gesture surprised him. He stopped and watched as Mirelle slipped past the boulder and under the arch.

The choice was sealed.

No jewels.

No elixir.

"I'm sorry, everyone," Rylan said. "I was spent."

Sephiri nodded. "Me, too."

Silence fell over them.

Peter turned toward Kira. "You stopped me." A tear formed at the corner of his eye as he whispered, "Why?"

Without answering, she pushed her hair off her forehead and turned back to the palace. She began her way up the stairs, moving slowly, leaning forward so far she pushed the steps with her good hand. Her injured arm was useless, covered in streaks of drying, oozing blood and pale with disease. Peter followed and tried to help her, but she waved him off. Halfway up the stairs, she leaned over into the rubble and picked up Rylan's bag, where he'd tossed it aside.

"Kira!" Peter strained. "Come on, we don't—" He choked on emotion. How much time did she have left? Hours? Minutes? The reaper poison's work was almost done.

Sephiri darted forward. "Now this is just crazy." She took the bag from her.

Rylan looped an arm around Kira's waist. "All right . . . where are we going?"

Kira managed a small smile and then continued up the stairs, leaning on Rylan as she went. They passed the golden doors to the empty entrance hall, walked up the stairs to the throne room, then passed through to the balcony where the rope bridge swayed in the breeze.

"Again?" Rylan asked. "I thought last time was the actual last time . . ."

"There's no way to get to the elixir," Peter said. "Not even Rylan could move the slab."

Kira climbed over the balcony railing and stepped onto the bridge. She moved her way across, slowly, legs shaking. Rylan paced behind her with one hand on her shoulder in case she lost her balance. Peter went next, and then Sephiri.

Kira collapsed as soon as she made it to the ledge. She slumped against the wall, head lolling as sweat poured off her.

"What are we doing?" Peter asked. He knelt by Kira's side. "Kira, please. What's going on?"

A small, dazed smile curled her lips upward. "The pack," she whispered.

Sephiri's eyebrow raised. She turned and sloughed the bag off for Peter to take it.

He furrowed his brow at Kira.

She grimaced and then groaned in pain as another spasm wracked her body. Her breath came in a shaky rattle. Peter moved to drop the pack, but Kira shook her head. "Open it," she said with a scratchy voice.

With trembling hands, he undid the clasp on the bag and pulled it open.

His eyes widened. Shock stole his breath away.

How did she do this?

Inside, the riches of Kytalia gleamed. The rare gems caught the sunlight, glittering and shining with every shift of the bag. The baltham coins knocked against each other. And there, in the center of it all, rested the golden bracer of King Xilxidor.

32

"No, way!" Rylan yelled.

Sephiri laughed. "We can put it back. We can still get the elixir."

Peter traced a finger over the snake's gleaming head.

Maybe they could put everything back *but* the bracer. That would be enough, wouldn't it? The jewels would all be replaced. It would just be one thing missing. They could throw in a rock to offset the weight. Then, they could heal Kira, and still be able to take proof of the city's existence back to Palenting.

"Peter." Sephiri shook her head. "Don't even think about it. Remember what the door said?"

What is left that remains great?

He could try to trick the system. He could try to take both— to save his friend and keep the treasure of Kytalia, but that would be greed. The one thing Kytalia disdained most. The reason the king sank the city into the mountains.

You may find death, or you may live.

He pushed the bracer back into the bag. They'd made it that far, and they had a chance to save Kira. He wouldn't lose her—not after everything they fought through to get there. If it ruined his chances of joining the army, he'd find another way. *There's always another way.*

Peter nodded, then lifted the lid on the chest in the alcove. He poured in the gems, the baltham coins, and the golden bracer at the end. Then he closed the lid and held his breath.

For a long moment, nothing happened.

They glanced at each other. Peter's heart pounded. Kira's eyes were half-open as she slipped in and out of consciousness. Her body shuddered with more pain.

Are we too late? But we didn't go through the arch. We made it in time. This can't be happening.

Beneath them, the mountain rumbled, deep and thick. The stone slab over the basin shuddered.

"Come on," Peter whispered. "Move."

With a slow movement, the slab retreated until it disappeared into the mountain, revealing the clear water.

The elixir.

Relief coursed over him like a cool breeze. *We made it. She's going to be okay.*

Peter grabbed the cup next to the basin and dunked it into the water, filling it to the brim. As soon as he pulled the cup out, the rumbling sounded again, and a new stone slab slid over the box of jewels.

He turned, cup in hand, and knelt at Kira's side, raising it to her chapped lips. He tipped it back so a few drops of the clear water slipped into her mouth.

"Please," he whispered. "Drink, Kira."

She startled. Her eyes flicked open, and one hand drifted up to fold over Peter's. A small swallow led to a larger one. After a moment, she gulped down the rest until the vessel was empty.

The cup clacked as Peter set it down. He watched and waited, barely daring to breathe.

Kira licked her lips. Her chest rose and fell in a shaky rhythm.

"Come on, Kira," Sephiri whispered.

Peter leaned in. "Maybe we need to—" He stopped.

The color of her cheeks changed, darkening from their pale hue.

"That's it!" Rylan shouted. "It's working!"

Once it began, the transformation was rapid and remarkable. The glassy sheen dissipated from her eyes. The swelling melted away in her injured arm, and color returned to the flesh. She took a deep, slow breath. Her eyes, newly bright, focused on her friends.

Then she smiled. "Hey, guys."

"It worked," Peter said, stunned. He hauled Kira into a tight hug. His eyes prickled with tears of relief. "You're okay. You're really okay."

She laughed as she returned the hug. "Yeah." Her voice was weak but brighter. "I . . . think I'm gonna be. Thanks to you all."

Peter pulled back. He shook his head as he took in her attentive eyes and her joyful smile. The only sign of the poison was the sweat drying on her brow and the old stain running down her arm.

Sephiri shoved Peter aside and dove into Kira's arms, along with Rylan.

When they all broke apart, Kira worked to her feet, shaky for a moment until her legs grew firm. She grinned and stretched both arms overhead.

The mountain rumbled beneath them again, lighter but still foreboding. A crack formed in the alcove's floor, beneath the box and the basin. It widened, and the recessed area gave way. The stone crumbled, and the crack spread like a spiderweb through the alcove. Unable to bear more, the floor shattered, and both the box of jewels and the basin of remaining water plunged down.

Peter rushed forward and peered down the cavernous hole where the alcove had once rested. The darkness was impenetrable. Far below, a faint squeaking sounded. He dove back just in time to dodge a sudden flurry of bats that burst out of the new opening. The four friends dropped into crouches, covering their heads as the bats flew by.

Unlike before, as the bats knocked against him, Peter wasn't afraid. Relief bubbled inside him, and he laughed. Soon, Sephiri joined in, and then Kira and Rylan, too. By the time the last bat flapped its way out of the mountain, the four of them sprawled on the ground, holding their bellies, and howling.

"I guess they call it the Mountain of the Bat for a reason." Peter wiped his eyes through the laughter, then propped himself up on one elbow.

Kira sat up enough to unwind the ruined bandage from her arm. She cringed at the crusty wrapping covered with old blood, dirt, and sweat. Residual ooze from the gash still covered her skin. She pulled out a clean bandage, dampened it with water from her canteen, and then wiped the worst of the grime from her shoulder. The wound itself was gone, with barely a blemish.

"Wait." Rylan sat up and blinked at the alcove. "If you had the jewels in that bag this whole time, what did Mirelle leave with?"

Kira grinned, her mischievous eyes shifting between the others.

"Kira?" Sephiri said. "What did you do?"

"You, uh . . . remember those snake eggs we found?"

Rylan's jaw dropped. "No way!" He started to laugh until his face grew suddenly serious. "Wait! So when I carried that pack with you up into the throne room . . . Inside it were . . . ?"

"Sorry," Kira said with a grin and a small shrug. "I was a little out of it."

His eyes grew, then a tremendous shudder racked his body. "Mirelle won't be happy when she finds that."

"So, you knew about Mirelle?" Sephiri asked. "This whole time?"

"Not the whole time. I suspected, though." Kira continued scrubbing at the grime. "You remember when she mentioned that the gang killed her parents?"

"When we first met her, yeah," Peter said.

"She said it was just her and her parents, three of them. But then later, on the boat, she mentioned a brother. That's when I realized she was hiding something. Then I glimpsed the brand on her arm. She was always so careful to hide it."

Sephiri frowned. "I never saw it."

"It looked like the pendant Renaud wore," Kira said. "I didn't get a close look, and her story still sort of lined up, you know? It was strange that she stuck with us despite everything that went on, so I just kind of kept an eye on her. I put the eggs in the bag as a precaution when I was resting."

"When did you figure it out?" Peter asked.

"When Gault held Mirelle captive, and you three came up here," she said. "They thought I was delirious and dying—and, well, I was. Their tension left as soon as you all did. They whispered, probably thinking I couldn't hear them or was too out of it to understand. They bickered about their plans like I wasn't even there. It was pretty obvious."

Peter nodded. "So when we were fighting by the arch . . ."

"I got the bag of treasure Mirelle tossed aside," Kira said. "Thanks for distracting everyone. No one was even looking at me. They probably assumed I crawled to the boulders to die, and honestly, it kind of felt like that. On my way up the steps, I realized there was no way I would make it. So, when I found Rylan's discarded pack, I made the switch."

"I can't believe you figured that out while you were on death's door," Rylan said. "I had no idea."

"Neither did I," Peter admitted. "I really . . . I trusted her. I'm sorry, to all of you."

Sephiri sighed. "I wanted to trust her, too."

"I don't know why I didn't suspect anything."

"You want to see the best in people. It's one of the reasons I like you." Sephiri blushed as if the words had snuck out.

A rush of warmth crept up Peter's neck. He couldn't hold back a half smile.

"I mean—" Sephiri sputtered. "It's better than assuming the worst, you know? When you grow up like I did, you learn to be a little more suspicious."

Both guilt and relief churned in Peter's stomach. *I'm lucky to have the friends I do. If we'd lost Kira . . .* He shook his head. That reality was too terrible to think about.

"Let's get out of here," he said. "I'm looking forward to some nights in a proper bed."

"Tell me about it," Kira agreed. She stood up and shook out her arms. "And after this, I never want to cross this terrible bridge again."

The four of them traversed the creaking rope bridge for the last time. Once Peter made his way across the bridge and onto the balcony, with all his friends at his side, he turned and looked back at the ropes swaying over the chasm.

"Should we leave it?" Kira asked.

"There's nothing up there," Rylan said.

Somewhere, deep in that pit inside the mountain, King Xilxidor's bracer rested in the darkness. There was no way of knowing how far down it was, or if it could be found again. Maybe it sank into quicksand, like the sand by the lake. Maybe the fall had destroyed it. Or maybe it was somewhere in the bats' lair, lost in the dark. If someone else found Kytalia, would they try to find the lost gems? Drop into the darkness and look for the treasures King Xilxidor wanted to remain hidden?

Peter unsheathed his sword and sliced through the two

knots tying the bridge back to the balcony railing. The bridge fluttered down and hung flat against the far mountainside.

"It feels right," he said.

Kira nodded with a knowing smile. "Let's go."

They passed through the throne room, then descended the stairs into the empty entrance hall. Peter took one last look around the high ceilings of the gleaming room before he pushed open the doors. No one would ever believe that they'd been there. Not the Palenting leaders, and certainly not Commander Isert. All he'd have left were the memories.

They made their way down the staircase, toward the blood-stained landing. As they approached the archway, a figure emerged near the boulders.

"Who's that?" Rylan asked. He paused, holding out his hand to stop Peter.

A man crouched between the rocks, rooting around. At the sound of Rylan's voice, he straightened up and then waved.

White shirt, stained slacks, and an exhausted, worn-out expression. Peter's muscles tensed. *Adrian.*

"You four," Adrian called, head cocked. "Where are the others?"

"What's it to you?" Peter drew his sword and hurried down the last few steps.

"Whoa." Adrian raised both hands in the universal sign of surrender. "I'm not here to hurt you." An unfamiliar confidence filled his voice. He stood with his shoulders squared and his feet wide, like a soldier instead of the meek medic Peter had known.

"Then why are you here?" Kira asked.

"Glad to see you're feeling better," Adrian said.

"Just a little reaper poison," Kira said. "Nothing I couldn't handle."

Adrian's eyes grew. "So the stories are real—the healing power of Kytalia."

Peter stepped closer, his sword still outstretched. "You know the stories? Is that why you followed us?"

"Calm down," he said. "Let me explain. My name is Adrian Damsgaard. I'm with the Rynorian Historical Society." He reached into his bag and pulled out a silver medal, wrapped in dark velvet. He held it out toward Peter like he lured a skittish cat.

Peter stepped forward, keeping his sword in hand as he peered at the medal. The symbol of Rynor was carved into one side, and the king's personal seal filled the other.

"I apologize for not telling you sooner," Adrian said, "but my business was with the Norivonne and, specifically, with Mirelle. The Society learned that one of the Denton brothers obtained the legendary Key of Kytalia and that the gang sought the city itself. They sent me to learn what information the Norivonne had found, and then to protect the city as a historical site, were it to be discovered."

"That's why you attacked her in the lake," Peter said as the pieces clicked together in his mind.

Adrian nodded. "She was too close. I was less worried about the intentions of you four, but she and her gang would have destroyed this city and ravaged it to serve their greed. I was confident that the Society could find the city from where we were. I wanted to keep her from alerting her gang to its presence."

"Why'd you run?" Kira asked. "You could have told us all of that. We could've helped."

"I didn't want Mirelle to find out who I was," Adrian said. "It was a snap decision—one I'm not proud of. But I was the only member of the Society there. I couldn't let that information be lost, should she find out and try to get rid of me—or all of us." He nodded toward the stairs. "I saw some Norivonne fell. Looks like there was a bit of a scuffle."

"That's putting it lightly," Rylan muttered.

"They're taken care of," Peter said.

"Impressive." Adrian raised his eyebrows. "Mirelle, too?"

Peter pursed his lips. "She, uh . . . She's—"

"She's taken care of, too," Kira interrupted.

Adrian glanced between them, but none of the four offered any more details. He shrugged, then looked up to the palace. "So you were inside? Were the myths true? I noticed the golden buildings are actually sunsbeite. Was there anything real in the palace?"

"There was," Peter said. "But it's gone now."

"Gone?"

"We couldn't take both," Rylan said. "Either a pile of treasure or a healing elixir. We had to pick."

Adrian's eyes widened as his gaze settled on Kira. "You healed her instead of taking the riches."

Peter sheathed his sword. "Of course."

Adrian nodded. "You're good friends." He reached into his bag and pulled out the golden dagger.

"The Key!" Peter said.

"I found this between these boulders. You were the ones who brought it here, weren't you?"

Peter nodded.

"I hate to say it, but this knife is the only proof we have that the city exists. I'll take some samples of the sunsbeite, do some sketches, and map the exact location, but I need to include the Key with my report as well."

"That's ours, though!" Rylan said. "We *actually* bought it!"

"And it was stolen before that, right?"

Rylan squirmed.

"There's not much monetary value to it," Adrian said. "It's much more valuable to the Society as a historical artifact. But I recognize that the four of you are the ones who found this city in the first place. I have some pull in Bromhill—I can ensure you're rewarded."

"Really?" Peter asked. *It may not be the riches of Kytalia, but a reward is better than nothing.* He exhaled. He'd barely had a moment to catch his breath and think about what all had happened. Kira was at his side. They'd found the lost City of Gold. He would've been happy with that. A reward would be the icing on the cake.

"What kind of reward are we talking about?" Rylan knocked shoulders with Kira, grinning.

"What do you need?"

"Does the Society have any baltham coins like the ones we just lost?"

Adrian's eyebrows lifted. "There were coins made of baltham?"

The mention of baltham sprang an idea into Peter's mind. "Actually . . ." He raised a hand. "Before we left Palenting, we were in a bit of a . . . legal issue with the constable. It was all a big misunderstanding, but we were in trouble. Is there anything you could do to help us clear that up?"

"Come on!" Mirelle called over her shoulder. "Keep up!"

She led the way through the tangled vegetation. Roots of the tall trees tugged at her feet. She slapped her way past the hanging vines and thick bushes.

"I'm coming," Renaud grumbled, trudging behind. "Don't forget, while you were lounging on that boat and prancing through the jungle, the rest of us were hoofing it on foot with little sleep or food for the last three nights."

She clenched her teeth, fighting to keep from snapping back at his gross simplification of her experience. Despite having been together for a year, Renaud grated on her increasingly each week.

Lost in her fuming fit, her toe hit a rock. She tumbled

forward into the dirt, catching herself on her palms and grimacing.

"Get up!" Renaud shouted. He hoisted the pack closer into his body as he shouldered his way through the vines and passed her. "Do you want those brats to catch up with us?"

"You're one to talk," she snarled, climbing to her feet. "If they do, I'll kill them myself. I'm already regretting not putting them out of their misery. I'm sure they'll show up in Marris, eventually, so we'll have to keep a lookout."

"Gah!" Renaud shouted, his back arching. With a stiff torso, he tumbled to the ground, hitting the dirt.

Mirelle barked a laugh. "You're telling me to get up? Stop messing around. We've got a lot of ground to cover!"

Renaud slumped prone into the dirt. He thrashed and cried out in pain.

Mirelle rolled her eyes. "What did you do, twist your ankle?"

A violent spasm wracked his body. His back bowed, and his eyes rolled back in his head. Flecks of foam beaded at the corners of his mouth.

Mirelle's eyes widened. *What happened?* She glanced around the undergrowth. *Did he step on a scorpion?*

Renaud collapsed back down and fell still.

Mirelle cringed. She poked her toe into the side of his body. "Renaud?" No response. She kicked him a little harder. "Hello?"

He was dead.

She laughed, quick and callous. *Bad luck for him.* A grin formed. One less person to share the wealth with. One less person to manage.

With Renaud out of the picture, she could lead the Norivonne as she always wanted, and the riches would be hers alone.

What were these riches? The stories of Kytalia mentioned gold and gems and priceless things beyond one's wildest imagination, but in their rush to escape, she hadn't yet looked.

She stepped over Renaud's motionless body and grabbed the pack. One peek, then she'd get moving.

Mirelle opened the bag, but it was dark—too dark to see. She leaned closer.

Hissing, a tiny tartis viper inside leaped from its cracked eggshell and onto her face.

33

"My beloved," Rylan said. "My closest friend. The love of my life. My one and only." He dropped his bag in the doorway of the Garrison and then walked, arms wide, to the rug spread out in front of the hearth. He flopped down onto it and smushed his face against the fur. "Oh. It's even better than I remember. It's the softest rug in the entire world. How did I ever live without it?"

"We weren't even gone that long, Rylan," Sephiri said, smiling with a shake of her head.

"Yeah, but we slept outside the whole time!" The rug muffled his voice. "It's amazing. It's like magic."

"Wait until we get the fire going." Kira walked to the hearth and stacked some wood.

Rylan rolled onto his back and stretched like a pleased cat. "It's so good to be home."

Peter stretched his arms overhead and rolled his shoulders.

"How's your shoulder?" Sephiri asked. "Better?"

He nodded, then rubbed where Gault's blade had sunk deep into the muscle. "It's still stiff, but better every day. If I keep stretching, I'll be fine in no time."

The first day of travel back to Palenting had been hard. Peter had been wracked with guilt, then sadness, then guilt about *being* sad. He was the one who pushed for Mirelle to join them, willing to take any risk for the chance of finding the lost City of Gold. His selfish desires had driven him forward. He'd clung to the hopes of proving the city's existence and bringing that proof back to Palenting to secure his future. His place in the army.

Peter returned empty-handed. He had no proof to give Commander Isert—nothing besides the stories of the golden city and Kira's miraculous healing. He didn't even have the golden dagger anymore.

Yet, as they'd traveled, they'd fallen into the easy rhythms of friendship again. The journey wasn't as arduous with Kira in good health. His wish of joining the army seemed to slip through his fingers like sand, and yet, he didn't ache for it. He was grateful they were all alive.

No one seemed to harbor any ill will about Peter's series of mistakes, so he was almost afraid to broach the topic, lest he invite any residual bad feelings up to the surface. As he set his bag down in their home, the desire to talk pulled at him.

"Seph," he said, "can I talk to you for a moment?"

She followed him into their training area. They unpacked the sword and Kira's bow and sat down near each other to scrub the blade and the arrows clean of dirt and blood. "What's on your mind?"

"I owe you an apology. I mean, I owe everyone one, but you, especially."

"No, you don't," Sephiri said. "I meant what I said back in Kytalia."

"Which part?" Peter scrubbed a rag over the blade of his sword. "That Kira's a genius?"

Sephiri offered a small smile. "That part's obvious. I meant the part about you seeing the best in people."

Peter sighed. "I try to, but . . . I put everyone at risk with how quickly I trusted her, and I didn't listen to your concerns. I'm sorry."

"I mean, she did save us from the Norivonne, to begin with." Sephiri shrugged. "Even if it was a ploy, she played it pretty well."

"I should've been more careful." He looked up from the blade.

Sephiri watched him with her brow slightly furrowed and dark, focused eyes. "None of us are perfect, Peter. When she showed her true colors, you didn't hesitate. That's what matters."

"I did hesitate, though. I couldn't kill her. She still felt like a friend, you know? I couldn't do it." Shame tightened his throat. "I had my sword right there, and I couldn't do it."

"That doesn't make you a bad person," Sephiri said. "That's why the four of us work, isn't it? Kira figured out how to get the jewels back. You handled that guy with the big scar. Me and Ryan handled the rest of the gang." She scooted closer and nudged her foot against his leg. "We're a team. We all work together."

"More than a team. We're a family." Peter's heart lifted. Sephiri was right. Even though Peter had made his own mistakes, his friends were there to fill the gaps. He wasn't alone. He never had been.

"Exactly," Sephiri said. "So . . . relax. We made it back, didn't we?"

"Did you think we wouldn't?" Peter asked.

Sephiri paused. "The Straith Mountains are vast and unforgiving. I knew it would be hard, but I can't tell the future, as much as I would like to. All I could do was hope."

"Well, I'm glad you trusted me. Even though I screwed up on this one."

They shared a small smile and went back to cleaning their

weapons. The silence was comfortable and familiar, broken only by the sounds of Kira and Rylan laughing as they prepared dinner.

He thought there had been something between him and Mirelle. There was a connection between them, a chemistry that felt new and intoxicating—more than a mere crush. She was pretty and smart and could climb a rope like nobody's business. It hurt when the truth came out. That connection was different from what he had with Sephiri, but he couldn't define what it was. His heart tugged in a thrilling pull. *And Sephiri's still here.*

Once his sword was clean, he slipped it back into the stack with the other weapons.

"Come, eat!" Kira called. "While it's hot!"

Sephiri and Peter joined Rylan and Kira at the large wooden table. Kira doled out servings of rich, fragrant garront stew. It was simple, but after days of eating dried provisions on the road, it was the best thing he'd ever tasted.

"Good to be back," Rylan said. "I wish we had some of those jewels, though. Might have been nice to upgrade the training area."

Kira sighed. "It would've been nice. I'm sorry—"

Three overlapping voices drowned out her apology. Then they broke into laughter.

"Seriously, Kira," Peter said, "There was never another choice. You think we'd let the poison get you?"

"And at least we have that letter." Rylan blinked. "We still have it, right?"

"Of course we do." Kira pulled the envelope from her pocket and set it on the table. "Once we deliver this to Baron Hamlin, we should be in the clear."

"I hope so," Sephiri said. "They can't be happy with us, though. The crown . . . breaking out of jail . . ."

A knock pounded on the door. "Fairfield!" an unfortunately familiar voice shouted. "Open up!"

Peter cringed. "He could have let us finish eating first." He grabbed the letter off the table. "I'll handle this."

Before Peter had made it halfway across the Garrison, the heavy wooden door slammed open, and Constable Eastling marched inside. The silver buttons on his uniform gleamed as he marched inside, flanked by tall, broad-shouldered soldiers in leather armor. Trailing behind them, grinning like a loon, was the well-dressed and irritating Ashton Dunn.

"We got word that the four of you had re-entered the city," the constable said.

"Hi Kira," Ashton said with a snooty wave. He turned to the constable. "See? I told you they were back."

"Take them away," the constable said to his soldiers. "Back to the jail where they belong."

Peter lifted his hand. "Hold up."

"You think this is a negotiation?" The constable raised his eyebrows. "After what the four of you did? Not only did you break into the museum and steal the Tarvinian Crown, but you also dared to break *out* of jail and flee the city. That crime carries its own punishment. Between the two, you'll be in jail until you've gone gray!"

Peter held out the letter, his mouth pulled up in a smile. "This will explain."

The constable snatched the envelope, unfolded the letter, and read, "'The Rynorian Department of Justice pardons Peter Fairfield, Kira Lancaster, Rylan Burton, and Sephiri Feather-stone for the purported theft of the Tarvinian Crown from the Palenting Museum and their subsequent escape from jail, due to their recent service to the kingdom.'" He waved the letter in the air. "You expect me to believe this?"

Peter's brows pinched together. "Of course! Look, it has the official seal! It came from the Department of Justice."

Peter tried to snatch the letter back, but the constable scoffed and held it out of reach. The man nodded to one of the soldiers. The man stepped forward and grasped Peter's arm, twisting it behind his back. His shoulder throbbed at the rough motion.

"Hey!" Sephiri shouted. "Let him go!"

The other guards marched forward and wrangled the other three as well. Near the door, Ashton cackled with delight.

"Quiet, you," the constable snapped.

Cowed, Ashton fell silent.

"You're a fool if you thought I'd fall for this cheap forgery."

"It's not forged!" Peter argued.

"It's real!" Kira said. "Write to the Department, they'll confirm everything—ask for Adrian Damsgaard in the—"

"Quiet!" the constable snapped. Holding the letter with both hands, he tore it in two and let it flutter to the ground.

"No!" Peter shouted. *After all we've been through, it can't end like this!* "If you would just listen to me—"

"I've had quite enough of your antics. Load them up!"

The soldier dragged Peter to the front door. As he passed. Ashton waggled his fingers in a teasing wave. "Nice to see you again, Peter," he said. "Have fun in jail."

Outside the Garrison, the constable's wagon waited, and a man threw open the back door. The soldier leading Peter wrangled both his arms behind him and tied them together with a rough coil of rope.

"Please," Peter said. "I can explain." It was pointless, though —no one listened. No one cared. He was just another thief, another kid, another lowlife they'd let rot in jail.

All of that journeying, all of that work . . . for nothing. The Constable could still ruin his life with a snap of his fingers.

Then, just as Peter was being loaded into the wagon, hoofbeats thundered down the dusty road toward the Garrison.

"Commander!" Peter called.

Commander Isert guided his enormous brown horse down the narrow road with expert ease and pulled it to a stop next to the constable. The animal tossed its head and pawed at the ground. Isert patted its neck, then hopped out of the saddle. He wore no armor, but his fine cloak fastened with a gold buckle bearing the Palenting seal, and his shined leather boots looked well worn. "Constable Eastling," the commander greeted. "Mr. Fairfield."

Peter's eyes widened.

"Commander," the constable responded sourly. "What brings you down to Lowside?"

"I received a missive from Bromhill," Commander Isert said, "from King Rasmus, and it included a letter for young Mr. Fairfield here as well."

The constable furrowed his brow. "From . . . the king? That can't be correct. These four are criminals. I'm taking them back to the jail now."

"From the king," Peter echoed in a stunned whisper.

"The missive mentioned a letter provided by the Department of Justice?" Commander Isert said. "I trust you have that in your possession, constable?"

Eastling paled. "Commander, you must understand, it's likely such a letter is a fake. This group of thieves has—"

"Where's the letter?"

The constable huffed, then scurried back into the Garrison. Before Peter could work up the nerve to say anything to the commander, the constable returned with both halves of the torn letter.

The commander raised his eyebrows. "I see."

"It's almost certainly a forgery!"

"Then why would the king reference it?" the commander said. "Untie them."

"Commander—"

"That's an *order*, constable!"

Eastling nodded at the soldiers, even though he fumed. The bonds around Peter's wrists were untied as quickly as they had been fastened. He rubbed the skin around his wrists.

"This was addressed to you." Commander Isert handed him an envelope with Peter's name written on the back in fine calligraphy. The wax seal of the king on the front.

Wide-eyed, Peter opened the envelope.

"Read it out loud!" Rylan said. "Is it really from the king?"

"'To Peter Fairfield and friends,'" Peter read, his voice wavering only a little, "'The Kingdom of Rynor thanks you for your service.'"

"Whoa," Kira whispered.

"'A copy of your official pardon has been provided to the king. As a gesture of appreciation, enclosed is a credit from the King's Treasury. King Rasmus welcomes your visit to Bromhill any time.'"

"A credit?" Rylan said. "What does that mean?"

Tucked inside the envelope was another piece of parchment, thicker than the letter, and stamped again with the king's seal. It had a fine letterhead and tiny calligraphy, and at the bottom an amount for . . .

"Twenty sol!" Peter nearly dropped the paper. "Is this real?"

"It came from Bromhill, so I would assume so," Commander Isert said. "The king had received a messenger bird and sent his fastest courier right away. That suggests this pardon is real as well."

The constable crossed his arms over his chest. "But, Commander, after *breaking out of jail*—"

"It's a full pardon, Constable. I believe it's best you be on your way." The commander peered at the door of the Garrison. "You as well, Mr. Dunn."

"Sir," the constable said. He shot a dark, fuming look at Peter, and then motioned for his soldiers to go. They rode off toward the center of town, and Ashton skulked away on foot, but not before spitting a curse at Peter under his breath as he passed. It all might come back to haunt him when the commander wasn't around to ensure they were left alone, but for the moment, Peter enjoyed the rush of watching the constable ride off with his tail between his legs.

"Peter, I'd like to speak to you privately," Commander Isert said.

His friends didn't move. Only when Peter nodded at them did the others walk toward the door. *They've always got my back.*

The door to the Garrison swung closed, and Peter stood in the dusty street with just the commander and his restless mare.

"The missive from Bromhill didn't contain specifics about what these services were," the commander said. "Does it pertain to what we discussed prior to your arrest?"

Leaving Kytalia empty-handed had led Peter to believe he no longer had a chance at joining the army. But now, here was the commander, opening the door right back up.

"If you did find the City of Gold," Commander Isert continued, "the Palenting army would be interested in seeing what artifacts you uncovered."

"We found it," Peter said.

Isert's eyes widened.

"The city is mostly sunsbeite, not gold," Peter said. "But . . . we did find a chest of jewels—emeralds, rubies, diamonds, and coins of baltham. We also found King Xilxidor's golden bracer. It was incredible!"

"You have all this?"

Peter frowned. "We couldn't take them with us. We had to choose." He glanced toward the door to the Garrison before turning back. "We could either take the chest of jewels or a healing elixir."

"And you chose an elixir?" The commander furrowed his brow. "Disappointing, but an interesting choice. Give it to me, son, and I'll pass it along to the army alchemists. With some luck, we should be able to uncover how it works and recreate it for our soldiers."

"Um . . ." He shuffled his feet. "We don't have that either, sir."

"What did you do with it?"

"My friend," Peter motioned toward the Garrison. "Kira. She had reaper poison in her system, and it was the only way we could save her. After she drank it, the rest of the elixir just —" He waved a hand. "The city took it back."

The disappointment radiating off Commander Isert was nearly tangible. "It took it back?"

Peter shrugged. "It got sucked into the mountain."

"So, you have nothing?"

"We had an artifact, the Key of Kytalia, but a man from the Historical Society took it with him. I think it's in Bromhill."

Commander Isert's unwavering gaze made his nerves crawl like bugs over Peter's skin.

"We didn't have a choice," Peter continued. "We had to save Kira."

"You always have a choice. If these resources you speak of existed, you chose to abandon them."

"Abandon!" Peter balked. "You don't understand, the reaper poison is fatal—"

"Don't lecture me! If you had brought that elixir back, imagine the *other* lives it could have saved."

"You can't know that," Peter said. "You don't know if you'd be able to replicate it."

"And now we won't find out. Nor will we have the wealth of Kytalia to strengthen our forces, all because you chose your desires over those of Palenting."

Peter was stunned to silence. His *desires*? Kira had been *dying!*

"I'm not sure you understand the meaning of sacrifice," the commander said. "A loyal soldier of Palenting would've brought the power of Kytalia back home with him, even if it meant losing a life for the greater good of the city. Do you understand what I mean, Peter?"

"I think I do," Peter said. "You think I should've let my friend die so I could bring the money or the elixir back to you."

"All soldiers lose people. It's part of the price we pay. But the lives saved and defended are worth it."

Was that what the army said before they killed Sephiri's parents? Nausea turned his stomach. If being a soldier meant they expected him to leave his friends behind and sacrifice their lives for the greater good, he didn't want any part of it.

Peter crossed his arms over his chest. "Well, I guess I'm more of a treasure hunter than a soldier."

Commander Isert frowned, then nodded. "I suppose so." He hooked his foot into his saddle stirrup, then mounted his horse. "Keep your nose clean, Fairfield." He snapped the reins. The horse reared up, and then Isert galloped away from the Garrison.

Peter watched Isert until the horse turned a corner and disappeared out of sight, carrying with it his hope of joining the army.

But it had never been a wish, he realized. It'd been a fantasy.

He pushed open the door to the Garrison and stepped inside. Sephiri, Rylan, and Kira leaped up from the table.

"What'd he want?" Rylan asked.

Kira doled out mugs of tea, with water freshly boiled over the still-roaring fire. Peter hurried over to the table and joined them. "He wanted to know if I had any artifacts from Kytalia."

"Tough break." Rylan grimaced. "Did you tell him what happened?"

"Mostly, and he said I should've let Kira die so I could bring the treasure back."

Sephiri gasped. "He was serious?"

"Dead serious," Peter said.

Kira hummed. "That doesn't surprise me."

"What?" Rylan asked. "That's madness!"

"Let me guess," Kira said. "He said you should've been thinking about what those treasures could've done for the army, right?"

"Almost word-for-word, yeah."

"I get it. People talk that way around my parents all the time." She sighed. "What's my life matter to him when he could've had all that money? All that power?"

"Who cares what he thinks?" Sephiri said. "Your life matters to *us*."

"All of us," Peter said. "Plus, I bet King Xilxidor wouldn't have wanted his treasures in the army's grasp, anyway."

Kira smiled. "That's true."

"What else?" Rylan asked. "Did he try to recruit you?"

Peter shook his head. "The opposite, in fact. I don't think I'll be joining the army anytime soon."

Sephiri leaned closer over the table. "Seriously?"

"I feel like it's kind of lost its luster. If that's the way the army is going to be . . ." He paused and noted the sparkle growing in Sephiri's eyes. "Then I don't want anything to do with them, either. I'd rather spend my time with you three, any day."

"And now we've got a whole lot of sol—from the king himself!" Rylan took the note from Peter's grasp and peered at it, still in awe. "I can't believe it."

"What are we going to do with all that money?" Sephiri asked.

"About that." The other three heads turned to Peter as the corners of his mouth pulled up. "I had an idea."

Rylan's hand shot up. "I'm in!"

"Rylan." Kira swatted his arm. "Listen to him."

Peter folded his hands on the table. "We found the city on

our own, and we found the Amulet before that. We're getting good at this, don't you think?" Peter peered at each of them.

Kira tilted her head. "Are you suggesting . . . ?"

"I think we should keep doing this. Keep looking for lost artifacts, treasures from the past, the things no one can find." He grinned. "This is already paying better than working for the mason."

Rylan matched his grin. "I'm in! Let's quit the mason. I can put together some better travel kits."

"And I'll quit the museum," Kira said with new anticipation. "I can focus on the research."

Sephiri nodded with an eager grin.

"We can look for leads in Palenting," Peter said. "And Bromhill, too. The king said we were welcome."

"We should make it a business," Kira said. "Attract clients, split the rewards."

Peter grinned. "I love it."

"We'd need a name," Kira said, "for the business . . . so people know we're serious."

Sephiri tapped her forefinger to her chin. "Hmm." The three of them fell silent. She caught Peter's gaze, and her dark eyes sparkled with excitement. "How about . . . the Treasure Hunters Alliance?"

EPILOGUE

Wagon wheels rattled over the uneven, rocky terrain. The man clutched the reins and flicked them once, twice, urging the horses faster and faster. The proximity of the bluff's edge made his hands sweat. Rocks kicked from the wheels, tumbling over the precipice and falling into the churning sea below. The sound of waves crashing into the rocks filled the air. Salty foam sprayed up high into the night sky and fell as a mist over the wagon. The horses thundered on. He leaned forward, shoulders pressing into the freezing air.

He risked a glance over his shoulder. The canvas covering the wagon's cargo flapped in the wind. Past the vehicle, darkness stretched as far as he could see. He narrowed his eyes, attempting to pierce through the gloom. He strained for any sound of pursuit. There was only silence and the black void.

He pulled against the reins, slowing the horses. Sweat frothed on their bodies. They tossed their heads as they slowed to a trot, their breaths fogging in the cold air.

The man glanced back again. *Nothing.* He risked a half smile. *Did I make it?*

He pulled again on the reins, and the horses slowed to a stop. They pawed at the ground and bobbed their heads, restless and exhausted. He exhaled, attempting to settle his nerves. Only the roaring of the sea leaping toward the cliffs filled the air, rhythmic like the pounding of his heart.

He jumped off the wagon bench and reached for the canvas flap. Moonlight glinted off the pile of gold and silver coins beneath until he stretched the flap over the wagon. He pulled the fabric tight over the cargo and retied the knots, tighter than before. He ran his hand over the cargo, clinking the coins together.

The beasts breathed heavily, recovering from the frantic gallop to which the man had pushed them. He rested a hand on the closest one's flank. It trembled and shook, snorting and huffing. He frowned. *I'll give them a second.* A loud crash of a wave drew his attention. He took a few steps toward the edge of the bluff, then peered down.

The dark sea churned below and spread in every direction. As he looked out to the horizon, where the sea blended with the night sky, a chill ran through him, irrespective of the cold. *What will they do if they catch me?*

He shifted his weight, and the earth gave way beneath his foot. He slipped, then stumbled backward, falling as the rock and earth that had been under him crumbled into the bluff and fell to the sea below. The man scrambled backward, gasping, as more earth broke off.

He panted for air, his heart racing as he leaned against a wagon wheel. The collapsing ground in front of him stopped. He strained his ear, listening to the sound of skittering rocks growing fainter. He blew out his breath, then wiped at his brow. A chuckle escaped his lips. "That was close," he said, turning to the horses.

The animals pawed at the ground. He stood and ran a hand down one of their necks, but the gesture did nothing to calm them. He glanced at the wagon, and a watery feeling ran through his gut. *If my feet can cause the ground to break . . .*

A fresh urgency returned. He jumped back onto the bench and took the reins in hand. As he was about to crack the reins and send the horses running, a low, rumbling growl filled the air.

The horses nickered and shook their heads. Their nostrils flared with each steaming exhale.

The man whipped his head around, seeking the source of the noise. "Who's there?" His voice shook. He saw nothing but darkness.

One horse tried to rear up, but the yoke constrained the motion. The wagon rocked under the force of it, rattling the mountain of coins. The man swore under his breath, then shushed the horses.

He pulled a knife from his belt and climbed back off the wagon. He strained to hear the noise again, creeping into the darkness, padding behind the wagon with the knife outstretched. The weak light of the waning moon did little to light his way. *Did I imagine it?*

Another growl rumbled through the night. It sounded as if it came from everywhere around him, and yet nowhere at all. Quieter than the roar of the sea, it made his whole body shiver. The man stopped moving. The knife trembled in his clammy palm.

The horses whinnied and thrashed. One attempted to rear again.

"Calm down!" the man shouted.

The wagon tipped to one side, then slammed back to its original position. His cargo clattered. The horses pulled forward, but the wagon didn't move. They whinnied again and strained hard as they pulled.

The man whirled back to the wagon. The back wheel was caught in the mud. He cursed and sheathed his knife. Standing next to the wheel, he attempted to lift, but the heavy vehicle wouldn't budge. A gurgling sound filled the air. His stomach dropped as he watched the wheel slide deeper and deeper into the thick mud.

On the other side of the wagon, the ground fell away, melting into the darkness below.

"No," he whispered. It's not just mud. It's a sinkhole. The weight of the wagon crumbled the delicate earth below. He had to move it—had to get it out.

He rushed forward and grasped the front of the wagon, digging his heels against a rock and pulling with all his might. His arms and back burned as he pulled, but it did nothing at all. The wagon sank farther, deeper into the ground. It covered one wheel, then sucked against the body of the wagon.

He was going to lose the whole vehicle. He was going to lose the treasure. Everything he'd been through to obtain it would be for nothing.

The growling returned, closer, louder. His head thrashed in each direction. "What is that?" he shouted. The horses whinnied again and pulled hard against the yoke. "Yes!" he cried. "Pull, pull!"

He tugged again at the wagon. The horses strained, their hooves digging into the dirt. Their muscular legs strained as he cried for them to pull harder, harder. If he could free the wheel . . .

CRACK!

The leather connection from the yoke to the wagon snapped in two. The horses bolted.

"No! Wait!"

He stared after them as they disappeared into the gloom. The thundering of their hooves faded, replaced by the crashing of waves.

The wagon lurched backward, snapping him from his stupor. "No!" He clung to the wagon, desperately holding to the wooden frame. The coins beneath the cargo shifted and rattled as the wagon tipped.

A sudden smell of decay flooded his nostrils. The growling was closer now, close enough to bring with it a smell, rancid and hideous. The hair on his neck stood on end as he tugged at the wood.

Mud burbled, and the wagon jerked, caught as if in a whirlpool. The motion dragged the man forward and his foot sank into the mud. He thrashed and clawed at the wagon to pull himself up, but the mud was like a riptide. It sucked him deeper, up to his knee, and then his other leg slid inside. The wagon tipped, pointing toward the sky. The treasure clattered down and strained at the canvas. He clawed at the dry ground, sinking his hands into the dirt, trying to pull himself up and back to safety. Dragging himself forward, he fought the powerful sucking force.

Behind him, the sinkhole swallowed the wagon.

Then he saw it, emerging from the darkness. The source of the growling.

Terror lanced through the man like a blade. An icy feeling turned his insides to water. The sucking pulled at his legs. His fingers slid through the dirt, weak and useless as he stared, wide-eyed at the horror in front of him. The smell of rot swirled into his sinuses. The rattling growls puffed his hair back, on top of him, like a rolling crack of thunder.

Mud tugged him down. He reached for help that wasn't coming. The ground broke around him, and then he was falling, falling, falling, not through water or mud but through air, through darkness, until darkness was all there was.

PETER, Sephiri, Kira, and Rylan will continue their treasure-hunting adventures soon. Want to be notified when the next book comes out? Sign up for Michael Webb's newsletter at www.subscribepage.com/michaelwebbnovels

LOOKING for books to read while you wait on the next one? Have you read Michael's Shadow Knights series yet? If not, pick up the Last Shadow Knight on Amazon https://getbook.at/amazon_tlsk

"Wow! That book was doggaly great! I'd tell everyone by leaving a review, but I can't type...my paws are too fluffy. Can you help me out? Can you leave a review since I can't?"

PLEASE LEAVE an honest review on Amazon or wherever you got the book from. Do it for Charlie.

ACKNOWLEDGMENTS

Writing this series has been an absolute blast! I don't think I'll ever get tired of treasure hunting and adventure. I want to thank a few people who helped make this book happen:

- Alpha/Beta Readers - Tara, Jeff, Laura, Dad, Aden, Beckham, and Eli. I could not craft a story like this without your help in keeping the plot and writing in line. I can't express enough how much I need and appreciate you!

- Kate - for pushing me to build depth into the story. Some of the ideas you came up with were crucial to building the tension and story arc it needed. Thank you for your help!

- Julia and Eli - You both are proud of me no matter if I sell 1 or 1 million copies. Thank you for your neverending love and support! No books would mean anything without you two to share life with at the end of the day.